Ramon Lull

Blanquerna

translated from the Catalan
with an introduction by

E.A. Peers

Edited with a chronology and
bibliography by

Robert Irwin

DEDALUS/HIPPOCRENE BOOKS

Published in the U.K. by Dedalus Ltd.,
of 9 St. Stephen's Terrace, London SW8 1DJ.

ISBN 0 946626 23 5 (Hardback) 0 946626 22 7 (Paperback)

Published in the U.S.A. by Hippocrene Books Inc.,
171 Madison Avenue, New York, NY10016 USA.

US ISBN 0 87952 376 7

Printed by The City Printing Works (Chester-le-Street) Ltd.,
Broadwood View, Chester-le-Street, Co. Durham DH3 3NJ.

British Library Cataloguing in Publication Data

Lull, Ramõn
[Blanquerna, English] Blanquerna
— New ed.
I. [Blanquerna English] II Title. III Irwin, Robert.
849'981 08 PC3937 L6

ISBN 0 946626 23 5
ISBN 0 946626 22 7 Pbk

THE TRANSLATOR

Edgar Allison Peers was born in 1891 and died in 1952. From 1920 onwards he held the Gilmour Chair of Spanish at the University of Liverpool. He specialized in Spanish mystical writing and in Catalan literature. These interests combined in his work on Ramon Lull.

THE EDITOR

Robert Irwin is a medieval historian, novelist and critic. He is the author of "The Arabian Nightmare", (Dedalus — £3.95) a fantasy set in medieval Cairo, which The Guardian described as "particularly brilliant", and "The Limits of Vision", (Dedalus/Viking — £8.95) described by the New York Times as "an immensely intelligent and delightful novel."

He has edited Gustav Meyrink's **Golem**, Barbey D'Aurevilly's **Les Diaboliques** and Huysmans' **Là-Bas** for Dedalus.

RAMON LULL: A CHRONOLOGY OF HIS LIFE AND TIMES

(Note: In many cases the dates given for events in Lull's life and works written by him are conjectural or approximate. Lull's literary output was prodigious and only a few of his major works are listed here.)

c. 1235 Lull born in Palma Majorca. In that year Ibiza conquered by James of Aragon, thus bringing all the Balearic Islands under Aragonese control

c. 1257 Lull marries Blanca Picanay.

1263 Lull, hitherto a profligate young man attached to the Aragonese court, converted to penitence by a vision of Christ on the Cross, experienced while Lull was trying to write a poem to his current mistress.

c. 1265 He commences the study of Arabic, which he has undertaken with a view to preaching to the infidel. In that year Dante Alighieri born.

1270 Louis IX's Crusade to Tunis.

c. 1272 He translates his **Book on the Contemplation of God,** (a treatise on practical theology) first written in Arabic into Catalan.

1273 He writes **The Book of the Gentile** (a fictional disputation between a Christian, a Jew and a Muslim).

1274 The General Church Council of Lyons.

The Moorish slave, who had been employed by Lull to teach him Arabic, blasphemes against Christianity, is punished by Lull and commits suicide.

In retreat on Mount Randa Lull experiences mystical illumination and conceives of the Ars Magna — a symbolic notational system designed to reveal the truths of Christian philosophy (and a primitive precursor of the modern computer).

c. 1275 Writes **The Book of the Order of Chivalry** and **Doctrine for Boys.**

1276 Foundation, at Lull's instigation, of the College at Miramar for Friars to study Arabic for missionary purposes. Lull teaches at Miramar.

1277 Lull visits Rome.

1280 Peter of Aragon establishes a protectorate over Tunis.

c. 1283 **Blanquerna** written.

1285 Lull visits Rome again.

1286 **Felix,** or **The Book of Marvels** written.

1287 The nestorian Rabban Sauma arrives in the West on a mission from the Mongols.

c. 1287 **The Book of Beasts** written.

1289-9 Lull in Paris and Montpellier.

1289 Tripoli captured by the Mamluks

c. 1289 **The Art of Finding the Truth** written.

1290 Expulsion of the Jews from England.

1291 Lull goes on his first preaching mission to Tunis. He is condemned to death by a Muslim court, but then reprieved and deported. Acre and the last remaining Crusader possessions in Palestine and Syria are lost to the Mamluks.

1291-2 Lull suffers a spiritual crisis. In 1292 he visits Naples to agitate for a new crusade.

1293 Election of hermit Peter of Morrone as Pope Celestine V. Lull tries to get the new Pope's sponsorship for increased missionary activity in the Muslim and Mongol lands, but later that year Celestine V abdicates.

1294 Benedict Caetani becomes Pope Boniface VIII.

1295 Lull writes **Disconsolateness** (perhaps his greatest poem). Lull becomes a Franciscan tertiary.

1297 **New Treatise on Astronomy** written.

c. 1298 Marco Polo dictates his travels.

1299 **Song of Ramon** written. James II of Aragon gives Lull permission to preach in the mosques and synagogues of his kingdom.

1300 Lull in Cyprus.

1305 **Book of the End** (on conversion and crusading) written. Bertrand Got becomes Pope Clement V.

1305-8 **The Ars Magna** written

1306 Lull meets Duns Scotus in Paris.

1307 Lull goes to preach in Bougie, a Muslim town east of Algiers and he spends about six months in prison. The arrest of the Knights Templar in France on the orders of Philip IV. John of Montecorvino becomes Archbishop of Peking.

1309 Lull tries to interest Pope Clement V in his missionary projects.

1309-11 Lull in Paris, lecturing and campaigning against Averroism in the University.

1311 Lull attends the Church Council of Vienne. One of its decisions is to establish chairs of Arabic and Mongol at the Universities of Paris, Louvain and Salamanca. Lull returns to Majorca.

1313 Lull goes to Sicily.

1314 Jacques de Molay, Grand Master of the Templars burnt at the stake in Paris.

c. 1314 Dante begins writing his **Divine Comedy.**

1315 Lull goes to Turin to preach the Faith again. Then moves on to preach in Bougie. Allegedly Lull makes a prophecy about the discovery of America.

1315 or 1316 Lull is stoned to death by angry Muslims.

1376 At the urgings of the inquisitor Nicholas Emeric, Lull's doctrines are condemned as heretical in a papal bull.

1417 Pope Martin V annuls the bull and Lull is rehabilitated.

BIBLIOGRAPHY

Aziz Suriyal Atiya, **The Crusade in the Later Middle Ages,** (London, 1938)

A. Bonner (ed.) **Selected Works of Ramon Lull,** 2 vols. (Princeton, 1985).

Martin Gardner 'The **Ars Magna** of Ramon Lull' in **Science Good, Bad and Bogus** (Oxford, 1981).

J.N. Hillgarth, **Luss and Lullism in Fourteenth Century France,** (Oxford, 1972).

Benjamin Z. Kedar, **Crusade and Mission: European Approaches towards the Muslims,** (Princeton, 1984).

E. Allison Peers **Ramon Lull: A Biography,** (London, 1929).

Lynn Thorndike, **A History of Magic and Experimental Science,** vol. 2, (New York, 1923).

Frances A. Yates, **The Art of Memory,** (London, 1966).

Frances A. Yates, **Lull and Bruno: Collected Essays, Volume 1,** (London, 1982).

INTRODUCTION

INTRODUCTION

I

Ramón Lull, the "Apostle of Africa," is undoubtedly one of the most noteworthy characters in Europe of the thirteenth century. He was a native of Palma de Mallorca, where he was born, soon after the conquest of the Balearic Islands from the Moors, perhaps on January 25th, 1235.[1] Of good birth, an only son, and in favour with the royal house (his father having played a prominent part in the recent campaign), he received the advantages of a courtly training; when he was of age to marry, the King,—James I, the "Conqueror,"—who showed considerable interest in him, found him a bride. Before this, however, young Ramón had given himself up to the life of a profligate. "When I was grown," he tells us in his autobiographical poem *El Desconort*, "and knew the vanities of the world, I began to do evil and entered upon sin, forgetting the true God, and going after carnal things." The story runs that, in spite of his wife's affection and the boy and girl that she bore him, he was passionately enamoured of a Genoese lady, who, however, spurned his advances. On one occasion he is said to have ridden on horseback into a church where she was engaged in hearing Mass. The lady endeavoured to persuade him by means of letters to desist from following her, and, as this proved useless, she summoned him to her presence, and revealed to him the breast which he had so often extolled in his verses, and which, all unknown to him, was being slowly consumed by a malignant cancer.

Another story goes that while Ramón, who at this time was about thirty years of age, sat composing verses to some woman of whom he was enamoured, the image of Christ crucified appeared to him. Struck with astonishment at the vision, he dropped his pen, and fell into a supernatural

[1] The day of the year is known, but there is considerable uncertainty as to the year itself. Some make it 1232, others 1233 and 1235.

sleep. Five times in all (and this we read in his own writings) did Christ appear to him before his conversion was complete, but, once converted, he never looked back.

Naturally enough, when the overpowering desire came to him to spend his life in the service of God, his thoughts at once turned to the conversion of the race which for so long had inhabited his native island. To acquire learning, preach to the unbelieving Moors, debate with them upon religion, write books which should convert them, and suffer martyrdom for his faith, if need arose—these were Ramón Lull's new ambitions. After much time passed in prayer and meditation, and a period the duration of which is uncertain spent in freeing himself from temporal cares, he set aside part of his wealth for the needs of his family, gave the rest to the " poor of Jesus Christ "—as *Blanquerna* calls them—and set off to obey the promptings of his conscience.

He first undertook a comprehensive pilgrimage, embracing Montserrat, Santiago de Compostela,[1] Rome and the Holy Land, where he gained without any doubt much experience which is reflected in his books. This concluded, after an absence of about two years, he returned to Mallorca, and later retired to the solitude of Mount Randa, devoting himself to study and contemplation, until he should be fitted to undertake what may be described as a crusade of learning against the Moors.

There is so much of Ramón's own thought and experience in *Blanquerna* that it is hardly necessary to describe in detail his long and varied life. One of his principal ideas was to compose an *Art General* which should convert the whole world to Christianity, and in planning this he believed himself to have been directly inspired by God. Another, and an extremely practical scheme, which was continually in his mind, was the establishment and endowment of colleges for the training of missionaries, especially in Arabic and in theology. Such a college was actually

[1] See *Blanquerna*, Chap. LXXXVIII, § 8.

founded in 1275 by King James II, and to it, and the friars minor who were trained in it, Lull refers, as will be seen, more than once in his didactic romance.

All his desires, however, were unfortunately not so literally fulfilled. Indeed, from one point of view, the life of Ramón Lull is a record of disappointment. He presented his various schemes to Kings and Popes, and was sometimes dismissed as a visionary, a fanatic or worse. He travelled incessantly in Italy, France, Cyprus, Egypt, Armenia, Malta, Tunis—one hardly knows where he stopped—preaching, pleading, lecturing, disputing, teaching and begging. Again and again he conducted campaigns in Africa in which he endeavoured to prove by argument, or at least to present in the light of probability, the fundamental truths of the Catholic Faith. It was on one of these expeditions, when he had passed his fourscore years, that he was stoned by a mob at Bugia; he died from the effects of this, and according to a tradition, which may not be correct, his death occurred on St. Peter's Day, 1315, when he was returning by sea to Mallorca, and was within sight of the island.

One likes to think that such a death was his: he might well have been foretelling it symbolically, in his *Book of the Lover and the Beloved:*

> The birds hymned the dawn, and the Lover, who is the dawn, awakened. And the birds ended their song, and the Lover died in the dawn for his Beloved.[1]

Then it was that " the Beloved revealed Himself to His Lover—stretched out His Arms to embrace him, and inclined His Head to kiss him."[2] With the crown of martyrdom which for so long he had desired, he entered into the joy of his Lord.

[1] *Book of the Lover and the Beloved*, 26 (and see note, p. 415).
[2] *Ibid.*, 91.

II

It scarcely seems possible that Ramón Lull, with so many other activities absorbing his mind, could have been a prolific writer. Yet he is credited by some authorities with nearly five hundred works, and by tradition with many more. In the monumental *Histoire littéraire de la France*, an annotated list of three hundred and thirteen works is given, all of which the compiler believes to be by Lull.[1] They are written, some in Latin, others in Catalan, and a number in Arabic—a few in all three: their subjects include metaphysics, theology, ethics, logic, medicine, mathematics and the natural sciences. Some of them are well worth reading still, and it is to be hoped that these may all be soon translated into English. More than one resembles *Blanquerna* in having a basis of narrative: such is the *Book of the Gentile and the Three Wise Men*, an intensely interesting volume. The *Book of the Order of Chivalry* was translated long ago by Caxton, and though short, and in parts commonplace, makes an appeal to the student of chivalry. Much longer, and in some respects Lull's masterpiece, is the enormous *Book of Contemplation*, of which the Catalan version has recently been republished in five large volumes. The short *Art of Contemplation*, which forms part of *Blanquerna*, gives some idea of its nature.

Other of the best-known works of Lull, the titles of which fairly describe their contents, are the instructional *Doctrina pueril* (Book of Doctrine for Boys), the *Book of the Philosophy of Love*, the *Book of the Holy Spirit*, the *Hours of Our Lady Saint Mary*, and the *Book of the Tartar and the Christian* (commenting the hymn " Quicumque vult ").

The verse of Lull, though in many places less poetical than some of his prose, has a particular interest as being partly autobiographical. In this connection the *Hundred Names of God* and the shorter verses are of less attraction

[1] *Histoire littéraire de la France*, Paris, 1885. Vol. 29, pp. 67, 386.

than the *Song of Ramón*, and that intensely pathetic record of disillusion entitled *El Desconort*. In this last, Ramón tells, in the bitterness of his soul, how all his efforts to carry out his own plans for the conversion of unbelievers have been of no effect.[1]

III

Blanquerna, as we know from the text itself, was written at Montpellier,[2] and in all probability between the years 1283 and 1285, which Lull is believed to have spent in that city. In Chapter LXV there is, as will be seen, an allusion to King James II as still reigning in Mallorca, whereas in Chapter XCII his deposition is referred to. Since this event took place in November, 1285, it follows that the latter part of the book was in process of writing about that time, and we may well believe, in view of Lull's manifold activities, that its composition was spread over the greater part of the period of his stay.

[1] It begins:

This is the *Desconort* which Ramon Lull composed in his old age, when he saw that neither the Pope nor other Lords of the world would give heed to his many and diverse petitions concerning the conversion of unbelievers.

When I fell to considering the state of the world, how few are the Christians therein and how many the unbelievers, then the thought came to my mind to go to prelates, kings and religious to the end that . . . our faith might be greatly exalted, and the infidels converted. And this I have done for thirty years, and truly I have achieved nothing.[3]

. . . . . .

Wife, children and lands have I left, and for thirty years have lived in weariness and trials. Five times have I been to the Court [of Rome] at my own cost; thrice have I attended general chapters of Friars Preachers, and thrice those of Friars Minor.[4]

. . . . . .

That which I urge at the Court [of Rome] passes unheeded by the Pope and his Cardinals, who do but delay, whereat I am exceeding sad, and cannot be comforted. For I urge upon them, and demonstrate quite clearly how the world may be ordered and that right soon; but they despise and mock me, as though I were a fool who spoke idly.[5]

[2] See Chap. XC, § 7.

[3] *Desconort*, III.

[4] *Ibid.*, XIV.

[5] *Ibid.*, XLVII.

These points, and others related to the composition of *Blanquerna*, are discussed by Mossen Salvador Galmés in his Preface to the edition which is here translated. The reader is referred to this for a fuller account than can now be given; something, however, must be said of one striking trait in the book which would probably occur to many who read no more than a summary of its contents. In 1294 occurred the dramatic renunciation of the papacy by Celestine V. The fate of this pontiff was less happy, it is true, than that of Lull's fictitious parallel, but in other respects there is a marked similarity between the two happenings, and the question at once arises whether *Blanquerna*—or rather the latter part of it—can have been written during a later sojourn of Lull's in Montpellier, namely in the year 1303. But there is no evidence to support the rather too obvious deduction which leads to this view, and against it is the quite conclusive fact that in *Blanquerna* the destruction of Lull's fondest dream—the College of Miramar—is not mentioned: on the contrary the foundation is spoken of with pride, as still flourishing. As this blow fell on Lull before the year 1295, when he refers to it in the *Desconort*, it must be laid down that, whatever the date of *Blanquerna*, it is earlier than 1295, and that therefore the episode of the renunciation of the papacy is introduced into the book only by a coincidence and has no set reference to the abdication of St. Celestine.

Unlike the remainder of Lull's prose works, *Blanquerna* has won for itself a definite place, and a very high one, in Catalan literature. It is unusually mature for the age in which it was written—for let us realise that it is a century older than Froissart's *Chronicles*, Chaucer's *Canterbury Tales* and Wyclif's translation of the Bible, and a full two centuries than Caxton and Malory and Commines. Two hundred and fifty years separate it from the masterpiece of Rabelais, which occasionally resembles it in minor detail. In Spain, Lull is roughly contemporary with Alfonso the

Wise and Juan Manuel, but was older than almost all the men who are commonly spoken of as the founders of Spanish prose. Where, it may be asked, in English, French or Castilian prose of the thirteenth century can one find such a book as *Blanquerna?* Even when we look towards Italy,—where genius flowered early,—though Dante, Petrarch and Boccaccio are each and all greater writers than Lull, we must remember that if the first was but slightly his junior, the second and third were born about the time of his death, and belong to the century after that of *Blanquerna*.

The worst faults of the story, considered as narrative of the class to which it belongs, are its *longueurs* (which persisted in European prose fiction for centuries after its age), the leisurely pace and the prolixity of certain parts of the story and the few failures in characterization which it contains. Let us admit at once that the preternatural wisdom of the rather forbidding Natana, and (in the early chapters) the colloquies between Evast and Aloma, are, for the most part, wearisome and dull: we can also, however, claim that no ground of reproach on this score is given once Blanquerna's adventures have fairly started. "Examples," pithily related, enliven the more didactic portions of the book; and the longer instructional narratives illustrative of the virtues and vices, whether or no they were penned with the same intention, fulfil it none the less. One example from among many is the story (in Chapter XIV) of the plebeian but ambitious draper, at which Ramón will hardly rebuke us if we smile.

Natana apart, the principal characters of *Blanquerna* are all well drawn. Evast and Aloma are admirably paired together, for if Evast is too unyieldingly ascetic to seem quite natural, he serves the better as a foil to Aloma, who is exquisitely human, and the most purely moving character in the book. In her desire for a son—in her stubborn refusal to be separated from her husband, who thinks to free himself so easily from his matrimonial vows—in her quick wit which conceives the daring plan of persuading her son into a marriage—in the shrewdness with which she foresees Evast's opposition and tells him only when the deed is done—and, most of all, in the touching farewell scene which contrasts her so sharply with her husband: in each of these, Aloma is all but a perfect character of early fiction, and, did she not degenerate into insignificance after Blanquerna's departure, she would be a perfect woman indeed.

The secondary characters have less charm. Narpan is the bold, bad man of fiction: an obvious invention. Pure inventions, too, are the shadowy opponents of the hero: the naughty cellarer, the ingenuously wicked archdeacon, the obstinate and reactionary chamberlain, and the rest. Natana's mother comes into the same category, though she proves to be her daughter's own mother when she reforms! The numerous canons and cardinals who move in turn across Lull's varied stage are hardly ever presented with the vividness of some of the less exalted personages of the drama. Many readers will lose their hearts to the Ten Commandments, or weep with Faith and Truth, or enlist in the service of the lady Valour. They will be less at their ease in the streets and squares of Rome than in that astounding "forest," where palaces spring up at their creator's good pleasure, where emperors sit on the grass and devour dry bread, or walk about with *juglares* and would-be hermits as naturally as can be. The epilogue to the book, in particular, has always struck us as wonderfully modern, and of especial skill.

IV

If *Blanquerna* is to be described as a *Utopia* (though is it not more like a Catholic *Pilgrim's Progress?*), the use of the word must not be taken to imply either a fantastic or a destructive purpose. Lull thought less of pulling down and rebuilding the habits of Church and society than of revivifying them with what he conceived to be the truly Christian spirit. Somewhat late in life he professed as a Franciscan tertiary—it had been a sermon heard on the feast of St. Francis that first quickened his desires into action—and there is much of the spirit of the "little poor man" in the social ideals of *Blanquerna*. Lull is devoted to the principles of the Sermon on the Mount: whole chapters of the book are commentaries, in effect, on its precepts. The Franciscan ideal of poverty, in spirit and letter, with its insistence on detachment from the world, and on the perils of the "vice of ownership," dominates the narrative, especially in the section which describes the lives of Evast and Aloma. "Sell that thou hast and give to the poor, and come, follow Me" is a literal command, to be literally obeyed. What, then, can be said of a monastery that rejoices in its possessions, a bishop who feasts like a king, a canon who enjoys a large income, and despises the "poor of Christ"? And there are worse offenders than these, nor are any spared. Laymen, as well as clerics, are examined in the light of Christ's precepts: wealthy and gluttonous merchants, deceitful tradesmen, drivers of hard bargains, hypocrites, lustful men, vain women, unfaithful wives and husbands—all are made to look at themselves as keenly as their creator looks at them.

The chief didactic element in *Blanquerna* has already been hinted at: its expression of the missionary spirit. To those who come to the book with receptive minds, there will be no room for anything but admiration of the persistence with which Lull returns again and again to this theme. It is so distressingly real to him. All kinds and classes of unbelievers are journeying daily (so his vivid phrase has it) toward the everlasting fires. It is the bounden duty of all —how can any doubt it?—by any and every means to save these souls, and no less so to recover the Holy Places from the unbelievers. When the Church and when Christian states have recovered the Christian spirit—which to a large extent (so runs his theme) they have lost—they will burn with love, and be filled with overwhelming desire to reconquer Palestine and convert infidels the world over. To preach Christ, and, if need be, to suffer martyrdom for Him, must be the goal of every true lover:

> The Beloved said to His Lover: "Thou shalt praise and defend me in those places where men most fear to praise me." The Lover answered: "Provide me then with love."[1]

> The marks of the love which the Lover has to his Beloved are, in the beginning, tears; in the continuance, tribulations; and in the end, death.[2]

So much is evident. Hardly less so is the method which Lull would employ to accomplish his purpose. He may or may not have directly denied that, as St. Thomas in particular had taught, there are truths which are incapable of proof, and can only be believed and defended. He does not, at any rate, deny this in set terms in *Blanquerna*, which alone concerns us here. But he does hope to establish throughout the world his crusades of learning, in which properly trained apologists and linguists will be able so powerfully to defend the mysteries of the Faith by argument that they will succeed in converting, directly or indirectly, the entire world. He is a convinced believer in polemic, and in the service which Reason can render Faith, though abundant evidence shows that he was equally convinced of the efficacy and need of prayer.

The practical nature of Ramón the Fool, however, devises more skilful means of attack than the sledge-hammer of argument. Some of these seem to us in modern days extraordinarily naïve, if not ludicrous—though one can never, of course, be sure how far they are merely in character, and how far they represent Lull's own views. Others are universally recognised as sound to-day: our modern training

[1] *Book of the Lover and the Beloved*, 135. [2] *Ibid.*, 233.

colleges, and facilities for learning the languages of other nations, would have delighted the panegyrist of Miramar had he found them in one of the fantastic lands of his fancy or the real ones of his travels.

V

Of the two smaller books which form part of this romance—*The Book of the Lover and the Beloved* and *The Art of Contemplation*—we have written elsewhere.[1] Together they form a noteworthy contribution to the study of Lull as a mystic. *The Book of the Lover and the Beloved* reveals something of the mystical life of Lull himself, under the fiction of reproducing certain of the experiences of Blanquerna. The *Art of Contemplation*, which illustrates Lull's love of method, is a practical manual of devotion. It makes no claim to describe in detail the substance of Lull's own contemplation, for such a thing, as it warns us,[2] would be impossible.

> The contemplation and devotion which Blanquerna had, and the art and manner thereof, none can tell it neither explain it, save only God.

But it gives some idea of the lines on which he worked, and incidentally sets down certain of his meditations and prayers, thus serving as a map or guide to the lower slopes of Mount Carmel, the mystical heights of which it would seem that he had been enabled to scale.

The two little books, then, are complementary. The first shows the mystic in his life; the second reveals the mystic as a teacher. Lull did well to make them part of *Blanquerna*, for without them the book, though interesting as an example of early didactic narrative, would entirely fail to

[1] In the introductions to the separately published editions of the *Book of the Lover and the Beloved* (S.P.C.K., 1923) and the *Art of Contemplation* (S.P.C.K., 1925).

[2] e.g. *Art of Contemplation*, III, 12; XIII, 7.

present one of the most important aspects of the life of Lull. Like his great fellow-Spaniard, St. Ignatius Loyola, who has much in common with him, though he lived two hundred and fifty years later, he was before everything else a *practical mystic*. Each of those two words must be duly stressed before the complete Lull can be in the slightest degree understood: the *Book of the Lover and the Beloved* and the *Art of Contemplation* convey the stress required.

The former is the greater of the two. It seems likely, indeed, that it will take a high place in the near future among the various mystical classics by foreign writers which have been translated into English. The vividness, picturesqueness and simplicity of the great majority of its aphorisms have commended them to many whom the profundity—even the obscurity—of a few of the later ones repels. And every reader is attracted by the fervour and devotion which inspires them. The greatest can hardly be forgotten: their very brevity imprints them upon the mind.

> Said the Lover to the Beloved: "Thou that fillest the sun with splendour, fill my heart with love." And the Beloved answered: "Hadst thou not fulness of love, thine eyes had not shed those tears, neither hadst thou come to this place to see Him that loves thee."[1]

> Said the Lover: "O ye that love, if ye will have fire, come light your lanterns at my heart; if water, come to my eyes, whence flow the tears in streams; if thoughts of love, come gather them from my meditations."[2]

> The Beloved clothed Himself in the raiment of His Lover, that he might be His companion in glory for ever. So the Lover desired to wear crimson garments daily, that his dress might be more like to the dress of his Beloved.[3]

[1] *Book of the Lover and the Beloved*, 6.
[2] *Ibid.*, 173. [3] *Ibid.*, 262.

VI

Lull is always a poet, and none of his books is wholly didactic for long. He is also, as a rule, a conscious artist: in places he reaches heights to which justice has not yet been done. Unfortunately, it is impossible in translation to convey a worthy idea of one of his principal merits,—that of style.

The charm of Lull's style is its simplicity. Except in the two opuscules which form part of *Blanquerna*, he seldom rises in this book to the pitch of eloquence. All his narrative is in the natural, unaffected tone of conversation,—the tone, less of a professional preacher, or a learned master in the sciences, than of a wandering friar—simple, naïve and picturesque. The amazing thing is that it should be the style of one whose synthetic and encyclopædic mind conceived schemes and subtleties innumerable, who was a "doctor illuminate," a "master universal in all arts and sciences." No part of the narrative of *Blanquerna* suggests such a man. Most of it might be a tale told round the fire in winter, by some unlettered follower of Christ, whose only art was love.

This translation of *Blanquerna* into English is not only the first ever made, but probably the first of the book in its entirety into any other language but Castilian. It is dedicated by a humble member of the Sociedad Menéndez y Pelayo to the memory of that great author, critic and son of the Church, in whose honour the Society was founded. Every student of Spanish literature owes a debt to Don Marcelino, for there is no field in which he has not to consult his works. But never does he need the guidance of the master more than when studying the Spanish mystics. Ramón Lull was a favourite theme for Menéndez y Pelayo's pen. He eulogised him in almost his first critical essay—the famous Academy discourse; discussed his work with the acumen of the born critic, in the *Origins of the Novel* and elsewhere, and edited a translation of this very *Blanquerna* into Castilian. For this last enterprise, it is true, the best version of the romance was not then at his disposal, but both his edition and the essay which precedes it will remain of permanent value. He approached Lull's work in Lull's own spirit, as all must do who would rise to his heights and penetrate to his depths. Only readers who are untouched by the mystical fervour of the Fool of Love, and deaf to his simple eloquence, will put it down unsatisfied. And for these may be repeated, in Menéndez y Pelayo's own language, the much-needed warning that its beauty and strength lie, not on its surface, but beneath:

> Let none attempt to read this book who sees in what he reads no more than a fleeting diversion. Let none attempt to read it who has no mind to penetrate beneath its surface. . . . And let none so much approach it unless he be prepared to appreciate the simplicity and sincerity which in its primitive pages he will surely find.

GLORIOUS LORD GOD, ONE IN ESSENCE AND THREE IN PERSONS! TO THY PRAISE AND HONOUR, WITH THY GRACE, VIRTUE, AND BLESSING, BEGINNETH THE BOOK OF EVAST AND ALOMA AND BLANQUERNA THEIR SON: THE WHICH IS MADE WITH INTENTION THAT MEN MAY LOVE, COMPREHEND, REMEMBER AND SERVE THEE, WHO ART VERY GOD, LORD AND CREATOR OF ALL THINGS.

PROLOGUE

IN signification of the five Wounds which our Lord God Jesus Christ received upon the Tree of the True Cross to redeem His people from the bondage of the devil and the captivity wherein they lay, we would divide this work into five books. And herein will we give instructions and rules of life in a manner according to the which there are distinguished five estates of persons who may find profit herein. The first is of matrimony, the second of the religious life, the third of prelacy, the fourth of the apostolic estate of the Pope and his Cardinals, and the fifth of the life of the hermit.

BEGINNETH THE FIRST BOOK WHICH IS OF MATRIMONY

CHAPTER I

OF THE MATRIMONY OF EVAST AND ALOMA

In a certain city it came to pass that a goodly youth, of right noble lineage, the son of a gentle burgess, became, through the death of his father, very wealthy in temporal riches. This youth, Evast by name, had been brought up and instructed by his father in right good manners: he was well-favoured in person, noble of heart, well equipped in all things, and knowing so much of letters and sciences that he had a passing great knowledge of Holy Scripture. Greatly was this Evast sought by men of religion in the city that he might become one of themselves, and by certain worldly men[1] also who desired to be allied with him through matrimony. Now while he was thus importuned by religious men and by men esteemed in the world, he gave thought one night to the order of religion and the order of matrimony, and it came to his will that he should embrace the religious life in order to flee the vain delights of this world. But he remembered the abundance of temporal riches which his father had bequeathed to him and how it was laid upon him to maintain the great house and to continue the almsdeeds which his father had made while he lived this present life. For all the which reasons, and because, moreover, he was the head of his line, he inclined to the order of matrimony, determining, for so long as he was in that estate, to give good doctrine and example to all that were likewise therein. He desired also to have sons who should be servants of God, to whom he might leave the temporal goods that he possessed, that before his death he might serve God in some religious order.

[1] The meaning is hardly more than "laymen."

2. When Evast had conceived and deliberated in his will how that he should embrace the order of matrimony, he said to certain of his kinsfolk, especially to those in whom he had the greatest trust, that they should seek in the city some damsel of noble lineage,—for by nobility of lineage the heart is fortified against wickedness and deceit. He desired further to have a wife who should be sound and well-formed in body, that nature might give good constitution to their offspring. And, above all, Evast besought his kinsfolk to seek out for him one that was humble and well brought up, and whose parents, together with herself, should be well pleased and honoured by the alliance.

3. There lived in that city a lady that was much honoured, and of great courtesy, who for long had been a widow, and had a daughter, by name Aloma. Throughout the city it was reported that this damsel ruled and directed all her mother's house, and moreover that she was right virtuous: the good lady that was her mother gave her this authority that she might know in what manner to maintain and govern her house when she should be wedded, and she gave her occupations also, that no foolish and evil thoughts should enter her mind through overmuch leisure and incline her to base deeds.

4. All the qualities that Evast desired in his wife were found in Aloma; and those that sought a wife for Evast according to his will were certified of her virtuous life. And so by the will of God the matrimony of Evast and Aloma was accomplished.

5. Throughout all the city was noised abroad the day of the wedding of Evast and Aloma, and many were the men and women that desired upon that day to do them great honour. But Evast would have none of it, for he desired to give to the people an example of humility, the which virtue is wont to be despised upon such days, and pride, vanity and vainglory to be favoured. Wherefore, upon the day of their wedding, Evast and Aloma went to the church

with but few persons, to signify by such means their humility; and that the Sacrament of the Mass should not be thought of less account than themselves, they were clothed in humble raiment. Together with them were devout and holy persons, that their prayers might be the more surely heard, and that God might be the better pleased with the oblation made by Evast and Aloma of their persons and of the possessions which He had given them.

6. The Mass on that day was celebrated by a holy man, that through his holiness the grace of God might rest upon Evast and Aloma. This holy man preached and declared to them the intention for the which matrimony is ordained, and gave them good doctrine, setting before them how they must live and fulfil the sacrament of matrimony and the promises which they had mutually made, that God might be served thereby and His grace through them be shown forth to all men.

7. Throughout that day were prayer and devotion made, and a great feast for the poor of Jesus Christ, who praise and bless God when alms are given to them. Through these is Jesus Christ represented at a wedding, whereto the poor are called and such wealthy men turned away therefrom as bear not in mind the Passion of the Son of God, wasting and squandering those temporal goods which the poor sorely need, and spending them in the service of men full of worldly vanity, like unto themselves.

8. On that day of their wedding Evast and Aloma served the poor of Jesus Christ, and in remembrance of the humility of our Lord Jesus Christ they washed the hands and the feet of thirteen poor men, kissing their hands and feet, and clothing their naked bodies with new raiment. And it was proclaimed throughout that city that every poor man who desired to receive alms for the love of God should come to that wedding-feast.

9. The kinsfolk and the friends of Evast and Aloma likewise served the poor of Jesus Christ on that day at the

wedding-feast. After which they departed to dine, each in his own house, that they might not take the viands from the poor, and Evast and Aloma dined together at the table of the thirteen poor men. And when they had dined, Evast went to a monastery of religious men to spend the rest of that day in prayer and contemplation, and Aloma went to another house wherein was an order of women, to praise and call upon God our Lord. And to each of these two houses, and to all the other religious houses of that city, Evast made a gift, and commanded abundant victuals to be given on that day of his marriage.

10. Evast honoured his bride as it behoved him, and treated her with much respect, to the end that love and fear might be increased within her, for these two things are well found in the heart of a woman. He gave her authority and management of the possessions of the house, and himself resolved to engage in trade, that in humility he might bear some office and not be idle, and ever have temporal goods for the maintenance of his house. For by overmuch leisure man comes to poverty and pride and indolence, and many a time, through over-great confidence in their nobility and riches, men of the city come to failure and poverty and give themselves to vice.

11. In the house of Evast and Aloma were no servants that were ill bred, lest their ill breeding should make some evil thought to be born in the mind of Aloma. Each day Evast and Aloma went to hear and behold the Holy Sacrament of the Mass, and, returning to their house, gave alms of the possessions which God had bestowed upon them. After this they were occupied in the maintenance of their house. During the week, and upon days of festival, they went gladly to sermons and to hear religious men, that they might listen to the Word of God and receive doctrine whereby they might continue in the estate of holy life.

12. The whole city was advantaged by the life and good estate and example of Evast and Aloma, for by their example

were greatly edified both those who dwelt in matrimony and likewise the religious; and by all men in the city they were loved and honoured. So greatly were they respected in that city that men and women alike found counsel and favour in them, and consolation in their necessities.

13. For much time and long Evast and Aloma lived together and had no children; and it chanced one day that Aloma considered the passing of this present life, and remembered the intent wherein she had entered the estate of matrimony, namely to bear children who should be servants of God. Then her eyes filled with tears and her heart with grief and sadness because she had no children. And she went into a fruitful[1] orchard which belonged to the house, and kneeled before a tree which was near to a fair water-spring; there she wept for a great space, praying to Almighty God, the Lord of all, that in His sovereign mercy He would give her a son, who should be His servant, and take from her the grief and sadness which was hers because she had no children.

14. While Aloma wept thus, and besought the God of Heaven and earth to hear her prayers, Evast after his wont entered the orchard and beheld Aloma weeping sorely, whereat he greatly marvelled, and spake to her as follows: "Wherefore weepest thou, Aloma, and why art thou so sad? What can I do that thou mayest be comforted? I marvel greatly to see these thy tears, and thy countenance revealing to me such sadness of heart, when never until now have I seen in thee a sign of trouble or displeasure. Aloma, my beloved, tell me now, wherefore is this? I had thought to know all thy desires, but it seemeth now that there hath entered into thy mind that which thou hast not revealed to me."

15. Aloma considered the words of Evast her lord, and had shame to reveal to him her thoughts, for she feared and

[1] *lit.* "bearing many flowers": the orchard was still in blossom

loved him greatly. But lest Evast should harbour some suspicion or doubtful thought concerning her, she resolved to tell him the reason of her tears, and she said: "Evast, my lord, never in all my life, since I entered thy power, have I had in my heart thought or desire which constrained me so greatly as does now my desire to bear a son; for it would be a grievous loss if the good things that we possess were inherited by any other than a son of our own body. And God gives much grace and honour to a man when He gives him sons to serve him, whereby his name and lineage may be preserved. And therefore, when I think upon death, and see that I have no son to whom may be bequeathed this house, and who may maintain these possessions, and the alms that are given of them, I cannot choose but weep, neither can my heart in aught find consolation."

16. Evast answered Aloma and said: "Through the virtue of God are all things created for the service of man; and God denies to man many things which he desires, to the end that he may know the greatness of His Power and Will, and have patience, and submit his will to the Will of God. All these things and many more does God ordain, to increase the occasion and means whereby man may have great merit, that Divine Justice may grant him great happiness in the glory of Paradise. And since this is so, foolish indeed is the person and the soul that considers not all these things; and it is but a mark of pride to wish to have all that may be desired. Thus for a man to have patience when he may not obtain that which he desires is a greater and a better thing than is the good which follows from the fulfilment of his desire to possess all things soever that may be loved. And if it were certain that all men loved and served God, then to have sons would indeed be good, and my soul would desire it greatly; but since it is in doubt whether they would be obedient to God or no, therefore do I greatly hesitate in desiring to have a son."

17. Many other weighty arguments and sound examples did Evaſt expound to Aloma that he might comfort her and drive the sadness from her soul; and through their great love Aloma was comforted by the words of Evaſt her husband, and she spake these words: " I bless and adore the Sovereign Lord Who has and holds all things in His power. Blessed be He Who gives me to know my low eſtate, for I am unworthy to have all that I desire, and as for the good things that God hath given me, I have neither deserved them nor can I thank Him for them as I ought. Let then my desires and wishes be ever subject to His Will. Throughout all the days of my life I know that it behoves me to wish only that which is good and pleasing in the sight of God; and so greatly at fault is my wrong desire that I will ever love and hope in the wondrous mercy of God."

CHAPTER II

OF THE BIRTH AND GOOD UPBRINGING OF BLANQUERNA

In charity, patience and humility lived Evaſt and Aloma ever, and on Sundays and great feſtivals Evaſt went to the monaſteries of the city, and with the monks therein he sang and praised his Creator. Even so likewise did Aloma in the convents with the nuns; and they went to the hospitals, doing service to the unfortunate that were therein, and visited the poor and needy to whom they secretly gave alms, and the orphaned children they put to some trade, to the end that, when they were of age, their poverty should not give them occasion to sin.

2. While Evaſt and Aloma did these and many other good deeds, God, Who is the fulness of all good and grace, was mindful of the desire of Aloma, and of her humility and patience, and gave her a fair son who received the name of Blanquerna. Great was the pleasure and joy and gladness of Evaſt and Aloma at the birth of Blanquerna, and Evaſt, delaying nothing, went to the church to give thanks to God

for the son that He had given them, and to pray that Blanquerna his son might serve Him all the days of his life. On the day that Blanquerna was born, Evast made many alms to the poor of Jesus Christ; and on the eighth day the child received baptism, having for his godfathers and godmothers persons of holy life, that through their sanctity God might bless Blanquerna with His grace. On that day Evast caused Mass to be sung solemnly by a holy chaplain, the same that gave the sacrament of baptism to Blanquerna; for that sacrament should be given by no miserable sinner that is unworthy of conferring it, since it is the beginning of life and of the road whereby man travels to everlasting rest.

3. Blanquerna was given a nurse that was healthy in her person, that he might be nourished with healthy milk, for through poorness of milk children become weak and sickly; and the nurse was honest and of worthy life, for in suckling children it is greatly to be avoided that the nurse should be sickly or sinful or given to vice, or of evil humour, corrupt of body or in any other wise unhealthy.

4. During all that year wherein Blanquerna was born, Aloma gave naught to her son save only milk, for by defect of strong digestion infants in their first year can digest no other food, such as bread sopped in milk or oil, which parents give them, or other such food which they are made by force to eat; and for this reason children have pustules or scabs, ulcers or boils, and the humours begin to rise up, and destroy their brain or their sight or cause in them many other infirmities.

5. This child Blanquerna was brought up with great diligence. Aloma his mother clothed him in such manner that in winter he felt somewhat of the cold and in summer of the heat, for the elements whereof the human body is composed should accord with the seasons in the which they have their operations, to give a tempered condition to the body, that the evil humours may not rise therein. And Aloma kept her son Blanquerna with her until he could

walk and play with other children, and she constrained him to naught that is contrary to that which nature requires of children at such an age: till the age of eight years she left him to the course of nature.

6. When Blanquerna was eight years of age his father Evast put him to study, and caused him to be instructed in the contents of the *Book of Doctrine for Boys*,[1] wherein it is related how in the beginning a man should instruct his son in the mother tongue, and impart to him sound doctrine and knowledge of the articles of the faith and the ten commandments of the law and the seven sacraments of Holy Mother Church and the seven virtues and the seven deadly sins, and the other things that are contained in the said book.

7. It chanced one day that Aloma gave to Blanquerna her son for breakfast, before he went to school in the morning, roast meat, and afterwards a flawn to eat in school if the desire for it came to him. When Evast his father knew this, he reproved Aloma straitly and said to her that to children should be given naught but bread to eat in the mornings, lest they become dainty and gluttonous, and lose the desire to eat at table when the hour comes to dine; for by eating only bread children find not therein such relish that through excess of eating the operations of nature are constrained; and even bread should only be given to children when they ask for it.

8. Of all things that were provided at table was Blanquerna accustomed and made to eat, lest his nature should be habituated more to one sort of viand than to another. He was forbidden to drink wine that was strong, and wine that was overmuch watered, and to take strong sauces that destroy the natural heat. A tutor, who was given to Blanquerna for guardian and for master, took him every day to church, and taught him to pray to God and to hear Mass attentively and devoutly; and after Mass he took him to the school of music that he might learn to serve a sung Mass well.

[1] *Doctrina pueril*,—a book of instructions written by Lull himself.

9. Blanquerna learned so much grammar that he was able to speak and to understand Latin, and afterwards he studied logic and rhetoric and natural philosophy, to the end that he might the better know the science of medicine wherewith to keep his body in health, and the science of theology whereby he should know, love and serve God and guide his soul towards the everlasting life of Paradise.

10. When Blanquerna had learned the *Book of the Principles and Steps to Medicine*,[1] whereby he gained sufficient knowledge to learn to govern the health of his body, his father caused him to go to the school of theology, wherein he continually heard Holy Scripture, and was catechized from time to time in questions of theology.

11. While Blanquerna studied thus, Evast nurtured him in fear and in love, in the habits of the which two virtues children and youths should ever be nurtured and brought up, with fasting, prayer, confession and giving of alms, and humility of speech and conversation and companionship of good men; and in other things like to these. Evast instructed his son Blanquerna, to the end that when he should be grown and arrive at man's estate his manner of life should by nature and good habit be pleasing both to God and to man, and that he should not rebel against the customs which befit good breeding and which good citizens and men of gentle birth must ever bear in mind.

CHAPTER III

OF THE QUESTIONS THAT EVAST PUT TO HIS SON BLANQUERNA

By the grace of the Divine illumination, Evast bethought him of the time when he desired to enter an order[2] of religion, and he sought to prove his son Blanquerna, and to discover if he could rule himself and the house in such a

[1] Another book by Lull,—the *Libre dels principis e graus de medicina.*

[2] *orde.* This word has sometimes the general meaning of "state," sometimes the more restricted sense of "order."

way as to serve and please God, that himself and Aloma his wife might severally enter religious orders, and leave the world and forsake their temporal possessions. While Evast considered thus, Blanquerna his son returned from the school. Now Blanquerna was a gentle youth, comely and pleasant to look upon, and he had reached the age of eighteen years, being ever obedient to his parents, of right good habits and gentle upbringing.

2. "Fair son!" said Evast. "I would have thee answer me this question: Near to this city there stands a castle, at the entrance to a great wood. It chanced that a huntsman went into the wood to hunt deer and wild goats and such like beasts, as was his wont. And with an arrow he wounded a stag, but all that day he could neither lay hands upon it nor find a trace of it. Now as the hunter returned to the city he met a traveller who bore in his hand an arrow. And the hunter enquired of the traveller whence he had that arrow. The traveller answered that he had found it in a dead stag which he had sold to a butcher. And there arose a dispute betwixt the two as to which of them should have the price of the stag; for the hunter said that it was he that had killed it, and that if he had not wounded it the other would not have found it dead. The traveller said that fortune had given it to him, and that the hunter had already despaired of finding the stag, for he was returning to the city. Each of them (said Evast) brought forth many and great arguments the one against the other. Now I would fain know, son Blanquerna, what thy judgment would be, as to which of these two had the right to receive the price of the stag, or if it should be divided between them."

3. Blanquerna answered his father Evast, and said: "My lord and father! Thou knowest well that occasion is more powerful than fortune,[1] because in occasion is the final

[1] Modern English would rather say "design" and "chance," for "occasion" and "fortune," but in mediæval literature the words here used are of common occurrence.

intention whereby the stag was wounded and killed, and fortune has no intention either of itself or in its action upon another. And since by fortune the traveller found the stag, but by occasion it was killed, and the occasion lay with him that killed it, therefore, according to right and justice, to preserve the superiority that occasion has over fortune, the stag must be adjudged to the hunter; for, were it adjudged to the other, an injustice would be done to occasion, and fortune would be honoured in a fashion that befits it not. For the which reason I adjudge the price of the stag upon every ground to the hunter, provided that he can first prove the arrow to be his, for it might be that the arrow was that of another huntsman who killed the stag, and not of him who said that he had killed it."

4. Then Evast asked his son if it were just that the stag should be returned to the huntsman, or the price which he had received for it. Blanquerna answered and said that the butcher by right and justice should have the stag, for he had bought it according to the usages of his trade, believing it to belong to the seller. And since the traveller had sold it in the belief that the price should be his, an injustice would therefore be done to the butcher if the gain which he would receive from the stag should be taken from him. And ill-seeming would it be if the traveller should receive injury in place of thanks, the which thing would follow if he gave satisfaction to the butcher together with the price of the stag and returned the stag to the hunter; for the which cause it was right and just that to the hunter should belong the price of the stag alone.

5. Evast said further to Blanquerna: "Tell me, my son, if the hunter is obliged to give the other aught of the price of the stag." "My lord and father!" said Blanquerna, "Two kinds of law in general are there in the world, from the which proceed all the categories of law in the particular; the one kind is according to God, and the other according to the world. The manner of law that is ordained

and disposed according to the law of God is more subtle and the occasion of more scruples than that which is of the world. Wherefore by this distinction between the two rules aforesaid, I may know that, according to the nobler right, the hunter is constrained to give to the traveller somewhat in consideration of his labour and in respect of charity, fraternity and conscience, and furthermore, of good breeding and courtesy, and against avarice, injury and envy. But that the huntsman freely, and of his own will, may have the virtues aforesaid, giving to the traveller some part of the price of the stag, it is ordained by divine ordinance and temporal justice that the huntsman by temporal law be not constrained to give any part of the price to the traveller; for, were he so constrained, there would follow none of the freedom which pertains to merit, whereby man may have the virtues aforesaid, nor would temporal law be set below divine; in the which case God would have abased the nobler law to magnify the less noble, which is a thing ill-beseeming and to be rejected by all reason."

6. Evast said to Blanquerna: "Tell me further, my son, if the hunter, by giving naught to the traveller, commits sin for which he merits the pains of hell." Blanquerna answered: "There is a difference, my lord and father, between sin mortal and venial; and if the traveller had any right to a part of the price of the stag, the ordaining of the two kinds of law aforementioned would be contrary to justice and to God, and this is a thing impossible; by the which impossibility I may understand and know that the hunter commits no mortal sin if he give naught to the traveller. But since he will use therein no courtesy nor charity, as is fitting, to mortify the conscience, therefore he commits venial sin, whereby he merits not everlasting damnation, yet merits less of eternal glory."

7. All these questions, and many more which it would take over long time to relate, did Evast put to Blanquerna his son, and Blanquerna replied right perfectly to them all, answering them with effective argument.

8. So when Evast saw that his son shone thus in knowledge, and was adorned with good breeding and habits, he was greatly pleased thereat, and he entered a chapel in his house, wherein he and Aloma prayed to God secretly and were wont to hear Mass daily, and to give thanks to God when they had risen from table. The altar-piece was of St. Andrew, in whom Evast and Aloma trusted greatly that they should receive grace and blessing from God.

9. When Evast entered the chapel, he kneeled before the altar and made the sign of the cross as was his wont. Then he spake these words: "O glorious Lord God, Who hast not forgotten Thy servant that so oft has desired to serve and honour Thee in the state of religion! Blessed be Thou, O Lord, and blessed be Thy mercy, which in pity and condescension has deigned to grant me all my will in my son Blanquerna. For long have I hoped and desired that my temporal goods might be entrusted to him, and that I and Aloma might be enabled to contemplate, love and serve Thee in a religious order, making remembrance of Thy holy Passion and grieving for our faults and sins. I adore, O Lord, Thy goodness, Thy greatness and Thy power, Thy wisdom, and love, and the other virtues wherein Thou art one God in essence, Father and Son and Holy Spirit. Blessed be Thou, O Lord, in Thyself and in all Thy virtues and honours, for that Thou hast given me a son so worthy and so prudent, to whom, from this day onward, I may entrust and leave the conduct of this house. To Thee, O Lord, as is my bounden obligation, I commend him."

CHAPTER IV

OF THE DISAGREEMENT THAT WAS BETWEEN EVAST AND ALOMA

Evast considered long how he might reveal to Aloma his wife the desire of his heart, and induce her to enter the estate of religion, for he feared greatly lest she should wish to delay. On the day following, after Mass, Evast and Aloma remained in the chapel, and when all the rest had left it, Evast spake to Aloma these words: " Aloma, my beloved! By the grace of God, our son Blanquerna is endowed with great wisdom and moreover is of right worthy habits and gentle breeding, and he has come now to an age when we may leave to him the care both of himself and of all our possessions and the management of this our house. And the time is come for Blanquerna to take to himself a wife, and for ourselves to leave this miserable world and enter the estate of religion that we may live in greater sanctity. And as by good living we have until now enlightened and instructed those that are in the estate of matrimony, even so by the sanctity of a good life let us give example henceforward to all such as are in the estate of religion. Therefore is it fitting that we make division of our temporal possessions, and for the love of God bestow them on the poor of Jesus Christ, and that thou choose that convent for women which shall please thee best, while I by thy leave will enter also a religious order as I have so greatly desired."

2. Very strange seemed to Aloma these words which Evast spake to her, wherefore she turned pale, suspecting in her heart that she had in some manner displeased him and given him cause to desire to leave her. Wherefore she took counsel with herself ere she replied. Then Evast spake to her these words: "Aloma! Wherefore answerest thou me not? And why is it that thou hast such thought? Hast thou not heard my words?" " My lord!" answered Aloma. " Thy words have I heard indeed, and thou hast given me to suspect that thou hast ill-will or displeasure against me, for the which cause thou wouldst fain leave me. If it seem to thee that in aught I have been in fault or have sinned against thee, I pray thee that thou wilt in some other manner be avenged, rather than leave me at the end of my days, for greater need have I of thy aid and governance than heretofore."

3. "Aloma!" said Evast, "Thou mayest be certain that at no time has my will been displeased or angered with thee or with any work of thine. Rather would I have thee know that since it pleased God to unite us twain in matrimony, I have given thanks to Him every day of my life for granting me thy sweet companionship. For among the gifts that God has given in this world to them that love Him, for the which they are bound to make continual thanks, is companionship that is loyal and true. And therefore, Aloma, think thou not neither fear in any wise that I am displeased at aught that thou hast done; and not only so, but I would crave thy pardon if ever I have wronged thee or done aught that seemed to thee evil. But since we have come to the end of our days, and since the state of religion is of greater sanctity than the state of matrimony in the which we now are, and since all men should approach God by good works as nearly as they may, and we ourselves have now both time and disposition, therefore I pray thee, who hast never been disobedient to my words or prayers, to consent to this prayer which I make thee, that we may both of us enter the life of contemplation, leaving the conduct of this active life entirely to our son Blanquerna. So can we do our utmost that by the grace of God we may dwell together, world without end, in the eternal glory of Paradise."

4. "My lord Evast!" said Aloma. "With shame and fear must I needs reply to thy words, and the God of glory knows well that never was it in my mind or thought to disobey thee in any matter soever, nor to desire disagreement betwixt my will and thine. But since the beginning of our union was in the state of matrimony, and the beginning must ever have regard to the end[1]—that is to say, that together we should ever be and remain till death come at last to divide us—know therefore, my lord Evast, that in no wise will I act contrarily to the beginning of this first estate

[1] *ha tots temps esguart a la fi*, i.e. "looks ever towards the end (which shall complete it)."

wherein God has placed me, and wherein He has kept and preserved me from sin against the estate of matrimony. In all things else, do with me as thou wilt, so that God be served and praised, and thou thyself have pleasure therein. To each and every thing will I gladly consent. But never will I abandon the estate in the which God has placed me, nor shouldst thou, saving thine honour, counsel me to enter another estate to the which I am less devoted than to that of marriage wherein I now am; for lack of devotion causes many a man and many a woman to despise their state of life, and to forsake it. I pray thee to tell me wherefore thou lovest the estate of religion more than that estate of matrimony wherein thou art."

5. "Aloma!" said Evast. "Thine answer grieves me greatly; but I think that thou speakest thus to the end that thy submission may please me the more, and that I may understand how thou forsakest the estate wherein thou art against thy will, and enterest the religious life for love of me, wherefore I am the more thy debtor. But thou needest not to seek my greater indebtedness or pleasure, for thyself and thine affection well content me. Let us rather strive to win favour and merit of God, to Whose judgment-seat we each must come. And all that I know of thy saintly life, and of my own faults, which are many and great, assures me that thy gladness at passing to the holy estate of religion will be greater than mine."

6. When Aloma perceived that Evast thought her to be excusing herself from his request to the end that she might try him or have thanks of him, her eyes filled with tears, and she fell to weeping bitterly. Then, deeply sighing, she answered him in these words: "My lord Evast! God alone can tell all that is in the heart of man. Know thou then indeed that my heart hath never suffered such grief or pain as now that I see myself opposed to thy will; for the love which I have ever borne thee constrains me so greatly that the tears of my heart rise even to mine eyes, and mine eyes

have shame to be in thy presence, and my conscience would compel me to believe that this thing, wherein there is no fault, is sin. Wherefore, O my lord, I would have thee know that I answer thee according to my present estate and my will: for my will constrains me and makes me to suffer because I obey thee not, yet it makes me to abhor the parting and the separation that there would be between us if we entered into diverse estates. And thy parting would be grief to me because my will would fain have thee alway, and mine eyes desire alway to see thee; so that my heart is heavy because I cannot fulfil that which thy will desires, since it would ever displease and afflict me."

7. "Aloma!" replied Evast. "Both thy arguments and thy affection please me, and I am sure of this, that the love of man and wife is the will of God. And for all these reasons, and for many beside, my heart will have much grief if I leave thee. Whensoever I see thee I am glad, and greatly cheered in countenance and joyful of heart when I remember thy worthy upbringing and devout practices or hear that men speak well of thee. But since it behoves me to love God my Creator and Saviour more than thee or aught beside, and since I fain would offer and receive His glorious Body, therefore the strength of this great desire makes me to forget the affliction that I shall have in losing thee. Yet know that in my heart is great suffering when I think that I should be the occasion of aught that displeases or grieves thee. But since the love of God gives man strength and power to bear many trials and to despise the world, therefore I exhort thee to the end that love may make us both to bear and suffer the pain of our separation, to the greater love and service of God."

8. "My lord Evast!" said Aloma. "True it is that in this world there is no office so noble and profitable as to celebrate Mass and to consecrate the sacred Body of our Lord Jesus Christ; yet although it be so noble, for no man is it lawful to enter upon so holy a mystery except he be

thereto duly ordained; and to this end he must do no wrong nor cause trial to another, in whom may be engendered wrath and occasion of sin. And every man is not worthy, neither should he hold himself worthy, to serve in so glorious an office. Wherefore if thou, my lord, desire to be a clerk and to sing Mass, it suffices thee to go daily to the church with the friars, and to assist at Mass and the other offices, aiding them in the singing and reading of psalms, lessons, responses and antiphons, and serving the priest that says Mass, according to the custom which now thou observest, desiring with all thy heart to be a minister at the altar. But hold thyself not worthy so to be, for this thou art not, since God hath not placed thee in that estate but in the estate of matrimony. And I will go day by day to the convent according to my wont, joining the nuns in singing and responding at Mass, in honour of the holy Sacrament of the Altar. Let us in this wise do all that we may, and not leave that estate of matrimony wherein we are and wherein God has placed us."

9. "Aloma!" said Evast. "Wearied and fatigued am I by the possession and handling of temporal wealth, and my prayers thereby are impeded. Into my heart has entered the desire to leave carnal delights and to give myself so earnestly to prayer that naught else shall be in my heart or in my thought save God alone. I would make penance and satisfaction for my faults and for the evil that I have done; for, both clothed and shod, in my meat and drink, in the comfort of soft beds, and in many and divers matters more have I erred and strayed. And I have the most earnest will to preach the word of God and the Passion of His Son Jesus Christ our Lord. And since the religious life is an estate more fitted for all these things than is the estate of marriage, therefore would I leave the life wherein I am, and pass to that of the blessed religious, doing penance with them and performing all the things aforesaid. And if thou didst take from me that happiness which the religious life can give me,

then wouldst thou be an enemy to the increase of my happiness."

10. "My lord Evast!" said Aloma. "If thou wilt forsake the world to serve God the better and leave to Blanquerna all thy possessions, I am content, so that thou and I remain still together. In this chapel we can adore, bless and pray to God. We should neither need to have commerce with temporal goods nor concern ourselves with the necessities of the body, since with all this Blanquerna is able to deal. For these causes therefore we need not to enter another estate. If thou wilt do penance and lead an ascetic life, there is a place more nigh at hand in thine own house than in a house of religion, and thou canst do all these things more secretly in the married state than as a religious. Likewise I am prepared to go with thee to a desert place or a mountain, that there we may both do penance, and the harder the life that we lead to serve the King of glory, the greater will be the content within my soul. Let us both live chastely, knowing not each other according to the flesh. Instead of preaching, thou mayest live a holy life, and by thy good example preach to all that are in the estate of marriage, edifying also such men as are in the estate of religion. What thing soever that thou pleasest mayest thou do with me, provided that thou wilt have me do naught that is against the sacrament which binds us."

11. "Aloma!" said Evast. "Great virtue is it to be obedient, to give and to submit thy will to another for the love of our Lord God." "My lord Evast!" answered Aloma. "Great virtue is it to be lord of thine own will, and to rule it well, which each can do better in himself than in another."

12. "Aloma!" said Evast further. "Great merit is won by him that forsakes all things for the love of God, devoting himself to His service." "Evast my lord!" said Aloma. "Great merit has he that is in the world and possesses temporal things without sin, and devotes himself to the service

of the poor of Jesus Christ; and great merit has he that is rich in the goods of this world yet poor in spirit; and if it be virtue to beg for the love of Jesus Christ, it cannot be a vice to give to the poor who beg for love of Him; and of doubtful wisdom is it to leave so many riches to Blanquerna, who is young and has not yet proved his fitness to administer the possessions of this world. Therefore I think it good that we do in this house the penance that thou desirest, and if it seems well to thee that we go not without the house, I am content. Let us show our son Blanquerna how he may rule himself and these our possessions, that they may be kept and preserved for the poor of Jesus Christ, who receive support daily in this house with the alms that thou givest them."

13. "Aloma!" said Evast. "Many arguments both weighty and true have I set before thee, wherefore thou canst and shouldst obey my requests. I pray thee then that thou excuse not thyself, neither resist my wishes, but make me glad and joyful, granting me that which for long I have desired, and bring not grief nor sadness nor displeasure to my soul, knowing how loyally I have ever loved thee."

14. "My lord Evast!" answered Aloma. "I have heard thine arguments, and I have enquired of my heart if I could consent to thy commands and prayers, but I can find no way whereby I may so consent. And since anger and ill-will are oft-times engendered when one man obeys not the prayers of another, therefore I pray thee that thou speak no more to me henceforward of this thing, for I may not further answer thee, and I fear lest between us there be engendered ill-will. Let us then return to our former conversation, and speak of God and of His works, as is our wont. And at whatsoever time thou wilt perform those things which I set forth at the first, I am ready to follow thy will."

15. Greatly was Evast displeased when he could not convert Aloma his wife to his will, and many were the days

and the hours wherein he spake to her further, using the words aforementioned. But each time he caused her grief and pain, and never could he in any wise move her; wherefore Evast had compassion upon Aloma because of the pain which he gave her, and resolved never more to speak to her of the matter, but to commend it wholly to the hand of God and to His Will. So he purposed inwardly to please Aloma by doing penance in their house, to remain therein and never again to leave it, lest they should see and hear the vain things of the world without, which impede the soul from the remembrance, understanding and love of God and of His honours. When Evast had thus resolved in his will, on the next morning, after Mass, he called Aloma as he was wont, and Aloma began forthwith to weep, thinking that he was about to speak the same words as before, which brought grief to her soul. "Aloma!" said Evast. "Weep not; for since thou hast so high and resolute a spirit, and wilt for naught incline to my prayers, therefore will I bend my heart to thy will to obey thy wishes. Let us then endeavour ourselves to lead a life of rigid penance secretly in this house all the days of our life, even for so long as shall please the will of God. And let us give full authority to our son Blanquerna over all our goods, saving such as we shall retain, for the need which we have thereof to sustain our lives while it shall please God that we live. Let us give him all that remains, and seek for him a wife forthwith. To-morrow, after Mass, let us call him and acquaint him with our design, after the which we can arrange our own affairs and draw up a rule whereby we may live in penitence."

16. Greatly joyed Aloma at these words which Evast spake to her, praising and blessing God that He had given these desires to Evast her husband. And she answered Evast that she was ready to fulfil all that he had set forth in the words aforesaid, and that she thought it well to do penance secretly in the house and to draw up the rule which should bind them.

CHAPTER V

HOW EVAST AND ALOMA DESIRED TO LEAVE THE CHARGE OF THE HOUSEHOLD TO THEIR SON BLANQUERNA

ON the next day after Mass, Evast and Aloma called Blanquerna before the altar where stood the sign of the holy Cross, and Evast spake to Blanquerna these words: "Well-beloved son Blanquerna! It behoves us to remember whence we are come, by Whom we are created and whither we must return; and to bear in remembrance also the favours that we have received from the Most High. Now has the time arrived for Aloma thy mother and me to forsake this world and renounce temporal riches. Our age and the feebleness of our bodies warns us that we draw nigh unto death. Now, therefore, henceforward is it meet that we lead a life of austerity and that all our days be spent in bewailing our sins, in prayer and in penance. We make thee, then, fair son, inheritor of all our temporal goods, and in the prayers and the good works that we shall do we give thee a part, and from henceforth art thou lord of all our goods. Do thou rule and govern this house in such a manner that the goods distributed therein be not lost, and that we ourselves receive sustenance in our lifetime, and that such children as thou shalt have may be nurtured in a way well-pleasing unto God."

2. When Evast had said these words, and many more, to his son Blanquerna, he took his seal, and Aloma took the keys of the house, and they desired Blanquerna to receive the seal and the keys. But Blanquerna took not that which Evast and Aloma would have given him, but began to look upon the Cross, and remembered the sacred Passion of our Lord Jesus Christ, and how He and His Apostles were poor in this world and despised temporal possessions. Long did Blanquerna think upon these things ere he answered Evast, and after his cogitation he spake these words:

3. "My lord and father!" said Blanquerna. "Great is the honour that thou and Aloma would do to this your son Blanquerna, who is unworthy such great honour to receive. And great faith and confidence have ye in your son, being willing to entrust to him so many things, or ever ye have proved him in loyalty, charity, justice and the other virtues. For the honour and the favour that ye do me, may ye be rewarded and have thanks of God. But as for me, know ye that from henceforward I will have in my heart neither honours nor riches nor pleasures of this world nor other thing soever, but only God Who has created me and made me to be His dwelling-place. Wherefore a grievous wrong would be done to God if He were cast out from the place wherein He would dwell, and sorely would it pain my soul to cast out God."

4. Great marvel had Evast and Aloma at the words of Blanquerna their son, to whom Evast replied: "What then dost thou intend, and the words which thou speakest, what deeds do they signify? Greatly am I amazed at thy words. I pray thee, tell me thy will." "My lord!" said Blanquerna. "By the Divine light is my soul moved to remember, comprehend and love the life of poverty, and of the hermitage, and the renunciation of this world, that it may the more perfectly contemplate and love the Son of God, Who came to this world for us sinners, and suffered most grievous Passion, which the sign of the Cross portrays to my bodily eyes. By the which sign I your son Blanquerna would fain follow the life of Elias and Saint John Baptist and the other holy fathers that have passed from this life, the which fathers did penance and led lives of discipline in mountain and desert that they might flee from the world and vanquish the flesh and the devil, and be not impeded in contemplating and loving the God of glory, Who is the beginning and end of all good."

5. "Blanquerna!" said Evast, "Right glad and joyful are we at the holy devotion which has entered into thy mind.

Many a time did I fear to pray God that He would give me children lest they should be sinners and live contrarily to His commandments. But now I know that the desire of Aloma thy mother to have thee for a son was good, since thou desirest to be a servant of God. I reprove thee not for thy devotion; but since thou must needs requite thy parents for the benefits that thou hast received of them, therefore it behoves thee to remain in the world until thy mother and I have passed from this life, when thou mayest fulfil the devotion and the desire which by the Divine virtue is in thee."

6. "My lord Evast!" answered Blanquerna, "Well do I know the natural benefits that from thee and from my lady Aloma I have received, and how ye have brought me up and instructed me to the utmost of your power. But greater than all these are the benefits that I have received from God; and the reason of all others for the which I am in the world is that I may know and love and praise and contemplate God. And since to be in the world is a thing that is perilous, most chiefly of all to a man that is young, therefore from the world am I fain to flee. I would go to God Who calls me: father, mother, honours, riches, happiness and all things would I leave for love of Him. For if I have but God in my heart I shall want for naught; and if God were not in my heart, who could give me the fulfilment of that which my soul so greatly desires?"

7. "Beloved son!" said Evast, "If thou obeyest not my prayers and my commandment, thou wilt do an evil deed both to me and to Aloma and likewise to the poor of Jesus Christ. For these last receive much alms from the possessions of this house, which will be lost if thou dost leave us. And thine will be the fault if we thy parents Evast and Aloma, for want of one to govern their possessions, are compelled to leave undone the penances that they desire to perform. Thine will be the blame for the trials which we suffer in our age; and since detriment and injury

done to others are displeasing to God, therefore, fair son, neither in justice nor in charity canst thou or must thou leave the possessions of this house to perish, nor be the occasion of our trials, nor cause the benefits which will follow from our penance to be lost."

8. "My lord and father!" said Blanquerna. "God wills that man should travail in His service even until death. Therefore it appears to me, having regard to your ages, that thou and my lady Aloma may yet travail and administer your possessions in this world and give therewith alms. And though to your years the travail of this world is ill beseeming, yet the greater for that very reason will be your merits if ye serve God thereby. Wherefore do thou and Aloma persist in your present estate, despairing not of the help of God, neither renouncing temporal wealth, after the fashion of many, that ye may find rest, the which rest is peril and travail to other men. At the end of your days, when ye have no more strength, commend ye your possessions to some trusty man who shall do good therewith even as ye do, or divide them all among the poor of Christ. Impede not, my lord, my happiness or my desire; set me not in peril for things that are temporal, fleeting and corruptible; reprove me not where ye should give me your blessing; and be not sad at that for the which ye should rejoice."

9. "Blanquerna!" said Evast. "Assay thou first in our midst to do penance and lead a life of austerity, rather than go to do penance in solitary[1] places. Do thou prove thy will also to persevere at length in that which it makes thee to desire. A great thing is this whereupon thou desirest to enter, and thou shouldst in no wise enter thereupon suddenly. For oftentimes it befalls that a man thinks to continue in a life of penance before he feels how grievous and how wearisome it is for the body to suffer. And when he feels this, he returns to the bodily pleasures and the vain delights which were aforetime his. And in such case he

[1] *agrestes*, lit. "rustic."

receives of men naught but disdain and reproof. Wherefore, beloved son, be thou not over-hasty, but curb thy will, and give thou heed to my words."

10. "My lord Evast, that a man should try and prove himself in the bearing of pains and in the life of penance is without doubt not engendered by lack of perfect devotion and love; for such things are lightened by the strength of devotion and love, and the severer is the life of a man, the greater and the nobler in him are love and devotion, as also are patience, strength, justice, hope and the remaining virtues. Wherefore there is naught that can trouble my soul save that my trials and austerities should be less."

11. Many arguments did Evast use with his son Blanquerna, that he might cast out from his mind the thought and the design which he had conceived. But the more he begged him, and the stronger were the arguments that he alleged, the greater was the assurance and determination that he found in him. Wherefore Evast ceased from speaking, for he feared that his words might be displeasing to God, and considered how through Divine grace Blanquerna might well be inspired by the Holy Spirit. While Evast thought upon these things, Aloma began to speak, and she spake these words to her son Blanquerna, weeping and being greatly moved in her spirit:

12. "Beloved son!" said Aloma, "If thou goest to the hermitage, what wilt thou eat? And if these garments of thine be torn, wherewith wilt thou be clothed? And if thou fall sick, who will tend thee? Fair son Blanquerna! Have a thought to thy body which I so carefully have nourished. Take pity on Evast thy father and on me, for in thy absence and with the fear of thy death and of thy sufferings we too shall suffer, who had hoped for help and comfort from thee at the end of our days. And now, when we trusted to have had of thee comfort and joy, and are wishful to give thee to wife a fair and goodly damsel of noble breeding, honoured ancestry and great riches, thou

wouldst forsake us, and give thy body over to death for no fault of thine; for thou hast done no such grievous wrong that thou needest to torment both thyself and us, neither have we done harm or wrong to thee." All these words and many more said Aloma to her son; and so devoutly and with so many tears did she speak, that Evast and Blanquerna wept likewise, and all three were for long in tears ere Blanquerna could answer Aloma his mother.

13. When Blanquerna had wept for long and nature had rendered him her due,[1] his soul had in no wise forgotten its sacred devotion, neither did fortitude delay in strengthening his mind to resist his bodily nature. And by the virtue of God, Blanquerna spake to his mother Aloma, and to Evast, in these words: "With the suffering of a mind constrained by the strength of love I must resist the desire of thy soul. Love has captured my will and makes me to disobey thy desires, though thou hast so long and so dearly loved me. I am thy son: from thee and from my father Evast have I taken my being. Ye have brought me up,—and better ye could not. All that ye have, would ye give me. Even your own bodies would ye put into my power. And I cannot serve you, nor gladden you with my presence: nay, my absence will bring you sorrow. I cannot reward you for the good that ye have done me and the love that ye have borne. For I am not my own; rather do I belong to Another, Who has captured me. Were I but lord of myself, I would give myself to you to serve and honour you all the days of my life. If God has captured me and withdraws me from your presence, and from the pleasures of this world, and makes me to be alone in the woods and the great forests, among wild beasts, and in places where there is lack of food and raiment and companionship and of many things necessary to man, then God, Who has given to the birds and the beasts in such places the wherewithal to eat, to drink and to be clothed, and Who keeps them in

[1] *i.e.* when nature had paid the tribute of tears.

health, will give to me also all that my body needs to sustain its life. Wherefore my soul will be able to contemplate Him in His honour and glory; and if my body should die for lack of that which it needs, then will God have worked His will with that which is His own, and my soul will have used hope, charity and fortitude towards her Creator and with respect to the trials of the body, and her profit will be so exceeding great that the trials of the body will be esteemed as light afflictions and as naught. All my life long will I pray for you to the God of glory; and if God for my merits should will to give me aught, I will pray Him to grant it to you. I beseech you to forgive me in that I cannot obey you and am the occasion of your trials. And I beg of your favour to forget me, that for my sake ye may suffer no more trials. Bestow on me then your blessing, for I would go to that place which God has given me to desire."

14. When Blanquerna had said these words and many more, he kneeled before Evast his father and Aloma his mother, and begged their blessing, since he desired to go to a hermitage to serve God. "How now, son Blanquerna?" said Aloma. "Wouldst thou indeed depart?" "Beloved mother!" said Blanquerna, "I would fain take leave of you, that I may go to those places to the which God and my fortune may be pleased to guide me. Wherefore I pray you to give me your blessing and in no way to delay my journey, for the longer I am with you, the greater will be your longing for my presence, and the yearning of my heart for yours. And the greater freedom I give to the desire of my soul, the greater will be my affliction and my sorrow."

15. "Fair son Blanquerna!" said Aloma, "Thou shalt remain with us all this day and night, for it beseems not that our farewells be so brief. Let all this day and night be spent in leave-taking and in tears, in mutual love and in grief at thy departure. In the morning, after Mass, thy father Evast and I will give thee our blessing, and then

shalt thou take leave of us for our whole life long: may it please God that we find thee and know thee in His holy glory. If thy absence give us now in this present life trial or grief, may God in glory eternal make us glad with thy presence so greatly beloved."

CHAPTER VI

OF THE TEMPTATION WHEREWITH BLANQUERNA WAS TEMPTED BY THE MAIDEN NATANA[1]

WHEN Aloma had ended these words, she went from the chapel to the house of one Naštasia, a widow. This lady had a right fair and gracious daughter, by name Natana. And Aloma enjoyed great friendship with Naštasia and her daughter Natana. Aloma went secretly into a chamber apart with Naštasia and Natana her daughter, and began to weep sorely, saying these words: "Ah, unhappy, wretched one that I am! For ever am I to be without comfort, and I had thought to be glad all the days of my life. I have lost my son Blanquerna whom I have loved above all things in this world, save only God. If in you I find not counsel and aid whereby I may recover my son, my soul will be in grief and sorrow all the days of my life."

2. Greatly marvelled Naštasia and Natana, and to great pity were they moved by the tears and by the words of Aloma. "Sister and friend!" said Naštasia. "Weep not; for if we can aid thee in aught, we will do it with all good will and pleasure and with all our might, provided only that it bring us no shame or evil repute among men." Then Aloma answered Naštasia, and related to her all that had passed between herself and Evast and Blanquerna their son; and she told her how Blanquerna would neither obey her

[1] This is the Cana of some versions of the story. She is so called in the introduction to the *Book of the Lover and the Beloved* (London, S.P.C.K., 1923, p. 15).

words nor give ear to her entreaties, and how he purposed on the morrow early to take leave of them and to depart to desert places alone to do penance therein all the days of his life. " Therefore," said she, " the counsel and the aid that I ask of thee, if thou wilt do me pleasure, is that thy daughter Natana shall speak with my son Blanquerna, to the end that perchance she may turn him from his present will and incline him to the state of matrimony, if he be pleased to take her to wife. All our possessions would we give, both Evast and I, in such a case, to Natana and to Blanquerna."

3. So they debated, and agreement was made between them that Aloma should bring Blanquerna to the house of Nastasia after the hour of dinner; and that, when they were within the house, Aloma and Nastasia should leave Blanquerna and Natana in the room alone; and that Natana should speak loving words whereby Blanquerna should know that Natana would fain be his wife, and had loved him for long with an inward love; and that in this manner they should turn Blanquerna from his former will, and incline him to the estate of matrimony. When this agreement had been made, Aloma returned to her house, and entered the chapel, where she found Evast, with his son Blanquerna, weeping for the parting which was to be between them. Then Aloma spake these words: " Now it is the hour to dine. Come then and let us to table, and afterwards we shall have leisure to weep for as long as we will."

4. Many were the meats that were placed upon the table, but little did they eat thereof, either Evast or Aloma or Blanquerna. When they had all dined, Aloma took her cloak and commanded Blanquerna to accompany her, for she desired to visit a lady of her acquaintance with whom she had to speak. So Blanquerna accompanied Aloma his mother to the house of Nastasia, and Aloma with her son Blanquerna entered a room wherein they found Nastasia and Natana alone. Natana was richly clad in costly gar-

ments, and adorned by nature with wondrous beauty. So Aloma said to Natana: "Hold company, if it please thee, with my son Blanquerna, while I speak with thy mother Nastasia." Then Blanquerna and Natana remained alone in the room, and Aloma and Nastasia entered another room to speak together.

5. While Blanquerna and Natana were sitting the one beside the other, and Blanquerna was thinking upon his journey, Natana began to speak to Blanquerna in these words: "For long, O Blanquerna, have I desired a way wherein I may speak to thee of that which is in my heart and reveal it. For long have I loved thee inwardly with all my soul, and above all things I desire to be thy wife. It is the strength of my love that now constrains me to speak to thee these words. If thou, by virtue of thy lineage and wealth, art deserving of a richer or more honourable wife, do thou consider the love wherewith from the depth of my heart I love thee, and do thou consider likewise the good intention wherewith I would be thy wife, for this comes of no intemperate thought. And may God fulfil the desire of my will to have sons of thee, who shall be servants of God, and be like unto thyself in the holy life which thou dost lead by the grace of God, and by the doctrine and example of thy father Evast and thy mother Aloma, who are of greater sanctity than any other persons in this city."

6. Fair was Natana, and prudently and with a semblance of great love did she speak these words to Blanquerna. Yet for all that he neither forgot not cast from his heart the holy desire that was his, nor did the fire of the Holy Spirit which had kindled his whole soul tarry long in coming to his aid. So when Blanquerna had thought for a brief space on the words which Natana had spoken to him, he spake to her these words: "The King of all kings, Who is the Hope and Consolation of all sinners, and Who forgets not His servants in their necessities, even that Lord do I adore and bless because from to-day temptations begin to assail me,

and the Divine Virtue aids me against evil counsel. Glad is my heart at this the beginning of my temptations, and hope bids me look to the strength which now I feel, that it may help me in all other temptations that assail me." Greatly did Blanquerna praise and bless our Lord God thus ere he made answer to the words of Natana.

7. Natana perceived that Blanquerna rejoiced and blessed God, and answered not her words; wherefore, exalted somewhat within herself, she spake to him after this manner: "Why, O Blanquerna, repliest thou not to my words? And what is this that thou sayest? And wherefore is thy soul made to rejoice?" Blanquerna answered Natana and said: "With the light of grace hath the Holy Spirit illumined my soul, making me to desire the life of a hermit, that I may have within my heart God alone. When thou, Natana, didst reveal to me thy heart, the lust of the flesh began to tempt my soul through my bodily nature and the work of the evil spirit. But forthwith my soul turned to the remembrance of its Lover, and the Divine Light illumined my soul with Divine Love, which made me to know that God forgets not His servant. And His love makes me so greatly to despise thy words, that I marvel, as I follow thine arguments, how in one so fair as thou there can be so foolish a thought as this of thine which counsels me to forsake the love of my Sovereign Lord for the love of thee. At certain times I have doubted if God will aid me against the temptations that will come to me in the desert, but now I know and doubt not that which I doubted aforetime. Let any temptation come that may: this my good beginning will cause me to despise it."

8. Greatly did Natana marvel at the sanctity of Blanquerna and his constancy of mind, saying: "Blanquerna, my friend! How is it that thou answerest not my words?" Blanquerna answered: "If thou wilt speak to me of God or of doctrine wherewith I may greatly love, honour and serve Him, then will thy words be very pleasing unto me.

But speak to me henceforward no vain words soever; suffer me rather, while my mother Aloma speaks with thy mother Nastasia, to think upon my journey."

9. "Blanquerna!" said Natana. "How couldst thou for so long endure the bitter life of wild and desert regions? And how dost thou purpose to endure it without first knowing if thou art able?" Blanquerna answered: "Who enabled Saint Catherine, Saint Eulalia, Saint Margaret, and other holy virgins and martyrs, to endure trials, torments and death, for these of their own will were put to suffering and torture, were killed or burnt alive, for love of my Beloved, Jesus Christ. And if these, who were young girls, frail[1] and of tender years, by the grace of God bore all these things and desired to endure yet more, shall not I, a man, endure hunger, thirst, cold, heat and fear as a hermit for love of God? And is it not beyond comparison a surer and a nobler thing to put my trust in the help of God in the desert than in this city to trust in the help of Evast my father, and of Aloma my mother, and in the riches of this world?"

10. "Oftentimes has it come to pass," said Natana to Blanquerna, "that a man among his kindred and his friends has purposed right valiantly to accomplish or endure some great feat or trial, and for this to be praised and rewarded exceedingly. But later, when the trial comes upon him, he shrinks from it; and that which he purposed becomes irksome to him, and he flees from that trial which he believed himself able to endure. Even so, when thou, Blanquerna, art in the desert, tasting that bitter life and looking upon wretched and scanty victuals, and grieving at the absence of Evast and Aloma, and of thy other kinsfolk and friends, being alone among wild beasts, then wilt thou be of another mind than that wherein now thou art, and then wilt thou fear things which now thou fearest not."

[1] So V (*fragils*). The alternative reading *frèvols* seems less appropriate.

11. "Natana!" said Blanquerna, "I go into the forest to contemplate my Lord God Jesus Christ and His Virgin Mother our glorious Lady Saint Mary; and for my company I have Faith, Hope, Charity, Justice, Prudence, Fortitude and Temperance. Faith I need that I may believe the articles of the holy Catholic Faith according to the Roman Church, and to aid me against the temptations which come through ignorance. Hope I bear in my company that I may hope and trust in the strength and help and mercy of Him Who alone can aid me. Charity my heart bears, and it will bear me to regions wild and make it to appear that this city and other regions inhabited are unpeopled and desert: with Charity man conquers and vanquishes all things. Justice makes me turn body and soul to God because He is the Creator and Benefactor both of me and of all things that are. Prudence makes me to know and despise this world that is full of deception and error and is of brief duration, and makes me to desire eternal happiness. Fortitude strengthens my heart, in the might of the Most High, to endure every trial for His love. Temperance I bear with me that it may rule my mouth, my appetite and my belly. If in the desert places I may not have these virtues, then shall I be compelled to return. And if I could not in such places endure hunger, thirst, cold, heat, nakedness, fear, poverty and temptations, where would be the virtues or the works without which I could not and would not live, either in these places or in any other? And thus, Natana," said Blanquerna, "thou wouldst affright me with those very things which I desire to endure for His love Who for love of me endured trials more grievous than those whereof thou speakest; and my desire to endure these trials and many others drives me from my home to those places where I may find them and have them; and I would neither be nor dwell in any place wherein they are not to be found."

12. "Blanquerna!" said Natana, "Greatly do thy words please me; for ever would I be with thee; may it

please thee then to take me in thy company, that we may live as penitents together in whatsoever place seems to thee best." Blanquerna answered: "It would be ill beseeming that either thou should be in my company or any other, for no company will I have save that of God, and of trees, grass, birds, wild beasts, fountains and streams, banks and meadows, sun, moon and stars; for none of these things may hinder the soul from contemplating God."

13. "Blanquerna!" said Natana, "If I am in thy company and there comes to thee at times an inclination towards carnal desire, the greater will be thy merit if thou abstainest and the farther wilt thou be from lust, which is a vice, and most displeasing to God. The greater will be thy strength if thou dost subdue thy flesh; and if thou dost take me and hast confidence that thou wilt subdue thy flesh, the greater will be thy hope. The greater the merit thou canst gain, the greater will be thy wisdom, and the more sternly thou subduest thyself, the greater love wilt thou have towards God. Wherefore, for all these reasons, and for many beside, it is good that thou take me in thy company." Blanquerna answered: "It is forbidden in the law for man to tempt God, neither should a man tempt himself according to the manner that thou sayest; for it is a manner of pride and vainglory, and therein is peril by reason of the lightness which is in man, who has fallen through the corruption of sin. When it comes to pass that a man by some accident falls into occasion of sin, then indeed does it behove him to use the virtues even as thou sayest. But for naught upon the earth would I take thee in my company: rather do I counsel thee to forsake the world and find companionship among women in one of the religious orders, in the contemplation, remembrance, understanding and love of the holy virtue of God, the vileness of this world and the glory which is everlasting."

14. "Blanquerna!" said Natana, "In our former speech love made me to love thy body and thy fair features,

but now has my soul risen to love the virtues of thy soul. By the virtue of thy words hast thou transformed my mind; my soul hast thou illumined with Divine Virtue; my heart hast thou given to God; and, whereas aforetime I desired to be thy wife, thou hast given me now for a Spouse Jesus Christ." While Natana spake these words to Blanquerna, Aloma and Nastasia gave ear and heard their speech. Nastasia was greatly angered at the words of Natana, and she said to Aloma: " Lady Aloma, I will not suffer Blanquerna henceforward to speak with my daughter." So Aloma and Nastasia entered the room, and the words of Blanquerna and Natana ceased.

15. Blanquerna took leave of Natana. And love, unfeigned and pure, caused Natana to weep before Aloma and Nastasia, and to say these words: " Forget me not, O Blanquerna, in thy prayers, for thy words make this room in the which I now am to be even as the dwelling whither thou wouldest go." Then Blanquerna expounded to Natana the manner wherein the seven virtues would preserve her virginity all the days of her life. And afterwards Aloma and Blanquerna left the house of Nastasia and returned to their home. Aloma related to Evast that which had passed between Blanquerna and Natana, and the reasons for the which she had led Blanquerna to the house of Nastasia. Evast said to Aloma that from that time forward they should in no wise hinder Blanquerna from his journey, for it was the Lord's doing, and a dreadful thing is it to set hindrances before those that would serve God.

16. All that night were Evast and Aloma in the chapel with their son Blanquerna. Their tears and the devout words that passed between them, who may recount them? And the profitable words that Blanquerna uttered that night concerning God and His glory, who may tell them? And the blessings that Evast and Aloma gave to their son, who can write them? And who is he that could have refrained from tears had he but heard their words?

CHAPTER VII

OF THE CONDUCT THAT EVAST AND ALOMA GAVE TO THEIR SON BLANQUERNA

On the morrow, after Mass, Evast sent word to his kinsfolk and friends that they should come and do honour to his son Blanquerna and give him conduct upon his way. And when all were assembled Evast recounted to them how that the Divine blessing had caused his son Blanquerna to be enamoured of the life of a hermit, so that he would fain depart to contemplate God in rustic places and in regions uninhabited by man. Great marvel had they all at these words, and prayed Blanquerna that he would remain rather than sadden Evast and Aloma by leaving them, saying that after the death of Evast they would make Blanquerna to be among their rulers and chief men even as they had made Evast. But Evast said to them that it was no longer fitting to speak of that matter, for so surely had Blanquerna received the Divine inspiration that he would for naught on earth desist from his journey.

2. "My lord Evast!" said Blanquerna, "For the avoiding of vainglory, and that men may not count as vainglorious the honour that ye and these worthy men would do me, and because I am unworthy to receive such honour, it would be well, if it please thee, that I should take leave in thy house of thyself and of Aloma and of these other worthy men, and go upon my journey secretly with the blessing of God." "Blanquerna!" said Evast, "By reason of the vain words of men, it is unseemly to refrain from giving a good example, the which thou dost give us all in thus loving and serving God and in despising this worldly life. More profit will ensue from the good example which men will have of thee than any harm from aught that they may say. And thou for thy part wilt be the farther from vainglory, and in the time to come thou wilt

not consent, for any temptation of the devil, to leave thy hermitage."

3. So Evast and Aloma, and a great company of people, followed Blanquerna, and great was the fame of Blanquerna throughout the city. Many blessings had he of the people; many a sinner was convicted of his sin, and many a virtuous man desired to multiply his good works in honouring and serving God. Many, moreover, had great pity for Evast and Aloma because they would see Blanquerna no more, and many lamented that he would have to endure a life of penance and trials in abundance in the solitary places wherein he would find none of those things which are needful for the support of bodily life.

4. Fair and white and ruddy was Blanquerna; right good was he to look upon, for nature had given him every quality which in the human body is goodly and pleasant to the eyes. Young was he in years, yet was his soul full of virtue. In his heart night and day dwelt remembrance and love of the Divine dominion. The holy purpose which his will so fervently desired filled all that saw him with fire and the love of God; devotion and piety brought tears from their hearts even to their eyes, and from their eyes the tears flowed down.

5. When Blanquerna and they that gave him conduct were without the city, Blanquerna prayed his father and his mother and the other persons that they would return. But Aloma answered, and said that she would in no wise leave Blanquerna before they came to the forest into the which Blanquerna was to enter. Evast and all the rest were of the self-same mind, so they followed Blanquerna one and all. And while they followed him, Evast enquired of Blanquerna what was the chiefest of the reasons for the which he had conceived the desire to be a hermit and to forsake the world. "My lord!" said Blanquerna, "Through the will of God it has come to pass that ye have caused me to be instructed in theology and in other sciences whereby I

have had knowledge of God, Who is revealed by the representation of the working of His virtue in the creatures; and since this world is a hindrance to the contemplation of God and the consideration of His high virtue, therefore this world do I forsake. That which I have learned I take with me to my mountain dwelling, and I will be a hermit that I may not be hindered in loving, knowing, praising and blessing God with the aid of that which I have learned in the world. This, my lord, is the chiefest reason for the which I leave the world. Other reasons are there in plenty; and among them is this, that I see in the world scarce any man doing his duty in honouring, loving and knowing God, or in rendering Him thanks for the good which he has received, seeing that all the world has gone after vanities, after evil, falsehood and error. Wherefore I had rather be among the wild beasts and the trees and the birds, which are sinless, than among so many men that know not God and have blame as touching the benefits that they have received of Him."

6. When Blanquerna had ended these words, Aloma begged him that he would make her a gift. Blanquerna asked of her what gift she would have. "My son!" answered Aloma, "I ask not of thee as a gift that thou shouldst desist from thy journey, but rather a gift that thou canst grant me." "Ah, Aloma, mother and lady mine!" said Blanquerna, "Well knowest thou that there is naught that has remained in my possession, save to follow the will of Him Who has made me to love the contemplation of His glories. Therefore if the gift which thou cravest be in accordance with the will of God, let all that I can give thee be thine." "Son!" said Aloma, "I ask of thee that thou promise to return for a time to me before thy death or mine, after which thou canst return to thy hermitage; or if thou wilt not come to me, make me to know by a messenger the place of thy habitation, and I will come to be with thee for so long as thou hast thanks and pleasure of my company."

Blanquerna answered: " Well knowest thou, Aloma, that I have no certain knowledge either of my life or of thine. Wherefore, if I should promise to come to thee, and afterwards died, then mightest thou think that I had not been true to thee; and if I returned to thee, then would the sorrow caused thee by my departure be renewed. No messenger could I send to thee, for all my life is to be lived alone, with company of no man; wherefore that which thou dost ask have I no power to give thee, according to the manner wherein the Divine Will has ordained me to obey His commandments."

7. " Son! " said Aloma, " What is the place where thou wilt build thy dwelling? And to what parts wilt thou go? " " Mother! " said Blanquerna, " I cannot certify thee of those things that I know not. I must wander through forests and over high mountains, to seek some place wherein is water and wild herbs wherewith I may sustain my body. Where the country is to be, and the place and the surroundings, let all be in the hand of God, for in Him is my hope, and in Him do I trust to direct me to a fitting place, where I may love Him and know Him all the days of my life, and pray for thee and for Evast my lord and father."

CHAPTER VIII

OF THE FAREWELL

While Blanquerna spake thus with Aloma his mother they came to the place where Blanquerna should enter the forest. At this place Blanquerna and all the rest made halt. Then Blanquerna kneeled first to Evast and begged that he would grant him grace and blessing in place of his worldly inheritance. And Evast kneeled and prayed to God for Blanquerna, saying these words: " Divine Essence, that art infinite in goodness, greatness, eternity, power, wisdom, love and perfection, and virtue in all things without difference! I adore Thee in Thy Virtue and in Thy virtues. My son Blanquerna goes to serve Thee and to contemplate Thee in Thy honours. In what place he will dwell, I know not; but well do I know that Thou, in what place soever he may be, art in essence, power and presence with all virtues, with all powers and with all fulness. O Divine Essence, that comprehendest all things, to Thee I commend Blanquerna my son. Guard Thou him, since he has placed in Thee his devotion and his hope. Fill him with love in Thy service, and reveal Thy Virtue to his understanding, that his will may love Thee the more fervently. Thou that art eternal, receive my son Blanquerna, that he may persevere all the days of his life and think upon Thy bliss. Impute not my guilt to my son Blanquerna, and, if in him there be guilt or sin, may it please Thee that I for him may do penance. Forget not how my soul delights that Blanquerna my son goes to serve Thee nor how my body suffers at his absence. O Simple Essence, pure act without end or beginning! Thou hast given me my son Blanquerna, and according to my power I have brought him up to serve Thee. Virgin is he in body and in mind. To Thee I give and commend him in the grace of Thy Trinity, in the blessing of the human nature which Thou didst assume. To the Son of the Heavenly Father Who is in Thee I commend my son Blanquerna. May the Queen of Heaven and Earth, our Lady Saint Mary, Saint Michael and all the angels, Abraham, Isaac, Jacob, Saint Joachim and all the patriarchs, Saint Peter, Saint Paul and all the apostles, Saint Lawrence, Saint Vincent and all the martyrs, Saint Francis, Saint Dominic and all the confessors,—may all these be for the protection and help of my son Blanquerna. In the hands of Elias and of Saint John Baptist, who were hermits, I place him, that Thou by their merit may preserve my son in his hermitage."

2. When Evast had ended his prayer, Blanquerna begged him to rise, that he might do to him the honour that was

meet. So Evast rose, and Blanquerna, kneeling, kissed the hands and the feet of his father Evast, and Evast kissed his son Blanquerna, and made the sign of the Cross over his head, and gave him his grace and blessing, weeping with great suffering of mind. When Blanquerna had received the blessing of his father, he kneeled before Aloma his mother, craving her blessing and grace through the favour of the King of Glory.

3. Blanquerna, kneeling upon his knees, regarded his mother Aloma with devout countenance, while she, as she stood, gazed upon the goodly features of Blanquerna her son. And the fervency of her love, together with her yearning for her son, constrained Aloma so that she could not speak. So Aloma and Blanquerna remained for a great while in that state, that neither could speak a word to the other. Finally Blanquerna, who desired to go upon his journey, gathered strength of mind and said: "It is the hour of my departure, and I must needs be away." And he said to Aloma that he awaited her farewell and her blessing.

4. Then by the virtue of God was power given to Aloma to speak to her son, and she spake these words: "Beloved son! I must needs make remembrance of the Queen of Heaven, Mother of the Son of God, Jesus Christ, that she may aid thee in all thy necessities." Then Aloma kneeled, and kissed the ground, and raised her hands and her eyes to Heaven, speaking with great devotion and many tears, in these words: "Glorious Queen and Virgin, who through thy glorious Son art in so many places honoured and invoked! All alone goes from me Blanquerna my son, I know not whither. To serve and make remembrance of thy Son he goes, to love and to obey Him. Since he goes to honour and love thy Son, do thou protect, defend and love my son. Thou art with thy Son in glory. Thy Son it is that makes my son leave me, and makes me to remain alone and comfortless. I will love thy Son, for thou lovest Him; thou

wilt love my son, for he is loved by me. Sorrowful is my soul at the departure of my son, but in the Presence of thy Son thou art joyful. I have had but one son, and he it is that thy Son takes from me. In peril of evil men and of wild beasts He makes him to go; alone He will make him to be all the days of his life; raw herbs he will eat; his clothing will be but his skin, and his locks, and the air around him. Do thou look down and see how fair is my son Blanquerna in his person and in his mind: think thou how sun and wind and nakedness will darken him and destroy the beauty of his features. When he is cold, who will give him warmth? When he is sick, who will tend him? When he hungers, who will give him to eat? If he fears, who will strengthen him? If thou aidedst not my son, even without my prayers, where would be thy pity and thy mercy? Let the grief that I have for my son, as I behold him going to his death, in affliction and penance, alone in the forest, I know not whither, call to thy mind the grief that thou hadst for thy Son when thou sawest Him done to death and crucified. If thy Son died for love, without sin, what sin has my son, save love, that makes him die? From that which I understand of thy Son and mine, and from the hope which I have in thee, there will surely proceed some virtue which will be profitable to my son."

5. These devout words and many others of pure and unfeigned sorrow did Aloma speak to the Queen of Heaven. While Aloma adored, Blanquerna raised his eyes to the sun and saw that night was drawing nigh; so he said to Aloma that it was time that she and Evast should return to the city with all the rest, and that he should go upon his way. Then Aloma rose, and Blanquerna kissed her hands and her feet, and she kissed the eyes of her son and his mouth and his cheeks, and over his head she made the sign of the Cross and gave him her blessing and her grace. And again she kissed her son, and spake these words: "Fair son Blanquerna! I offer and commend thee to the care and support

of the glorious Virgin and of her virtues, whereby multitudes of sinners gain help and protection. May her mother Saint Anne, and the holy man Joseph of Arimathæa who begged the Body of Jesus Christ, be to thee protection; to Saint Catherine, Saint Mary Magdalen, Saint Margaret, Saint Clare and all other sainted women[1] I commend thee: be thou ever in their hands! And by the grief and sorrow that I have and shall have at thy departure, may all that can aid and defend thee have pity upon thee and help thee against thine enemy, even against the Spirit of evil. And do thou, son, as thou art of so noble temper, continue in thy holy life, that, by the grace and virtue of God, I and Evast may see thee in the glory that knows no end." When Aloma had said these words, she embraced and kissed Blanquerna her son and fell in a swoon to the ground.

6. When Blanquerna had received from Evast grace and blessing, and Aloma had recovered her consciousness, he kneeled, and looked up to Heaven, weeping and raising his thoughts and his hands to God, Whom he adored in each of the fourteen articles of the holy Catholic Faith, saying these words: " Lord God, Who art Unity in Trinity and Trinity in Unity! In Thee I adore Unity of Essence and Trinity of Persons, without composition soever and without diminution. I adore, O Lord, the Father Who in His infinite goodness, greatness, eternity, power, wisdom, love and perfection, engendered a Son Who is infinite in goodness, greatness, eternity, power, wisdom, love and perfection; this Son I adore in Himself and in the Father, and the Father I adore in Himself and in the Son. I adore the Holy Spirit, Who proceeds from the Father and the Son infinitely in goodness, greatness, eternity, power, wisdom, love and perfection; this Holy Spirit I adore in Himself and in the Father and in the Son, and the Father and the Son I adore in the Holy Spirit. And the three Persons and

[1] *santes.* The reference is to canonised women, for which no single word exists in English.

the three essential Virtues aforesaid I adore in Essence and Unity; and the Essence and Unity I adore in the personal virtues. Lord God! (said Blanquerna) I adore Thee as Creator that hast created out of nothing the world and all that is, that Thou mayest be known and loved and that in Thy glory we may share in Thy bliss, and Thou mayest glorify us. I adore Thee, O Lord, as Restorer[1] and Saviour. I adore Thy Conception through the operation of the Holy Spirit in the womb of the Virgin Saint Mary, whereby two natures were united in one Person called Jesus Christ. I adore Thee in Thy Nativity and in the virginity of our Lady Saint Mary, who before Thy Birth was a virgin, and after Thy Birth remained a virgin also. I adore Thee, Lord, in Thy Passion which Thou didst endure on the Cross to redeem the human race; and I adore Thy Soul which descended into Hell to bring thence Adam, Noah, Abraham and the other prophets who for so long had desired Thy holy Advent. I adore Thee, Lord, for that it pleased Thee to rise again and to reveal Thy glorified Body to the Virgin, that Thou mightest comfort her, and be to us an earnest of the Resurrection. I adore Thee, Lord, for that Thou didst ascend to the Heavens, and dost sit for ever in glory at the right hand of the Heavenly Father. I adore Thee and fear Thee, Lord, because at the Day of Judgment Thou wilt come to judge the good and the evil: the good Thou wilt send to glory without end and the evil to eternal torment."

7. When Blanquerna had adored God in the articles aforesaid, he adored and blessed our Lady Saint Mary, and blessed the angels and the apostles and all the saints in glory, and commended himself to the protection of God and the whole court of Heaven, and gave thanks to God and to all the company of the saints. For Evast and Aloma he prayed for a great space to God. And his prayer and the

[1] *Lit.* "Re-creator." "Re-creation," in the sense of Redemption, also occurs in this book.

manner of it were so pious and devout that all who were with him wept, and begged the God of Heaven to guide Blanquerna that he might have a long life and enjoy the protection of God.

8. When Blanquerna had ended his prayer and asked the pardon of Evast and Aloma for the grief which for his sake they were suffering, he took from a messenger of the house of Evast the mean garments that he was wearing and gave him his own. He took also seven loaves in significance of the seven virtues, which he desired to have with him all the days of his life. Thereafter he made the sign of the Cross before his eyes, and turned his face towards the forest, and went forward saying these words: " In the Name of the Father and of the Son and of the Holy Spirit, One God: may He be the Beginning of this my journey, the Continuance and the End."

9. Then Evast and Aloma and all the rest remained in that place where Blanquerna had taken leave of them, looking after him as he went, until he was within the forest. And Aloma said: " Alas, unhappy that I am! Now have I lost from sight my son Blanquerna, and never shall I see him more in this present life." Then with great weeping and sorrowing did Evast and Aloma and all the rest return to the city, speaking of Blanquerna and of the great devotion which God had given him above that of all other men that they had seen at any time soever in their lives.

CHAPTER IX

OF THE FURTHER HISTORY OF EVAST AND ALOMA

After Mass on the day following Evast and Aloma remained in the chapel speaking at length of the ordering of their lives, and they composed and set down a rule which they should keep all the days of their life, the which rule is as follows. In the beginning thereof it was ordered that all their goods should be commended to a faithful religious lay brother, their needful expenses alone to be kept for their own use, and the overplus of their income to be given to the poor of Christ. That they should wear humble raiment; that on three days only of each week they should eat flesh; that they should wear no garment of linen nor lie between linen sheets; that they should know one another nevermore in carnal pleasures; that at Matins they should rise and say their Hours; that after Mass they should remain to pray and hold converse concerning God; that ere they ate they should wash the feet of thirteen poor men at the table from the which they ate; that they should not leave their house; that at night they should search their consciences to see if they had erred against God or their rule; and that the one should give discipline to the other, each accusing himself of his misdeeds. This then is the rule which was made by Evast and Aloma.

2. Very careful were Evast and Aloma to find a friar to whom they should commend their property, for none such could they find conveniently in all the precincts of the city; and Aloma proposed to Evast that they should make some man overseer who was of their own kindred. But Evast said that this was not wise, because kinsfolk are wont to have overmuch pleasure in possessions commended to them, and think and plan how they may be made the heirs. Then Evast remembered a monk who was a priest, an old man, of good life and a native of other parts. So Evast prayed the abbot to give him this monk for governor, that he himself might continue in the rule aforesaid, which monk also would be confessor to him and to Aloma. This monk was accordingly sent to Evast and Aloma, and they remained in that estate which the rule that they made describes.

3. While Evast and Aloma were in the estate aforesaid and all the city had a lesson and an example in their lives, it came to pass by the will of God that Evast fell exceeding ill, so that he thought to die of his sickness. Then Evast

called Aloma his wife. "Aloma!" said Evast, "With thy counsel and good will I would fain draw up a testament, and I would have thee tell me thy mind as to how my possessions should be ordered to the service of God; I pray thee also to tell me thy will as to how thou dost purpose to live after my death." Greatly was Aloma distressed at the sickness of Evast, and long did she weep ere she was able to make reply. Then said Aloma: "My lord Evast! In all thy will there is naught that I may or would dispute. Dispose thou thy possessions and mine in what manner soever thou wilt, and dispose thou also of me as seems to thee best. For my will is wholly subject to thine."

4. "Aloma!" said Evast, "Among the things that men do in this world for the love of God, it is worthy of praise to give alms in perpetuity to the poor of Christ; wherefore am I minded to leave all my possessions for the building and endowment of a hospital wherein the poor and destitute may be tended, and I would that thou aid in the administration of this hospital and in the service of the poor, to the end that by thy merits God may have mercy upon me a sinner and continue His blessing upon thee and upon Blanquerna. Let the chaplain and the administrator of this hospital be the holy man who now administers our possessions; and after his death, let there be sought out some other religious man, meet to have care of the hospital, and let this ordinance be kept in the hospital after the manner aforesaid." Greatly did the words and the ordinance of Evast please Aloma, and she said to him that she was in his power to obey all his commands. So Evast made his testament as aforesaid, and according to the above named form commended the hospital to the care of the prince of that land, and of the bishop, and of the chief men of the city. He commanded likewise that after his death his body should be borne to the church humbly, without pomp or vainglory, and that none of his kinsfolk should follow him to the church who thought fit to weep or show signs of

sorrow for that which was according to the course of nature and to the work of the Divine Will.

5. Then Evast confessed, and received the Body of Jesus Christ, saying these words: "I adore Thee, very Flesh and very Blood of Jesus Christ, which to my bodily eyes are represented under the form of bread. The bread I adore not, but I adore and bless the holy Body of Jesus Christ which in this bread is represented to my spiritual sight. I adore Thee, Son of the living God, Who didst bear upon the Cross that Body which I spiritually behold, the which Thou didst unite with Thyself. This glorious Body represents to my soul Thy great and infinite power, which beneath the form of bread makes very Flesh and very human being to exist, and this form Thy great humility takes before me a sinner, that from it I may have grace and blessing. In Thee, O holy and glorious glorified Body, I trust and hope, in Thee I believe, and to Thee I pray for forgiveness. I receive Thee because Thou wilt receive me in Thy Kingdom through the knowledge and contemplation of Thy Virtue; and in Thy Virtue I am delivered from the hands of my mortal enemy."

6. When Evast had adored and received the sacred Body of Jesus Christ and had done all that pertains to a faithful Christian, he slept, and by the virtue of God and the merits of Aloma and Blanquerna, who prayed to God for him daily, God restored to him his health. When Evast was whole and freed from his sickness, he returned to the rule wherein he had lived. Now one day he was seeking a letter in a chest, and he found the testament which he had made, and he read it. Long did Evast consider the good which would follow, after his death, from the ordinance which he had made. And Evast called Aloma, and said: "Herein is written the good that would have been done to the poor of Christ had I passed from this life; and because God has been pleased to lengthen my life it is not just that injury should result to those who beg for love of Him. Wherefore,

if thou wilt have it so, it is good that we execute the testament in our lifetime; for perchance after our death others might be less diligent than ourselves, and we might both die very soon, with the result that the good that would follow the establishment of the hospital and the acts of mercy to be done therein would be hindered." Greatly did the words which Evast spake please Aloma, and she said to Evast that she was subject to his will to obey it in those things and in all others.

CHAPTER X

OF THE HOSPITAL

EVAST sold his house, and received for it much money. Then in the most convenient part of the city he built a hospital: with all his income he endowed it, and in that hospital Evast and Aloma lived long as servants of the poor of Jesus Christ. Evast made the sick men who lay in the hospital his care, and Aloma the women. When they had tended the sick and it was the hour to dine, Evast and Aloma went together to beg for the love of God that which they were to eat on that day, or they dined with some person who might bid them for the love of God. Of naught that belonged to the hospital would they eat nor squander it upon their persons, so they begged for the love of God that whereof they had need to sustain their lives.

2. Great was the example of the worthy life which Evast and Aloma led, and through their merits God bestowed favours upon many men, and heard the prayers of many sinners in that city, and healed many sick folk in the hospital through the intercessions of Evast and Aloma. Through the good example of Evast many that had been hardened sinners became penitents, and many men entered the religious life. And all the things that Evast and Aloma did were for a rule and example and exhortation, and caused

remorse of conscience in the men that saw them, and by that which they did they mortified in sinners the seven deadly sins after the manner following.

CHAPTER XI

OF GLUTTONY

It came to pass one day that Evast and Aloma had attended to their sick folk, and went to seek some person who would give them food for the love of God, for Whose love they had given food to many that were sick in the hospital. Now as they went along a path that was near to the palace of the Bishop of that city, the Bishop came riding by with many of his canons and clergy from taking his pleasure without the city. This thing the Bishop did daily that his health might profit and his appetite be the heartier at table. Afterward he caused Mass to be sung, and after Mass he went to dine. When the Bishop saw Evast and Aloma, he bade them dine with him, so they dined with the Bishop on that day.

2. When they had dined and were ready to give thanks to God, a burgess of that city, the same that had bought the house of Evast, brought a roast peacock, well basted, to the Bishop, who as yet had not risen from table. The Bishop fell to eating once more and tasted the peacock, and sent a portion thereof to Evast and Aloma, who were sitting humbly upon the ground before the Bishop like poor folk. All those to whom the Bishop sent a portion of the peacock to eat, partook thereof, save Evast and Aloma, who would not taste it. Then the Bishop enquired of them wherefore they tasted it not. " My lord ! " replied Evast, " It is the ordinance and will of God that man should eat to satisfy his body according to his needs, and that which is not needful to the body is not ordained of God and may be the cause of sickness and death, and belongeth unto gluttony, which is contrary to temperance. Wherefore, since we have

satisfied the body, as is fitting, neither for a peacock nor for other meat will we act contrarily to the will of God and to temperance, neither will we be to ourselves the occasion of sickness or death."

3. All that day did the Bishop think deeply upon the words which Evast had spoken, remembering the noble and honourable estate wherein Evast and Aloma had lived, and how they had forsaken the world and sold their house, which was among the noblest and most ancient in the city, and how it had been bought by that man who had sent the peacock to him. As the Bishop thought in this manner and considered the great good which Evast and Aloma did, he felt an uneasiness within him[1] because he had eaten to excess, which uneasiness came to him many times through repletion and often caused him sickness. Wherefore, so deeply did the Bishop consider the good estate of Evast and Aloma, and so fervently did he reproach himself and avow his sin, that thenceforward he sang Mass himself each morning before riding abroad, and was chastened for the vice wherein gluttony had held him captive; and such temperance had he that his other virtues were increased and he lived for many years in health and did many good works.

CHAPTER XII

OF LUST

In that city wherein Evast and Aloma lived as penitents, it came to pass that an old man, who was given to lust, took a wife that was young, and a woman of ripe age was wedded, for the sake of carnal pleasure, to a gallant youth, who took her to wife because she was rich. The youth and the damsel were neighbours, and saw one another often, and the devil, who strives with all his might to lead men astray, treated with them till they were vanquished by the sin of lust. While both were in that state of carnal sin, and knew each

[1] Lit. *ell senti en son ventre alcún destemprament. . . .*

other therein, it chanced that upon a feast-day the old man and the youth with their wives were in the church at Mass. Now as they heard Mass, the rain descended heavily. Evast and Aloma were standing at the doors of the old and the young man, asking alms for the sake of Jesus Christ as was their wont, when from each house came forth a servant bearing a rain-cloak and over-shoes for her lord and lady. The one servant said to the other: "Let us give alms to these two poor folk, and let them bear the cloaks and shoes to the church that we be not harmed by the rain." Each of the servants thought it well, and gave bread to Evast and Aloma, telling them to take the cloaks and shoes to their employers.

2. So Evast bore the cloaks and the shoes of the men, and Aloma those of the women. And they entered the church, which was filled with people, and in the presence of all performed their errand. Great marvel had the people at the humility of Evast and Aloma, and greater than all was the marvel of the two men and the two women to whom Evast and Aloma had brought the cloaks. And because the holy lives of Evast and Aloma were known throughout the city, and the noble and honourable estate of their former days was very great, therefore the youth and the girl resolved that they would know each other carnally no longer, nor commit the sin of lust. The older woman also repented of the intent for the which she had wedded the youth, and likewise did the old man; and each one, through the good example of Evast and Aloma, grew to love chastity and religion.

CHAPTER XIII

OF COVETOUSNESS

It happened one day that Evast and Aloma went through the chief square[1] of the city, that some man might bid them to dine, and they found none who bade them. Now in that

[1] *plaça.*

square[1] there lived a wealthy money-changer who had ever much gold before him, and he was a man whose covetousness knew no bounds. Evast and Aloma begged him for the love of God to give them food, or else some piece of money wherewith they could buy it. The money-changer, who was enslaved by the sin of covetousness, answered them and said that he would give them no food, nor aught beside of all that he had. Then he rose from the table at the which he sat, and went to visit a shoemaker, to the end that he might make him some shoes.

2. Evast and Aloma went through the streets begging for the love of God, and it chanced that they passed before the house of the shoemaker by whom the money-changer was being shod. The shoemaker called Evast and Aloma, saying: "It is the hour to dine. I am a poor man, and I have a wife and children who live on that which I gain; there is a little meat in the pot and I can spare a coin for some wine. But in my house there is not bread sufficient for all; for the love of God, I pray that one of you will dine with me and take a share of that which God has granted me to gain."

3. Evast said to Aloma that she should dine that day with the shoemaker, and that he would go and seek to dine elsewhere. But Aloma, who loved and honoured Evast greatly, said that she would go and seek elsewhere, and that he should remain. Charity and love was there between Evast and Aloma, and each had compassion on the other, for the cold was great and the rain fell heavily, so that they went through the streets with great distress. They strove then together thus, and each desired the other to remain; but Evast at all hazards resolved that Aloma should remain. So Aloma, who was ever obedient to the will of Evast, remained, and Evast went elsewhere to seek alms for the love of God.

4. While Evast and Aloma gave proof of the love that each had toward the other, and the shoemaker recounted

[1] *plaça.*

to them his poverty and bade one of them to dine with him, the money-changer thought upon his great riches, and upon death and the justice of God, and spake within himself these words: " Alas, thou wretched one! How hast thou lived up to this present time in blindness? And wherefore art thou the captive and slave of the sin of avarice? And how do thy riches and thy money avail thee without love? And where is the thank that thou hast toward God for the goods that He has given thee? All this that thou hast is of less worth than the good-will of the shoemaker towards the friends of God. Nor couldst thou with all thy wealth buy the love and charity which is between Evast and Aloma." Deeply did the money-changer think upon the holy lives of Evast and Aloma; and through their good example and the good-will of the shoemaker he freed himself from the bondage of avarice, and from that time forward was a generous and liberal friend to the poor of Christ; and through the virtue of liberality which was in him he had increase of many other virtues.

CHAPTER XIV

OF PRIDE

WHILE Aloma dined with the shoemaker, and Evast went seeking food through the town, he passed by the door of a man who was exceeding proud and wealthy. That man was a draper,[1] who was making a great feast, for he desired to give a daughter that he had to a knight greatly honoured in that city. Evast saw at the door of his house many of the poor who tarried there till one should give them as alms the remnants that were left from the table. So Evast sat among the poor, to whom he spake many good words, com-

[1] The Catalan word *draper* has the general meaning of a merchant or dealer in cloth, and is therefore not exactly identical with the English word here used to translate it. As will later be seen, the cloth-merchant had a bad reputation in Lull's country, especially when he was an itinerant.

forting and consoling them in their poverty, and putting them in mind of the poverty and humility of Jesus Christ and of the apostles who loved poverty.

2. When it was the time and hour at which all in the house had dined, the remnants from the table were brought to the poor. Each poor man had his cup and his plate wherein he received that which was given him for the love of God. Evast had naught wherein to receive the green stuff which was given to him, neither had he cup nor jug for the wine, so he asked one of the poor men to allow him for the love of God to receive his share in his own plate and cup. Thus were companionship and fraternity made between Evast and this poor man, and they ate together at the door of the lord of the house. While Evast and the poor man ate, the master of the house came out with his honoured guests, and beheld Evast seated upon the ground among the poor.

3. Great wonder had the draper and all his companions at the humility of Evast; and through the great humility whereof Evast gave proof before the draper and the rest of those that knew of him and of his holy life, the draper called to mind his own haughtiness, and remembered how that he was indulging it as concerning his children, by desiring to give his daughter to a man of greater honour than befitted her. And by the virtue of God and the good example of Evast, the draper was freed from the bondage of pride, and came to love humility, and gave his daughter in marriage to another draper.

CHAPTER XV

OF SLOTH

Sloth had in his power a man of great wealth who dwelt in the city wherein Evast and Aloma lived as penitents. This man had no wife, nor was fain to have, and his possessions were a profit neither to him nor to any other. All day he sat in the square and mocked at the people who passed by. When he saw any do good works he was wrathful; but he was glad when he heard evil spoken of any, whether of men or of women. One day it chanced that as that slothful man went to dine, he found Evast and Aloma who were in the street through the which he was passing. And two women whom Evast and Aloma had dowered, for the love of God, were contending concerning Evast and Aloma, for each of them wished to give meat to them on that day.

2. The slothful man passed by and saw the hospital of Evast and Aloma, which was very great and right well builded. In that hospital were many that were poor, and many servants who served them with great diligence; each one of the poor therein lay in the fairest of beds, with as much food before him as he needed. This slothful man began to think upon the great good which Evast and Aloma did. His conscience began to enquire of him if he had done any good thing, for the love of God, with the possessions that God had given him, and he could not assure himself that all the alms that he had done in his life were in value as great as the food which the sick folk in the hospital had before them on that day.

3. " Alas, wretched man that thou art! " said the man that was in the bondage of sloth, " how much harm hast thou done for so long to the poor of Jesus Christ! And where are the merits that await thee after thy death, to present thy soul to the Lord of Heaven and Earth, and to defend it from thy mortal enemy, who after this death awaits it that he may send it to fire everlasting? Miserable wretch! What man is there in this hospital as sick as art thou? " While he spake these words within himself, he saw at the end of the room two beds that were made but of branches of the vine, together with a small quantity of straw, and one covering only. So this man went to one of the beds, undressed and put himself therein, and bade them bring him

food, for he was sick, and had come to that hospital to be healed of the sickness which he had.

4. Of all that he desired to eat and drink the man that was sick of sloth had plenty, and he lay in the bed until nightfall, when Evast and Aloma came to lay themselves there. Thus Evast found the slothful man in his bed. "Brother and friend!" said Evast, "Who art thou that hast placed thyself in my bed? Go thou and lie in the other beds, for they are better than this." "Sir!" answered the sick man, "I desire not to leave this bed until I am whole." Evast and Aloma enquired of the sick man what was his sickness. "Sir!" said the sick man, "Sloth has imprisoned my soul, and suffers me not to do good with the possessions which God has entrusted to me; and I have faith and hope in thy prayer and in that of Aloma, that if ye pray God to deliver me from the slavery wherein Sloth now holds me, God will grant your petitions."

5. Said Evast: "Neither sloth nor other sin is of strength enough in man to destroy his free will, which God has created in so great strength and power that by no sin can it be conquered or subdued. But since thou hast faith in our prayers, albeit we are unworthy that they be heard, we will pray God to call to thy mind His glory and honour, and the sacred Passion of Jesus Christ, and the vileness and short duration of this world, that henceforward thou with thy person and with all thy possessions mayest serve our Lord God all the days of thy life."

6. Right devoutly and with great contrition of heart did the sick man repent, and prayed to God together with Evast and Aloma. When their prayer was ended, the sick man perceived that he was cured of his sickness and prayed Evast and Aloma to lead him to the altar. So they led him before the altar of Saint Andrew, and there he offered himself in person, and with all his possessions, to be for all time a servant of that hospital.

CHAPTER XVI

OF ENVY

THERE was in that city a very wealthy man, who had desired to buy Evast's house. That house, which was very beautiful, was situated in such a place that at all times when that rich man went out of his house he saw it, and greatly envied it; and so great was the envy that he had of that house, that he desired mortal injury to its owner, and daily he considered how he might acquire it.

2. For long this man bore envy and ill-will. While he was in this state of sin, it came to pass by the ordinance of God that the rich man who had bought the house of Evast passed from this life. At his door were many poor folk awaiting alms, according to the custom whereby, when a man is to be buried, alms are given to the poor at his house for the good of his soul. Among these same poor folk were Evast and Aloma, who waited there in expectation of alms.

3. Great was the humility and great the example which all the chief mourners who had followed the body had of Evast and Aloma, whom they saw among the poor awaiting alms, and much speech had they concerning them. And while they spake of Evast and Aloma, extolling the good works which they did, the man that was envious heard them, and knew and remembered his sin, and spake within himself these words:

4. " O foolish and senseless man! Of what avail is this house to him that was lord thereof? And which has the better fame, whether he that is dead or Evast who has sold the house and with the money has builded the hospital wherein so great alms are done? Sinful, envious man that thou art! What evil did that dead man to thee, for the which thou hast for so long and without reason soever borne him evil will? Wretched man! How canst thou make satisfaction for this sin, for the which Envy has held thee

so long time at the gates of everlasting fire, which never ceases to torment all those that in the sin of envy die? Couldst thou do naught that would keep envy from thy heart for ever?"

5. While he considered thus, and reproached himself for the sin into the which he had fallen, he purposed in his heart to do, while he had the good will, some notable thing, that he might be strengthened in charity and virtue by the grace of God and that envy should thus have no more power over him. Wherefore, in the hearing of all the mourners who had come to honour the dead man and were about to depart, he spake these words:

6. "O my lords, and ye that have come to this place to honour the man who aforetime was master of this house! I beseech you, by God and by Saint Mary, that ye follow me to my dwelling, and that Evast and Aloma, and all these poor men, come with us." So Evast and Aloma, and all the men and women that were assembled there, followed him to his house. And when he was come to the entrance of his house, he threw wide the doors, and there in the street, before them all, he confessed his sin. Then he put Evast and Aloma in possession of his house, which was very noble, and gave it to the hospital. And he said before them all that he had desired to make this gift in their presence and to say that which he had said, that he might be led thereby to abjure envy and become subject to love, and that he might the more be punished for his sin.

CHAPTER XVII

OF WRATH

In the hospital of Evast there was a sick man who suffered from an ulcer in the leg and could not be cured. And that man was greatly constrained by his sickness. It came to pass one day that he was suffering exceedingly by reason of the grievousness of his sickness, and considered for how long a time he had borne it. Wherefore such wrath entered his mind that he desired death, and cursed himself, and the day of his birth, and the life which he led. And so great was his wrath, that in his mind he cursed both God and all things that were.

2. While the sick man was thus wrathful, Evast, as was his wont, together with the physician, tended his leg. When the physician had placed by him the powder which he was accustomed to give him, Evast bound up and dressed his sore, and, kneeling down, kissed his feet, according to his daily custom.

3. Through the great humility and charity which was in Evast, God enlightened the conscience of the sick man and showed him the sinfulness of his thoughts. And the sick man thought upon the great humility of Evast, and, remembering his own transgression and his wrath, spake these words: "Alas, thou wretched one! How strange a thing is this! For thou art the enemy of God and of all things, by reason of the wrath that is in thee! Evast gives himself to the service of God, but thou servest the devil." Greatly did Evast marvel at these words, and he begged the sick man to tell him their meaning.

4. "My lord!" said the sick man, "So great wrath has entered my mind through the sickness which I suffer, that I desire death rather than life; and so greatly has wrath taken hold upon me that it has caused me to curse God and myself and all things. But thy humility, piety and charity make me to think upon my transgression, and to consider the great favour which God has shown to me in giving me as servant such a man as thyself. And since my ingratitude and my wrong-doing are so great, it is neither just nor right that from henceforth thou shouldst serve and keep in thy hospital so guilty a sinner as am I."

5. "Brother and friend!" answered Evast. "God wills that I should win merit in serving thee, and that thou

shouldst win merit through patience. Thou mayest know the vileness and the misery in the which we live in this world; wherefore thou shouldst have pleasure in that which makes thee wrathful. Thou hast come into this world that thou mayest have merit whereby God may justly call thee to His glory. Wherefore the greater the increase which God gives to thee of sickness, the greater is the occasion which thou hast of patience and of keeping in remembrance the grievous Passion which He bore by hanging on the Cross for thee and all mankind." So devoutly did Evast speak to the sick man and so piously admonished he him, that he repented of his sin, and spake these words:

6. "Ah, patient God! Who could conceive such great patience as Thine, Who by patience hast so conquered my wrath that I submit myself thereto from henceforward and for all the days of my life! The more Thou dost cause me to suffer, the sweeter to me will be my life, and the more clearly will Thy love and Thy dominion be manifested to me." These words and many others the sick man spake, beseeching pardon of God and rejoicing in His mercy.

CHAPTER XVIII

OF VAINGLORY

On a certain great festival it came to pass that a friar had preached in a church wherein was assembled much people in honour of the feast-day. A great company of notable men followed the friar to his monastery to do him honour. And it pleased the friar that they followed him, that the other friars might see how he was honoured by the notable men that gave him conduct. As they went, the friar made conversation of a kind that should cause them to extol his sermon. Greatly did they laud the sermon which the friar had preached, and great pleasure had he thereat in his mind.

2. While the friar had vainglory in his mind at the words which he heard concerning his sermon, they met the young wife whom the good example of Evast and Aloma had freed from the bondage of lust. When the friar saw her, he remembered how for long he had striven to free this girl (whose confessor he was) from sin, and that neither his sermons nor her confessions had availed as greatly as the good example of Evast and Aloma. While the friar considered thus, he knew that he had been guilty of vainglory, and he resolved to chasten himself and to undergo some penance that his sermons might never more be to him an occasion for vainglory.

3. After he had considered thus, a lay brother who was a companion of the preacher enquired of him: " Which sermon bears the more fruit—a sermon of words or a sermon of good works and good example? " The friar answered: " Since it is a greater virtue to do good works, and since to do them costs a man more than to tell another how to do them, therefore is the fruit of a good example greater than the fruit of words. It is but a short time since Evast and Aloma through their good example converted a woman to chastity whom I was able to convert neither by preaching nor by exhortation."

4. When the friar had ended his words, he took leave of the notables who would have followed him to the monastery, for he desired their escort no longer. And by the virtue of God, and the good example of Evast and Aloma, the friar determined in his mind that his future works should be like to the good words which he spake in his sermons.

5. According as ye have heard, by the grace of God Evast and Aloma by their good example mortified the sins aforesaid; and a long time would it take to recount all the good that resulted from the lives of Evast and Aloma. And while they were still serving and loving God with all their might, it pleased our Lord God to call Evast to His glorious

bliss, and to take him from the perils and the misery of this world.

6. Dead was Evast in this world, but living was he in glory. Aloma was left, and daily she prayed to God for Evast, and besought Him to take her from this world when her penance therein was ended. Grieve she dared not, for she feared to disobey the will of God: console herself she could not, since she had neither Evast nor her son Blanquerna. So she grew old, and her body, through affliction and age, caused her much trial for so long as she lived. Then God, Who forgets not His servants, called her to His happiness, wherein she found the soul of Evast her husband whom she so greatly loved.

ENDED IS THE FIRST BOOK OF EVAST AND ALOMA

BEGINNETH THE SECOND BOOK WHICH IS OF RELIGION

PART THE FIRST

CHAPTER XIX

OF THE STRIFE THAT WAS BETWEEN NATANA AND NASTASIA

AFTER Blanquerna had left Natana, she was ever wrapt in thought concerning the words which Blanquerna had spoken to her, and she thought upon the Passion of Jesus Christ, and upon the trials and deaths of Saint Catherine, Saint Eulalia and Saint Margaret, which they endured in this world for the love of God.

2. By the virtue of God, and by the nature of cogitation, which inclines the will toward that upon which man thinks, Natana conceived an ardent desire to forsake the world and to enter the estate of religion.

3. Nastasia observed that her daughter was all the day long deep in thought, and changed completely from her former condition. Therefore, supposing her to be enamoured of Blanquerna, she spake to Natana in these words: "Beloved daughter! Wherefore art thou sad and whereon dost thou think so deeply? It seems to me that thou hast remembrance of Blanquerna. Now if thou wouldst have Blanquerna for thy spouse, desire it no longer, for Blanquerna is gone to be a hermit all the days of his life, as thou knowest. If thou wouldst wed, an honest burgess has a son that is still young, and him thou canst wed, for thy dowry is great and thou comest of honoured lineage. Further, thou art fair in person and of good upbringing; therefore canst thou seek out from all the city the best and most honourable man yet unwed, and him canst thou have for thy spouse."

4. Natana enquired of Nastasia if she knew any man in the world who was fairer, nobler and more powerful than

all other men that are in the world, and if that man would be her spouse; for she felt herself to be so rich and so noble in her mind that she would not from the city alone choose the fittest man to be her spouse, but from the whole world would she choose a man, and that man, come what might, she would have for her husband and her spouse. "Daughter!" said Nastasia, "The best man in the world—who could choose him or know him? Nor art thou so rich or so nobly born that kings and emperors and other princes would give thee one of their sons in marriage." Said Natana: "If I lack the riches or honour or noble breeding needful to fit me to be the wife of a king's son, can there be no king's son that thou knowest who would humble himself to be my spouse?" Nastasia answered and said that she knew no son of a king or of a prince who had humility so great that he would lower himself by taking her to wife.

5. Then Natana spake to Nastasia and asked her if she had never heard men speak of Jesus Christ, Who is the Son of the King of Heaven and Earth and of all that is, the which Jesus Christ is the noblest and the fairest and the wisest and the most truly to be loved of all men that ever were. In Him (she said) is such humility that His Divine Nature was pleased to humble Itself to be a person with human nature. Such courtesy and humility has this Jesus Christ that pity and love made Him humble Himself to be poor, to be tormented and to be killed, so that sinners who could not be saved or receive the blessing of God should come to eternal life and escape the torments of hell which are likewise everlasting. "Mother!" said Natana. "It is this Jesus Christ Whom I will have for my Husband and Spouse, and I pray thee to grant Him to me so soon as thou canst, for greatly do I desire Him. And fear thou not concerning Him because He has so much honour and power, for oftentimes already has He humbled Himself as much as I ask or more."

6. Greatly was Nastasia displeased when she knew that her daughter had conceived a love for religion,[1] and she spake ill to her of the religious life, extolling the estate of matrimony. So there was a dispute between Natana and Nastasia as to which was the worthier, whether the life of religion or the life of matrimony. Nastasia extolled the estate of matrimony, saying that it was made by God in Paradise; and that by it is the world governed, for if all were in religion, the world in a short time would be without men; and that religion comes through matrimony, and matrimony can exist without religion. Natana answered and said that as God made the order of matrimony after the body, even so after the spirit by the light of grace did He make the mind of man to conceive the order of religion. And if matrimony is an estate whereby men come into the world, religion is an estate whereby men come to glory. And although the fruit cannot exist without the tree, it follows not that the tree is better than the fruit, since God created the tree for the sake of the fruit.

7. While Natana and Nastasia disputed concerning the estates of religion and matrimony, Nastasia said to Natana that she herself had desired to enter the religious life, but certain religious and certain dames of a religious order had dissuaded her and counselled her to take a husband, and therefore she thought that there are trials in the religious life which are grievous to bear, while in the life of matrimony there are pleasures which are agreeable exceedingly.

8. "Mother!" said Natana, "The men and women who are in the state of religion are of diverse wills; and so noble a thing is the religious life that it permits not any evil soul to be stained with vain concupiscence. Wherefore the greatest trial that man can have in the religious life is when that life displeases him and he desires the vanities of this world; and the greatest pleasure that a man can have in

[1] Here, as often elsewhere in the book, by "religion" is meant the "religious life,"—*i.e.* of a monk or a nun.

this world is that of a religious who loves his order and considers that he has escaped from the perils and vanities of this world, and in his mind has ever God and His honours."

9. "Daughter!" said Nastasia to Natana. "In this city lives a noble youth of right good upbringing, and as I have heard from his mother and from other persons he would fain have thee to wife, for he is deeply enamoured of thee." "Mother!" said Natana, "This youth, is he so powerful that he can forgive my sins? If I am sick, can he heal me? Or can he give me heavenly glory? Or if there is famine upon earth, can he give generous abundance of temporal possessions?" When Natana had vanquished and overborne Nastasia thus with her arguments, as is set forth above, Nastasia ended her words, lest Natana should be yet more strongly confirmed in her devotion, intending at another season to extol the order of matrimony. So she rose from the place where she was seated, and went to the window to look out at the people who passed along the street.

10. While Nastasia was at the window a damsel with a great company of people passed by, on her way to pray to God in the church, for on the morrow she was to be a bride. Right fair was she and nobly clad, and she rode upon a palfrey. Many honourable men followed her and many noble ladies; jesters and tumblers who sang and played instruments of music, and men who danced, did honour to this damsel. Nastasia called Natana to come and stand with her at the window. So Natana went to the window. "Daughter!" said Nastasia, "Thou seest how fair a sight is yonder damsel, and the great company that attends her." While Nastasia spake thus, there passed a corpse that was carried to the church for burial. The grief and the tears of the wife of the dead man, who could express them? "Mother!" said Natana, "Seest thou how great is the sorrow of yonder woman that has lost her husband?" Nastasia answered not these words, but rose from the

window that Natana might also depart and gaze no longer upon the grief and tears of this woman.

11. While Nastasia and Natana were still in the room, a servant came to them weeping, and enquired of Nastasia if she desired to go and do honour to a woman that had died in childbed, and whose body they had opened to take from it the living child. "Mother!" said Natana, "Dost thou hear these words?" Nastasia made no answer, but went from the house to the woman, who was to be buried on that day. While Nastasia was without the house, Natana thought upon her mother's words, and how she had tempted her to embrace the estate of matrimony. Natana feared the devil, and the lightness of the mind of woman which so easily is swayed, and she feared lest her mother by some skilful art should take from her the devotion which she had to religion. Wherefore Natana sent a secret message to the abbess of a convent of good fame that she should send two dames of the order to fetch her on the morrow when her mother would be at Mass, for she wished to visit her that she might speak with her certain words.

12. When Natana had sent this message, she returned to the window to see the woman who wept for the death of her husband come back from the burial. While Natana was at the window, she heard a crier proclaiming that all should come to see justice wrought upon the son of a burgess who was to suffer the penalty for having killed a man. This man who was being led to execution passed before Natana; his father and his mother and a great company of his kinsfolk followed him. The lamentation which they made, who could recount it? While Natana was at the window and saw all these things, she beheld Nastasia coming. And Nastasia, meeting the man that was being led to execution, wept for the sorrow of the woman that was bewailing her son. When Nastasia was once more in the house Natana said to her: "My lady! I perceive that thou hast wept, and that thy heart has been moved to devotion. Hast thou

had contrition of heart, and does thy conscience reproach thee because thou hast chidden me for the holy devotion which God has put into my soul?" "Daughter!" said Nastasia, "Speak to me no more such words as these, nor conceive of any estate save that of marriage; for if thou dost so, thou wilt be disinherited and likewise beaten, and thou hast kinsfolk whom I will cause to give thee many strokes and blows." "Mother!" said Natana, "Thou wouldst have me resemble those holy women, the saints who bore many trials in this world for their Spouse Jesus Christ, Who Himself endured a grievous Passion and Death that He might give them glory without end. Threaten me not, then, with that which I fain would have; rather do I pray thee to give me to endure that which my will desires."

13. All that night Nastasia thought deeply how she might give to her daughter a husband, who should be to her as a son, and whom she might adopt, bestowing on him the great riches which her husband had left to Natana her daughter, of the which riches she would bewail the loss if her daughter entered the religious life. But Natana thought all that night how she might enter a religious order. On the morrow early, when Nastasia went to Mass, the abbess sent to Natana two nuns to give her escort to the convent. When Natana left the house, she told the servant that she purposed to go to the convent, and commanded her to tell this to Nastasia, that she might not think she had gone to some place of ill repute.

CHAPTER XX

OF THE MANNER WHEREIN NATANA ENTERED A HOUSE OF RELIGION

WHEN Natana reached the convent, the abbess and all the sisters received her with great honour. She went into the chapter-house with the abbess and the sisters of the house. Then Natana spake to the abbess and to the sisters these words: " The Divine Virtue has conquered in me the false temptation of the devil which caused me to tempt Blanquerna to be disobedient to the Divine inspiration which called him by means of the life of a hermit to contemplate and love Him. Blanquerna has commended to me seven ladies whom I would serve in this convent among you. These seven ladies are the seven virtues, whereby man serves God and Jesus Christ, journeys towards bliss, and flees from the seven devils who are the seven deadly sins which Evast and Aloma mortify day by day in this city. I would fain eat bread and drink water in this convent all the days of my life. I would flee from the world ere it enslave me, and hinder me from the service of these seven ladies whom I cannot serve as well in the world as in religion."

2. Weeping and with great devotion of heart did Natana thus speak, and so devout and noble-minded were her words that the abbess and all the sisters were moved by her good example to devotion and tears. The abbess answered Natana and said: " Blessed be the Name of Jesus Christ, and praised be His Virtue, Who has sent us so good an example and mirror of life to inspire us to love our order and despise the vanity of this world." Then said she to Natana: " Welcome art thou, my daughter! The Divine Brightness has illumined thy mind, and by this same light dost thou illumine us that we may persevere in good works. Greatly do I joy at being in thy company, but I must enquire of all the sisters, as is our wont, whether or no it be their will that I receive thee among us."

3. So Natana went to the church to pray the Queen of Heaven to beg grace of her Son that the abbess and the sisters might be pleased to receive her into their order. While Natana prayed thus with tears, the abbess enquired of the sisters whether or no they desired and counselled her to receive Natana. And all the sisters were glad that Natana should become one of them. One of the sisters said that

Natana was wealthy, and that by her wealth much good would come to the convent; but the abbess and the rest reproved her, and said that when a person is received into an order, no thought must be taken as to temporal riches, for wrong is done to the person received if she be received because of the riches that she forsakes and despises, and not rather for the virtues wherewith she joins the order.

4. The sacristine[1] said to the abbess that Natana should be proven for a time with respect to her devotion before she was clothed; but the abbess answered that many a one for shame remained in an order until she had conceived devotion which made her love to be in religion. While the abbess was saying these words, she sent for Natana to come, saying that she and all the sisters would receive her into their company.

5. The abbess enquired of Natana if she desired to take the habit immediately, or to remain for some time in the convent, that she might make trial of the austere life which the sisters lived in afflictions of the body, and see if she found the enclosure or the routine of the convent to be over-irksome. Natana answered and said that she had no need to make trial of her devotion, for He that had implanted in her the devotion that she had to religion could keep it there for so long as He willed, according to His grace and mercy. Natana desired to take the habit so soon as she might, to the end that if her mother or her kinsfolk wished to reclaim her, the convent, according to its privilege, could forbid them.

6. While Natana received the habit of religion, and promised to observe the rules of the order, and the abbess gave her her benediction according to custom, Nastasia had returned from the church thinking to find her daughter. But the servant said that she had departed with two sisters from the convent. Greatly was Nastasia displeased, and she went immediately to the convent and demanded to be

[1] *Sacristana* (*fem.*).

taken to her daughter. So the abbess took her to Natana, who was clothed in the religious habit. Nastasia wept bitterly and uttered many threats when she saw her daughter thus attired, and she returned to her house and sent messages to all her kinsfolk and to the kinsfolk of Natana's father.

7. These all assembled in the house of Nastasia. Greatly were they moved with wrath against the convent; and took counsel together, and made agreement, that if the abbess delivered not Natana to them they would drag her thence by force, and would rase to the ground and demolish and burn the whole convent and put all the sisters to death. So Nastasia and all the others came to the convent to demand Natana: the abbess answered that they could not have her. Then all of them together cried out and said that if she delivered not Natana they would burn the convent and all the sisters. Greatly was the abbess dismayed, and even so were the sisters, and the abbess answered that they would take counsel together whether they would give up Natana or no.

8. So the abbess and all the sisters went into the chapter-house. Natana wept and prayed, and begged the abbess and the sisters that they would in no wise cast her out from the order and deliver her to her mother, who desired to enslave her to the vanity of this world. In great fear and peril were the abbess and all the sisters, and great was their terror, and many cried out that they should deliver up Natana. While the abbess and the sisters were in this state of doubt, a sister said that it would be more prudent for them to give up Natana than to die every one of them, and have the convent destroyed. Then Natana answered, and spake these words to the abbess and to the other sisters:

9. "Ye have all heard that our Spouse Jesus Christ, for love of us and to redeem us, desired death and martyrdom. God was pleased to give devotion to the apostles, to show that the Son of God has servants who fear not to die if

thereby they may do honour to His honour and show love for His love. God gave devotion to Saint Catherine, Saint Eulalia, Saint Margaret and the other martyrs so that they desired for love of Him to suffer death, and to give example to all men of how they loved to die to honour God. If ye for my sake do die, ye will die to honour God, ye will be martyrs, and will give good example to men; but, if ye suffer me to be dragged by force from the order, ye will give example and precedent to the people, so that they will for ever menace you if ye receive any women against their will." Thus earnestly did Natana beg her sisters not to forsake her, nor to show that they lacked devotion; she recalled to their minds the Passion of Jesus Christ, and gave them remembrance of the martyrdom of Saint Catherine, Saint Eulalia and Saint Margaret, and of the other virgins who died to honour Jesus Christ.

10. So many devout words did Natana speak to the abbess and the sisters, and so great was the power thereof, that they determined to suffer death rather than to deliver up Natana, and they trusted in the words of Natana, having hope in God, Who ever defends His servants when such is His will and pleasure. Yet neither the abbess nor any of the sisters dared answer Nastasia and the rest concerning the resolution which they had taken through the power of the Holy Spirit.

11. The abbess and the sisters fled, and hid themselves, and had great fear of death. But Natana made before her eyes the holy sign of the Cross, and having strength and nobility of mind, spake these words: "Hope, Strength, Charity, Justice! Since ye have made me to be your servant, it is time that ye aided me against your enemies, who because of me would destroy this convent and the sisters who have no part in my sins." As Natana said these words, she went up with the keys to a window above the doorway, and from the window she showed herself to her mother and to all the rest, and spake these words:

12. " Welcome be ye, my lady mother Nastasia, and all ye that are here. I greet you all; I make over you the holy sign of the Cross, whereby ye remember the Passion of the Son of God Who for us men was pleased to become Man, and was delivered up by men to death for our salvation. On behalf of my lady abbess, and all this community, I greet you, and make you to know that they desire to suffer death rather than have you rescue me. They would fain show you that Jesus Christ has daughters who will die for His love. In God they trust, and the justice and power of God they remember. They are women: ye need not to bring arms against them: they have no mind to resist you. See, here are the keys of the door: do what ye will." Natana threw the keys to Nastasia, and prayed that the first woman to be killed should be she herself, since she would be the occasion of the death of them all, and of the destruction of the convent.

13. But Hope, Charity, Justice and Strength had not been virtues if they had failed Natana. God, Who forgets not them that praise and love Him, put such power into the words of Natana that Nastasia and all the rest wept for the devout words that Natana spake, and for the holy lives of the abbess and the other sisters in the convent, who had chosen death for the love of Jesus Christ. So the hearts of Nastasia and the rest were turned, and their ill-will departed; and devotion came to them, with conscience of their fault, and with abstinence, charity and justice. All of them repented, and they praised and blessed God, Who had given such virtue to Natana and to all the sisters in the convent. They greeted and saluted Natana every one, bidding her have no fear of them, and begging her to pray for the pardon of God upon them for the foolishness and the wrong which their wills had conceived.

14. In the presence of Natana they all turned and departed, and Natana went to ring the bell, that the abbess and the sisters might come to the chapter; but for the fear

that they had they would not come. So Natana went through the convent seeking them, and she told them of the mercy and the pity of God, Who forgets not those that put their trust in Him. Great was the joy of the abbess and all the sisters. The abbess looked from the window and saw that they had all departed. Only Nastasia remained at the door alone, weeping and lamenting loudly, and saying these words:

15. "Alas, thou wretched one! Where are the thanks and the gratitude that thou hast towards God, Who has given thee so noble a daughter? And what crime had the abbess or the sisters of this convent committed against thee that thou wouldst have had thy kinsfolk destroy them? Is there any crime equal or like to thine? Can the pity and mercy of God be greater than thy sins? Would the abbess and the sisters of this convent pardon thee or humble themselves to receive among them so sinful a woman as thou?" Very pleasant and agreeable were the words of Nastasia to the abbess and to all the sisters, and above all to Sister Natana. So Nastasia gave the keys to the abbess through the window, that the door might be opened, and she might enter the convent to ask pardon of the abbess and all the sisters.

16. The abbess and the sisters received Nastasia very graciously, and together they went to the church[1] to praise and bless the name of God. Hearty thanks gave they to God, Who had delivered them from death. Then Nastasia went to the chapter-house with the abbess and all the community. First, upon her knees, and kissing the ground, she asked pardon of the abbess; then, in like manner, she asked pardon of all the sisters. They forgave her every one, and all the sisters kissed her. When Nastasia came to her daughter to beg for her forgiveness, she kneeled and wept bitterly, and spake these words to her daughter who kneeled before her mother and kissed her hands and her feet, and

[1] This, though called "church," would seem to be the convent chapel.

with weeping and tears kissed the ground, praising the virtue and the mercy of God.

17. "Beloved daughter!" said Nastasia, "It is a custom among us that the daughter should kneel before the mother and ask her pardon. But I by my sin have offended so grievously against thee that I am not worthy to ask thy pardon, nor even to be in thy presence, since I have desired to make thee the occasion of death to all the sisters of this house. Daughter! If in thy heart thou hast aught of pity or of mercy, wilt thou pardon me? Canst thou gladden and console me with thy friendship and company? And will God, by thy prayers and merits, be pleased to have remembrance of me and call me to His glory?" These words, and many more which it would take long to recount, spake Nastasia to her daughter Natana, and kissed her many times. Natana was so full of joy, of devotion and of charity, that she could not speak; only her eyes and her hands did she raise to Heaven and to the crucifix which was in the chapter-house, and kissed the hands and the feet of her mother many times. Not alone did Nastasia and Natana weep, but the abbess and all the sisters wept likewise for the words of Nastasia and Natana.

18. "Daughter!" said Nastasia, "Whereon is set thy mind? Hear thou my cries, make answer to my words and remember not transgressions that are past." "My lady!" said Natana, "Thine is my soul, and thine am I myself. There can be no sin in a heart to the which God has given such great devotion as to thine. Pardoned thee already are thy sins and thy transgressions. And if thou hast no sin, why shouldst thou implore pardon? If thou wilt have aught that is of me or in me, do thou have it all."

19. On that day the Name of God was greatly blessed by all the sisters in the convent. Nastasia begged that they would give her the habit of religion. But because she was old, and of such feeble health, the abbess and Natana and the sisters counselled her to build a house without the con-

vent and before the door of the church, that there she might abide and eat and have a pittance for her body, which she could not have in the convent. This counsel did Nastasia observe, and she lived in the manner aforesaid and gave example of good to all the sisters that saw her. And her dress was humble and in some wise like to the dress of the sisters in the convent.

CHAPTER XXI

HOW NATANA BECAME SACRISTINE

IN a short space of time Natana learned perfectly to read, and afterwards to sing and to recite the office. All day she would be at prayer in the church, and she delighted to aid the sacristine. The abbess took knowledge of the duty which pleased Natana most, that her service might be most pleasing to her. And, since Natana loved to be in the church and to help the sacristine, therefore the abbess, with the counsel of all the sisters, made Natana sacristine, saying these words:

2. "Natana!" said the abbess, "It is time for thee to serve in some office; and since thou delightest to look upon the Cross and the Altar which call to mind our Saviour Jesus Christ, Who is the Spouse of thy soul, and since moreover thou wilt keep the church clean, together with all that is used therein to honour Jesus Christ in the service of the Church, therefore is it the will and the prayer of the whole community that thou be sacristine."

3. Natana gave hearty thanks to the abbess and to all the sisters for the honour that they desired to do her, but she prayed that they would not grant her that honour, whereof she was not worthy; neither had she come to the convent to be honoured, nor did reason consent that she should usurp the office of the sacristine, with whom was to be found no fault.

4. The abbess answered Natana, saying that it was according to reason that the fittest person should serve in each office, that the rule of the order might best be preserved; and when any sister had laboured well in her office then was the order wont to grant her indulgence. And since the sacristine was old, and had laboured well as sacristine, therefore they would now have her to rest, and in patience and humility to see her office given to Natana, and their will was that Natana should labour in that office and be obedient to the command of the abbess.

5. So Natana was made sacristine and served right well in her office. With Nastasia her mother she was ever at prayer in the church, and they spake together of God, of His power, of His honour, of the Passion of Jesus Christ, of the glory of Paradise and of the pains of Hell. "Mother!" said Natana, "More seemly words by far, and more pleasing to God and to the saints in glory, are these which we use daily, than those that we used while we were in the world and spake of worldly things." Nastasia, answering, blessed the Name of God, Who had set her in that state and given her the consolation and companionship of her daughter Natana.

6. "Sacristine, my daughter!" said Nastasia, "Well do I know that in no wise could I have had thy companionship, hadst thou remained in the world and taken a husband, so well as I have it now that thou art in religion. Now see I how the eyes of my understanding were darkened, when I sought to turn thee from entering the religious life. It would be well that we should divide the temporal goods which we possess among the poor of Christ." Natana answered, saying that she was considering how distribution of the worldly possessions that her father had left her could well be made, to the end that for a long time to come they should yield abundant fruit. "And therefore," she said, "I consider daily, having regard to the condition of this convent, in what way we may enrich it with our temporal wealth."

CHAPTER XXII

OF THE DEATH OF THE ABBESS

THE mercy and justice of God desired to bestow upon the abbess her reward, for she was of a great age and had laboured well in the service of God. So God was pleased to call her to His glory that He might show her what manner of Master she had served: He desired to show her how His power could reward His servants. So He was pleased to give to her Himself in glory and to be therein her glory, since she had given herself to Him in this world. The messengers that He sent to bring her to Him were the trials that she bore patiently in her sickness, the which trials God gave to her that she might have patience and obedience, purify her body of all sin, and straightway, after this life, go to her eternal rest.

2. While the abbess was sick, an agreement was made among the sisters that they should beg her to counsel them in the election of one to succeed her after her days were done; for she had better knowledge of the sisters, and of their obedience, than had any one of themselves. So certain of the foremost among the sisters prayed the abbess secretly to assign to themselves one of them as superior according as seemed to her the most fitting. The abbess answered and said: "As it seems to me, the sister most meet to be superior is Sister Natana, for I have found her ever obedient and devoted to her order; and she has left great riches and honours for the sake of religion. And since I am at the gate of death, as well I know, ye may be assured that I cannot speak falsely; wherefore I counsel you that ye make Sister Natana abbess."

3. It pleased God now that the abbess should pass from this life to that glory which endures for ever. Right honourably was her body disposed in burial, and great was the honour which the chiefest citizens and the ladies of the

city and the religious orders paid on that day to the abbess. Greatly was the abbess mourned by all the people, and by the sisters of the convent, and most of all by Sister Natana. Many masses were said for the abbess on that day in the monastery; and such was her holy life that in all the churches of the city masses were sung for her soul. All that day was a day of weeping and prayer among the sisters, who had lost that which they most loved in this world. And they agreed that in the chapter-house, after the sermon which a friar was to preach concerning the abbess, one of themselves should comfort all the rest with words of consolation.

CHAPTER XXIII

OF CONSOLATION

It was the will of all the sisters that Natana should speak words of consolation concerning the death of the abbess. So Natana rose to her feet, made reverence before the holy crucifix, and gave thanks to God and to the sisters for doing her this honour over all the rest. Natana said that there were many sisters in the chapter who knew more of consolation than she, but that, since it so pleased them, she would speak according as God should give her grace. So Natana began, and spake after this manner:

2. "My will is to give comfort and consolation to myself, and that by my consolation ye may have a manner and example of consolation to your own selves likewise. This is the new method of a wise religious, who preached right nobly by communing with himself."

3. "Dead is my superior. Charity and justice move my soul to yearn and weep for my lady abbess. My soul moves my heart to bring tears to my eyes. Fain would I weep, for tears and love agree well the one with the other. Justice wills that a man should weep for his superior. I must weep if I would console myself, for without tears I

may have no consolation. I weep because I see her no more who loved me and was wont to point to me the way of salvation. But I must be glad for her joy and happiness, and for gladness too must I weep; for there is no perfection of gladness in this world without weeping. Loss and emptiness have come upon us because our lady has been perfected, and has won eternal rest. I must rejoice at her bliss, and be sad at my own loss and emptiness; and therefore, for joy and sorrow alike, I must weep. If for two reasons I should weep, then must I weep doubly; if I weep not because reason wills it, then must I of necessity weep for my sin in weeping not. My soul forgets not itself that it may weep. If justice would make me lose my consolation and punish me, then let it not allow me to weep; and if it would comfort and reward me, I pray it to let me weep for long with all my will."

4. "My will was created that it might have pleasure in the Will of its Creator. If my will desires not that which its Creator wills, I must needs have no more comfort. If for my own necessities I would have had from my superior that which was imperfection, what is become of the charity which my superior made me to love? If I have grief at the death of her body, I must comfort myself because of the good of her soul, which makes me to rejoice. My superior has gone from this life of peril: hast thou then wrath, O my soul, that she is here no more? If thou, O body, that art a creature by nature beast-like, wouldst take from my soul consolation for the loss of that which is like to thee,[1] then will my soul comfort me by reason of that same likeness.[2] Weep thou, my body, if weep thou wilt; for in thy tears my soul will find consolation. To thee, O body, it pertains to weep; to my soul it is given to remember the virginity, the perseverance, the sanctity, the worthiness, the good

[1] *i.e.* the body of the abbess.

[2] *i.e.* because the soul of the abbess, which is like to the speaker's soul, is saved.

works and the holy end of my superior." Thus devoutly, and in words that by their nature accord with consolation, did Natana console herself, and so piously did she weep, that she moved all the sisters to pity and tears, and consoled them all with her devout words and her tears. And all the sisters praised and blessed God and His power, saying that it was a time to love and to weep and to have patience, and praising the Will of God Who had been pleased to manifest His power. And their tears and love became to them an occasion and cause of consolation.

CHAPTER XXIV

OF THE MANNER WHEREIN NATANA WAS ELECTED ABBESS

NATANA and all the sisters who had a voice in the election of an abbess went into the chapter-house. "Above all things," said Natana to them, "is it needful to have a worthy superior, for through the goodness of the superior God gives virtue to those that are beneath her. Wherefore, since our abbess has passed from this life to the next, it is needful, according to nature and reason, that we seek from among us the one that is chiefest in holiness of life and the love of God, for she is worthy to be our pastor according to the ordinance and the will of God."

2. All the sisters desired to elect an abbess according to their accustomed manner, but Natana said that she had learned a new way of election, which way is by art[1] and by numbers; and this art follows the conditions of the *Book of the Gentile and the Three Wise Men*, which follows the *Art of Finding Truth*.[2] "After this manner," said Natana, "is found truth, and this truth will reveal to us which sister may best and most fittingly be made abbess."

3. So Natana was desired by all the sisters to tell them the manner whereby through an art they might discover

[1] *i.e.* method: the word is a common one with Lull.
[2] Works of Lull's: see pp. 311, 327.

and elect the sister who was meetest to be abbess. Natana answered, saying these words: "Of the art of election I will tell you in brief manner the beginnings. This art is divided into two parts: the first part is of choosing the electors who themselves elect their pastor; the second part is of the manner wherein their superior is chosen. Wherefore I will tell you first of the first part, and afterwards of the second."

4. Natana said: "We number in this chapter twenty women, who have a voice in the election of a pastor. According to the art, we must elect from these twenty sisters an odd number, which may be five or seven, for this number is more fitting than any other for an election, and the number of seven is more fitting than the number of five. Therefore let an oath to vote truly be taken first by all the sisters; then let the first sister be asked secretly which of the nineteen are most meet to be of the seven electors; and afterwards let the second be asked, and the third, and so in order down to the last; and each time let the answer of each sister be written down. Finally, let it be seen which sisters are they that have received the most votes, and let those that have had most votes be the seven who shall elect the abbess."

5. "The second part of the election consists in the choice by the seven electors of their pastor. First, it is meet that the seven electors agree upon a certain number of persons, and upon certain names for election, as seems to them good, and let each be compared with the other according to four conditions, namely: which of them best loves and knows God, which best loves and knows the virtues, which most knows and hates the vices, and which is the meetest in her person."

6. "Each of the seven electors may choose one person to be in the number of those to be elected superior, and each elector herself shall be of that number. In order that ye may the more clearly understand the art, let us suppose

that the number of persons, whereof our pastor is to be chosen and elected, be nine. First, then, it is meet that the seven be divided into two parts: two of the one part and five of the other. The five must decide which of the two shall be elected, and the name of her that has most votes shall be secretly written. After this, another of the five shall be compared with her that has received most votes; let her be set in the place of her that has been defeated by lack of votes; and let that defeated one be set in the place of her that is compared with the first or with the second. And let this be done in order with all the rest, and to this number let there be added the eighth candidate and the ninth, namely, the names of those that are not of the electors. Now, if we take this number, there will be six-and-thirty compartments,[1] in the which will appear the votes of each. Let her be elected that has the most votes in the most compartments."

7. When Natana had expounded the art of election, one of the sisters asked her: "If it should chance that the votes in these compartments are equal, what does the art in this event ordain?" Natana answered: "The art ordains that from the number of these, whether two or three or more, chosen by art alone, be chosen that one who best accords with the four conditions aforesaid, and she who best accords with the conditions is worthy to be elected."

8. Greatly did the art and manner of election please the sisters, and they all said that by following this art there could be no error in the election. So they all determined that for ever thereafter they would make elections in the art and manner which Natana had described, and to this end they set themselves to study the art, and they learned it. After a few days they made election according to the art,

[1] Majorcan Lullists disagree as to the sense of the word *cambres*, which is here translated "compartments." The most likely alternatives are "divisions of the ballot-box" (as in § 9) and "cells."

and by the art it was revealed to them that Natana was to be abbess.

9. So Natana was elected abbess. Greatly was she displeased at being thus honoured. She blessed God for that He had been pleased to honour her above all the rest, but she feared lest the sisters had erred in the art, and desired to see the six-and-thirty divisions of the ballot-box, so that if they had erred in the art and she should not be abbess, they might elect that one whom the working of the art might indicate. So Natana and the sisters who were not of the seven electors examined the way which had been followed according to the art in the election, and found that they had followed the art as was meet. Then Natana began to think deeply how she might learn and be able to rule herself and the sisters, and she meditated daily how she might direct the convent in right ways.

CHAPTER XXV

OF THE MANNER WHEREIN THE ABBESS MADE ORDINANCE CONCERNING THE FIVE CORPORAL SENSES, AND FIRST, OF HEARING

The abbess caused the bell to be rung that the sisters might assemble in the chapter-house, for she desired to ask counsel of them as touching the manner wherein they might use the sense of hearing in that convent, that the rule of their order should be the better served. While the abbess was in the chapter-house and the sisters were assembled for the chapter, a sister who in the city begged for the love of God came to the chapter-house and related to the other sisters that she had seen a bride right fair and nobly apparelled, who with great honour was being led to the church. The sister related these things gladly, and gladly did the other sisters hear her. The abbess perceived in these words the unruliness which results when sisters who beg speak of temporal pleasures to their companions.

2. In the chapter-house was the abbess with the sisters. In the presence of them all the abbess blessed God and said these words: "Long has my soul reflected, and sought how my mother Nastasia and I may give back to God the possessions which He has entrusted to us. Now by the virtue of God is my soul enlightened concerning the manner wherein we may give our riches to this convent, namely, upon this condition, that henceforward no sister shall go to beg in the city, nor relate any temporal matter which she sees or hears; for to hear of temporal pleasures makes the vanities of this world to be remembered and desired, and by such desires are hindered prayers and meditations upon the Passion of Jesus Christ."

3. A rule was made that no sister should leave the convent without great necessity; and the possessions which the abbess and her mother gave to the convent were so many that they sufficed to satisfy the necessities for which they were wont to beg. These possessions were administered by lay brothers, old and worthy men, already proven in another order. These provided the convent from their administration without entering therein, and if the abbess or any sister needed any private thing, which they had need to conceal from the friars, there were widows living alone in the city, devout and honest women, and these attended to their needs.

4. A certain fixed number of sisters were enrolled, and beyond that number thenceforward no more were to be received. This rule was made that the possessions which the abbess gave to the convent might suffice, and that they might have excuse for refusing requests to receive too many sisters. If any lady desired to enter the convent, or to send her daughter, she might do so by payment until the death of some sister; and that payment would cease at the death of a sister whose place on the foundation she could take.

5. Each day the abbess went through the convent, to see if aught could be found that concerned the ordinance of

hearing. One day the abbess entered the orchard and saw two sisters who were spinning apart, and another who was spinning alone. Then she entered the dormitory, and thence went into the other rooms where the sisters were accustomed to spin, and she perceived that they span not in one place together. On the next day the abbess convened a chapter, and made a rule that all the sisters should spin in one place, and that one of them should read aloud from some book that was in the mother tongue, that the other sisters might listen. This book was to treat of the Passion of Jesus Christ, and the lives and martyrdom of the saints,[1] both men and women, and of the lives of the Holy Fathers who were dead. In this book also should be the miracles of my lady Saint Mary and of the virgins and martyrs and the other saints; and this book should be read both at festivals and on other days by each sister in turn and order. The book was procured, and the ordinance was established in that convent, and likewise in others that took example therefrom.

6. The abbess desired most earnestly that this ordinance should be kept, that by the hearing of this book the minds of the sisters should not think upon vanities nor upon immoderate imaginings which should incline them to sin, and that each of them should grow to love the good lives of the saints departed. For as by seeing fair things the soul is moved to love, even so by hearing pleasing words it is moved to desire.

CHAPTER XXVI

OF SEEING

THE abbess went into the chapter-house with all the sisters of the convent, and spake these words: "Forasmuch as the Divine ordinance has been pleased to ordain that man should have the use and governance of his corporal sight which, rightly ordered, may lead to a spiritual life, there-

[1] *dels sants e de les santes.*

fore is it well that a rule and ordinance be made among us that we may know how to use the sight of the body. Let our eyes, then, be ordered well to gaze upon the Cross, and upon the image of our Lady Saint Mary, and upon other figures which present to us the lives of the saints who have passed from this world. Let us do honour to all these, invoking them whensoever we see them, and remembering in our souls those things which they signify to us."

2. "Let our apparel be humble; let there be no subtlety neither any adornment in our features, but only that which Nature has set there according to the will of God. When women of the world come to see us or to hear our words (as was said in the chapter concerning the hearing), when we see their proud apparel, and their features subtly painted, then must we praise and bless God for that He has chosen us to be the servants of humility and kept us from the vanity of this world. Then must the eyes of our spirits see how Jesus Christ our Spouse, and our Lady, and the Saints, wore humble apparel. Each one of us may win much merit if she can remember this when she looks upon proud apparel. Let us furthermore beg the women of the world that they come among us humbly apparelled, and that in their features there be no subtlety nor adornment, that they may not tempt our souls to covet the vanities of this world."

3. "When we behold the graveyard, then is it time to think upon death; and with the eyes of the spirit we may look upon the worms that shall gnaw and consume the eyes wherewith we see, and the ears wherewith we hear, and the tongue wherewith we speak. When we behold the vileness of our bodies,[1] then is it time for us to think upon the vileness of our natures, that pride may be mortified in us and humility exalted. If we enter the orchard and see the ass drawing the water-wheel,[2] and look upon the trees and the

[1] Lit. *Com serem en les latrines e veurem la sutzetat que ix de nostre cors.*

[2] The water-wheel (*cenia*) is the *noria* of St. Teresa's *Book of her Life*, Chap. II.

plants, then is it time for us to render thanks to God, Who has created us to be of a nobler nature than the beasts or the trees or the plants; for, had He so willed it, He could have created us after their kind."

4. "Let us look up to the heavens and behold how high they be; let us gaze upon the sun, the moon and the stars. Let us meditate upon the sea and the earth and upon birds, beasts, plants and men. Let us praise God Who is so great, for if God has created so many, so various and so lovely creatures, how much greater than them all is He, their Creator! And if all these creatures have been created by God for the service of man, how great should be our thanks toward God for all these things and for many beside." The abbess prayed the sisters after this manner to use the eyes both of the body and of the spirit, that their souls might rise to the love of God and incline neither to error nor to sin.

CHAPTER XXVII

OF SMELLING

"To smell roses, lilies and other such flowers gives delight and pleasure to the body, and in this pleasure there is peril, lest the soul incline to desire some vanity of the flesh. Wherefore it is good that we who dwell in this convent to the end that we may live lives of austerity and penance should have no flowers save those that we place on the altar that it may be the better adorned. When we smell the perfumes, of musk and of amber, which women of the world carry in their dress, then is it good for us to remember the sponge and the gall and the vinegar wherewith our Spouse Jesus Christ quenched His thirst on the day of His Passion. Further, we may remember the stable wherein He was pleased to be born, and give ourselves thereby an example to take no delight in odours which move man to sin."

2. "When women of the world sit among us, and we smell the various dyes wherewith they have adorned their features, then is it time to remember the wickedness of their minds, and it is good that we reprove them. For if they feel no shame in making manifest in our midst their foolish purpose, in no wise should we have shame in rebuking them, since shame is but meet in matters wherein is error and sin."

3. "To inhale evil odours is a thing to be shunned, forasmuch as they corrupt the air, by the which corruption are engendered in the body sickness and death. But even more to be shunned is the friendship of a woman who in her face or dress bears odours that signify the sins for the which she longs. For if through breathing corrupted air the body is exposed to risk of corporal death, no less so, through the friendship and intimacy of an evil woman, is the soul oftentimes inclined to think and desire evil works, whereby the will and remembrance become the occasion to man of eternal punishment." In this manner and in many others did the abbess ordain that through the sense of smell there should be no occasion in the convent whereby should be lost that bliss which is supreme and eternal.

CHAPTER XXVIII

OF TASTING

The abbess spake to the sisters in these words: "The chiefest reason for the which we live the religious life is that we may contemplate God, and adore Him, and serve Him; and among the things which most impede contemplation and prayer is superfluity of eating and drinking: wherefore the ordinance is good which commands us to eat and drink with temperance. Nevertheless there must be among us no hypocrisy, such as is found among those that join an order and make a show of austere living in respect of meat and drink, when in truth they eat and drink delicately and with superfluity."

2. "If flesh be forbidden to a religious, it is a thing ill-beseeming that she give savour and pleasure to her palate, whether with fish or with other viands, through using sauces or other things such as these. If it be good to fast, it is unlawful to eat as much in one hour of the day as do others in two; for were it not so, there would be no great virtue in fasting. If our raiment and our beds give significance of religion, the bread that we eat and the wine that we drink must likewise signify austerity of life."

3. "Superfluity of eating and drinking engenders boils and bad blood, and occasions sickness and death. Through superfluity of victuals the body is to the soul an occasion of desire for carnal delights. Many a religious house is poor and in debt through exceeding superfluity of victuals. If any that is of a religious order eats better and more delicately than when he was of the world, then did he more of penance in a worldly habit than he does in the habit of a religious. To suffer patiently hunger and thirst is to mortify sin and give health to the body, since nature consumes in the body superfluity of evil humours."

4. "Let us eat and drink that we may have life to love and serve God; let us not live that we may eat and drink. If we are servants of God because we are His creatures, and because He has redeemed us in the Incarnation of the Son of God, let us not be the servants of the belly which pardons not nor grants respite to its slaves. Let us not trust rather in the meats which nourish the body than in the virtues which feed the soul." All these words and many more spake the abbess to the sisters, to the end that each of them should afflict her body by hunger, thirst and meagreness of victuals, and that by virtue of their austerity of life God should pardon those in the world that are in bondage to the sin of gluttony.

CHAPTER XXIX

OF FEELING

"TOUCH is a feeling which pertains to the whole body. The whole body is a creature of God: the whole body, then, should feel affliction for the love of God. If we are in winter, we ought to feel the cold, and if in summer, the heat, for the love of God. If we flee from feeling cold and heat, and flee not from feeling hunger and thirst, then do we do injury to the mouth. In like manner as the lord wills to be served by his vassal, even so God wills to be served by the body, which is His own. If the body endures not suffering, where then is the service that it renders to God? For as God has given bodily objects for our eyes to see, and that the soul through the same may have spiritual sight, even so has God given feeling to the body that by the self-same feeling the soul, which is the form of the body, may have patience."

2. "Rough clothing, hard beds and the religious life agree well together: even so do white[1] raiment and soft beds agree with the life of the world. If we feel vermin[2] in our beds and cannot sleep, it is signified to our understanding that our prayer has been brief, and we have kept too little vigil in praying to God. Far better is it to pray to God and keep vigil than to desire sleep and be hindered therefrom by vermin. If then we would not feel vermin, let us desire to keep long vigils: much sleep and religion are opposed the one to the other, for were they in accord, then would there be no difference between religion and the habits of the world."

[1] *blancs vestiments.* But this may be an error for *blans vestiments*, "soft clothing." Cf. *blan lit*, the words which follow, and are translated "soft bed(s)."

[2] Lit. *puces ni menjança.*

3. "If we desire to feel[1] carnal delights, then in our conception of carnal thoughts is our virginity defiled. The virgin body deserves to feel the fires of hell, if the soul desires its corruption. To be conscious rather of the nature of the body than of the virtue of the soul signifies that the body is lord of the soul. If Jesus Christ felt for our sakes grievous trials and the agony of death, let us for His love endure a life of austerity. If we have come together in this place to escape from the feelings of the world, let not us that are in this place be in the world by virtue of our desires for its vanities. If thou wouldst feel vanities, for the which thou mayest be condemned to feel everlasting flames, put thou but thy finger in the fire and see if thou canst suffer the fire for so much as an hour."

4. "Sickness, whether of fever or of pain or of other kinds, makes the body to suffer, through the which suffering, if thou hast patience, thy soul may exercise its virtue. If God wills that thy body should endure suffering, and thou hast not patience, call to mind in thy soul whether thy will is in conformity with the will of God or in opposition thereto. If thou dost feel in thy mind desire and yearning for thy kinsfolk, seek thou in thy mind if thou feelest therein God. If thou dost feel temptation or thought of folly in thy soul, then it is that God would make thee feel His virtue, through prayer and remembrance of His Passion; for through such temptation He wills that thy soul may awake in contemplating His blessing."

5. When the abbess had made a rule and had given instruction to the sisters concerning the manner wherein they should use the five senses of the body, then spake she to the sisters these words:

6. "By the will and ordinance of God it came to pass

[1] It will be noticed throughout this chapter that the words "feel" (*sentir*) and "feeling" (*sentiment*) are used where English would prefer such words as "endure," "undergo," "desire." This emphasis on the word used in the title of the chapter is, of course, intentional.

that Blanquerna commended to me seven queens, and bound me to them in service and honour, the which queens are the seven virtues to ourselves most needful. Wherefore since it pleased you that I be abbess, I beg and command you all in common that these seven queens be held in great esteem among us, and that we be obedient to them in all our works. And if any of you commits deception or fault against any one of them, let her in chapter before all the rest sue for pardon and forgiveness, to the end that she may have the greater shame for her fault and return not again to a like sin, and that the rest of you take example thereby and be ever opposed to the enemies of the seven queens." All the sisters approved of that which the abbess said, and they set apart one hour of the day when they should assemble in chapter, for each one to examine her conscience as to whether she had done aught that was displeasing to the seven queens, or agreeable to the seven deadly sins.

CHAPTER XXX

OF THE SEVEN VIRTUES, AND FIRST, OF FAITH

It came to pass one day that through the vigilance of the devil a sister was tempted against faith, as she meditated upon the Holy Trinity of our Lord God, and the virginity of our Lady Saint Mary, and the sacred transubstantiated Host of our Lord God. While this sister was tempted concerning the articles of faith aforesaid, she called to mind the rule and ordinance which was established by the abbess and the sisters of the convent, according as is related above. When the abbess and the sisters were in chapter, the sister who had been tempted in this wise rose and asked for discipline, saying these words: "It is ordained of God that when the soul is assailed by a temptation it betake itself to God and to the virtues which He has given us that they may aid us in our necessities. My soul was given up

to

lightness and poverty of faith, that the power of God might be made known through its sin, and that strength and hope might fortify faith in my soul. But since my soul forgat the hope and the strength of God, it doubted concerning the Trinity of the Most High, and I pondered how there could be in God unity of Essence and plurality of Persons Who should be diverse without diversity and composition of Essence. And not alone was this doubt in my mind, but likewise did I doubt concerning the Incarnation of the Son of God, cogitating how such great humility could be in the Divine Nature, Which was pleased to unite with itself human nature to be with it one Person. Concerning the Divine virtue and power my soul doubted, cogitating how before the birth of Christ and likewise after His birth our Lady Saint Mary could have been a virgin. In all these manners my mind has fallen into doubt, and most of all as to the nature of the sacred Host, which has the colour and taste of bread, yet beneath its colour and taste is the Flesh of our Spouse Jesus Christ. For having doubted thus I beg a penance, and before the whole community I confess the lightness of my faith, to the end that all the sisters may take example from me and know how to preserve themselves in like case from temptation. And I would have an exposition made to me concerning this matter of my doubt, that doubt may never more return to my soul."

2. The abbess answered: "It behoves not that our minds should comprehend the manner of the work that God has in Himself, wherein the Father begets the Son, and the Holy Ghost proceeds from the Father and the Son; for if our mind comprehends not all that God has created, which is a matter complete and finite, how much less can it comprehend all that God works in Himself. Wherefore that which we understand not in God is that which our understanding suffices not to comprehend, and therefore God wills that by the light of faith we believe that which we cannot understand concerning His Trinity and the re-

maining articles. Nevertheless God has given to the understanding a virtue whereby through the creatures we may have understanding of God; for even as the understanding can comprehend that man is one person composed of two diverse natures, to wit, body and soul, even so, and beyond all comparison more easily, can God be One in Essence yet in Persons Three, and the Three Persons be one Essence; and if God had not such power, it would follow that He had greater power to unite plurality in the creature than in Himself, and this is a thing that can in no wise be granted."

3. " All that which God has made in the world, has He made to show forth to us His virtues, that He may be known and loved of us, and through our knowledge and love He may have reason to use in us justice and mercy, and so may give to us eternal glory. Therefore did the Son of God take our nature that He might use toward us humility and give us an example of how humility may be ours. He desired to show His Power and His Love; for His Power and Love are better shown through the Incarnation of the Son in human nature than through the creation of the world out of nothing; and we are constrained to love God more because He was pleased to take our nature and to die for us, than we are so constrained for any other thing that He could do for us whatsoever. Wherefore, even as according to physical nature it seems to our understanding impossible that the Son of God should become incarnate, even so in spiritual wise does our understanding perceive, according to the great humility, charity and power of God, that God had the will and the power to become incarnate. For if He desired not or were unable to unite with Himself our nature, it would be manifest that in Him there was a lack of will or of power, whereby He might charge us[1] to know and love Him. For all these reasons, therefore,—

[1] Both P and V strengthen this phrase: V reads, " He might compel and oblige us."

and for this further one, that God can unite soul and body to be one person together, even if the nature of the soul be one thing and that of the body another,—for all these reasons our souls can mortify the doubts which they might have concerning the Incarnation of the Son of God."

4. "God created Adam in the Earthly Paradise, and made Eve his wife of a rib that He took from him: this work was not performed after the course of nature, but according to miraculous working. So the Conception in the Virgin,—being, as she was, a virgin,—of the Son of God, Who came within her as Man and God, and was born of her, Man and God, albeit she was a virgin: this was a miraculous work opposed to the working of nature, showing that God has greater power and virtue and will than nature, in that He works that which nature has no power to work, and shows Himself in this way Lord over nature. And if God used not such supernatural working, He would not give proof that His power was above nature."

5. "With the eyes of the body man cannot be seen; for man is composed of soul and body, and the eyes of the body can see but a part of man,—that is, the body. But with the eyes both of spirit and body can man be wholly seen, for the understanding sees the soul, as the eyes of the body understand and see the body. Now with the eyes of the body man sees in the sacred Host the form and colour of bread, and with the spiritual eyes the Flesh of Jesus Christ; for as the eyes of the body see physical things, so the eyes of the spirit see spiritual things; and as the bodily eyes see the Host by means of light and as to colour, so the spiritual eyes see in the Host, through the virtues of God, the Flesh of our Spouse, Who wills with infinite will, and power omnipotent, and wisdom wherein is all fulness, that beneath that form and colour of bread should be the very Flesh and Blood of Jesus Christ. And if God willed it so, and it could not be, it would follow that His power, will and knowledge had not infinity, neither all fulness; and since our under-

standing sees all fulness and infinity in the virtues of God, therefore it sees with the virtues of God that which with the eyes of the body we cannot see."

6. According to this and other manners, the abbess mortified the doubts into the which the sister had fallen concerning faith. So this sister and all the rest were gladdened thereby in their minds; and their faith was so severely strengthened against the temptations which should assault it, that thenceforward no power which the demon had could make them to doubt the Faith or its articles. All the sisters praised and blessed God Who had endowed the abbess with so great wisdom, and to them had given so good a pastor, who by her knowledge and her holy life instructed them so deeply in the love and knowledge of their Spouse Jesus Christ and of His works.

CHAPTER XXXI

OF HOPE

THERE was a sister in the convent who had been a great sinner in the world, and had afterwards entered the life of religion: this sister had committed certain deadly sins. One day she remembered the great justice of God and the sins that she had committed, both in the world and in her order. So deeply did she think upon her sins, forgetting the mercy of God, and such remorse did she feel for them, above all for those that she had committed in the convent, that she began to despair of the forgiveness of God, and said within herself that, whatever were the good deeds that she did, she could not have the blessing of God.

2. While the sister reflected thus, her will was moved to return to the sins of her former life; but through the merits of the penance which she had done, and through the saintliness of the abbess and the sisters, God was pleased to look upon her with eyes of mercy, and to call to her

remembrance that which the abbess had ordained concerning hope and the other virtues. In chapter, before the abbess and the whole community, she confessed the temptation against hope which had assailed her, and begged forgiveness and counsel against this temptation whereby she was so greatly vexed.

3. The abbess answered her in these words: "The sin of despair is of such a kind that it causes man to think God to be more just than merciful, and after this manner many a sinner falls into despair. And since God is merciful, and greater than any creature, it must needs follow that man, who is a creature, cannot sin in the degree that the mercy of God can pardon. Wherefore it is a needful thing that when man thinks upon his many sins he should think also upon the great mercy of God, to the which they do honour and glory[1] that make it equal to the great justice of God. And through this honour and glory Mercy forgives man his mortal sins, giving him contrition and sorrow for them."

4. "To remember the Conception of the Son of God and His Passion quickens hope and mortifies despair; for if God willed to join and unite with His Nature our human nature, and if He willed to condemn to great suffering and to death that nature which He took that He might redeem us from the devil, it follows that He wills to pardon us if we trust in His pity and mercy. When a soul despairs, this is for lack of charity, because it remembers not the sacred humility which God showed in taking human nature, neither remembers His Passion: thence comes it that despair arises and conquers hope. But, when charity and hope unite against despair and sin, they move God to pardon, forasmuch as they make man to love and trust. Wherefore for one that can use hope with charity in his remembrance, understanding and will, it is a light thing that all his sins be forgiven him."

[1] Lit. *honrament e honor.*

5. While the abbess spake these words, the cellaress[1] said to her that she herself sinned often against hope by thinking upon the expenses of the convent and doubting if their store of money could suffice. The abbess answered that the virtue which is contrary to that sin which caused her to despair was an occasion to her how that she should remember the wealth and bounty of God, Who to so many creatures gives all things that they need; for if God gives the means of life to beasts, birds and fishes that have no reason, and to men of the world that love a worldly life, it would be a wrongful thing if He gave not these likewise to themselves, who were gathered in that convent to flee from temporal delights, and who trusted in God. Wherefore (she said) is it virtue to think upon such things and to trust in God; and such virtue and such thought must they have whensoever they were tempted by the sin aforementioned.

CHAPTER XXXII

OF CHARITY

BEFORE the abbess and the whole community, a sister of the community confessed her sin, which for long she had committed against charity; for she had loved God less for Himself than for the glory that He was to give her, and she had feared Him more lest He should condemn her to eternal torment than by reason of His goodness. The abbess spake to that sister in these words: " So greatly ought God to be loved and feared for the excellence of glory and virtue that is in Him, that He is the rather to be loved and feared for Himself, than for the sake of winning glory or fleeing from hell. For in loving glory man loves himself, and by reason of the love of man for himself is it that he fears the pains

[1] While the duties of the cellaress were in part such as her title implies, they also included, as this paragraph shows, a wider supervision over the temporal business of the convent.

of hell. And because man should love God more than himself, therefore is it contrary to charity and justice that man should fear God because of that which is the less noble; rather should he love and fear Him because of that which is the more noble, since He is more worthy and noble than are all the creatures."

2. When the abbess had shown the reason for the which man should love God, and had shown likewise the manner wherein man may love glory and fear the pains of hell, another sister said that she had sinned against God and against all the other sisters, in that the intention for the which she had entered the order was not for the love that she had to God and to the sisters, but because in the world she was poor and had not the wherewithal to live. The abbess answered and said that in one and the same action man can rule his intention both wrongly and rightly; for if because of poverty he enters the religious life, he may yet chiefly have love to God and to his order, and but secondary intention to the self and its needs. "But since," said she, "thou hadst intention to thyself alone when thou couldst have entered the order for love of God and the community, therefore art thou blameworthy before God and the sisters, and for this thou shouldst do penance."

3. "Truth is it," said another sister, "that I desired to be abbess, and that, rather to honour myself, than for charity and love to God and the sisters." The abbess answered: "To love high place for thine own honour is pride and vainglory, and contrary to the life of Jesus Christ, Who in this world willed to be poor. But to love it that God may be served, and the unruly lives of others may be guided and governed in the way of salvation, is to love God and thy neighbour, and is charity agreeable and well-pleasing to God. To mortify that foolish desire, namely the love of high place for the honour which it brings, thou shouldst remember the life of Jesus Christ and of the saints who loved poverty, as also the trials of a superior in govern-

ing those that are beneath her, and her servitude to those that are beneath her. Furthermore, thy foolish desire was contrary to liberty, for the sister in a convent is subject to her superior only, but the abbess is the subject and servant of all the sisters. Were it pleasing to God and the sisters, and hadst thou an ordered will, I would willingly exchange my office for thine."

4. "Lady abbess," said another sister, "for long have I desired how I might have charity towards God and my neighbour. So I pray thee to teach me the manner wherein I may have it." The abbess answered: "Whoso would have charity according as is meet, must know how to understand and remember; for, except he have wisdom in remembrance and understanding, his will cannot be in charity. Wherefore his remembrance and understanding must oftentimes be directed towards God, and towards His power, knowledge and will, and His works and His virtues, and the vileness of this world, and the glory of the next, and the pains of hell, and he must consider the wondrous love of God for us, and how we are all of one nature, one flesh and one blood, the which nature and flesh and blood the Son of God was pleased to take for us, when He willed to suffer for us and to die upon the Cross. By this remembrance and understanding the will conceives charity and love, and by forgetfulness and ignorance of these things, charity departs from the will, and anger, ill-will, falsehood and wrong-doing enter it."

5. When the abbess had said these things, she exhorted the sisters that before all things they should strive to have charity, for charity resists none that would fain possess it, and none can have thereof as much as he would. With charity man can suffer trials, and endure with patience that which is hard to bear, and rejoice at that which is pleasant and desirable, whensoever the memory and understanding are directed thereto. So lofty and noble a virtue is charity, that it made God to descend from heaven to earth, and made

Him also to take our flesh, weep, labour, suffer and die. And charity moved Him to create the world and all that is, and His charity it is that sustains us, giving to us all the creatures whereby we live, and all the creatures that do serve us. And Divine charity has created for us Paradise whereto it calls us, and wherein we may have eternal glory and escape infinite pains. Wherefore, as by charity we have boons so many and so great, and as it is given to whosoever would have it, a great sin and a great wrong is it if we have no charity in our minds.

CHAPTER XXXIII

OF JUSTICE

THERE was a sister in the convent grievously sick. The abbess, according to her custom, enquired daily throughout the convent to see if in aught she could minister to its well-being, or if her presence could anywhere be of advantage. She entered the sick room, and there found the sister that was sick, who bore her sickness with impatience, and spake words which signified to the abbess that justice was not in her soul.

2. The abbess enquired of this sister what had been the work within her of justice and of charity, fortitude and patience. The sister answered: "So greatly does my sickness constrain me that in my soul there is no place for virtue, but I am oppressed by wrath so great, that I had rather be dead than living."

3. "O, foolish one!" said the abbess. "I desire thee to answer me and tell me which thing would torment thee more: to be upon a great mountain full of fire and sulphur, or to bear this sickness? If thou die without justice, then will thy soul be borne to the fires of hell which are eternal. Who is He that giveth thee this sickness? When thou hast not patience, thou dost hate God, Who gives thee sickness

that He may punish thee for thy sins. Thou dost oppose His justice since thou hatest His works. No fortitude is in thy mind, for thy sickness casts out from it charity and justice and sets therein impatience and wrong. When God gives thee sickness, He asks of thee that thou thyself give justice to Him with charity and patience, that He may give to thee the eternal blessing of salvation." With such good words did the abbess exhort the sister that was sick, that charity, justice, fortitude and patience took possession once again of her soul which they had lost, and the sister spake these words:

4. " I adore and bless Thee, O Divine virtue of justice, because Thou chastisest me, and yet sparest me in that Thou chastisest me not according to the multitude of my sins. Worthy am I to suffer these trials and many beside. Do with me that which is pleasing to Thy will: may my will be one with Thine. I am not worthy of glory: sins have I for the which I merit everlasting torment. If Thou be pleased to punish me, Thou willest to use Thy great justice. If Thou be pleased to pardon me, Thou willest to use Thy great mercy. Whether Thou dost punish or pardon, I adore and bless in all things Thy great justice, and in all things I hope for the tender mercy which the Queen of Heaven prays Thee to have upon us all." While the sister spake these words, she felt within her such great fervour and devotion, which were given her by charity, justice, fortitude and patience, that she was enabled thenceforward to bear her sickness lightly.

5. When the abbess had comforted and instructed the sister that was sick, she entered into a secret chamber wherein was in durance a sister that had grievously strayed and sinned against her honour and her order. When the abbess entered to see that sister, that she might console her in her penance, she found her in tears, upon her knees, saying these words: " O sacred justice of God, that hast all things in Thy power! I adore Thee and bless Thee, for

in the trials that I suffer I have knowledge both of Thyself and of my sins. From this knowledge comes gladness to my heart, making me to love Thy justice and lament my transgressions. Wherefore the more are the trials that Thou sendest, the more dost Thou reveal Thyself to my knowledge, and makest me to remember the wondrous mercy that is in Thee. In this bodily affliction would I ever be, that my soul may know Thee and love Thee and learn to be glad in Thee." So devout and holy were the words which the sister spake that they moved the abbess to devotion, to mercy and to pardon. And the abbess, weeping, spake these words:

6. "There can be no defect in that wherein the holy justice of God would participate or be. Disposed am I to pardon thee, and to pray the sisters to pardon thee, since Divine justice pardons all those that praise Him and bless Him in His works. Starved and afflicted is thy body through thy many trials; poor are thy garments, poor and scant is thy food. Thy bed is of branches of the vine, thy companions as to the body are solitude and darkness, but thy soul doth company with the Divine brightness that makes thee to love and to know the Divine justice. Thou dost ask and it shall be given thee; thou dost repent and shalt be forgiven. And thou art nobler through thy repentance and devotion than am I through my virginity."

7. Devoutly and with tears the abbess ended her words, and the sister thanked her fervently, saying these words: "It is the nature of a good master that he love the blessing of his subjects. My bitter life and my imprisonment are an instruction to the sisters that they may beware lest they have sin and wrong-doing in their hearts. My happiness is to afflict my body and contemplate God in His justice. I repent me of my sins, and I beseech His pardon. All the days of my life would I continue in this penance wherein now I am. The more do I suffer in my person, the more is my soul exalted in God: may God be in my soul, and penance and trials in my body."

8. The abbess went into the garden, where she saw a sister that was weeping beneath a tree. This sister had enjoyed in the world great riches and honours, and because of the delicateness of her former life she bewailed the austerity of the life which she led in the convent. The abbess enquired of the sister why she wept and was thus disconsolate, and the sister related to her all that her mind desired. " O foolish and unjust soul ! " cried the abbess, " Hadst thou never knowledge of justice, that in a religious order chastises with austere living those that have tasted delicate victuals in the world, and humbles with lowly garments those that have worn proud raiment, and with a hard pallet tortures those that have lain in noble beds ? Foolish one ! Why goest thou not into the church to weep ? Lift thine eyes to the Cross and behold our Spouse, Jesus Christ, Lord of Heaven and earth,—in what a bed He lies ! See His garments that are dyed with crimson,—with the crimson blood of His Body. See how He is naked, and tortured and forsaken. He thirsts : see how His thirst is quenched with a sponge filled with salt, gall and vinegar. See what a crown of honour He wears,—how His Body is scourged and wounded." So severely did the abbess thus admonish the sister, that thenceforward she conceived no more the foolish thought that she had had aforetime.

CHAPTER XXXIV

OF PRUDENCE

A CERTAIN sister was in sin, and had no sure knowledge whether the sin was mortal or venial, neither would she ask nor enquire whether that sin was mortal or venial. And this she did because she loved to be in sin, and feared, if she knew that the sin was mortal, to forsake it. One day it came to pass that, while the abbess held a chapter, this sister became conscious of the wrong that she had committed against wisdom, according to the manner related above. The abbess answered and spake these words:

2. "God has given to man reason and discretion that he may use his reason against sin, and may love the virtues. Therefore, when a man uses not his reason lest he should become conscious of the sin wherein he dwells, the justice of God acts according to reason in punishing man, and taking from him discretion and consciousness for so long as he lives in this world. A great sinner in this world is the man who has blinded the eyes of his understanding, so that from henceforward he may have no consciousness of his sins nor repent of them. Wherefore we see many men dying in a state whereby we may know their damnation, insomuch as they make no restitution for their wrongdoing, neither have repentance for their sins at their latter end. That there may be friendship and companionship, therefore, between justice and wisdom, justice punishes those that love not and honour not wisdom."

3. While the abbess spake thus in the chapter, there was present a sister who had a son that was a prosperous advocate in that city. This son, before he became an advocate, had desired to take orders and learn the Divine Scriptures. But his mother had put him to study law,[1] that he might remain in the world and take to himself a wife. This sister remembered how ill she had behaved to her son in respect of his studies, and therefore she had consciousness of the faults that she had committed against wisdom, and she spake these words:

4. "A sinner am I against wisdom, and against the Holy Scriptures whereby man has knowledge of God." So this sister besought pardon and forgiveness for her transgression, according as we have said above. The abbess said to the sister that she had very greatly erred against the wisdom and understanding that the Holy Spirit had given, for the desire of her son to be a religious and to understand

[1] *leys e dret.*

the Scriptures of God was given to him by the Holy Spirit, Who was pleased to put wisdom within him that He might be known and loved of him, and to grant him celestial bliss. Wherefore the sister was guilty of that sin and of all the sins that her son would commit by his ill using of the science of law, so that he would have the less of glory if he came to salvation, and, if he came to damnation, the greater torment. Greatly was the abbess moved against this sister, and heavy was the penance that she gave her.

5. While the abbess was speaking of the gifts of the Holy Spirit, a sister became conscious of her ignorance, in that she knew not the fourteen articles, nor the seven gifts of the Holy Spirit, nor the eight beatitudes which Jesus Christ promises in the Gospel, neither did she know the seven virtues wherewith man goes to Paradise, nor the seven deadly sins which send him to the fires of Hell, nor the ten commandments which God gave in the Law. Of all these things was that sister ignorant, the which things are very profitable to be known. For this ignorance she besought forgiveness, and prayed that these things aforesaid might be shown her.

6. Straitly did the abbess reprove this sister, saying these words: " She that knows not the fourteen articles, wherein is our faith, cannot hold or use the faith as is meet. And she that knows not the seven gifts which the Holy Spirit gave, how can she thank the Holy Spirit for them? And she that knows not the eight beatitudes, cannot desire eternal glory. And she that knows not the seven virtues, where is the light that shall guide her in the way of salvation? And she that knows not the seven deadly sins, from what shall she guard herself, how shall she repent and confess, and where is her contrition? And she that knows not the ten commandments, wherein shall she be obedient to God? And if she be disobedient, how shall she know it?" Let all who would know the things aforesaid re-

member that they and many more are written in the *Book of Doctrine for Boys.*[1]

CHAPTER XXXV

OF FORTITUDE

As we call prudence, wisdom, even so do we speak of fortitude as strength, that women may the more easily comprehend it. Now a certain sister, who adored God continually, beseeching Him to give her the seven virtues wherewith to serve Him, and to defend her from the seven deadly sins, was tempted many times by vainglory concerning the goodness of her life, and the devoutness of her prayers, wherein charity and contrition for her sins made her to weep and to remember the mercy of God.

2. So strongly was this sister tempted to vainglory that she believed that God would work miracles on her behalf, and that He would honour her in His glory above all others. It came to pass one day that while this sister had vainglory in her prayers, she became conscious of her sin, and marvelled greatly how that such wickedness as vainglorious thoughts could enter her soul while she was so devoutly engaged in prayer. So this sister asked the abbess in chapter, and before the whole community, whence came to her the sin aforesaid. The abbess answered and spake these words:

3. "Companionship and fraternity exist between one virtue and another, so that the virtues are exalted one by another, and the vices mortified. Now as charity, justice, faith and hope are present in a high degree when the soul is at prayer, and contemplates the virtues of God, prudence and fortitude would fain be of their company. Therefore when the soul is tempted by vainglory, and has the wisdom to be conscious of the temptation, and reason is strong to oppose it, and remembrance is led to comprehend the

[1] See p. 39 above.

misery whereto sin leads us, and understanding seeks to comprehend the nobility of God, then wisdom puts forth its lofty virtue and is virtue[1] in the company of the other virtues. But when vainglory is victorious and the soul forgets its wrong-doing and comprehends not the virtues of God and is consenting to vainglory, then by defect of wisdom, and of strength of mind, the other virtues fall into sin."

4. When the abbess had described the manner wherein vainglory tempts those that are in good works, another sister said that she had many times been tempted to leave her order. The abbess answered that that temptation comes through defect of strength in the mind, where there is lack of charity in loving the order and despising the world; and, because the memory remembers the world and forgets the honesty and holy life of sisters of religion, therefore is fortitude mortified in the will. Wherefore should a man forget the cause for the which temptation comes, and should remember other things.

5. Another sister said to the abbess that she was tempted every day to eat and drink and speak against the rule of the order. And the abbess said: "God has been pleased to ordain that the creatures should be many and various, to the end that, in many and various manners, they may serve man; and to man God has given them, that in many and divers manners he may serve God. So this temptation comes that fortitude by means of abstinence may conquer gluttony and unruliness of speech, the which conquest it makes when charity and justice aid it against sin. Wherefore that temptation is occasion for the virtues to use that virtue which God has given them, that the soul may have thereby greater glory."

6. There was a sister in the chapter, very comely and of right honourable lineage, who had left great riches for the

[1] So V. The various versions all differ among themselves: this is probably the best reading.

sake of her order. That sister was tempted daily by pride, and she begged the abbess to give her counsels against pride. The abbess answered her and said that whensoever that temptation came to her she should enter the garden and look upon an ass drawing the water-wheel and think how dearly she longed to be that ass. The renunciation of esteem that she would make in order to think herself an ass would strengthen her inwardly against pride, by causing her to think upon God Who could make her to be an ass if He desired. When she had meditated thus, she should go to the graveyard and think upon the dead, and remember the putrefaction of their flesh and the filth of their bodies[1]; and afterwards she should go into the church and look upon the Cross, that she might remember the humility wherewith it pleased God to humble Himself. All these words and many more spake the abbess to that sister, that she might teach her to fortify her mind against pride, and cast away all things rather than commit any sin against God.

CHAPTER XXXVI

OF TEMPERANCE

The abbess was with the sisters in chapter, and she spake these words: "By the virtue of God we have spoken and made ordinance concerning six of the virtues. Now must we speak of temperance, and I would fain know if there is any one among us who has sinned in any wise against temperance." A sister answered and said that she had had no knowledge of temperance, wherefore she knew not if she had erred against it. The abbess said to this sister that temperance is the virtue of the mean betwixt much and little; by "much" let human comprehension understand the greatness of God, Who is greater than all things without immoderateness in aught, and as to the "little," let it

[1] The original reads: *lo fems de son ventre.*

understand that in God is naught that is little. Now, superfluity and littleness constitute the mean in the creature, but in God there is no temperance, in that He has naught in Himself that is either superfluity or littleness.

2. "Furthermore," said the abbess, "God has created temperance between two limits, that is to say, in order that it may be the mean whereby man may be able to use wisdom, justice, fortitude and the other virtues; for in eating, drinking, speaking, sleeping, watching, walking, dressing, spending, meditating and all things else, he has need of temperance that wisdom in him may have knowledge of that which is too much and that which is too little, and that charity may love the mean, and that justice from the two vices may take temperance and give it to charity, and fortitude be in the mind of man in opposition to superfluity and littleness, as accords with temperance, whereby fortitude may have agreement with the virtues which accord with temperance."

3. When the abbess had shown the agreement that is between temperance and the other virtues, the sister remembered her sins against temperance, and spake these words: "Alas, sinner that I am! How great is my guilt! For in eating, drinking, speaking and many other things have I erred in ignorance against justice, charity, wisdom, fortitude and temperance. For justice gave me conscience, and wisdom revealed to me superfluity and littleness, that charity might love temperance; and, since my will had no fortitude, it inclined itself to superfluity or littleness, and used not temperance. And as God has given liberty to the soul, which can use the virtues aforesaid, and my soul has not desired to use them and has used the vices, therefore am I in error, and I beg for penance and pardon and confess myself guilty."

4. The abbess said to the sisters: "There are three powers in the soul, to wit, memory, understanding and will. All that the soul does, it does with these three powers.

Therefore, that there may be ordinance of the five bodily senses which must be ruled by the soul, and likewise of the seven virtues of the soul, let there be ordinance even as we have said, the which we shall have if we be ordered in respect of the three powers. First, then, let us speak of memory."

CHAPTER XXXVII

OF MEMORY

" Memory is given to the soul that it may remember the Sovereign Good, from Whom come all good things, Who has created us all, and to us that are gathered in this convent has given grace to remember Him and to forget the vanities of this world. To receive benefits from another and to forget them is in the soul a grievous sin. Now we have received benefits from God, and He to save us has taken our nature and in it has suffered great trials and grievous death; wherefore we are bound to remember these things daily and at every hour of the day, and I desire and command each of you to call to remembrance the goodness, greatness, eternity, power, wisdom, love and perfection of God, and likewise His Incarnation, Passion and all else that pertains to Him, and to put each other in mind thereof. For by such remembrance do ye flee from temptations, and your trials are lightened and your souls illumined by the light of benediction."

2. " It behoves us to have remembrance of the glory of Paradise that we may desire it; of the pains of hell, that we may fear them; of death, that we may be prepared for it, for we know not when it will come, but only that with certainty we must die. Let us remember whence we have come, that there may be among us no pride; let us not forget the corruption and putrefaction of our bodies, that we may have humility; let us remember each other in charity and justice, that peace may be among us. If we

learn to remember, we shall learn to forget; if we learn to forget, we shall also learn to remember; and if we learn to remember and forget, we shall learn to understand and love. Let us remember our sins that we may remember the justice and mercy of God: let us remember the virtues that we may love them for the sake of God."

3. "It behoves us not to remember that which we have done in the world, lest by that remembrance the will be moved to desire the world. If we suffer temptation, let us turn to remembrance of God and Our Lady and the saints in Paradise, and ask their aid. Let each of us remember the angel that God has given her to defend her from sin, and let each do some honour to her angel daily. Let each of us remember some especial saint who may be her advocate in the court of Heaven: let us remember also the lives of the saints, both men and women, that we may grow to love the lives which they led. Let us remember the unbelievers, praying God to send them the light of understanding and faith, that they may know it, and love it, and be led in the way of salvation. At night, after Compline, let each of us have remembrance whether in aught she have offended her Creator; in the morning, after Matins, let us remember in what state we have been during the night." In each of these manners and in many besides did the abbess teach all the sisters remembrance, that they themselves might be remembered in the sweet and pitiful mercy of God. And all the sisters praised and blessed God, Who had given such wisdom, love and holiness to their abbess Natana.

CHAPTER XXXVIII

OF UNDERSTANDING

Sister Natana the abbess said to the sisters that understanding is the light of the spirit, which illumines the soul that it may understand truth concerning its Creator, and

His works, and that the will, before it be moved to desire or hate, receives light from the understanding that it stray not in its works. For even as blind men, by defect of bodily sight, do err in the ways wherein they walk, even so does the soul go astray in its memory and will when it receives not light from the understanding.

2. Oftentimes it comes to pass that by overmuch remembrance and desire the understanding suffers disturbance, and therefore he that would receive spiritual light must have temperance in his will and memory and understanding. He that would understand, let him learn to remember and will, and he who would remember and will, let him learn to understand; for much understanding is engendered of much remembrance and will, and much remembrance and will of much understanding, when man can make accord between the works of his remembrance and of his understanding and his will.

3. If we would have understanding as touching God, we must first use faith and afterwards understanding, and believe in excess of that which we can understand, and understand that God in His Essence and His works is greater than we can comprehend: for if the understanding suffices us not to understand all that we ourselves are and do, how much less beyond all comparison can our understanding suffice to comprehend God and His works! And were it not thus, it would follow that we ourselves in our essence and our works were greater than God; which is a thing impossible.

4. There is no defect in failing to understand that which we cannot understand, but there is defect in the man or woman that has understanding and has never learned to use it in respect of that which he can understand, or that desires not to use understanding in that which he might understand, or rejects the use of the best of all the creatures that God has created, or has no mind to enjoy that excellent delight which comes to the soul through understanding, or

fears not the sadness which comes to the soul through ignorance. The stronger is the working of the understanding, the greater and nobler and loftier is it by virtue of that working. But by overmuch remembrance, the power of the memory may become less, even as by overmuch loving or hating the power of the will may grow less. He, therefore, that desires not to understand what is within his comprehension,—how should he desire to remember or love it?

5. The will must not desire that the understanding may comprehend that which is beyond its power, but it should desire it to be ignorant of the same. And if the understanding comprehend truth, the will must love it, and if it comprehend falsehood, the will must hate[1] it; and if the understanding comprehend the will, the will must love it, for even as the understanding is made to comprehend the will, even so is the will made to love the understanding. And if the memory often remembers without understanding and willing, the imagination is wont to be exercised in such a way as to drive a man mad.

6. While the abbess taught the sisters thus concerning the use of the understanding, a sister enquired of her in what manner the memory could remember without willing or understanding. And the abbess said to this sister that as a man may first remember one thing and afterwards another, he often remembers one thing and afterwards another so that the will has no time to love or hate, nor the understanding to comprehend. Then the memory works by hazard in its remembrance, and by this use the imagination becomes disordered, and by this disorder of the imagination is destroyed the virtue of the memory.

[1] *desamar*, more literally "un-love," since the verb is the simple contrary of *amar*.

CHAPTER XXXIX

OF WILL

The abbess said to the sisters that God has given will to man, and to beasts, birds, fishes and all living things; but the will that He has given to men and women is nobler than the wills of the beasts, and the other creatures that have no reason; the end whereof is that the human will must desire nothing without reason. Therefore, when it comes to pass that a man or woman loves or hates without reason, such a one has a baser will than any other creature.

2. "It beseems the will to love that which is good and to hate that which is evil. When a man loves that which is the lesser good more than that which is the greater good, then does he order his will to love that which is evil and to hate that which is good." Now, while the abbess with much subtlety spake these words, a sister said to her that it was not a lawful thing that women should speak with such subtlety. And the abbess answered and said "that since the understanding could comprehend such words as these which she had spoken, it beseemed the will to desire that the understanding should soar in its comprehension, and that the will thereby should be the better able to contemplate and understand God and His works. For if God had not willed to be contemplated by love and understanding, He would not have placed such great virtue in the creatures nor in the memory, understanding and will, the which virtue He has placed in them that He may be the better comprehended, and thereby the more loved. And if through the direction of will and understanding toward some subtlety there be engendered doubtfulness, then must recourse be had to faith and fortitude, whereby the human mind may be strengthened to believe that which it may not understand."

3. "Liberty in this world accords better with will than with memory and understanding; and obedience is more seemly in religion than in the world or apart from religion. And this is because liberty is more constrained in religion than in the world, inasmuch as the will that loves of its own accord to subject itself freely to obedience has risen the higher and will have the more merit and charity and justice, than the will that is not under obedience. For, if it be a pleasing thing to love of one's own accord the Beloved,[1] a greater merit is it to love against one's own accord obedience to a superior; for in such a case the will is submitted to itself in loving that which inwardly it feels disposed to hate. And if thou darest not to think upon this subtlety thou dost doubt concerning the exaltation of thy faith, the which thou shouldst love that there may be in thee the greater fortitude and hope. And this which I tell thee signifies for thee some hidden thing, the which, at this present time wherein we live, I dare not give thee to understand."

4. "Each one of you has will and understanding; let each one submit her will to her understanding. And I desire and command that the will of each be bound and submitted to my will; and that my will and my understanding be bound and submitted in general to the understanding of all of you, for this is the proper function which pertains to the office of an abbot or an abbess in religion."

CHAPTER XL

OF PRAYER

The abbess was in chapter with all the sisters of the community, and she desired to know the manner of their prayers, for it is a thing most needful that prayers be duly ordered, because prayer is the noblest work in the religious

[1] *son amat*: "the Beloved," in particular, and "the object of one's love" in general.

life, and prayer without rule and order is very displeasing to God. While the abbess spake thus, a sister besought pardon because she had sinned many times against prayer, repeating but few words of prayer and setting her mind, while she prayed, upon vain things opposed to prayer. The abbess answered and said "that prayer is of four kinds. The first kind is of the heart that contemplates God while the mouth speaks no words. The second is when the heart and the mouth agree in prayer, and the heart understands that which is signified by the words. The third manner is of a man that leads a good life and commits no mortal sin, for all that such a man does is prayer. The fourth manner is when the mouth speaks words of prayer and the heart thinks upon other things. This fourth manner is displeasing to God, and bears no fruit, and signifies defect of charity, wisdom and fortitude, through the which defect the soul is forgetful of itself and knows naught of that which is signified by the words. In such prayer man must have recourse to the virtues aforesaid, with the aid whereof the soul may unite with the words, and understand, remember and love the words which the mouth speaks."

2. "Ye have heard how Blanquerna adored God in the fourteen articles, and how Evast adored Him in Essence and in virtues, and how Aloma prayed for her son Blanquerna to our Lady Saint Mary. Now the great affection and love which these had in their prayers accorded with their words; and we also should love God and His works so fervently that the soul and the words may unite to pray to God and the tears rise from the heart to the eyes and flow down therefrom, and the virtues conquer and vanquish our sins, and our souls take comfort from weeping and find joy in devotion, giving glory and blessing to God."

3. "When we are in prayer, we must remember, understand and love the virtues and the works of God, and with faith, hope, charity, justice, wisdom, strength and temper-

ance we must order our souls and bodies that we may be able to raise the memory, understanding and will to contemplate and desire His glory, and after this we must remember, understand and hate[1] our sins and the vileness of this world. Thus, by this work, and by the aid of the fire of the Holy Spirit, our souls will be illumined to pray to God aright, and our prayers heard by the justice and mercy of God, in Whom is all perfection and in Whom every perfect prayer finds virtue[2] that leads to the bliss of salvation."

4. "We must pray for the Holy Apostolic Father, for the cardinals, for prelates, princes and all Christian people, that God may give them devotion and that all their lives may be spent in the knowledge and love of God, and that through them may return the holy devotion which to the greater exaltation of the faith was once in the world, that is, in the earthly lifetime of our Spouse Jesus Christ and the Apostles."

5. "Let not our souls, in their prayers, forget the unbelievers, for they are of our blood and of like form to our own. Their ignorance of faith and of knowledge comes from their lack of teachers, for so far as we can see they have none. They know not God, neither love Him nor believe in Him, neither do they render thanks to God for the blessings which He gives them. Many of them daily blaspheme our Lord Jesus Christ, believing Him to have been a man that was deluded and a sinner. Great virtue would it be that one should confess before these men the Name of God and His virtue, and the honour which is in our Spouse: well-pleasing to God would be one that taught these men to honour Him who now do Him dishonour. And on the Day of Judgment those that suffered that they might exalt the Name of God would come to the Court with garments like to those of Jesus Christ."

[1] *desamar.*
[2] P: "perfection of virtue." V: "fulness and virtue."

6. " Let us render thanks to God for that He has given us this our human life and made so many creatures to do us service. Never can we thank Him enough for all the good that we have received of Him and receive of Him daily. Let us pray our Lady Saint Mary and all the angels and saints of Paradise to give thanks for us. Let us accuse ourselves of our sins and sue for pardon. Let us count ourselves unworthy of the good that we receive and the glory for the which we hope. Let us render thanks to God, Who has brought us from the bondage of the world and gathered us together in this place to live lives of penitence. Let us beg of God virtues whereby we may be defended from the vices. Let us by the holiness of our lives adore our Saviour. Let us continue in love and tears, in contrition and devotion, never wearying of adoring, loving and praying to Him Who has given us hearts to love, eyes to weep and mouths to praise His virtue and His works." In all these ways, and in many more, did the abbess instruct the sisters in the prayer, adoration and contemplation of God.

CHAPTER XLI

OF WATCHING

In the presence of all the sisters the abbess spake these words: " Mindful am I inwardly of how I once was wont to look upon my lady the abbess, (to whom God grant forgiveness) and to hide certain matters that she might have no knowledge thereof. Wherefore, in order that at all hours of the day your souls may fear the justice of the order, I desire, after taking counsel with you, to make a new establishment in this convent, to wit, that each week we make secret election of one sister who shall be a spy, to keep watch over all that ye do, and that none of you shall know which is she, to the end that each of you may fear the other as though she were my own presence. And in chapter that sister shall recount all that she has seen you do that is evil or contrary to our order."

2. "Further, I will ordain that we set spies in the city who may observe if any of our sisters enter therein for reasons of need, and take note of their behaviour and of the places whither they go; lest of them or of any of you they hear dishonourable words or aught whereby sin may be imputed to us."

3. "And I would not only that there be watchers set over you, but also that there be one set over me, that I may be the better kept from every error. Therefore I desire that three sisters be chosen each week and that these make secret election of one that shall take note of all that I do and that I know not which is she that keeps watch over me. And I desire that in chapter she accuse me before all the sisters if she have seen me do aught that is unseemly or contrary to my order; and before all things it is good that I do penance for this and sue for pardon." All the sisters found that which the abbess said to be good, and they confirmed all things soever that she was pleased to ordain.

4. For long years did the abbess Natana dwell in that convent, following all the ordinances aforesaid; and through her holy life and doctrine were found therein many good sisters. Moreover, many a lady in the city took good example from her, and many more convents followed the rules and customs which she established.

ENDED, BY THE GRACE AND HELP OF GOD, IS THE BOOK OF THE ORDER OF WOMEN

Now must we needs return to Blanquerna, whom we left in the forest, about to seek a place wherein he might adore, contemplate, love and have knowledge of God.

Part the Second

CHAPTER XLII

OF THE TEN COMMANDMENTS

For the whole of that day, after he had parted from Evast and Aloma, Blanquerna journeyed through the forest. At nightfall he came to a fair meadow, wherein was a beautiful fountain, beneath a tall tree. There did Blanquerna take his rest, and he slept all that night. Before dawn he began his prayers according as he was wont; and through the strangeness and solitariness of the place, and the heavens and the stars, his soul was highly exalted in the contemplation of God. When he heard the wild beasts roaming through the forest, his prayer was disturbed through his fears, but by hope and fortitude his mind was strengthened to trust in the sovereign aid of God.

2. Until sunrise Blanquerna remained in prayer. After it was day he set out afresh, and journeyed until sunset, when he came to a place wherein was a great multitude of trees. In that place was a fair palace right nobly builded. Blanquerna came to the door of the palace, over the which were inscribed in letters of gold and silver these words: "Thou shalt not have strange gods. Thou shalt not forswear thyself. Thou shalt keep holy the Sabbath day. Thou shalt honour thy father and thy mother. Thou shalt do no murder. Thou shalt not commit fornication. Thou shalt not steal. Thou shalt not bear false witness. Thou shalt not covet thy neighbour's wife. Thou shalt not covet thy neighbour's possessions. These are the ten commandments that dwell in this palace. They have been exiled in this forest; they are despised, disobeyed and forgotten by those that are in the world. In this palace they weep and

lament and bewail the honour that they were wont to have in the world, that God might have the glory and men come to everlasting salvation."

3. Greatly did Blanquerna marvel when he had read the words that were written above the portal, so he knocked at the door with intent to enter therein to see the ten commandments. The door was opened by a comely youth. Blanquerna was fain to enter, but the youth forbade him, and said that no man might enter the palace who was disobedient to the ten commandments. Blanquerna answered and said that he had cast all things else from his mind, and had given his whole soul to the service of God, the Lord and Creator of all good things. Then he related to the youth his story. The youth closed the door, saying that ere he could give him leave to enter the palace, he must ask it of the ten commandments. So the youth begged leave of the ten commandments, relating to them the story of Blanquerna. And this story pleased them, and they commanded that Blanquerna should have leave to enter and should be brought before them.

4. Blanquerna entered a great and beautiful hall wherein were written the names of those that are disobedient to the ten commandments. In that hall were ten chairs of gold and ivory fairly carven, in the which sat the ten commandments in estate of great honour. Right nobly were they clad in silks and gold; great beards had they and long hair, and in appearance were as aged men. Each one held upon his knees a book, and wept and bewailed very bitterly, saying these words:

5. "Alas, thou that art despised of men!" said the first commandment. "Dead are they that have loved thee, by whom thou hast been served with all honour. Many are the men in this world who believe in idols and make strange gods of the sun and the moon and the stars. To love one's son, one's castle or oneself more than the Most High is to make a god above Him that is Sovereign Good over all good

things. Alas! where are they that love God above all things? And who is he that to honour God will give himself up to death and to suffer all trials? The more do I think upon the multitude of men that are in the world, and the fewer men do I find who love God in truth, the greater grows my pain and the more are my griefs increased. Such sinners are had in remembrance by the mercy of God, Who preserves them and grants them these temporal possessions. But who is he that remembers the great justice of God? Or that gives thanks to God according as is meet?" When the first commandment had said these words, he read in his book, and wept, and as he read he bewailed himself and was sorrowful and full of grief.

6. Greatly did Blanquerna marvel at the grief which the first commandment suffered, and he enquired of him what he was reading in that book. "Beloved son!" said the first commandment, "In this book is written the great glory of the bliss of Heaven and the great pain to be suffered by them that are disobedient unto me. In this book are written the names of all that are obedient unto me and of all that are disobedient, and since the number of the disobedient is greater far than the number of the obedient, and there is no error or wrong in me whereby I merit disobedience, and those that disobey me most are they to whom God has granted the most of worldly honours, therefore now my disconsolateness and my grief grow greater whensoever I read in this book."

7. While the first commandment spake with Blanquerna, the second commandment wept and lamented so bitterly that Blanquerna gave ear to his words, and looked upon his tears, which moved him to pity and to contrition of mind. "Oh, neglected wretch!" said the second commandment, "To swear falsely by God is to despise thy Lord, and thereby is honour done to the creature above the lofty dominion of the Creator. God loves a single soul more than all the riches of this world; and a perjurer loves

that for the which he perjures himself more than God or the eternal glory which he may win."

8. In like manner did the third commandment weep and lament, saying these words: "God commanded the Jews to keep the Sabbath, and the Son of God incarnate ordained that Christians should keep holy the Lord's Day. But the Jews, who are blasphemers of our Lord Jesus Christ, and live in error, keep the Sabbath better than do Christians the Lord's Day: who then shall comfort my soul because of this sin? And men and women commit more sins on days of festival in eating and drinking and using vanities than on any other days of the week: who then is he that is obedient unto me?"

9. The fourth commandment likewise lifted up his voice and wept, saying: "God is the Father of all creatures by creation and grace; mother of all men is the Mercy and Justice of God: and I am the commandment which tells how a man should honour his father and his mother. Who is obedient to me, in honouring God as his Creator? And who is he that trusts in His Mercy? And who fears and loves the Justice of God?"

10. The fifth commandment could scarce contain himself as he gave utterance to these words: "Dead is charity in him that kills his neighbour; by his sin he destroys his soul when he is disobedient unto me. More deeply am I disobeyed as to spiritual than as to physical death; more is an earthly lord feared for his justice than is the God of Heaven. Dishonoured and despised am I by those that disobey me. Sad is my soul when it sees them travelling along those paths by the which they go to everlasting torments."

11. The sixth commandment said: "I am the commandment of God against fornication; I am ordained of God to combat uncleanness of mind and body, but women dye their eyebrows and their hair, daub colours on their faces and adorn their garments, to the end that I may be

disobeyed and despised. I have lost my inheritance and my dominion through lust in those to whom I am sent. If lust mine enemy has made me to be dishonoured, sad and disconsolate, then will my sister Justice have vengeance on them that have so dishonoured me."

12. The seventh commandment, weeping, began to speak, and said these words: "Friendship and love is there between me and charity and justice. Daily is theft the cause of evil-doing and deception; I am the commandment which forbids theft, that there may be charity among all men. Justice punishes thieves, but it makes me not to be obeyed for charity, but rather through fear of itself. The good things are stolen which God has given to them that are disobedient to me, for they render Him no thanks for the good things that He has given them. The good which is in them, they give and attribute it to themselves. If I endure suffering and grief in this world, they will suffer eternal torments in the world to come for the dishonour which now they show me."

13. The eighth commandment spake with suffering of heart, and said these words: "False witness persecutes me daily, and makes those to be disobedient by whom I thought to be honoured. False witness is made concerning the honour of God by him that loves rather the honour of his order than that of his God. To deny Trinity in God, and the Incarnation of the Son of God, is false witness against the goodness, power, wisdom, love and perfection of God; to increase evil report and to deny truth are contrary to my will. Daily am I, the commandment, given, and daily am I disobeyed; false witness has cast me out from mine inheritance, and to it are given the honours that I was wont to have. To love this world rather than the next is false witness given against the glory of God."

14. Envy has increased in the world, and the ninth commandment lamented the harm which envy and lust had done to him, saying these words: "If thou, Charity, hadst

such great power against envy, and if thou, Justice, didst incontinently punish all them that covet the wives of their neighbours, then should I be honoured and feared by them that hold me in dishonour and despise my virtue. If lust and envy have power against me, where is the aid that through you I possess? Let not Charity and Justice neglect to strengthen nobility of mind, that I may be honoured and obeyed in despite of envy and lust. Obedience, my friend! Forsake me not for envy and lust which make thee to be displeasing unto God and likewise to me, whensoever thou dost follow lust and envy."

15. Blanquerna was now in the presence of the tenth commandment, who lamented in this wise concerning fortitude and hope: "Alas! And who has set me in the wrath and displeasure of fortitude and of hope? For never in the past have I failed or deceived them. To covet the riches and the goods of one's neighbour is to be light-minded and to sin against hope, and not to hope or trust in the riches or the virtues of God. Too long do Charity and Justice and Prudence tarry in destroying my enemies, and in installing me once more in the friendship of Hope and Fortitude, the which friendship in former years I enjoyed. By those that were wont to aid me am I forgotten; by mine enemies, despised and dishonoured." These words and many more spake the ten commandments, and so bitterly did they weep and lament, that Blanquerna could not refrain from tears.

16. For long did Blanquerna weep and remain with the ten commandments, and he enquired of them if there were naught wherein he could aid them or be of avail to fulfil their desires and make their sorrow to cease. And the ten commandments told him that naught could relieve their great sadness save an exceeding devotion and affection of the mind in prelates and princes and religious men, to the end that with great fervour and love they should punish all such as were disobedient to the commandments.

17. So Blanquerna kneeled to the ten commandments, and begged of them leave and license to continue upon his way, and grace and virtue to keep them every one and with constant mind to be obedient to them in his hermitage. And each of the Ten Commandments blessed Blanquerna, and he left them with cheerful spirit, and went forth to seek the place wherein he might dwell as a hermit all the days of his life.

CHAPTER XLIII

OF FAITH AND OF TRUTH

Blanquerna set out from the palace wherein were the Ten Commandments, and journeyed through the forest from one part to another, seeking a place where he might build his cell. At the hour of none, when he had said his office, he sat down near to a fountain and ate one of the seven loaves which he carried with him. When he had eaten, and had drunk from the water of the fountain, he gave thanks to God and continued upon his journey. As he went through the forest, he saw lions and bears and wolves and wild boars and serpents and many other evil beasts; and because he was all alone and unaccustomed to seeing such beasts he had fear and was affrighted in his mind. But Hope and Fortitude recalled to him the power of God, and Charity and Justice strengthened his mind, and he fell to prayer, and gave thanks to God, because He had given him such company, whereby he remembered His power, and was enabled to trust in His hope.

2. While Blanquerna was journeying thus through the forest, there came from before him the sound of a most miserable and wretched voice. Greatly did Blanquerna marvel at the sound of the voice which he heard. When he had gone a little way he saw coming through the forest, with none other company, two ladies, right nobly dressed and very pleasant to look upon; but one of these ladies

wept and bewailed herself bitterly. Blanquerna went quickly to meet these two ladies, and enquired of her that was weeping what was the occasion of her tears and sadness. The lady that wept answered and spake these words: "I am Faith, and I have journeyed with this lady, who is Truth, into the land of the Saracens, that I might convert them into the way of salvation. And they have not been willing to receive me nor yet Truth; neither would they believe me, but made opposition to me and to Truth. Sad is my soul because God is not loved in those lands, neither honoured nor believed; and sorrow have I and pity for the damnation of those innocent men. Needs must I weep for the great ill that follows from the error wherein they live, and bewail the merit that is lost in those that will not present to them my brother and my sister."

3. Blanquerna enquired of Faith who were her brother and her sister. Faith replied: "This lady is my sister, and my brother is Understanding, to whom I am going now, that he may visit those people from whom I come, and demonstrate to them by necessary reasons the fourteen articles of faith; for the time has come when they will not receive the authority of the saints; and there are now no miracles such as those of old whereby they that knew not me nor my sister were enlightened. And since the people require arguments and necessary demonstrations, I go to my brother, who has power, by the virtue of God, to prove the fourteen articles."

4. Blanquerna answered her and said that Faith would lose her merits if her articles were demonstrated by Understanding, through the which articles Faith is enlightened to believe even against Understanding. But Faith said to Blanquerna that it was a thing ill-beseeming if the chiefest reason for the which man desired to convert the unbelievers were that greater merit thereby might be occasioned to Faith; and that this should rather be the secondary intention, and that the chiefest intention should be that God

might be known and loved. "Let Understanding use his virtue," said she, "that I thereby may be the greater and the more highly exalted; for even as Understanding may the higher soar by comprehending the articles, even so may I rise higher yet,—yea, above Understanding; for I can believe that which he cannot comprehend; and when men affirm that my sister Truth is not in these necessary reasons, they speak against me and my sister and my brother, albeit they can be calumniated by any light reason, comparison being made between me and my sister and my brother."

5. Blanquerna said that many a time friars and other men had gone to preach the Roman faith to unbelievers, and had not been able to convert them, because it seemed that God desired not their conversion; and when God desired it, then would it be a light thing to convert them. Faith answered: "If God desired not the conversion of men, wherefore would He have become incarnate? And wherefore did He will to suffer upon the Cross? And wherefore did He so greatly honour the apostles and the martyrs who suffered death to exalt me in the world? But God daily awaits those that will love Him, desiring them to come to Him of their own free will and not of constraint, that they may win great glory; and the people tempt God, and believe that, when God wills it, He will grant them the will to suffer martyrdom for love of Him. And what stronger demonstration can there be that God wills man to bear trials and death for love of Him, than that which is represented before our eyes by the Cross, or than the words in the Gospel that Jesus Christ spake when He said three times to Saint Peter that if he loved Him he must feed His sheep? Or what can error do against God, and against my brother and me and my sister? But since there is no perseverance nor continuance in disputations against the unbelievers, therefore does it appear to the people that error cannot be vanquished by us."

6. When Faith had straitly rebuked Blanquerna, she returned to her weeping, and began to lament and cry out as was her wont, and continued on her way towards Understanding her brother. Blanquerna followed Faith and Truth, and comforted Faith in such manner as he was able, saying these words: "Wise is God in all things, and His Justice fails in naught. Wherefore since God knows that thou, O Faith, hast done thine utmost in desiring the conversion of unbelievers, the Justice of God excuses thee; and hence must thou be comforted according to the wisdom and justice of God, and thy merit is as great as if thou hadst converted the unbelievers whose conversion thou didst so greatly desire." Faith answered Blanquerna, weeping: "Alas, wretched one that I am! Never did I think myself to be so greatly despised by men. And how can any suppose that I may be comforted while my Creator and my Light is despised, unknown, unloved[1] and blasphemed against by men? If I were comforted because of my merit and my powers, where would be charity in my will? Such consolation as this comes through defect of love, devotion and pity which are my sisters, to whose virtue my consolation would be opposed." Thus did Faith reprove Blanquerna, and shame and conscience overtook him. And meanwhile they had arrived in those parts where Understanding had his dwelling.

CHAPTER XLIV

OF UNDERSTANDING

In the shade of a fair tree laden with flowers and fruits, on the fresh grass near to a crystal fountain, was a high seat subtly carved and adorned with gold and silver and ivory and marble and precious stones. Upon this seat sat an ancient and reverend man, right nobly garbed in crimson

[1] *desamat.*

samite, whereby is signified the Passion of the Son of God. This man was Understanding, who was reading to many of his disciples in philosophy and theology. While Understanding read to his disciples, Faith and Truth with Blanquerna came to that place and greeted Understanding and his disciples, and were courteously welcomed by Understanding and by all the rest.

2. Understanding enquired of Faith and Truth how they did, and what they had accomplished of that purpose for the which they went upon their journey. With great compassion and grief, Faith answered her brother, and told him of the manner wherein she had journeyed among the Saracens, and how she had found men learned in philosophy that believed not in the articles of the Saracens, but neither would they receive the authority of the saints nor believe them. " And therefore," said she, " my sister Truth and I have come to thee, to pray that thou wilt go to them and by necessary reasons wilt show to them the truth, and lead them out of the error wherein they live, that God may be known and loved by them and my griefs be relieved."

3. So Understanding turned to his disciples and spake these words: " The time has come wherein our knowledge is exalted; the unbelievers demand necessary demonstrations and reasons, and refuse credence to aught beside. It is time for us to go, and make use of the science which we have; for, if we use it not as we ought, in honouring Him from Whom we have it, we act against conscience and against that which we know, and we desire not to have the merit and the glory which we can have if we use our knowledge. Very great is the doubt which the sages of the Saracens have in their belief; the Jews are in doubt by reason of the bondage wherein they live, and desire to have knowledge; and many idolaters are there who have no belief: it is time that we go. I would know now which of you desires to go in company with me and with my sisters. We have a new method of argument with the unbelievers,

by showing them the *Brief Art of Finding Truth*[1] ; and, when they have learned this, we shall be enabled to confound them by this art and by its beginnings."

4. When Understanding had ended his words, the disciples made excuses to him, saying thus: "A fearful thing is death and the endurance of trials and torments; a thing to be shunned is it to suffer hunger and thirst, to leave country and kindred and to go into foreign lands among people that kill and torture those that reprove them for their beliefs." When the disciples said these words, Truth could no longer hold her peace, and she spake as follows: "If all these things whereof ye speak are to be feared, much more to be feared is it to be an enemy of me and of my sister and my brother, and also of Hope, Charity, Justice and Fortitude! If my brother has given me to you, where is the honour that ye do me by opposing Falsehood, who has done me such grievous dishonour before so many people? And which of you is he that would fain be like unto Jesus Christ, at the Day of Judgment, in His crimson garments? And if ye died not natural deaths, which of you would fain die to honour his Celestial Lord?" Then Truth wept, and Faith began again to lament her bitter griefs, and Understanding said: "Alas! Where are the thanks of those to whom I have shown the truth!" And he said to Faith and Truth: "Go to Devotion, your sister, and pray her to come to these disciples, that are without piety, that she may teach them to love, and give them resolution to follow me upon that journey to make the which ye so greatly desire." So Faith and Truth, with Blanquerna, went to Devotion. And while Blanquerna followed Faith and Truth he praised and blessed God Who had set him in this place so that he had heard the words aforesaid, which he had never heard before.

[1] Another allusion to Lull's own work: see pp. 327, 332 below.

CHAPTER XLV

OF DEVOTION

FAITH and Truth, together with Blanquerna, came to a place where sat Devotion beneath a right beauteous pine-tree, and she was in prayer and tears, desiring the honour of Jesus Christ and remembering His grievous Passion. Devotion welcomed Faith and Truth, and greeted them with cheerful countenance, but Faith and Truth greeted Devotion with countenances that were sad and troubled. Wherefore Devotion feared lest her brother Understanding had some sorrow or grief, and she enquired of them concerning the estate of their brother. Faith and Truth answered Devotion by relating the happenings set forth above, and they told how Understanding their brother begged her earnestly that she would come to him to move his disciples to love to the end that they might follow him, giving praise to the Holy Divine Trinity and the Incarnation of the Son of God, that God and His works might have the honour among us which is fitting, and we ourselves be well-pleasing to Him, and they that are in falsehood and error be enlightened by faith and truth and understanding.

2. " How then ? " said Devotion, " Have they me not in their minds when my brother presents to them Truth my sister ? " " Contrary is it to nature," said Devotion, " to know God and His works, and not to have charity and devotion to honour God and His works. This contrariety is engendered by forgetfulness of the Divine Virtue, and the glory of Heaven, and the pains of Hell, and remembrance of the vanity of this world and fear of death. Alas, unhappy that I am ! Where are Hope and Charity and Justice and Prudence and Fortitude that they aid you not and aid not the wisdom of my brother ? " Greatly marvelled Devotion, and sorely lacked she comfort as she spake the words aforesaid.

3. While Devotion marvelled at this ignorance of the disciples, who feared death and trials borne for the honour of God and the gaining of celestial happiness more than they feared to have not Charity, Hope and Fortitude, Faith and Truth begged Devotion that she would go to the disciples, for there had been overmuch delay, and it was time that devout upholders of the Faith should preach to the unbelievers; for souls are hastening daily to the eternal flames even as the rivers hasten ceaselessly to the sea. Devotion answered: " Well know ye that no power avails over free will in the disciples of my brother, wherefore unless they will it freely I cannot be in them; for else would my works be contrary to Charity and Justice which accord with merit of glory and merit of blame. Therefore it is well that ye return to my brother and his disciples, and tell them that they may have me all the hours that they will in their company and in their mind whensoever they are pleased to have remembrance and desire for me. And to the end that they may desire me, there is figured upon the Cross the image of Jesus Christ, the which should cause them to have great shame because they desire not to have me that they may pay to Him the honour due."

4. Faith and Truth returned to Understanding right disconsolate in spirit. Blanquerna took courteous leave of them and went on in search of a habitation. And as he journeyed all alone through the forest, he remembered the words of Devotion, and praised and blessed the Charity, Wisdom and Justice of God, Who had charged faithful Christians, through the Incarnation and Passion of the Son of God, to fear neither trials nor death that God and His works may be honoured.

CHAPTER XLVI

OF DILIGENCE

BLANQUERNA went from one place to another in the forest, seeking the spot which he so greatly desired. His mind ceased not to love, nor his soul to remember, nor his mouth to praise the Name of God. While Blanquerna journeyed in this wise through the forest, he saw a man on horseback riding towards him with great speed. This man carried a goodly quantity of money. Blanquerna greeted him, and enquired of him why he went with such great speed. And he answered, saying that he was the minister of a king who had sent him to a certain city to make ready for him a lodging and to buy those things whereof the king had need for his honour in a great court that he purposed to hold with many noble barons. Blanquerna enquired of him many things, but the minister would not tarry with him lest he should be delayed in his journey, neither would he answer those things that were asked of him.

2. All that day Blanquerna journeyed till after the hour of none, when he ate of his bread and of some raw herbs that were growing near a fountain. While Blanquerna was eating, a squire came by upon a palfrey, which he rode with great speed. This squire came from the court and was going to a city wherein had been elected a bishop; and, since the election had been confirmed by the Pope, he went to bear felicitations[1] to the chapter of the city and to the kinsfolk of the bishop. The squire gave his palfrey to drink at the fountain which was before Blanquerna. While the palfrey drank, the squire related to Blanquerna his errand as aforesaid; but in such haste was the squire that he could scarce make Blanquerna to understand these words nor would he allow the palfrey to drink his fill at the fountain.

[1] P: "to bear the news."

3. Blanquerna ended his meal, and fell on his knees to give thanks to God. While Blanquerna praised God at the hour of none according to his wont, he saw a merchant, who had been robbed and stripped of all that he had, approaching him on foot, weeping, and lamenting bitterly, and saying these words: "Alas, unhappy one! How long hast thou laboured in many lands, how much hunger, thirst, heat, cold and fear hast thou borne to gain that which now thou hast lost! Miserable wretch! What wilt thou do? And how will thy wife and thy children fare? Now art thou robbed, and all that thou didst possess is taken from thee. Wilt thou make outcry concerning them that have robbed thee? Thou art in peril of death lest the robbers kill thee, for thou journeyest often and art ever in their hands." "Fair friend!" said Blanquerna: "Whither goest thou? And who has brought thee into this same great sadness that thy disconsolate appearance signifies?" The merchant related to Blanquerna how he had been robbed by a knight who had a castle near the place through the which he was passing, and how he was going to make outcry against that knight who had robbed him, and how he had lost all that for the which he had ever laboured.

4. After the merchant had been gone from Blanquerna a little space, there came on foot another man in great haste, laden with geese and hens which he was carrying on his back. Blanquerna asked him if in all that forest he knew of no place wherein he might dwell, provided only that it should be upon a hill and a fountain should be there and wild fruit growing, to the end that he might lead therein the life of a hermit. But that man answered not his words, for so intent was he upon a lawsuit wherein he was engaged that he thought that Blanquerna was asking him concerning his estate and his journey. Therefore spake he to Blanquerna in these words: "Sir!" said that man, "I am going along this way, to a town that is near to a castle, in

the which town I have a lawsuit against my brother. For I demand of him a vineyard that my father has bequeathed to me in his will. And these things that thou seest I bear as a present for the judge and for the advocates upon either side, and further I bear them money which I have borrowed at an exceeding great rate of interest. I pray thee for God's sake that thou aid and counsel me if thou knowest aught of the law."

5. For long did Blanquerna marvel at the surpassing great desire of that man to gain the vineyard, and he was mindful of the words of Faith and Truth and Understanding and Devotion, and of the wondrous diligence which he had seen in the persons aforementioned. So Blanquerna fell on his knees, and his heart was moved to devotion, and his eyes to weeping and tears, and he spake these words: "Oh strange will, contrary both to order and to nature, wherein is defect of courtesy and wisdom! Whence comest thou, that makest the honour and knowledge of God to be forgotten, and wilt not give devotion to them that fear to bear trials and death to the end that God may be honoured, and the erring led into the life of salvation! Foolish art thou, O will; small thanks hast thou to thy Creator, and little dost thou fear the pains of hell, whereby thou shalt never attain thy desire. Where is that good thing wherewith thou canst be rewarded by the minister of the king or by the squire or by the merchant or by the countryman? Foolish one! How is it that thou rememberest not the salvation that thou canst have in this world? Or why fearest thou not to lose in this world that which is irrecoverable in the next?" Greatly was the countryman amazed at the words which Blanquerna spake, and leaving Blanquerna he returned to his former cogitations.

CHAPTER XLVII

OF AUGURIES

FAIR was the day, and the sun illumined the whole wood through the which Blanquerna journeyed. On a high hill he espied a knight, mounted upon his horse and clad in full armour. That knight was cunning in the interpretation of auguries, and had come to seek omens which should signify the truth to him concerning a combat wherein he desired to engage against another knight that was his mortal enemy. While the knight watched to see if he might not espy an eagle or a crow or a sparrow-hawk or any other bird from the which he could learn the thing that he desired to know, Blanquerna ascended the hill to enquire of the knight if he knew of any place which would accord with the life that he desired to lead.

2. When Blanquerna reached the knight they saluted each other in right friendly fashion. Each of them enquired concerning the other's estate, and related the reason for the which he had come to that place. When Blanquerna had learned the reason of the coming of the knight, he spake to him these words: "Sir Knight! Art thou as strong and noble of mind as is signified by the goodly fashioning of thy body and of thy horse and of thy armour? Thou seemest to me right well able to defend thyself against another knight." "Friend!" said the knight, "I am strong of person, and full well armed, and I feel within me no fault which inclines me to evil-doing or deception; and by the grace of God I have long held the order of knighthood; wherefore it seems to me that I cannot be vanquished or overcome by any single knight."

3. "Sir Knight!" said Blanquerna. "All that is done in this world comes to pass by the action of two things, to wit, occasion and fortune.[1] Occasion is that which has

[1] For the use of these terms, cf. p. 41 above.

regard to the things to come according to the knowledge of discretion and reason through enlightened understanding or the enlightenment of faith; but fortune is a thing which comes to pass without occasion or prevision whatsoever. I ask thee, then, which of the two is stronger, whether occasion or fortune." "Fair friend!" said the knight, "Stronger of a certainty is occasion, which accords with reason and intention, than fortune, which accords with the matter itself without deliberation of reason and discretion and intention." Blanquerna answered the knight saying "that he had spoken well; but that his actions were contrary to his words, forasmuch as he was watching for omens; for the birds which go flying through the air fly by occasion to the end that they may catch their meat, but their flight is a matter of fortune with respect to the angle at the which they pass a man as they fly. Wherefore a knight that does battle with another, having first sought fortune from the birds, is neither as strong nor as wise according to the art of war as is he that does battle by the arbitration of reason, and the discretion of his understanding, which signifies to him the things that are to come according to the circumstances of war. By these words mayest thou learn that thine enemy is stronger against thee if he follow that which reason demonstrates to him than art thou against him if thou be guided by that which the birds chance to do, wherein is no necessity of reason which can use its virtue; the more so because such a usage is displeasing to God and is contrary to hope, fortitude and justice; wherefore thou hast the worse of thy battle."

4. Long mused the knight upon the words which Blanquerna spake; and through the merits of Blanquerna and the working of reason the knight took knowledge of his errors, and spake these words: "Many a time has it come to pass that reason has showed me how I should make certain attacks and perform stratagems of battle; but, because I believed in omens more than in my understanding,

therefore have I forsaken that which reason dictated to me, and followed the omens, which have caused me to act in contrary wise to reason and intellect. Blessed therefore be God, Who has sent to me through thee this knowledge! From this time forth no auguries nor omens shall have me in their power."

5. "Sir Knight!" said Blanquerna, "Another law of battle has God made, namely that since reason dictates and demonstrates how a man may do harm to his enemy, reason should therefore take thought if it accords with charity, hope, justice, prudence and fortitude; for all these virtues are the sisters of reason, and reason may not have effect in her thoughts if she be opposed to her sisters. Wherefore it behoves thee to have in mind the agreement that is between reason and the virtues aforesaid." Greatly did the words of Blanquerna please the knight, and he said to Blanquerna that he would indeed think after this manner, as he had never yet done at any time soever in his life.

6. Long did the knight consider if in battle he had used charity, justice and hope; and his conscience recalled to him the malice and the enmity which he had borne to his foe, and how he had set his hope on auguries, and how pride and vainglory had been in his mind in the stead of fortitude. Therefore, when the knight had thought for long upon these things, and upon many more whereby he had knowledge of his errors, then praised he and blessed God, and repented him of his faults. Commending himself to the care and service of reason and her sisters, he spake to Blanquerna in these words: "Blessed be God, Who has given me fortitude whereby in my mind I have vanquished my enemies. Never have I fought a fight that was so full of profit and of pleasure. Through the enemies whom I have vanquished in my mind I will vanquish my enemies in the mind of that knight whose mortal foe I have for so long been. Alas! What battle is well fought and won, but with charity, justice, patience, humility and fortitude

to overcome and vanquish malice, ill will, pride, evil doing and deception?" When the knight had ended these words, Blanquerna took his leave of him and continued upon his journey.

CHAPTER XLVIII

OF VALOUR[1]

BLANQUERNA continued on his way with great desire to find a place meet for his penitence. While he journeyed thus through the forest he espied a road along the which walked a jester[2] very poorly clad, his appearance and his manner bearing witness to his poverty and sadness of mind. Blanquerna enquired of the jester wherefore his countenance thus bore witness to sorrow and grief. "Sir!" said the jester: "I have come from a court wherein a noble baron of these parts has been of late dubbed knight. In that court I thought to find valour which should restore my poor garments, and should reward me for the sirventes[3] that I

[1] To translate the words *valor* and *desvalor*, "valour" and "disvalour" respectively are used, rather than "worth" and "worthlessness," which to modern ears express more of the meaning of the Catalan word. Up to the sixteenth century, the word "valour" was in general use to express the idea of a person's worth or importance in respect of his attributes or qualities. The full sense in which the word is used in this book will become clear as the reader proceeds with the narrative. In particular, Blanquerna's descriptions of the offices of valour will be noted (§§ 3, 5 below).

[2] The word *juglar* ("jongleur") occurs so many times from this point onwards in the book that, rather than burden the narrative with a continually recurring foreign word, we have thought it best to translate by "jester." The *juglar* was a well-known mediæval figure about whom much has been written both in Spanish and other languages. His accomplishments and qualifications were numerous, and varied greatly with circumstances. He could be juggler, acrobat, conjurer, satirist, buffoon, tumbler, singer, actor, reciter, mimic, sage, musician, and much beside. But his profession in its most general aspect consisted in *the giving of amusement:* "illorum officium tribuit lætitiam," say the *Leges Palatinæ* of the King (James II of Majorca) to whom reference has already been made. Hence the word "jester," which has in English a similarly extended meaning, seems suitable to translate *juglar*.

[3] The *sirvente* was a kind of song or poem, usually of a satirical nature. It has been remarked above that the *juglares* were often accomplished satirists.

have made for long against those that are enemies of valour, and because I praised those that in this world maintain valour; but there was no reward given for valour in that court, nor to any of its lovers. For this cause I have fallen to thinking how I may compose another sirvente, wherein I may speak ill of valour and its servants."

2. "Fair friend!" said Blanquerna: "Ere thou makest this sirvente, it behoves thee to have knowledge of valour and of those that are its servants, that thy words may contain truth." "Sir!" said the jester: "For long have I had knowledge of valour, and sought it in many lands, and it has never yet aided my poverty nor enabled me to leave the service of evil men." "Friend!" said Blanquerna: "If valour were that which thou sayest, it would of necessity be bound to help thee; for if it did not so it would not be valour. But it might be that that which thou namest valour is disvalour, evil and sin. Wherefore if evil, ill-speaking, ignorance and disvalour make thee to go about in poverty, then sayest thou wrongly that valour has done thee injury or wrong."

3. "Sir!" said the jester: "Since thou art so doughty a defender of valour I would have thee tell me what valour may be. Blanquerna answered and said that valour is valiancy[1] of virtues against vices, and it is that thing whereby comes utility and preservation against deception and sin. Comprehended in this valour are truth, liberality, courtesy, humility, moderation, loyalty, piety, knowledge and many virtues more, the which are daughters of faith, hope, charity, justice, prudence, fortitude and temperance: of these is valour the daughter."[2] While Blanquerna thus demonstrated the meaning of valour to the jester, a knight passed by on foot, bearing his lance in his hand, and upon his back his sword. When he was near to them, the jester

[1] *valença.* The word "valiancy" preserves the euphony and balance of the sentence, but the meaning is rather "utility," "usefulness," "worth."

[2] So V. Other versions have: "of whom is the daughter of valour."

said to Blanquerna that that knight was the emperor, for he knew him and had seen him many times. The jester and Blanquerna did reverence and honour to the emperor, who greeted them in very friendly fashion.

4. The jester enquired of the emperor what was the fortune that caused him thus to journey alone and on foot through the forest. The emperor answered and related to them both how that in the chase he had pursued a wild boar for so long that he had become parted from his companions; and how that he had followed the boar into a dense forest, and the boar had slain his horse and he himself had wounded the boar to death. When the emperor had related the adventure which had befallen him, he asked the jester and Blanquerna if they could give him aught to eat; for hunger constrained him greatly, because two days had passed, in the which he had neither eaten nor drunk. "Lord!" said Blanquerna: "Hard by is a fountain where thou mayest drink the pure water, and eat of the fresh grass which grows around it." The emperor answered saying that without eating he could not drink, and that it was not his custom to eat grass; but that he thought soon to die if he found not some thing to eat of a kind whereto he was accustomed.

5. Blanquerna led the emperor to the fountain; and they sat all three upon the fresh, green grass near by. Blanquerna drew out the three loaves that remained to him, and together they brake their fast and dined. While the emperor ate, Blanquerna enquired of him which thing was of the greater profit to him: whether the bread that he ate or his empire. The emperor answered and said that in that place the bread that he ate was of greater profit and worth[1] to him than his empire. Blanquerna replied: "Little is the worth[2] of an empire which is less profitable to its lord than the bread which he eats. From this, O jester, mayest thou take knowledge of that wherein true

[1] *més li profitava e li valia.* [2] *valor.*

valour consists. All valour consists in three things: the one is in earthly things which avail to sustain the body, the second, in the gaining of virtues and merits, and the third, in that all things are good in so far as by them God is served, known and loved, and is pleased to use His power in His creatures."

6. Then the emperor enquired of the jester and of Blanquerna what was this conversation upon valour into the which they had entered, and they related to him the words concerning valour which they were speaking when he met them. And Blanquerna said to the emperor: "Lord! Many are the noble deeds which oft-times thou hast done, whereby thou hast been a friend of valour. Now if thou hast done aught that is evil, and opposed to valour, it can in no wise aid thee in this forest wherein thou hast as little power as one of us. But if in thy soul there is nobility of heart, which accords with valour, the virtues whereof I have spoken are the daughters of valour and they can aid thee in this forest to have patience and humility and consolation in the hope of God Who can aid thee in this place and in others."

7. For long did they all three speak of valour, and for long did they walk together, until they came to a fair meadow surrounded by trees full fair. In the midst of that meadow was builded a beautiful palace, carven and walled with marble. Above the portal thereof were set these words: "This palace belongs to the lady Valour, and no man that is an enemy or a persecutor of valour must enter therein, nor can enter. In this palace dwells Valour, who is exiled from the world, and from her lovers, and from all them that are lovers of disvalour. Daily does Valour weep and bewail her wrongs, and fain would she recover her honour, and she awaits trusty helpers[1] who shall restore her to the world, that the honour of God may be multiplied throughout all lands. Comfortless is Valour, and evil-

[1] *valedors*. See note, p. 175 above.

doing and deception are increased. All men suffer from the dishonour which is done to Valour. If disvalour were valour, then would be greater in the world the honour of God. Valour welcomes him that remembers and loves her in his mind, and that laments the ill which she suffers, and that desires her honour."

8. When the emperor and Blanquerna and the jester had read these words, they wondered greatly at the significance thereof, and knocked at the door of the palace with intent to enter. A fair damsel appeared at the window, and enquired their will, and the condition and estate of all three. Each one told the damsel his name and his estate, and they said that they desired to enter the palace to the end that they might look upon Valour. So the damsel related to Valour the names and the estates of all three, and enquired of her if she would grant them leave to enter the palace. But Valour desired not that the emperor nor the jester should enter, for they were her enemies, and of the number of them that persecuted her in the world and made her to dwell in that forest. But because Blanquerna was her servant, she desired that he should enter and be given friendly welcome.

9. So Blanquerna entered alone into the palace, where he found Valour, who spake to him these words: "I Valour am created to signify and show forth the valour of my Creator and my Lord. God gives valour to plants, beasts, birds, heavens, stars, the four elements, and metals, that man may have valour over and above all these. And when man will not have this, he is in valour less than all these things or than any other creature, because he loves disvalour, the which he desires to have, believing it to be valour. Many men in the world have honours and riches, wherein is disvalour; and the friends of valour are despised and poor in the world. Many are the books wherein is written truth concerning the Incarnation and Passion of the Son of God, the which have valour in respect of redemp-

tion; but the books have no valour for infidels, who lack teachers. Many are they that hold the possessions of Holy Church, that they may exalt valour. But who is he that will exalt Holy Church in valour and in honour, against dishonour and error and infidelity? Many are they that desire God to have valour that they may gain honour; but few are the men that love valour to the end that God may have honour. If I have never done injury or wrong, wherefore is there done to me dishonour? And if Disvalour has never done acts of justice or bestowed rewards, wherefore is there done to him honour?" While Valour spake these words and many beside, her eyes were in tears, and her heart was in sorrow and pain, and she bewailed her wrongs bitterly.

10. Even till the morrow early was Blanquerna with Valour, comforting her and inspiring her with hope, and saying these words: "Strong above all other powers is God; His Wisdom has no fault; the world is His creation. Wherefore is it seemly that the world should come to its fulfilment, which could not be if disvalour went not to destruction and valour were not continually more highly exalted and went not ever recovering its honour. The mercy of God is not forgetful of sinners, and the justice of God has no friendship with the enemies of valour." With words such as these and with many more did Blanquerna bring consolation to Valour. With tears and devotion he took leave of her, vowing to submit his mind to her all the days of his life, and Valour took him into her guardianship and keeping.

11. Blanquerna left the palace, and, as he pursued his journey, he related to the emperor and the jester the tears and the despair[1] which he had found in Valour, and the words which she had spoken, making complaint of her enemies. Long did the emperor and the jester consider and think upon the words which Blanquerna spake con-

[1] *desconort*, "lack of consolation," "comfortlessness." See p. 19, above.

cerning Valour; and each was in constraint of conscience by reason of the sins which he had many times committed against Valour. While the emperor considered his sins, he enquired of Blanquerna concerning his history, and Blanquerna related it to him, together with that of Evast and Aloma, and he related likewise how that he was seeking to live as a hermit that he might have God and His honour ever in his mind, and flee from the world, which is the enemy of valour.

12. The humility of God moved pity and patience to pardon, and remembrance came to the emperor through the mercy of God. Contrition and repentance for his sins were in his heart, and he spake these words: "O guilty man and fool, that persecutest Valour and goest after wild beasts, setting thyself thereby in peril of death! thou that hast for so long served disvalour, yea, all the days of thy life, believing it to be Valour! For sin there must needs be made satisfaction, and for unruliness must atonement be made with rule"; wherefore in that place, in presence of Blanquerna, he vowed that in all his empire and in his person he would thenceforward serve Valour, that in himself and in others she might recover her possession, for so long lost. "Wherefore," said he, "I must needs make ordinance concerning my empire and my person in honour of Valour, that by my example Valour may receive her wonted honour, and return to live among us gladly and without sorrow."

13. As the emperor spake these words, they began all three to walk along a road which agreed not with the journey of Blanquerna. So Blanquerna said to the emperor that it behoved him to return towards those parts where he was seeking his hermitage. Beneath a fair tree he took leave of the emperor and the jester right courteously, and the emperor spake to Blanquerna these words: "Blessed be the hour when first I met thee upon my journey. Grievous to me is the parting from thy friendly presence.

It behoves me to put my house in order and the house of my lady the empress, and all my empire will I put in order, and commend it to men that love Valour, that Valour may have satisfaction according as I have promised. Of the ordinances of my realm will I make a book, and this jester and many others will I send throughout the world that they may proclaim valour in courts wherein it is despised, and persecute and cry out against disvalour in every place wherein it is praised. I will have them to take naught of any man, save of me alone, that they may the better exalt Valour. I will educate and bring up my sons right well, and then will I resign my empire, and serve God all my life together with thee in thy hermitage, that God and Valour may ever be in my mind. I beg thee to pray for me to God, that He may pardon me, and grant me thy company."

CHAPTER XLIX

OF CONSOLATION

In the neighbourhood of that part of the forest wherein Blanquerna journeyed was a shepherd keeping a large flock of beasts. That shepherd had a son of the age of seven years. For the great love which the shepherd bore to his son, he took him one day with him. It chanced that the shepherd slumbered beyond his wont, and the child strayed from the place where his father was sleeping, and a wolf came to the fold and found the child there and carried him off. At the cries of the child, when the wolf carried him away, the shepherd awoke, and saw that the wolf was carrying off his son. So he gave chase to the wolf with his dogs; but, ere he could reach him, the wolf had killed and mangled the child and devoured his heart within his breast. When the shepherd came to the place where he found his son dead, he was in despair, and cried out in these words;

2. "Alas, thou wretched one! Thou hast lost that which thou most didst love. Dead is thy son; and thou art the occasion of his death, for against the will of his mother didst thou bring him into this forest. So hast thou given to thy wife grief and sorrow all the days of her life. Despair above all despair else must be thine, and tears more than any yet shed. Needs must thou lament so bitterly that never more canst thou have consolation or joy. Shame and guilt with respect to thy wife are thine." As the shepherd lamented thus, he embraced and kissed his son, saying: "Son! Where is the fairness that thy countenance aforetime showed? And whither has fled the great delight that my mind was wont to have therein? O son! Thy death makes me to yearn for death also. Naught had I in my mind but thee; from henceforth, what will be in my mind? I am old and fain would die; grievous sorrow do I bear because I feel not death; my life is death by reason of thy death; no hope have I of comfort nor of pardon for my sin in being the occasion of thy death."[1]

3. So great were the cries and the complaints and the weeping of the shepherd that because of his cries and the barking of the dogs that fought with the wolf, Blanquerna made his way towards the sound of voices, at the which he marvelled greatly. When he arrived at that place, the shepherd was weeping and lamenting and ever embracing and kissing his son. Blanquerna desired to console him, but the shepherd gave no semblance of seeing him or hearing his words, so greatly afflicted was he by the anguish and the grief which he suffered.

4. Blanquerna saw that the wolf had killed one of the dogs, and held the other fast on the ground, and he thought that he would aid the dog, and that together they would slay the wolf, that by his death the shepherd might in some

[1] *Ma vida es mort en ta mort; no he esperança de conort ni quem sia perdonat lo tort que he de ta mort.* The prose rhymes, which are very characteristic of Lull, cannot be reproduced in English.

degree be comforted. So Blanquerna took a staff which the shepherd carried, and went against the wolf right speedily and as one that by the death of the child was moved to pity. The wolf endeavoured to flee, but the dog held him fast until he had been slain by Blanquerna. Then said Blanquerna to the shepherd: "Dead is thy foe, and by reason of his death should thy sorrow be turned into comfort."

5. Many words, devout and of great consolation, spake Blanquerna to the shepherd, but for all that he said or did the shepherd would not answer him nor cease from bewailing his grief with all his might. Greatly did Blanquerna marvel at the grief of the shepherd, and great was his pity thereat, and he perceived that the exceeding fury and sorrow of the shepherd had made his memory[1] to flee, and that he had no understanding of Blanquerna and of his words. Therefore, that he might give him consolation, and understanding of his words, through the which he might be the more inclined to consolation, he began to speak after another manner, which is according to natural reasoning; and he spake to the shepherd these words:

6. "Oh, caitiff, and fool, that art the occasion of the death of thy son! Wherefore weepest thou not, neither lamentest the harm that thou hast wrought? Hast thou no understanding, that thou consolest thyself thus lightly for the loss of that which thou so greatly lovest? Dead is thy son; and the wolf has slain thy wife and all thy dogs." The shepherd loved his wife very greatly, and supposed that Blanquerna spake the truth, and that he himself had not wept nor made lamentation as in fact he had done. While the shepherd reflected thus, he spake these words: "Is my wife in truth dead? And this that I do, is it to weep or to be comforted?" Blanquerna answered: "Come with me, and thou shalt see thy wife whom the wolf has

[1] Or, as we should say, his "wits": this is a mediæval use of the word "memory."

slain." The shepherd followed Blanquerna to the place where the wolf lay dead. "This is thy wife," said Blanquerna. Great was the wonder of the shepherd at the words of Blanquerna. and he thought that he had lost his senses and that the wolf was his wife.

7. When Blanquerna saw that the memory of the shepherd was beginning to return and to act once more according to its nature, and that his understanding had begun again to do its work, Blanquerna led the shepherd back to the place where his son lay dead, and took the child and began to kiss and to embrace it, and to weep and lament according as its father had done. Greatly did the shepherd marvel at the lamentations of Blanquerna; and the greater was his wonder, the more did his intellect, which he had lost, return. When the shepherd had recovered his wits, he went again to the place and knew that it was the wolf that was slain, and had joy because it was not his wife, and this joy in some wise restrained and assuaged his sorrow. Then he came to Blanquerna, who was holding the body of his son and weeping over it. "Sir!" said the shepherd, "Why weepest thou for my son? Give his body to me again and let me return to the tears that were mine." Blanquerna answered the shepherd and said: "It is a custom of the parts whence I come that a man takes a share in the lamentations and the weeping of others; wherefore I will share in thy weeping and lamentations, that thy bewailing of the death of thy son may be great, and indeed it is very right that thou shouldst lament greatly. And if thou desirest to follow the custom of my country I will show thee an art and method whereby thou mayest lament and weep for the death of thy son, since thou art guilty of his death." "Sir!" answered the shepherd. "Thy words are agreeable to me, and I pray thee to tell me the manner and the custom of thy country, according to the which I may greatly weep and lament while death yet suffers me to live, that I may endure the more torment in my lifetime."

8. Blanquerna answered the shepherd: "Ere thou canst know the manner wherein thou mayest fitly bewail thyself, thou must needs have knowledge of charity, justice, prudence, fortitude and hope, and thou must needs tell me the truth concerning that which I shall ask thee." "Sir!" said the shepherd, "All things will I learn of thee and all that thou askest of me will I tell thee, so that thou wilt but show me the manner wherein I may have such sorrow and grief as may slay me, over and above the despair that I must needs have concerning my son." Blanquerna conjured the shepherd to tell him the truth: which had he loved the more, whether God, or his son? The shepherd answered and said that he had had more love to his son than to God. Blanquerna said that it was defect of charity in a man to love any thing more than God; and that justice is that which punishes men that love God less than any thing soever. "As thou hadst greater love to thy son than to God," said Blanquerna, "therefore has justice punished thee in the death of thy son, and the Wisdom of God wills that henceforward thou love God above all things, that prudence may be in thee, and thou mayest have fortitude to aid thee against thy present wrath, and to mortify thy mind, and have hope of seeing thy son, who is in the glory of God."

9. The shepherd began to remember and understand the words which Blanquerna spake, and the more he considered them, even so the more did he feel relief from his sadness, and considered how that he ought rather to increase his grief. Wherefore he marvelled greatly, and spake to Blanquerna these words: "The more deeply I have remembrance of thy words, the less do I feel in myself of sadness and the more am I comforted. Where is the sorrow that by thy words thou desirest to increase in me?" Blanquerna answered and conjured the shepherd to tell him the truth: before the death of his son, which did he love the more, whether joy or sorrow? The shepherd answered

and said that he loved the rather joy. Then said Blanquerna: "If thou lovest sadness the rather, now that thy son is dead, then is death the mistress of joy and of sadness, according as thou lovest. Wherefore as death has been to thee so cruel a foe, thou shouldst not give to it such great dominion that it should make thee to desire sorrow more than patience and joy; but it behoves thee to be the greater enemy of death, now that it has robbed thee of thy son, than thou wert aforetime when thy son yet lived."

10. "Blanquerna!" said the shepherd. "How may I be the enemy of death, who has slain my son and who refuses to slay me?" Blanquerna answered: "With patience and consolation, by having joy in that which is done by the justice of God, and gladness of heart whence comes fortitude against sorrow. To have joy at possessing prudence, and to consider the utility even of hurt received as touching these earthly things, puts man in opposition to bodily and spiritual death, and in accord with that heavenly life which is everlasting even to the end of time."

11. Long would it take to recount the words which Blanquerna spake to the shepherd to console him; and by the art and method which Blanquerna used did he draw the shepherd from sadness and lead him to comfort and joy, the which joy the shepherd had as he spake these words: "Glad is my soul henceforward in knowing its Creator and in having the virtues which it was neither wont to have of old nor was able to use. For my son has departed from great peril, and is with his Lord in glory. May my will be ever subject in obedience to the Will of my Lord God." When the shepherd had said these words, and many more, he took the body of his son and kissed it and set it upon his back, and blessed and praised God, saying that greater was the profit that he had gained through the death of the child, by using the virtues aforementioned, than was the hurt which he had received thereby. Blanquerna and the shepherd took courteous leave the one of the other, and

Blanquerna prayed the shepherd to have God ever in his remembrance, and consolation and patience in his will, all the days of his life. The shepherd promised that he would have consolation and patience, but he was troubled as to how he should comfort his wife for the death of her son whom she loved above all things.

12. Blanquerna counselled the shepherd that he should comfort his wife according to the same manner wherein he had comforted him; and he told him to recount to his wife the death of their son, recounting together therewith the death of a brother of his wife, whom she greatly loved; and that afterwards the brother should come to comfort his sister, for in that he would yet be alive she would have as great comfort as the shepherd himself had had when he perceived that the wolf was not his wife.

CHAPTER L

OF FORTITUDE

In the forest through the which Blanquerna journeyed was a mighty castle, which belonged to a knight, who, by reason of the strength of his own person and his skill in feats of arms, was passing proud and did much harm to all those that lived around him. It came to pass one day that the knight, armed with his accustomed weapons and alone upon his horse, attacked the castle of a lady who had a fair daughter. It chanced that the knight found the damsel without the gates of the castle, together with other damsels, her friends, and he took her and placed her across the neck of his horse in her own despite and in despite of her companions, and escaped with her into a great forest. Loud were the cries and many the attempts that were made to take the damsel from the knight. As the knight bore her away she wept and lamented bitterly, and a squire who followed the knight challenged him and fought him, but the knight wounded the squire, and threw him from his horse, and slew it, and continued on his way with the damsel towards his castle.

2. It came to pass by chance that as Blanquerna was wandering here and there[1] through the forest, he came upon this knight. The damsel wept and cried and begged Blanquerna to aid her. But Blanquerna considered how that his bodily strength was light in comparison with the strength of the knight, and therefore he bethought him how he might aid the damsel with fortitude and charity which are spiritual forces. So he narrated to the knight this example[2]:

3. " It is said that once on a time a man right learned in philosophy and theology and the other sciences was moved by devotion to go to preach to the Saracens the truths of the Holy Catholic Faith, that he might destroy the error of the Saracens and that the name of God might be adored and blessed as is done among us. This holy man went to the land of the Saracens and preached and demonstrated the truth of our law and overthrew the law of Mahomet in so far as he was able. Throughout all that land there went forth the fame of that which he did. So the Saracen king commanded that holy Christian man to leave his country, saying that if he left it not he would be delivered up to death. The holy man obeyed not this bodily commandment, for charity and fortitude were in his mind, and made him to despise the death of the body. Great was the wrath of the king against him, and he made him to appear before him and spake to him these words:

4. " ' Oh, foolish Christian, that hast despised my commandment and the strength of my dominion! Seest thou not that I have power enough to cause thee to be tormented and delivered up to death? Where is thy power through

[1] *per un loc e per altre.*

[2] *exempli:* a short, frequently fable-like story used by moralists and preachers to illustrate a precept.

the which thou hast despised my strength and my dominion'? 'Sire!' said the Christian: 'True it is that thy bodily power can vanquish and overcome my body. But the strength of my mind may in no wise be vanquished by the strength of thine, nor by the strength which is in all the minds of all the men in thy land. And since strength of mind is nobler and greater than strength of body, therefore charity, which is in my mind, has such love for the strength of my mind, that it makes me to despise all the bodily strength that is in thy person and thy kingdom. Wherefore the strength and charity of my mind are ready to do battle with the powers of thy soul and with the souls of all them that are beneath thy sway.'"

5. "Great marvel had the king at these words which he heard, and he enquired of the Christian what was the occasion in his mind whereby he set at defiance all the strength and all the charity which were in the souls of the men of his country. 'Sire!' said the Christian: 'So great a thing is the Incarnation of the Son of God and the Passion which He suffered to save us, and so strong is truth against falsehood, that I have such charity and strength in my mind that in all thy land and among all the men that own thy sway there is no charity or fortitude which can by any arguments do battle with mine. And this is because ye are in error, and have not devotion concerning the Incarnation and Passion of our Lord God Jesus Christ.'"

6. "The Saracen king was greatly wroth against the Christian, and he commanded throughout all his land that the wisest men should come together, and they that had most of charity, and that they should vanquish in the Christian the virtue and charity of his mind, and afterward that they should cause his body to die a shameful death. So they all came together against the Christian, and he vanquished and overcame them all with spiritual strength and with charity; and he said to the king that he would do harm to their bodies if he parted them from their souls,

which had greater virtue in strength and charity than all the souls of his subjects, and that he would do injury to the soul if he rewarded not its merits."

7. When Blanquerna had related to the knight the example aforesaid, he enquired of him after this wise. "Sir Knight!" said Blanquerna: "Which, thinkest thou, is stronger and nobler in power, whether the strength of mind which overcame and vanquished so many other minds, or the strength of body which was greater in the Saracen king than in the Christian?" The knight answered and said that strength of mind is the greatest strength that is in man. "Sir Knight!" said Blanquerna: "Even as that strength is the greater and nobler, even so must it be the more fervently loved by charity. Well dost thou see that the strength of my body and the strength of the damsel whom thou hast taken are as naught by comparison with thy horse and thy arms and thy person; see therefore wherein there is more strength, whether in thy mind, or in thy horse and arms and person; for if thy mind be stronger against evil-doing and wrong and lust than are thy person and thy arms and thy horse, thou wilt return this damsel to that place from the which thou hast taken her, and thy mind will no longer be inclined to evil and wrong-doing. And as God has given strength to thy body, thou wilt have through the virtue of God strength and nobility of mind, through the which thou wilt have charity towards all good deeds wherein is loyalty and courtesy, humility and wisdom."

8. For a great space of time did the knight consider the words which Blanquerna spake, and he desired that no evil teaching nor villainy should vanquish or overcome his mind, wherewith he had many times vanquished and overcome knights in many attacks and combats. Wherefore the knight spake to Blanquerna these words: "Never by any man have I been vanquished or overcome. And, if I obeyed not thy words, wickedness and villainy would overcome my mind, which mind is by me very greatly to be loved, for

by its strength have I ever been victor over mine enemies. My mind is not vanquished by thy words, but rather does it vanquish and overcome in me the evil-doing and the villainy which was therein. Thou seest here this damsel: I pray thee, bear her to the castle of her mother. I have mortally wounded a squire from that castle, and therefore in good sooth I may not myself bear the damsel back within its precincts." And with these words the knight took leave of the damsel and of Blanquerna with all courtesy.

CHAPTER LI

OF TEMPTATION

GREATLY was Blanquerna displeased because he had perforce to leave his journey to accompany the damsel whom the knight had commended to him; but charity and fortitude made him to go with the damsel towards the precincts of the castle. Now while Blanquerna journeyed with the damsel, he felt within his mind temptation of carnal pleasure by reason of the surpassing loveliness of the damsel and the solitude wherein they were both together in the forest. But as soon as Blanquerna felt temptation, he remembered the means[1] whereby man mortifies all temptation,—to wit, God and His Passion, and the glory of Heaven, and the pains of Hell; and he fell to prayer, and begged the aid of the seven virtues that were in his company, and remembered the vileness and the abomination that is in the working of lust, and desired to have the nobler working that is in the virtues when they unite each with the others against the vices.

2. Many times was Blanquerna tempted by lust, for so long as he went with the damsel, and incontinently he gave himself to prayer, as is related above, and mortified the temptation. By the work of the evil spirit it came to pass

[1] *Lit.* "medicine."

likewise that the damsel was tempted to sin with Blanquerna, and she had not the means[1] of Blanquerna wherewith to fight temptation; wherefore she spake these words: "Fair sir! I am in thy power, and thy words have delivered me from the hands of the knight. No other reward can I give thee beyond this, that thou mayest command my person and do therewith all thy pleasure."

3. Blanquerna felt within himself his temptation increased through the words that the damsel spake, and he turned again to remembrance of God and the virtues, according to his custom. While Blanquerna considered thus in fortitude and in nobility of mind, through the light and inspiration of Divine wisdom, he remembered and comprehended how that God forsook many sinners, that they might be the occasion whereby just men should increase their virtues; wherefore Blanquerna perceived how that the damsel was forsaken by the grace of God, that he himself might have greater occasion of virtue, and be the stronger against temptation and lust, to the end that by greater fortitude he might have greater merit. So Blanquerna kneeled upon his knees, and adored and blessed God Who gave him so many occasions whereby he could greatly exalt His virtues. While Blanquerna adored and blessed God, it came to his will by the Divine Virtue that he should instruct the maiden as to how she should meet temptation whensoever she should be tempted by lust or other sin.

4. "Damsel!" said Blanquerna. "It is the nature of understanding to make that which is much remembered greatly to be loved or hated; wherefore whensoever man is tempted in any wise to sin, he must have much remembrance of the vileness and abomination of sin and the evils which follow therefrom; for even as a man has the greater remembrance after this manner, even so does the understanding make the will to love the sin no longer. Another manner is there of mortifying temptation, to wit, that a

[1] *Ibid.*

man should have remembrance of God, and of His goodness, greatness, power, wisdom, love, perfection, justice, and of how He has had great love to man, and of how He has prepared great glory for him, and of how noble a thing it is to use faith, hope, charity, justice, prudence, fortitude and temperance. The third manner is that a man should forget the sin and all the circumstances of his temptation; for by his forgetting sin is the will mortified as to the love thereof; wherefore he must have remembrance of other things. After these three manners aforesaid may every temptation be mortified." The damsel took knowledge that Blanquerna spake these words to her because he knew of that concerning the which she was tempted, and she praised and blessed God, because He had given such virtue to Blanquerna against temptation; and whensoever there came to her temptation concerning him, she used the doctrine which he had given her; by the which doctrine she mortified the temptation and accustomed her soul to the use of the virtues.

5. Long did Blanquerna and the damsel journey through the forest, even until the damsel was wearied with walking, and desired to rest beneath a tree, under the shade whereof she fell asleep. While the damsel slept, Blanquerna remained in prayer, and contemplated the Divine blessing. Now, as Blanquerna was at prayer, he heard a voice that lamented and wept and gave signs of great distress and sorrow. Blanquerna went towards the direction whence that voice came and found the squire who had been wounded by the knight, the which squire was returning in great distress.

6. "Fair friend!" said Blanquerna, "What aileth thee? And what needest thou to repair the injury that has been done to thee that thou mayest have consolation?" "Sir!" said the squire, "Distressed am I and angered because I cannot fulfil the errand on the which I have been sent." The squire recounted to Blanquerna how he had

followed the knight that he might take the damsel from him, and how the knight had wounded him and borne away the damsel. "Fair friend!" said Blanquerna, "Reason counsels thee to take comfort, since thou hast done all that was within thy power; for even so much thank oughtest thou to receive as though thou hadst recovered the damsel." "Sir!" answered the squire, "It is of the nature of charity that no man should take comfort for doing that which was within his power, if he brings not to fulfilment the thing which he desires; and because I desire to serve the lady who has bred me, and through my fault my desire has not been brought to fulfilment, therefore in her distress it is fitting that I have distress, albeit I have done that which was within my power."

7. Deeply did Blanquerna consider the words of the squire, the which words signified great perfection of charity and fortitude, and as he considered, even so did he remember how through defect of charity certain men who desired to give example of the Catholic Faith held themselves excused, insomuch as they did that which was within their power and could not bring to fulfilment that thing which they so greatly desired; through the which defect of fulfilment they should the rather be in distress for the dishonour which God has of those that know Him not and of those that honour Him not according as they know Him. While Blanquerna was considering thus, he said to the youth: "Fair friend! See thou there, beneath yonder tree, the damsel whom thou seekest; and since thou hast perfect charity, God wills that that which is in thy mind be brought to pass, and that thou have the merit concerning that thing for the which thou hast laboured." Then the squire drew near to the tree, and beheld the damsel sleeping, the which damsel awakened and returned with the squire to the castle; and they both took leave very courteously of Blanquerna.

8. Blanquerna set forth once more upon his journey, and, as he journeyed, he considered with much searching

of heart how he might find a place wherein to serve God as he desired. For two days Blanquerna went through the forest without finding aught that he might eat. On the third day he was in great distress by reason of his hunger; and the greater was the distress of his hunger, the greater was his hope and trust in God, that He would fortify him against hunger and temptation, whereby the demon might cause him else to sin against hope and patience, by means of impatience and despair. While Blanquerna with the help of the virtues strove thus with all his might against temptation and hunger, Prudence came to the aid of her servant, and enlightened the eyes of his mind; so that he considered how great affection and exaltation in prayer fortify the body through the influence of devotion. As Blanquerna considered thus, he endeavoured with all his powers to pray and to contemplate God and to use his virtues that he might have fruition of God[1]; and by the virtue of God and the nature of the understanding which should comprehend God and the will which should love Him, the eyes of Blanquerna were in tears and his heart was in charity and devotion; and so highly was Blanquerna enraptured[2] in his prayer, that he felt neither hunger nor thirst nor suffering, but his body was in great bliss, taking virtue and strength from his prayer. In such wise did Blanquerna adore God, and journey through the forest, neither eating nor drinking; and whensoever he felt hunger, even then adored he God according as is written above, and God sent him virtue and strength whereby his soul continually had devotion, and his body was strengthened and sustained.[3]

[1] *en fruir Deu.* [2] *tan altament fo rabit.*

[3] This passage constitutes one of the few clear references to supernatural prayer in *Blanquerna.*

CHAPTER LII

OF PENITENCE

BLANQUERNA journeyed through the forest remembering and loving his Creator and his God, singing: *Gloria in Excelsis Deo.* While he journeyed thus, he lighted upon a road along the which he went until the hour of none, when he met a squire coming from another direction, weeping sorely and giving signs in his countenance of great sadness. Blanquerna enquired of him wherefore he was weeping. The squire answered: " Sir! I weep because my master, Narpan by name, whom I served, has withheld from me my wages, and I have left him because I cannot serve him as he desires, for so evil and unruly is he in his customs that no man can suffer his wicked life."

2. " Fair friend!" said Blanquerna: " Where is this Sir Narpan of whom thou speakest?" " Sir!" answered the squire: " He is near to this place, in an abbey. In that house he has made his dwelling, for he went there to do penance; but the penance wherein he lives is like to the penance of the wolf." Blanquerna asked the squire what was the penance of the wolf. " Sir!" said the squire: " It came to pass once on a time that the wolf entered a yard wherein were many sheep which he killed and devoured. On the next morning, when the master of the sheep entered the yard and found that they were dead, he was very wroth against the shepherd, who had not watched the yard that night, and he killed the shepherd; and when he had killed him he bewailed the death of the shepherd and of the sheep. The wolf, who had beheld the shepherd slain, and heard the grief of the farmer, had contrition of heart and said that it beseemed him to do penance for the harm which he had done to the farmer and because he had been the occasion of the death of the shepherd. Now there was a vineyard near by wherein were many bunches of ripe grapes, which

belonged to the farmer whose sheep he had killed; so he went there to do penance by eating the grapes daily according to his desire. And in like manner the master whom for long I have served does his penance; for in the world he has been a sinner, and has killed many men and committed many sins, and he has come to this monastery where he eats and drinks and lies slothfully in bed according to his desire, and dwells in great comfort, so that from his life all the monks of that house have bad example and many of them also have envy of him."

3. "Friend!" said Blanquerna, "Thinkest thou that if I went to the monastery and dwelt for a space with Narpan I could convert him to a righteous life?" The squire answered: "If thou shouldst go to him he would take and do to thee even as was done to the parrot." Blanquerna besought him to tell him the story of the parrot. "Sir!" said the squire, "It came to pass in a certain country that two monkeys placed wood upon a glow-worm, thinking that it was a fire, and they blew upon the wood that the fire might kindle. A parrot was in a tree and he said to the monkeys that that which glowed was not a fire but a glow-worm; but they would not listen to his words. A crow said to the parrot that it was foolish to attempt the correction of those who would not receive teaching. But the parrot came down from the tree and placed himself between the monkeys, to the end that they should hear him, so one of them took the parrot and killed him. Even so wilt thou fare if thou seek to correct one that will not receive correction; and by his secret vices wilt thou too be corrupted against such good habits as thou hast."

4. Blanquerna said: "I put my trust in the counsel which the fox gave to the boar." The squire begged Blanquerna to relate to him that story. Blanquerna said: "A fox was journeying through a forest and he found a boar who was awaiting a lion with whom he had a mind to do battle. The fox enquired of the boar for whom he was

waiting, and the boar related to him that which was in his mind. The fox told the boar, who had only two teeth wherewith to fight the lion, that the lion had many teeth and claws to use against him; and therefore it seemed to him that the lion would have the better of the battle. The lion came and fought with the boar, whom he killed and devoured, because he had superiority of weapons. And in like manner have I superiority of weapons against Narpan, for I shall fight him with the aid of the Divine virtues and of the virtues created, while he will have nought but vices wherewith to fight against me, the which vices have no power against God and His virtues."

5. When the squire had heard this example, he left Blanquerna and went upon his way. Blanquerna considered the peril which might befall the monastery through the evil life of Narpan, who was feigning penitence therein; and charity and hope made him go to the monastery, where he found Narpan, of whom the squire had spoken to him. "Friend!" said Narpan, "Whence comest thou? Wouldst thou be for a year or more in the service of a master?" "Sir!" said Blanquerna, "I come from this forest, and I go in search of a sufficient livelihood, and I would fain serve a master with whom I can better my fortune, and who may have of me some advantage also. Wherefore, since thou hast enquired concerning my estate, I pray thee to tell me also of the estate wherein thou dwellest in this monastery."

6. Narpan answered Blanquerna: "I am in this monastery to do penance for the sins which I have committed in the world, from the which I have fled. My squire has left me, and for this reason I have need of another. Wherefore if thou wouldst live with me I will requite thy work in such wise that thou shalt be well recompensed for it." "Sir!" said Blanquerna, "If thou dost penance, and I serve thee, it follows that I also do penance; wherefore I will abide with thee for the space of a year in this form and

condition, that thou shalt likewise do penance." Narpan and Blanquerna agreed concerning their undertakings, and Blanquerna served Narpan for eight days according to his will, to the end that Narpan might be moved in his mind to love him and give the better credence to his words, and also that he himself might be the better acquainted with his customs.

7. On the eighth day Narpan commanded Blanquerna to kill a goose from among those which he had in the pasture, and prepare it for dinner. Blanquerna entered the place wherein were the geese, together with a great multitude of hens and capons, and he found a fox which had entered therein. Blanquerna killed the fox and skinned it wholly, excepting only the tail, and set it to roast; and when Narpan came to table Blanquerna set the fox upon a dish before him. Greatly did Narpan marvel, and he enquired of Blanquerna wherefore he had brought the fox and not the goose, for the fox was horrible both to eat and to behold. "Sir!" said Blanquerna, "Geese and hens have no enemy as mortal as is the fox; and since thou lovest geese and hens it is fitting that thou shouldst eat their enemy." Greatly was Narpan displeased with Blanquerna, and he said to him many evil things, because he had counselled him that he should eat the fox, and had not made ready the goose. "Sir!" said Blanquerna, "Even as foxes are opposed to geese and hens, even so are geese and hens and capons and dainty dishes opposed to penance; and as I am bound to thee, to serve thee according to the forms of penance, thou wilt be doing penance if thou dost eat the fox rather than the delightful and delicate meats that thou desirest."

8. All that day Narpan spent without eating flesh, and was greatly wroth with Blanquerna. At night, when he desired to enter his bed, Blanquerna had placed the pillow beneath the mattress, and the mattress beneath the straw pallet, and the blankets were beneath the sheets and the

counterpane.[1] Narpan enquired of Blanquerna wherefore he had not made the bed according to his wonted fashion. Blanquerna answered that that bed was made according to the work of penance, and that in no other wise could a bed of penance be made. But Narpan was a slothful man, and desired not that the bed should be made after this fashion. When he waited for Blanquerna to kneel and take off his shoes, according as he was wont, Blanquerna said to him that humility was a friend of all those that did penance. On that night Narpan lay in the bed which Blanquerna had made after his own fashion, and he could not sleep, and he thought for a great space upon the sins which he had committed in the world, and upon the words which Blanquerna had spoken.

9. At midnight, when the monks rose for matins, and Blanquerna heard the bell, he cried out to Narpan that he should rise for prayer, for the hour of prayer had come. Narpan answered him that he was not wont to rise at such an hour, but Blanquerna desired that he should rise at all hazards, so he took the sheets from him, and gave him first of all a scapulary of rough and coarse cloth, which Narpan was wont to wear above his under garment. Narpan obeyed Blanquerna, since he had spent the night with his thoughts, and contrition had begun to enter his mind. He clothed himself in this garment, which was of goatskin, and afterwards Blanquerna give him a skirt, which was of white Narbonne cloth, and then he gave him a tunic which was of a fine linen cloth and clothed him with it above the skirt.

10. When Narpan had risen and clothed himself, Blanquerna went with him to the chapel to be in contemplation and prayer. But Narpan said to Blanquerna that he had great shame that the Abbot and the monks should see him thus clothed. Blanquerna answered that shame and virtue

[1] *i.e.* to give a superficial appearance of comfort to a bed which was uncomfortable in reality.

accorded well with penitence, and that God had blessed those that had patience and humility whensoever they were scorned and reproved for doing works of penitence.

11. Narpan and Blanquerna remained in the chapel till it was day and the monks were ready to enter the chapter. After satisfaction had been made, and discipline was ended, they said Mass, which is said the more worthily when satisfaction has been made in chapter. When the monks entered the chapter and the Lord Abbot enquired of Narpan wherefore he went so strangely clothed and rose so early, Narpan answered that his squire had clothed him thus and had wakened him, and that from thenceforward he desired to be obedient to Blanquerna in all that he counselled him. Blanquerna said to the Abbot that he desired to repeat in chapter certain words of Narpan in the presence of the whole community. So the Abbot and Narpan and Blanquerna entered the chapter, and all the monks marvelled at the garments which Narpan wore.

12. When all were in chapter, Blanquerna rose and spake these words: "Three things agree with penance: contrition of heart, confession with the mouth, and satisfaction for the sins which a man has committed. In contrition it is seemly to weep and repent, and to remember and grieve for the sins which a man has committed, and to trust in the mercy of God, and to fear and love His justice. In confession it is seemly that a man should confess his sins and desire nevermore to return to them. In satisfaction it is seemly that a man return that which he has wrongfully held, that he afflict his body with vigils and prayers, coarse meats, a hard bed, rough garments of humility, and other things like unto these. Wherefore, since these three things aforesaid accord with penitence, and there is a bond and agreement between Narpan and me that I serve him according to penitence, therefore, in presence of all, I demand of Narpan that the relationship which is between us be preserved."

13. When Blanquerna had ended his words, Narpan said, in the presence of all, that he had been for long in a state of blindness, being ignorant of the conditions which accord with penitence, and that God had sent to him Blanquerna who had enlightened the eyes of his soul, and that, from that time forward, for all the days of his life, he desired to serve God and to do penance in every manner which should be pleasing and agreeable to Blanquerna. The Abbot and all the monks praised and blessed God, Who had thus shown forth His virtue in the words of Narpan and Blanquerna.

14. Narpan and Blanquerna went apart from the rest into the chamber of Narpan. Blanquerna was not unmindful of his journey, and he desired to continue his search for a hermitage; and therefore he spake to Narpan concerning that which was in his mind, and prayed him that he would free him from the promise by the which he had bound himself to serve him for the space of a year; and that, since Narpan had recognised his sins, he would return to him his bond and loose him from his covenant. Right displeased was Narpan when he heard that Blanquerna desired to leave him, and with devotion and contrition of heart he answered Blanquerna, weeping, saying these words:

15. "Enlightened am I by Divine inspiration, and moved to devotion by contrition, confession and satisfaction. If my evil customs seek to reclaim me, who will help me? If I remain without a master, who will bring me up to love, serve and honour God, Who is worthy of such great honour and before Whom I have so greatly sinned? I beg of Justice that the agreement that is between us, and the promise which thou hast made me, be kept. If I obey my master, why will my master become an enemy to me in leaving me? I desire to be the companion and servant of Blanquerna, and not his master according to our agreement. With my lord and master Blanquerna I would fain go to his hermitage; but I must needs remain in this monastery

to make satisfaction to the Lord Abbot and all the monks who for so long have served me. I must needs give a good example, that in my amendment of life the monastery may have some profit."

16. So devout and full of reason were the words of Narpan, and with such piety were they uttered, that Blanquerna was moved thereby to devotion and tears, and there came to him thoughts of contrition; and he considered how he might remain all that year with Narpan to keep him in his worthy estate of life, that both of them together might give good example to all the monks of that community. So on that day Blanquerna confirmed to Narpan the promise which he had made to him, and both of them made undertaking to wear hair cloth next to the skin and to remain as companions for the whole year in that monastery, giving glory and praise to God and doing penance. Great was the joy of Narpan and of the Abbot and of all the monks, when Blanquerna repented him of the intention which he had had to depart from them.

CHAPTER LIII

OF PERSEVERANCE

All that year Blanquerna and Narpan continued to live together doing penance; and Blanquerna sang with the monks in the chapel antiphons, proses, hymns and responses, and he expounded to the monks the Scriptures. The Abbot and all the community desired greatly that Blanquerna should become one of them and teach them grammar and theology and the other sciences which he knew, but Blanquerna excused himself from being a monk because he desired to continue in his former will to lead the life of a hermit.

2. Upon a feast day it came to pass that the Abbot desired to preach; but he feared to preach because he knew

not Latin nor was skilled in expounding the Scriptures, and he had shame concerning Blanquerna, knowing that he would take cognisance of all the errors in his speech. Now the Abbot and all the monks were in chapter, and Blanquerna and Narpan entered the chapter to hear the Abbot who was to preach. But before the Abbot could begin, the steward came into the chapter and told the Abbot that a great company of knights and other men had come to honour the festival and that they purposed to dine that day in the monastery. The Abbot commanded that a right worthy feast should be prepared for them, and that to their beasts should be given oats and all things whereof they had need, for such was the custom of that monastery. When the Abbot had said these words, he spake to Blanquerna as follows: "It had been in my mind to preach, but because of my ignorance I find that I myself am not prepared to preach according to the honour of the saint whose festival to-day we celebrate. Therefore I could greatly wish that thou, Blanquerna, wert a monk and might preach to us, and to all those that come to this monastery on days of festival; for if it be our custom to satisfy their bodies with meat by way of alms, we do harm to their souls if we satisfy them not with spiritual meat by sermons and by the word of God."

3. Blanquerna answered the Abbot, saying: "Perseverance is a virtue wherein is demonstrated the perfection of the other virtues, for without perfection of virtues perseverance can be no virtue. And inasmuch as I have bound myself to continue to be a servant of the virtues, therefore it behoves me to serve perseverance wherein the virtues show forth their works. If then I were to leave the purpose for the which I have forsaken my home, and to take another purpose, I should do injury to charity, fortitude and the other virtues; wherefore I pray the Lord Abbot and all the community to hold me excused."

4. "Blanquerna!" said the Abbot, "It came to pass once upon a time that a hermit entered a city. The king of that city was dead, and the custom was that the first stranger to enter therein on the third day after the death of the king should be made king in his stead. By the ordinance of God it came to pass that the hermit entered the city and was made king; but the hermit disputed the election because he desired to continue in his former life. And there was argument between the electors who had chosen him for king as to whether he could continue in the devotion which was his wont. And the electors gave judgment and sentence among themselves, saying that the hermit could more readily be excused in intention and in will from the office of king than he could live apart from people in rustic spots where he led the life of a hermit, and that in the office of kingship he could the better use fortitude, hope, justice and the other virtues, and hence would be the better servant of perseverance. Wherefore in like manner our judgment is that thou shouldst remain and continue with us who are hermits and would fain be thy companions."

5. Blanquerna answered and spake these words: "Ye may remember, sirs, how Saint John Baptist was a hermit, and dwelt alone in the forest, eating locusts and wild honey, and was clothed in the skin of camels; and Jesus Christ said that there was not born of woman a greater man than Saint John Baptist. Because Saint John Baptist remained alone in his hermitage and afflicted himself greatly, therefore God honoured him in His glory according to the word which He spake concerning him."

6. When Blanquerna had said these words, the Prior said to Blanquerna that Jesus Christ, Who is a greater Man than Saint John, went about and remained ever in company with the Apostles, signifying thus that perseverance in company with men when they are together is the nobler virtue, and that perseverance perishes not through the

company of other men, for it is not like to perseverance in a man that dwells alone. And therefore, he said, according to justice and hope, it behoved Blanquerna to obey and fulfil the prayers of the Abbot and of the whole community.

CHAPTER LIV

OF OBEDIENCE

The Cellarer[1] said to Blanquerna that in all the world there was no virtue of greater merit than obedience. Wherefore, since obedience is stronger in a man who is in submission to another, than in a man who lives alone in his hermitage, Blanquerna would be acting contrariwise to obedience if he forsook it in that wherein it has the greater virtue and is the better pleasing to God.

2. Blanquerna answered: "Once on a time it came to pass that a blind man had a son who led him from door to door begging alms for the love of God. The son of this blind man had a dog. The child died, and the blind man took the dog which led him from door to door, according as the child had been wont to do. Now it chanced one day that the blind man left one city to journey towards another. On the road there ran past a hare, and the dog desired to drive away the hare from the road, and the blind man followed the dog. The dog went in pursuit of the hare, and came to a great bank, and desired to go down the bank after the hare, which had gone down the side of the bank. The blind man followed the dog, and fell down the bank, and brake his leg, and spake these words:

3. "'Great is the favour which God gives to man when He grants him bodily sight, whereby the eyes of his under-

[1] The office of the *cellarer* in Lull's country was more comprehensive, as the narrative will show, than his title implies. He was bursar and overseer of the monastery, and frequently took a large share of responsibility for its administration. We learn, however, from p. 223 that this monastery had also a *tresorer*.

standing may obey that which is demonstrated by bodily sight in creatures that can see, to wit, the nobility of the Creator; but greater is the favour which God gives to the will, which obeys the eyes of understanding, comprehending thereby those things which the will is the more bound to obey; for a will obedient to him that has no understanding is like to one in my present state; and if understanding were obedient to will, the intellect would not be so greatly honoured if will were not the more bound to obey it.' "

4. When Blanquerna had said these words, and many more, the Sacristan answered: "Well do we know and understand the similitude according to the which thou speakest, signifying that the will is in peril when it obeys understanding wherein is defect of comprehension. Wherefore, according to thine own words, we would have charity and justice to give judgment." While the Sacristan spake these words, a messenger came to him, to bid him go to a lay brother who was sick unto death, to bear to him the Viaticum. So the Sacristan and all the rest followed the Body of Jesus Christ, and strengthened therewith the sick brother. When the Sacristan said to the sick man that he should believe that Host to be the Body of Jesus Christ, the sick man answered and said that he believed not that Host which he saw beneath the form of bread to be the Flesh of Jesus Christ.

5. Great was the grief of the Abbot and all the rest when they saw that the brother believed not and was in error; and they called Blanquerna and begged him to answer the sick man and to deliver him from his error. So Blanquerna asked the sick man if the human understanding is nobler in virtue than are the eyes of the body. The sick man granted to Blanquerna that there was more nobility in the understanding and intellect than in the eyes of the body and in sight. Blanquerna said to the sick man that since intellect was a nobler thing than bodily sight, it behoved

man to be obedient to intellect rather than to bodily sight that man might render to intellect its due honour; the which intellect understands in the Host the working of a miracle through the Divine power, even as it understands the world to have been created from nothing.

6. "By nature, beneath the form of man, are the four elements, the which are invisible to the eyes of the body, which see naught else save only the form of the man wherein they are compounded; and the first form is in the second as it were secretly. Wherefore since nature is sufficient for that work, how much more are the power, the wisdom and the will of God sufficient to make Flesh to be beneath the form of bread! And were it not thus, God would not have demonstrated His power to be above the power of nature." These words and many more spake Blanquerna to the sick man, who received the Body of Jesus Christ as a faithful Christian, praising, blessing and adoring God, for that He had brought him out of the error in the which he had lived. The sick man died and God received his soul; and the Abbot and the monks returned to the conversation in the which they had been with Blanquerna.

7. "Blanquerna!" said the Abbot, "This thing which has happened is to thee an example,[1] signifying that God desires thee to be His servant and company with us; for, hadst thou not been with us, that soul which to-day has passed from this world had been lost to God, and from his damnation we should have taken cognisance of the ignorance which is in us, forasmuch as we could not have said to this dead man the words which thou hast spoken to him. Many times has it come to pass that God has sent to us like incidents whereby we may perceive His will. Not only hast thou advantaged the soul of this dead man, but to all of us hast thou given instruction wherewith we may fight temptation if we meet it in like manner."

[1] In the sense of *exempli* or exemplary story, commented upon above (p. 189).

8. Blanquerna answered: "There is one manner more wherein he who has temptation concerning the Body of Jesus Christ may be turned from his error, to wit, by faith; for God desires that man should be obedient to faith, mortifying the imagination when it seeks to offer to the understanding false similitude against the operation of the Divine power, and this manner may ye yourselves employ, albeit ye have ignorance through defect of science." The Abbot answered Blanquerna: "A stronger and surer thing is it to combat error with intellect and with faith than with faith alone; and therefore justice accuses thy[1] conscience that it is opposed to thy words, the which excuse thee from companying with us."

CHAPTER LV

OF COUNSEL

Blanquerna considered deeply the words which had been spoken to him and that which had come to pass concerning the temptation of the brother that was dead. While Blanquerna considered on this wise the Abbot and all the monks prayed that he would become one of them. Narpan also, weeping, spake to Blanquerna these words: "Beloved friend Blanquerna! Whereof dost thou think, and wherefore obeyest thou not the prayers of the Lord Abbot and of all this community, and, above all, thine own understanding, which will make thee to have remorse if thou give not to these servants of God intelligence whereby they may have of Him better knowledge. For the higher rises the understanding to have knowledge of God, the more truly is the will prepared to rise to an exceeding great love of God and of His servants. Wherefore, if thou wilt devote thyself to the service of this monastery, I will devote myself to thee, and will be thy companion and servant, and thou wilt bring profit to thyself and to all the rest; but if thou

[1] V: "our."

livest alone in a hermitage, to thyself alone will be the profit."

2. Blanquerna answered him: "Wrong would be done to a contemplative man, who remains in solitude for the love of God, if his prayers profited not others but himself only. Wherefore have I fallen to considering this thing after another manner, to wit, through the remembrance of my mind that diverse wills are like unto sheep and must be subject to the enlightened and exalted understanding which is as their pastor; and this knowledge makes me to think upon devotion,[1] and consider the harm which those disciples of Understanding had because they had no devotion." Thus did Blanquerna speak to the Lord Abbot and to all the community, and he said that in all things a man should take deliberation and counsel, ere he should pass from one purpose to another, and that he himself should take counsel with the seven virtues, who many times had counselled him well. The Abbot and all the monks prayed to God that, in the counsel and agreement that Blanquerna had resolved to take, their rights and their needs might both be had in remembrance.

3. All that day and all that night were the thoughts of Blanquerna fixed upon other things, for man should ever think upon certain other things for a space before he takes with himself counsel; for the understanding begins to return to its power again concerning that which a man proposes to it, and hence the understanding comprehends it the more clearly having come to the matter twice. On the day following, after Mass, Blanquerna betook himself to prayer; and, when his prayer was ended, he gave himself to thought, and had remembrance of each of the virtues one by one, and remained in that thought until the hour of none. After dinner Blanquerna went to the garden for recreation to divert his mind, and after this recreation he slept, that his meat might be the better digested, and that

[1] Lit. *lo capítol de devoció*. The reference is to Chap. XLV above.

that night he might the better keep vigil to consider these matters. At vesper time he desired not to keep vigil, and he slept, that in the morning he might return yet again to his thought, and this the more especially since in the morning hours the imagination has greatest agreement with the understanding.

4. At the hour of matins, Blanquerna rose, and went into the garden to gaze upon the heavens and the stars, that he might have the greater devotion, and he knelt upon the ground and made the sign of the Cross, and lifted up his hands and his eyes to the heavens with affection of will, and prayed to God that it might please Him to remember His servant and to enlighten him concerning those actions which were the most pleasing to Him. And by the will of God it came to pass that Blanquerna resolved to become a monk, because he reflected that he could do greater service to God in the monastery than in the hermitage. And Blanquerna was strengthened in his purpose, and remembered that whensoever he had considered that matter he had conceived this same resolve, and that none of the virtues had opposed themselves to it; and Hope gave him consolation and trust that the time would come in the which he should be a hermit and live the life he so greatly desired; and Prudence demonstrated to him that the life which he would lead in the monastery would by its nature give him increase of holiness in his life as a hermit.

5. When Blanquerna had ended his devotions he went to the chapter-house, wherein he found the Lord Abbot and all the monks who were speaking with Narpan concerning the holy life of Blanquerna. Blanquerna knelt to the Abbot and the monks, and made his submission to the Order, and to all its commandments, without exception soever. Great was the joy of the Abbot and of all the rest; and Blanquerna and Narpan received the habit and the benediction of the Abbot with great honour, and made the vows which pertain to that Order.

CHAPTER LVI

OF THE ORDERING OF STUDIES

The Abbot and all the monks went to the chapter with Blanquerna to make ordinances concerning studies. It was ordained by them all that they should set aside a part of the monastery as a school and place of study, that there might be therein a place convenient for study. When they had ordained a place apart they made ordinance concerning times, for without ordinance of time no study can be profitable. After the ordinance of time they ordained certain persons who should teach, having regard to age and will and natural understanding and good breeding. After all this they made ordinance concerning the sciences, as to which should be those that they should study. Now as they were occupied in making these ordinances concerning the sciences, a man brought into the chapter a letter from two monks who demanded money for their expenses, and to buy books of law. This letter the Abbot read in the presence of all the chapter. The Abbot related to Blanquerna how that they had two monks in Montpellier studying law, that they might be able to assist them in their temporal business. As the Abbot related these things, a squire appeared before him, saying that in a farm belonging to that monastery a lay brother was gravely ill, and begging them to send a physician who should attend to him. The Abbot sent to the city for a physician, who would not go without great recompense, nor would he remain with the sick brother for more than one day. So the brother died, for need of a physician who should visit him continually. And the Abbot and all the rest were remorseful because of his death.

2. According as fortune ordained, a Bishop came to that monastery while the Abbot was in the chapter with all the monks. The Bishop entered the chapter, and the Abbot

and all the monks received him with great honour. The Bishop was a notable clerk, and learned in many sciences, and he made many questions and disputes concerning various sciences; and in that monastery was no man who could reply to the questions which the Bishop made, save Blanquerna alone, who resolved and expounded all the matters concerning which the Bishop made question. All that day was spent by the Abbot and the monks in company with the Bishop. And on the morning following, after Mass, the Abbot and the monks returned to the chapter to make ordinance concerning the sciences which Blanquerna was to teach.

3. "Blanquerna!" said the Abbot. "Which sciences seems it to thee that thou shouldst expound?" "My lord!" answered Blanquerna, "Once on a time it came to pass that a man was mortally wounded. This man had a wound in his face. The physician gave heed first of all to that wound which first of all he saw, but the wounded man had also a mortal wound in the belly, through the which he lost so much blood while the physician tended the wound in his face that from the worser wound he died. On another occasion it came to pass that a fox enquired of an eagle wherefore she had wings and feathers and beak and claws. The eagle answered the fox, and showed her the reasons for the which Nature had given her all these things, which were needful to her. By these similitudes and by many like unto them mayest thou learn which of the sciences is the most needful of all, and which are the sciences that thy monks ought to learn."

4. The Abbot and all the monks begged of Blanquerna that he would expound to them the words which he spake by similitudes. Blanquerna expounded the example of the wounded man by another example, saying, "Once on a time it came to pass that an abbot sent a monk to the schools. This monk when he left the monastery was full of good customs. But when he went to the schools and

companied with worldly men, he learned the customs of these men and forgot his own. When the monk returned to the monastery he was full of vice, and though he expounded science by doctrine, by his works he expounded vice. And by his vices he corrupted all the monks and led them into evil customs; so that they used in an evil manner the science which they learned." After Blanquerna had expounded the first of these examples, he expounded also the second by another example, saying that "once on a time it came to pass that a nightingale was in a tree which had many leaves and flowers. That nightingale enquired of the tree wherefore it had so many flowers and leaves. The tree replied that Nature had ordained that it should bear flowers and leaves that it might afterwards bear fruit. According to these words is it signified that, having regard to the end for the which we are in this place and have left the world, it behoves us to study many sciences, that we may learn the science of theology, which is the end and the complement of all other sciences."

5. When Blanquerna had expounded the examples aforesaid, the monks ordained that in the first place he should teach grammar, for the better understanding of the other sciences; that afterwards he should teach logic, for the learning and understanding of nature; and philosophy, that they might better understand theology; and that when they had learned theology he should expound medicine, and afterwards the science of law. While this ordinance was in the making, a monk made objection that it was a thing impossible for the disciples to learn all these sciences; but Blanquerna answered and said that they might learn a convenient quantity concerning each science; and that, at the end, they might learn in one year the beginnings and the art of the four general sciences which are the most necessary, to wit, theology and natural science and medicine and law, and by these beginnings, set forth according to art, they might use the sciences according to their needs;

for by means of elementary knowledge, ordained and set forth by art, man may make use of the elements of other knowledge.

CHAPTER LVII

OF VAINGLORY

Blanquerna expounded the sciences and the art thereof according to the order aforesaid. In the chamber of the Abbot one day were the Abbot and the Prior and the Cellarer, and they spake of Blanquerna and his disciples. The Cellarer said to the Abbot and the Prior that he feared that the time would come in the which they would be despised by the disciples of Blanquerna, forasmuch as science is an occasion of vainglory and pride, whereby they that have not science are despised. And therefore the Cellarer counselled the Abbot and the Prior that they should abolish these studies, the more so by reason of the great expense to which the studies led.

2. Long did the Abbot and the Prior consider the words of the Cellarer. Now the Abbot was a right devout and holy man; and, albeit he had no great learning, he had much natural sense mingled with devotion. Therefore spake he to the Cellarer these words: "In natural science there is a book which treats of moral virtues, and Blanquerna expounds under the head of theology the three theological virtues. Wherefore these virtues will be reason and doctrine to the disciples whereby they may have humility and justice, and may do honour to us who endeavour to provide and procure for them learning. And therefore I have trust that neither vainglory nor pride will incline their minds, as concerning us, to aught that may be wrong or evil."

3. Many a time had the Prior imagined and considered and desired that after the death of the Abbot he should succeed him; and he considered the matter, and feared that

because he had but little learning, if the Abbot were to die, Blanquerna or one of his disciples would succeed him; and therefore was the Prior daily in great sorrow, and he desired that the studies should be abolished. Now the Abbot was wise and observant, and took heed of the monks and of their estate, and he saw that the Prior was daily in great sorrow. So the Abbot desired to know for what occasion the Prior had conceived such great grief; for sorrow is an evil sign in a monk or a religious man, unless he be sad through remembrance of his sins, or of the evil which is in the world, whereby the honour which is due unto God is not paid to Him.

4. The Abbot commanded the Prior by his obedience that he should tell him his mind. The Prior answered and said that that whereon he thought was a secret matter and it behoved him not to tell it save in confession. The Abbot perceived that the sadness of the Prior had naught in it of virtue, and he remembered that day when the Cellarer spake the words aforementioned. Therefore the Abbot related to the Prior this example: " Once on a time it came to pass in this monastery that the son of a highly honoured burgess desired to dedicate himself to the religious life, and his father, with a great company of his friends, came to this monastery and dragged him from it by force, saying that they would not consent to his becoming a monk because there was in us defect of learning; but they consented that he should enter another order wherein there were right learned men."

5. While the Abbot spake thus with the Prior, and counselled him in many words to take comfort, and to cast aside his sadness, there came to the monastery two religious men who were notable clerks, to see the Lord Abbot, who was with the Prior, and they remained all four together for a great space of time speaking of the things of God; and the two friars put many questions to the Abbot and the Prior concerning Holy Scripture, the which questions they

could not answer. While they spake thus, the Abbot had remembrance of a monk who was of the disciples of Blanquerna, and who every day was very joyful, and gave signs of great happiness. So the Abbot sent a messenger to that monk begging him that he would come and reply to the questions which the two strange friars put. The monk came and resolved the questions, and put to these two friars many more which they could not answer. While they spake thus, the steward called to the two friars to come and dine. Now, after the departure of the friars, the Abbot enquired of the monk wherefore he was every day so joyful. "My lord!" answered the monk, "So great is the pleasure that comes to me from the science which I learn, through the which I find in philosophy occasion to have knowledge of God, and with such happiness do I remember that I am in religion, and have fled from the world, that by night and by day I have delight and joy, the more so since my science makes me so greatly to despise the world and vainglory, and to love humility and God."

6. The monk returned to hear the lesson which Blanquerna was giving, in the which lesson he was expounding by the natural arguments of philosophy how the creatures give knowledge of the Creator and His works. The Abbot remained with the Prior and related to him this example: "Once on a time it came to pass that there was a great discussion between the pine tree and the date palm and the fig tree, wherein each one set forth the greater nobility which Nature had given him above all the rest. The pine tree alleged that the pine fruit and the husk of the pine cone were within him, to the end that the pine cone might be preserved, and therein also the lineage of the species; and that therefore he was the most noble. The date palm alleged on his own behalf the sweetness of the date fruit, and further said that the date stone conserved his kind. The fig tree said that hers was the greatest right, forasmuch as all her fruit gave sweetness, and the whole of it was good,

and therefore was she more deserving than the rest. Now in like manner," said the Abbot to the Prior, "may thy soul find comfort; for we are the outer husk, and the pine cone and the seed are Blanquerna and his disciples; we are, as it were, that outer part of the date fruit which man eats, and the stone is the conservation of learning. And therefore, after our deaths, the time will come when all this monastery will be like to the fruit of the fig tree, and there will be many notable clerks in our Order, both abbots and other officers and likewise disciples."

7. When the Abbot had spoken these words, the Prior took knowledge of his error, and of how pride made him to desire honour and vainglory, and he confessed his sin to the Abbot, and his soul was enlightened concerning the trials which his sadness had for so long made him to suffer. And therefore he spake these words: "Once on a time it came to pass that a wealthy man was sick, and he lamented bitterly concerning death, forasmuch as it would cause him to leave his riches and his wife and his children; and through the sadness of his soul, and the fear which he had of death, he was tormented after a double manner, for the sickness tormented him in one wise and the sorrow of his soul in another." When the Prior by this similitude had revealed to the Abbot the thoughts which were in his heart, he begged of the Lord Abbot pardon and forgiveness and he left the bondage of sadness and returned to the state of joy which was his aforetime.

8. It came to pass in that country that the King held a great court, and asked counsel of his barons, and sent a messenger to the Abbot bidding him come to his court and bring with him the most learned monks that he had. The Abbot and the Prior went to the court, with Blanquerna and other monks; and, above all other counsels which were given to the King, the counsel of Blanquerna was chosen and followed. On that day Blanquerna preached to the King and to all the people and to many religious men

who had been summoned to that court; and his sermon pleased the King and all the rest very greatly. While the Abbot and the Prior were returning to the monastery with Blanquerna, the Abbot and the Prior spake with Blanquerna concerning that which he had said in the council and in his sermon. But Blanquerna spake with them upon other matters, that vainglory might be mortified. The Abbot said to the Prior how that great virtue was in Blanquerna, who was full of good customs, and how that day he had brought honour upon all the monks of that house, and how the King, through the profit and the pleasure[1] which he had of Blanquerna, had elected to be buried in that monastery.

CHAPTER LVIII

OF ACCUSATION

By Eastertide Blanquerna had ended his expositions, and so great was the labour which his studies had caused him that the Abbot and the Cellarer took him to visit the farms of the monastery, to the end that he might have some bodily recreation. The Abbot and the Cellarer prepared salted fish and sauces and other things to take with them. Blanquerna reproved them, saying that to carry such things upon a journey is contrary to hope and poverty, and that therefore it behoved them to go upon their journey with virtues only and to leave behind them such things as are contrary to a life of penitence and in accordance with the active life. Many things did Blanquerna cause the Abbot and the Cellarer to leave behind them which they had desired to take, but the Cellarer disputed greatly with Blanquerna, especially concerning the coverlets and cushions and the cups and jugs which Blanquerna had discarded from their baggage.[2]

[1] P: "and the good knowledge."
[2] P: "trunk." V: "mule."

2. As Blanquerna journeyed along the road with the Abbot and the Cellarer, they met a Bishop who also was taking recreation, and with him went one of his nephews whom he greatly loved, together with a great multitude of his companions who were hunting and carried with them hawks, falcons and sparrow-hawks, together with dogs of divers kinds. The Bishop invited the Abbot and his companions to accompany them, and they went into the city on that day, and dined with the Bishop. At table there were divers meats prepared in many ways: golden cups, jugs and basins of silver were on the table. Great was the company of people who daily dined in the palace. After grace, when they had risen from the table, came jesters[1] with divers instruments, who sang and danced, speaking words of a nature very contrary to those prayers which had been said at table. "My lord!" said Blanquerna to the Bishop. "Here are jesters who hold themselves bound to do thee pleasure, because thou hast given them to eat. I too have dined with thee, and if it please thee I would fain be as one of thy jesters and speak to thee certain words." It pleased the Bishop and all the company that Blanquerna should speak to them and say his words.

3. So Blanquerna rose and reproved the Bishop straitly for the superfluity of meats and the garments and the numerous trains of those that were present, and the ornaments of the table, and above all things he reproved the Bishop because he gave ear to jesters who were enemies of the honour of Jesus Christ, through Whom the Bishop himself was so greatly honoured and Who had created so many creatures to give him pleasure. Blanquerna bore on his person a crucifix, which he showed to the Bishop and to all the company, saying these words: "Jesus Christ has died, and dead is devotion. In the honour of Jesus Christ are created prelacies and canonries and prebendaryships:

[1] The word is *juglars* (see p. 175 above); this passage throws further light on their accomplishments.

but who is he that does to Jesus Christ due honour?" Blanquerna wept, and great was the shame of the Bishop and of all the rest, and the Abbot and the Cellarer were greatly displeased with Blanquerna for that he reproved the Bishop so straitly.

4. The Abbot and his companions came to a monastery, wherein they stayed; and there they found a worthy preacher who ruled and governed the monastery; and all the people of that district honoured and loved the monastery because of that friar. Right well were the Abbot and Blanquerna and the Cellarer welcomed on that night. The Cellarer spake that same night with the friar who preached so well, and counselled him to leave that Order and to come to their monastery and join their Order. When the Abbot and Blanquerna had left the monastery, the Cellarer related how he had endeavoured to persuade that friar to come and take their habit. Blanquerna reproved the Cellarer straitly, saying these words: "Envy, lack of charity, pride, avarice and wrong are in our company. These brothers with whom we have lodged in the night that is past have received us with right good cheer and with courtesy, and we have seduced and enticed from them an honoured brother who is of their number. For this sin it behoves that accusation be made in chapter, to the end that it be punished."

5. At vesper time they came to a monastery that was greatly honoured, and lodged there. While the Abbot and Blanquerna spake with the friars, who showed them the monastery, the Cellarer spake with a friar of that monastery, saying that the chapel and the dormitory and the chapter-house and the other parts of his own monastery were greater and fairer than the chapel and the rest of the buildings of that house. When they had striven concerning the buildings and the offices they discussed also the two Orders, and each of them praised his own Order and spake ill of the other. And Blanquerna kept the words of the Cellarer

in his memory, that he might make accusation concerning them in chapter.

6. As they went along the road, the Abbot and Blanquerna and the Cellarer passed by a goodly spot, wherein was abundant water, with fields and vineyards and trees and pastures. That place was the property of a rich burgess. The Cellarer said to the Abbot that whensoever he passed by that place he coveted it for their abbey, for it would make them a right noble farm. The Abbot enquired of the Cellarer if the Treasurer had money sufficient to buy it. The Cellarer answered that the money which the Treasurer had was needed to pay the debts which they owed by reason of a castle which they had bought; but that when these debts were paid they ought to collect sufficient money to buy this place, and abstain greatly in their meat that they might the sooner buy it; and that they had made like abstinence when they had bought the castle. Blanquerna kept these words in his heart[1] and said that envy, avarice and wrong had not yet gone from their company, wherefore he spake these words: "Alas! How great is the error of this world, for the religious is not kept from sin by his habit but by justice and charity. To eat beans, to drink stale and sour wine, to wear long garments and double cowls, to use stirrups of wood, to rise for matins, how is it that these things aid not justice and charity that they may company with us?" Blanquerna begged of the Abbot that they should return to the monastery, for his soul was in great travail, and he desired greatly to have recreation according as was agreed between them, and to have the company of his brethren, and solace in speaking with them words of God.

7. When the Abbot and Blanquerna and the Cellarer had returned to the monastery, and were in chapter, Blanquerna accused the Abbot and the Cellarer of the great display which they had made when they left the monastery;

[1] P: "mind."

and he said that a man who belongs to a religious order should delight in want and in the lack of certain things upon a journey; for such want is an occasion to him of hope, patience, penitence, poverty and humility, and is a good example to countrymen and to other persons whom he may meet upon his journey.

8. The Abbot and the Cellarer accused Blanquerna for that he had so straitly reproved the Bishop who had invited them to dine; but Blanquerna excused himself, saying these words: "Love, truth, justice and virtue moved me to reproach the Bishop, and this cannot do me harm, in the life either of the body or of the spirit. If I had shame of my reproof of him, where would be the virtues aforesaid? If I had shame and fear to speak, I should delight in keeping silence concerning the dishonour and wrong which has been done to my Lord and Creator and Saviour. To love and to die remembering Christ and His works, these things accord one with the other and are opposed to eating and living in forgetfulness of the honour and the gratitude which it behoves us to render to God."

9. Blanquerna excused himself well, for the right was his; and afterwards he accused the Cellarer who wished to entice the good preacher from the friars who had given them so honourable a welcome. Many reasons, both strong and true, did Blanquerna allege to prove that wrong, falseness, villainy and covetousness are in those who would persuade friars to leave one house for another; for it is against the law of community that a friar shall take another from an Order, and according to the vice of ownership may this fault be accused and punished.

10. That a man should praise his Order is permitted, and contrary to irregularity of orders; but to praise one Order above another is to speak ill concerning an Order and is contrary to the law of community and to the charity, justice, fraternity and unity of God. To have envy of towns, castles and farms is to sin through avarice and the vice

of ownership. To contract debt and to take loans in order to have riches and many farms,[1] is to make companionship and alliance between the religious and the worldly man, and signifies the servitude of the religious to the worldly man, and is a sin against the poverty of the monastery and the alms which are given therein to the poor. That a monastery should contract debt because it has lack of food, which has failed because of pestilence or want of rain or other natural cause, is a thing that may be permitted. Blanquerna said that he accused the Cellarer of all these things aforesaid, and he desired that in his presence there should be given to him the discipline.

11. So the Cellarer was condemned to suffer discipline: a monk brought many rods which were bound together, and prepared to give discipline to the Cellarer; but Blanquerna unbound the rods, and said that the use of many rods in giving discipline signifies vainglory, and causes harm to the person to whom it is given, and gives a feeling of suffering less severe than that which was given by one rod alone. Wherefore the Cellarer was beaten with one rod only, whereby he had greater suffering than he would have received from all the other rods. And the rule was made that discipline should ever be given with one rod only, upon the naked flesh.

12. Greatly was the Cellarer confounded, and great shame had he, and he excused himself concerning certain things, saying these words: "The argument whereby I am accused of envy and covetousness is contrary to justice and charity which move me to desire that the monastery should possess many towns and castles and farms, to the end that in this monastery there may be gathered many monks, and great alms may be made herein." Blanquerna answered: "Jesus Christ might have had in this world the companionship of many princes had He wished; but in token of humility and poverty He was pleased to elect the com-

[1] The reference is, of course, to the monastic, and not to the individual life.

panionship of few men, to destroy pride and vainglory. Wherefore is it a better thing to desire the holiness of a few men, than to gather together a multitude of men in whom is error and sin. Saint Sophia did greater alms in building the church in Constantinople than did the Emperor; for more pleasing to God was the mite which she gave day by day to the work, than were all the remaining gifts which were given by the Emperor, and by the which that church was built and completed; and as thou hast excused thyself against justice, repentance and contrition, it behoves that thou shouldst again make satisfaction through discipline." So the Cellarer was beaten again, because according to justice his excuse was of none avail.

CHAPTER LIX

OF THE MANNER WHEREIN BLANQUERNA WAS MADE SACRISTAN

For so long did Blanquerna continue to give instruction to his disciples that many grew they in number and marvellously did they learn of him, becoming noble preachers and masters. Throughout all those parts there went out fame concerning the greatness of the doctrine which Blanquerna taught, and many other monasteries sent monks to him to learn that doctrine which he taught, and many disciples did the Abbot send to divers monasteries to become teachers therein, and many men from those parts endowed in that monastery chaplaincies in perpetuity for the repose of their souls. Great was the increase of well-being in the monastery by reason of the science that Blanquerna taught.

2. Now while Blanquerna was a teacher there it befel that the Sacristan passed from this world to the next. Blanquerna desired to be daily in contemplation, which thing he could not be by reason of the hindrance caused by his studies, to the which he devoted himself very earnestly.

The Abbot and all the monks desired that Blanquerna should become Sacristan, and that another monk, who had become a master in the science which Blanquerna had taught him, should teach the disciples in place of Blanquerna. But a short space before this time, Blanquerna had been ordained priest; with great fear did he receive that office, whereof he thought himself not worthy, and humbly and in secret did he sing his first Mass, without show of vanity soever. Blanquerna was elected therefore to be Sacristan. He kept the chapel in great cleanliness and did all that pertained to his office, and sang Mass daily, and the greater part of each day he spent in prayer. At vesper-tide he lay down to sleep before the altar of our Lady Saint Mary. The tears and the prayers of Blanquerna, who may recount them? And the heights which he reached in his contemplation, who can tell them? And the art which he had as touching the exaltation of his soul to God, who may know it?

3. It came to pass one evening, after Compline, that Blanquerna was at prayer, and wept through the abundance of his devotion, and reflected that, even while the priest sings Mass, there are angels who do reverence and honour to the Holy Sacrifice of Jesus Christ their Lord. Very deeply did Blanquerna reflect after this manner. Now while Blanquerna reflected thus, he fell asleep, and in his dreams there came to him that which he had considered while he was yet awake. For by the influence of the strength of his imagination which he exercised while he was awake concerning the ministry aforementioned, it seemed to him as he slept that he was singing Mass and that Saint Michael and Saint Gabriel served it. Two or three times did Blanquerna wake from his sleep that night, and each time did that same dream return to him. At midnight Blanquerna rose to ring the bell, and he said Matins with the monks. After this, he fell to prayer, remembering that which he had dreamed on that same night. While he yet thought

thereon, he vested once more to sing Mass. And when he was before the altar, it seemed to him that at either end thereof was an angel with wings, and that each angel held in the one hand a Cross and in the other a Book. Great wonder had Blanquerna at that vision, and he believed that it was with him even as it seemed; but he desired not to proceed with the singing of the Mass until he had resolved his doubts. So Blanquerna fell once more to remembering the virtues whereby at every hour his needs were met: justice brought to his mind his unworthiness to behold the angels; prudence gave him intelligence as to how, through the influence of his thoughts, and the weakness of his brain, which had been enfeebled by abstinence, vigil, fast and great watching, phantasy had represented to him certain vanities under the guise of truth. Fortitude strengthened his mind against the imagination, which at times is of unruly imagining, whereby the bodily sight conceives certain vain similitudes which are contrary to truth. By all these virtues was Blanquerna aided, and he resolved the doubts which had come to him, and afterwards he sang Mass right devoutly as was his wont.

4. It came to pass one night that Blanquerna was in the chapel alone, and he thought upon the demons and upon the horrible shapes which they take when they desire to fill man with terror. While Blanquerna considered thus, he felt fear and terror enter his mind, and he had affright at being alone in the chapel, and had a mind to sleep that night in the dormitory; but he remembered that this was a temptation against fortitude, and against prudence, and that it was sent to him that fortitude and prudence might be exalted, the which exaltation they received when Blanquerna remembered the perfect power of God which could defend him as well in the chapel where he was alone, as in the dormitory among his companions. Wherefore Blanquerna was fortified against the temptation and the fear which had come to him, and he fell to prayer, and remem-

bered the great power of God, Who willed that he should be tempted after the manner aforesaid, that he might know that the power of God is as great in one place as in another.

5. In many a wise was Blanquerna tempted by day and by night, and as soon as he was tempted, he called to his remembrance the seven virtues, and according to that virtue which was the best fitted to mortify the temptation, he adored God in those virtues uncreated which presented themselves to him through the remembrance which he had of the seven virtues created[1]; and the more Blanquerna was tempted, and did battle with the temptation, the greater exaltation had his merits, and he praised and blessed God Who gave him the occasion whereby his merits should be the greater, that the justice of God might grant to him great glory. Even so lived Blanquerna and served God, all the days of his life. Great was the virtue that God for His part showed to Blanquerna, and Blanquerna was as a shining light and a good example, whereby all the monks and all the people of that country were of holy life. And, through the holy conversation of Blanquerna, God granted His blessing to all the people and all the parts of that region, with wealth, peace and abundance of fruits both spiritual and temporal. So all blessed and praised God, Who had given to one man such great virtue, that through him many men had received many virtues by the grace of God.

CHAPTER LX

OF THE MANNER WHEREIN BLANQUERNA WAS ELECTED ABBOT

The Lord Abbot grew old, and in his own person he could no longer satisfy the needs of the monastery. So the Abbot with all the community went to the chapter, and he begged

[1] A fuller idea of the meaning of this passage may be formed from the *Art of Contemplation*, below.

of them indulgence, saying these words: " For a long time great honour has been done to me, my brethren, by you who have held me as your superior. Such great honour I have ever been unworthy to receive. And now I have come to a time when I have no more strength in my person, by the which lack of strength I am more unworthy than before to be your pastor. I have come to the end of my days and I would fain be in submission to some one of you, that I may grow more obedient. I beg you to elect another Abbot and upon me to have compassion."

2. Counsel was taken by Blanquerna and all the chapter, and it was agreed that indulgence should be given to the Lord Abbot, in significance of charity and justice which willed that reward should be made to him for all the labour wherein for so long he had continued, that his flock might be served and kept. Charity willed that a fitting place should be given to the Lord Abbot in some farm-house where he might remain and live, and that a monk should serve him, and that some pittance might be given to his body whereby he should the longer live. The Abbot gave thanks to all the chapter for the indulgence which they had shown him, and he rendered up his seal and renounced the office of Abbot; and the monks made ordinance that another should be elected in his stead.

3. According to the manner of election whereby Natana had been elected Abbess it was determined that an abbot should be chosen. Now, when the electors enquired of Blanquerna who should succeed the Abbot, according to his opinion, Blanquerna answered in these words: " Our common brotherhood signifies charity among us. Wherefore, in significance that charity is with us a common virtue, and to give good example, it would be a thing most fitting that we should elect as pastor some bishop of these parts, who is holier of life than are other bishops." The electors answered and said that it was not the custom of their Order to elect as Abbot a man who was not of their Order, and

over and above this they thought that no bishop would forsake his diocese and pass to their Order to become an abbot, since a bishop has a wider rule than has an abbot.

4. Blanquerna said to the electors that it came oftentimes to pass that an abbot was elected to a bishopric; and that therefore it was in reason that a bishop might be elected an abbot, since the duties of an abbot accord better with the contemplative life than do those of a bishop, and the work of a bishop accords better with the active life than does that of an abbot. Wherefore since the contemplative life is better and nearer to God than the active life, if from the contemplative life abbots passed to the active, how much the more should bishops leave the active life to enter the life of contemplation! "Wherefore," said he, "to the end that we may introduce the custom that a bishop may be elected as an abbot, and that the contemplative life may be exalted and loved above the active, it is good, according to my mind and will, that we elect for our abbot a bishop."

5. One of the seven electors was the Cellarer, and he said to Blanquerna that if they elected as abbot a bishop or any other person who was not of their Order or monastery, it would seem that there was a lack in their monastery of fitting persons, and of persons worthy to be elected abbot; wherefore it behoved them not to elect a bishop as abbot, over and above the which he thought not that a bishop could be found who would leave his diocese to become an abbot. Blanquerna answered: "Pride and vainglory, lack of hope and the vice of ownership, are signified by the words of the Cellarer, which are contrary to justice, charity and hope; and since prudence wills that the fittest person be elected, charity gives one common aim even to the diversity of Orders, and justice condemns ownership where there should be common charity and fraternity, and hope moves us to remember that if our Lord and Pastor Jesus Christ

suffered death to save men that are bishops, it follows that we shall find some bishop who to honour Christ will leave his diocese to be an abbot."

6. The Cellarer ceased from the argument which he had made against Blanquerna, and he began to argue after another manner, saying these words: "It is seemly that an abbot be accustomed to eat of our meat, and to follow the rules and habits of our community, to the end that he may be a light and an example to us, whereby we may continue in our habits; but another man who is not of our Order is less fitted to be our abbot than is a man that is of our Order, and who for long years has followed in orderly wise the rule of our Order." "Cellarer!" said Blanquerna, "Still does thy will follow the path and track of despair; for God, Who has accustomed thee to thine Order, can so accustom and govern another religious that is of another Order, if he enter our own." While Blanquerna and the Cellarer disputed after this manner, the Bishop whom Blanquerna had reproved, as is recounted above, came to the monastery, and the words of Blanquerna and the Cellarer had an end, and the whole community went out to receive the Bishop, to do honour to him and his companions.

7. The Bishop desired to do honour to the monk who had renounced the office of abbot, even according to the honour which is due to an abbot; but that monk recounted to the Bishop the indulgence which had been granted to him by the chapter, and how he had renounced his office, and how a very delectable place without the monastery had been assigned to him, wherein he might live, and how in that place he would have a pittance for his body, which would be greater than that which he could have in the monastery. Then the Bishop and that monk went away to that place to live therein together. The Bishop sent away all his companions, and kept with him one squire only. And for a great space the Bishop lived in penance

with that monk, and they spake daily together of God and of His glory and despised the vanity of this world.

8. The Cellarer and the other electors returned to their former conversation, and made discussion, according to method and to their needs, which person of all the monks in that house was the most meet to be Abbot. To all the electors it was manifest that Blanquerna should be Abbot according to all the conditions which belong to that office, with the exception of one condition only, to wit, that Blanquerna was a greater lover of the contemplative life than of the active; and that the office of Abbot accords with the active life, to the end that he may the better provide for the needs of the monastery. So there was dispute among the electors if because of the condition aforesaid Blanquerna should be rejected from the office of Abbot. But one of the electors said to the rest: "Even as Blanquerna our master has shown us how with the virtues we may supply our needs, even so does it behove us in this case to have recourse to hope and justice, and to put our trust in the holy life of Blanquerna, the which through justice may satisfy us in the contemplative life, even as much as, or more than if Blanquerna had more of the active life than of the contemplative; and therefore let us not fear to make Blanquerna our Abbot and our Pastor, even as he has been our teacher."

9. So Blanquerna was elected Abbot. Greatly was he displeased at the election, and many reasons did he allege wherewith he excused himself from being Abbot. None of which reasons would the monks receive, but at all hazards they desired with common voice that he should be their Abbot. During all the time that he filled this office he continued in it as was his duty, according to the which he was bound to treat of temporal matters and to keep them in his remembrance, albeit they hindered him from the consideration of heavenly things. Oftentimes did Blanquerna weep for the servitude to the which he was come, and

desired liberty to contemplate God, and to think upon the Passion of his Redeemer. Wherefore he spake these words:

10. "O ye virtues, my friends, that were wont to aid me, and delivered and kept me from the servitude into the which my father Evast and my mother Aloma desired to place me! Whither are ye gone, and wherefore have ye not aided me against the servitude into the which I am come?" While Blanquerna spake these words, in his consideration thereof he found Fortitude and Prudence, who spake to him mentally after this manner:

11. "Strong is the mind that has no pride in the honour of the office of abbot and the dominion which it brings over many men. Obedient is an abbot through fortitude of mind, when he follows that which his understanding reveals to him, making inspections of the monastery and from time to time entering the infirmary." While Fortitude spake thus, Prudence answered him, and said that an abbot has a part in the merits of the monks, for he has perforce to order his will that he may be the servant and the subject of them all. "Great am I," said Prudence, "in the government of one person, but greater yet in the government of many persons; wherefore have justice and merit greater accord with me than they were wont to have."

12. Blanquerna was fain to rejoice because of those things which Prudence showed him concerning the increase of her glory; but Charity made him to remember that he was no longer able to contemplate the things of God as he was wont; and because he loved God more than merit and glory, therefore did Charity and Yearning make him to weep greatly. In this manner Blanquerna continued, and long did he rule as Abbot; and by reason of his desire for comfort and for contemplation he went from time to time to the farm-house, wherein were the Bishop and the monk who was aforetime Abbot, and with them he had recreation, and comforted his soul in the contemplation of our Lord God.

OF THE BOOK OF *AVE MARIA*

CHAPTER LXI

OF THE MANNER WHEREIN THE ABBOT BLANQUERNA MADE THE BOOK OF *AVE MARIA*

BLANQUERNA was Abbot in an abbey that was of great honour, which contained a great number of monks and which enjoyed great wealth. Daily did Blanquerna consider how after some new manner he might honour Our Lady. On a certain day Blanquerna was considering the honour of Our Lady, and through Divine virtue it came to his will that he should build in the monastery a chamber set apart from the rest, wherein should ever be a monk who should daily within that chamber give greeting to Our Lady, and eat and sleep therein, and follow not the rule of the monastery, but be free in all those things wherein he might the better give greeting to Our Lady and have contemplation concerning her. The Abbot Blanquerna caused this room to be built, and gave to it this name: Ave Maria. Then went the Abbot into the chapter with all the monks and spake to them these words: "All the greatest honour that a creature may receive from the Creator was done within the womb of Our Lady when the Son of God took human nature within her; and therefore it behoves our Order, which has Our Lady for its Head, to honour her with all its might. Which, therefore, of you desires to greet Our Lady and to live in that chamber which bears the name of Ave Maria?" Many were the monks who desired to be in that chamber and hold that office; but the Abbot said that the monk who should have it must be a great clerk, and learned in divers sciences, to the end that by their aid he might be able to raise his understanding to contemplate and greet Our Lady, and he must further be devout, and a man of holy life. Wherefore there was elected from among them all the monk who had in greatest measure the conditions afore-mentioned.

2. That monk dwelt in the chamber of Ave Maria, in the which he kept his books, making it likewise his cell, and placing therein an image of Our Lady. A lay brother brought to him daily his pittance from the monastery. That monk sang Mass in the chapel, and went through all the monastery, and spake with whomsoever he desired, and had many privileges besides. It came to pass one day that the Abbot entered the chamber of the monk, and desired to know the manner wherein the monk greeted Our Lady Saint Mary. So the monk knelt down before the image of Our Lady, and spake these words, and many more, as was his custom:

3. "'Hail Mary!' Thy servant greets thee on behalf of the angels and the patriarchs and the prophets and the martyrs and the confessors and the virgins, both men and maidens; and he greets thee likewise through all the saints that are in glory. Hail Mary! He brings thee greetings from all Christians, both righteous and sinners: the righteous greet thee, for that thou art worthy of greeting and art the hope of their salvation; the sinners greet thee, because they ask of thee pardon, and have hope that thy merciful eyes may look upon thy Son, to the end that He may have pity and mercy upon their sins, being mindful of the grievous Passion which He bore to give to them salvation and to pardon their guilt and sin."

4. "'Hail Mary!' I bring thee greetings from the Saracens, Jews, Greeks, Mongols, Tartars, Bulgarians, Hungarians from Lesser Hungary, Cumanians, Nestorians, Guinovins and Russians: all these, and many unbelievers else, greet thee through me who am their representative. I bring to thee their greetings, to the end that thy Son may desire to have remembrance of them, and that thou mayest beg Him to send to them ministers who may lead them to know and to love thee and thy Son, in such manner that they may be saved, and in this world may know and

desire thee and thy Son, to serve and to honour Him and thee with all their power."

5. "'Hail Mary!' These unbelievers, on whose behalf I greet thee, have ignorance concerning thy salutation,[1] and the honour which God has given thee. They are men. Like form and like nature have they to the form and nature of thy Son, Whom thou so greatly lovest, and by Whom thou art so greatly honoured and loved. They go through ignorance to the eternal fire; they lose the eternal glory of thy Son; for there is none to preach to them nor to show them the truth of the Holy Catholic Faith. They have mouths wherewith they could praise thee if they but knew thee; hearts have they wherewith they might love thee; hands have they wherewith to serve thee; feet have they wherewith to walk in thy paths. Thou art worthy to be known and served and loved and praised in all lands and by all men. They greet thee, and they beg of thee, through me, thy help and grace and blessing."

6. "'Hail Mary!' It behoves me to weep and to do penance, and to endure a life of austerity, and to praise and love and know and serve thee, that my greetings may be to thee the more acceptable." The monk wept bitterly as he greeted Our Lady thus. Blanquerna wept for the great devotion of the monk and the devoutness of the greetings which he made to Our Lady. The sweetness and the virtue which the Abbot and the monk had as they wept and greeted Our Lady, who can recount it?

7. "Beloved son!" said the Abbot, "Greet thou Our Lady, who is our health and blessing. By her aid are those men saved who without it had been damned. In our mother Eve was our damnation, and in Our Lady is our salvation. Mary is light and splendour, illumined and illumining alike. Hail to her, for she is a being without evil and without defect. Let us, then, greet her and love her. We have a Lady through whom we shall gain all the

[1] *i.e.* the angelic greeting.

virtues and conquer the vices. Remember, oh son! how many are they that greet Our Lady, and how blessed are they that are loved and remembered by her, who has such noble remembrance and such merciful will. Behold the Heavens, how great they are, and how wondrously illumined by the sun, the moon and the stars! The sea, the earth, men, birds, beasts, fishes, plants, herbs and all things living and all things that are,—all these are in the service of Our Lady and all these are of her Son Who has created them. Greet her and weep, for with such greeting Our Lady is well pleased. Greet her with remembrance, for she ceases not to love, remember and help all that greet her with understanding highly exalted and with effectual[1] will. Son! Call thou upon all the powers of thy soul, and see if thou dost use them all to greet Our Lady."

8. While the Abbot urged and inspired with all his might the monk that dwelt in the chamber of Ave Maria, that monk spake to the Abbot in these words: "Conquered is my power, and exalted is the honour of Our Lady. No more can I love, honour and consider those things that are above; I must needs behold my faults, which are below. If it might so be, I should desire the more to weep and love and have remembrance, in greeting the Queen of Heaven and of all the earth and the sea. Each time that I greet Our Lady she brings me consolation and joy. Her greeting is my companionship and my consolation and my comfort."

9. The Abbot marvelled greatly and had great pleasure at the words of the monk of Ave Maria, because he was able so worthily to greet and contemplate Our Lady, and many times in the week did he come to greet Our Lady with the monk, to do her honour, and that each might the better assist the other to weep, and that the soul of each, in the other's contemplation of Our Lady, might be the

[1] *efectuosa*. This is probably an erroneous reading for *afectuosa*, "affectionate," "affective."

more highly exalted. A man of such good life was this monk of Ave Maria that there were many monks in that house who, because of his example, served Our Lady with greater regularity; and as often as they had temptation, or distress of any kind, they came to this monk, to the end that by his words they might be comforted and instructed in the service of Our Lady.

CHAPTER LXII

GRATIA PLENA

On a certain occasion it came to pass that through want of rain there was a great dearth of corn in that country. Very great alms were made by the Abbot to all the poor who came to the monastery. For a long time they continued in that monastery to give alms, and through the report thereof which went through all the land, and because in that monastery they gave alms of bread and of vegetables to all that came there, the number of the poor who came to beg alms of them increased greatly. It came to pass one day that the Cellarer entered the granaries that were in the monastery, and went to all the farms, and found that the alms which the Abbot gave could not be continued for a long time thence, for they would not have corn enough to give until the new crops were harvested. Greatly was the Cellarer troubled, and he said to the Abbot that the alms must cease, because in the farms and in the granaries he had found so little corn that within a short time there would be a famine in the monastery.

2. Greatly was the Abbot troubled at that which the Cellarer had said to him, and he went to the farms and to the granaries, to learn if in truth there was so small a quantity of corn as the Cellarer had said. As the Abbot and the Cellarer returned to the monastery, the Abbot passed by a farm which was held by a lay brother who

above all things loved and honoured Our Lady Saint Mary. In all that farm there was no more than one granary full of corn. Greatly was the Abbot troubled at the lack of corn, and greatly did he sorrow at the thought that the alms must cease, and by reason of this sorrow his soul was in sadness and his eyes were in tears. The brother that held the farm enquired of the Abbot wherefore he wept. "Fair son!" said the Abbot, "I must needs weep at the deaths of the poor, for these poor folk will die if the accustomed alms which are given to them from the monastery cease, and cease they must by reason of the dearth of corn." "Lord Abbot!" said the farmer, "Continue ye to give alms in honour of Our Lady, for I will provide you with sufficient corn for all this year; doubt not this, but take ye as your surety Our Lady, who is full of grace." The Abbot answered: "Thy surety is seemly and sufficient, so much so that we should sin if we were to refuse it, and the alms were to cease."

3. The Abbot returned right joyfully to the monastery, and commanded that alms should still be given daily according to custom. For so long and to so many persons did he give alms that all the corn in the granaries and from all the farms was spent, excepting only the corn in the granary which was in the farm whose holder had taken Our Lady for surety. So the Abbot sent a message to the farmer that he should provide him with corn according to his promise. The farmer opened the granary and sent to the monastery one-half of the corn which was therein. Again at another time he opened it, and found that it was half full even as he had left it, so he sent all the corn to the Abbot. When the farmer had closed his granary, and the beasts who bore the corn had left the farm, the farmer said his Ave Marias according to his wont. When he came to the words "full of grace" he marvelled, because he had left the granary empty of corn, and Saint Mary had not filled it, albeit he had given her as surety to the Abbot.

4. While the farmer thought thus, he doubted whether Saint Mary was full of grace, for it was clear to him that, if she were so, the granary would at all times be filled with corn. Yet once again the Abbot sent to the farmer for corn, for that which he had last sent him was all spent. So the farmer put his trust in Our Lady, and yet once again he unlocked the granary and found it full of corn; and the farmer remembered how that Our Lady was full of grace. All that year did he find the granary full whensoever he went to it, and the contents thereof sufficed for the needs of the community and for all the alms which were given by them, until the new harvest. The Abbot and the monks praised and blessed Our Lady, who had been pleased to have remembrance of their needs.

5. It came to pass upon a feast day that the farmer went to the monastery to keep the feast. The Abbot enquired of him by what means he had found sufficient corn for their needs during the whole of the year. The farmer said to the Abbot that among the other words which are in the Ave Maria he had great devotion concerning the words "full of grace"; and therefore he put his trust in Our Lady, that she would keep the granary full of corn for so long as there was a dearth in the land. Long did the Abbot think upon the words which this brother had spoken concerning Our Lady, and upon the devotion which he had to the words "full of grace"; and therefore in a certain part of the monastery he caused a room to be made to the which he gave the name Gratia Plena (Full of Grace), and in that room he desired that this brother should remain all the days of his life, adoring and contemplating Our Lady who is full of grace.

6. Right holy and devout was the brother of Gratia Plena; and, according to his power, he adored Our Lady daily, considering the grace whereof she was so full; and by reason of the great age and of the holy life of that brother the monks came to him, and remained with him hour after

hour, listening to the devout words which edified them and moved them to devotion and charity, by the which they were comforted and made glad. All that monastery was enlightened by this brother and by the brother of Ave Maria, and many a time did the monk of Ave Maria and the brother of Gratia Plena visit each other, and the monk spake of the words "Ave Maria," and the brother of the words "Gratia Plena." The pleasure and the brotherly companionship of them both, who may recount it? And the good example which they gave to all the monks and friars, who can tell it?

7. The Abbot Blanquerna desired to weep and to contemplate Our Lady; for the many temporal affairs wherewith he had perforce to occupy himself in the monastery had greatly inclined his thought toward the things of earth; wherefore the Abbot went alone one day to visit the brother of Gratia Plena, and desired to know the manner wherein he contemplated Our Lady. When the Abbot entered the chamber wherein was that brother, he found him kneeling before the image of Our Lady, weeping and saying these words:

8. "Full art thou, O Mary, of the Plenitude which is thy Son, Who is the fulness and plenitude of all that is. In thee, who art all fulness, is the fulness of the remembrance and understanding and will of my soul. The whole world cannot attain to that fulness which thou containest. And knowest thou why? Because through thy Son thou mayest have more fulness than the whole world, since the whole world is not so good as art thou. Thou art full of grace, that we may recover the grace which we have lost. In thee is there fulness of our faith, hope, charity, justice, prudence, fortitude, temperance. We have fulness because of the fulness that is thine. And he that remembers and loves thee is full of grace likewise; and he that is remembered and loved by thee has no defect."

9. "'Full of grace!' Filled with grace wert thou in respect of God and of man, when the angel Gabriel gave thee greeting. That One, God and Man, Whose mother thou art, is full of eternal and infinite goodness, and of infinite and eternal power, knowledge and will. Wherefore if thine abundance is eternal and infinite in goodness, greatness, power, wisdom and will, thy plenitude may not be voided nor lessened nor multiplied. Wherefore, as thou that art full of grace art that same Mary that has such fulness, my soul is filled with charity, whereby it may fully know and love thee, and mine eyes are filled with weeping and tears, that they may do honour to thy honours, and weep for my sins and my transgressions."

10. According to these words, and to many besides, was this brother adoring and contemplating Our Lady as the Abbot came to visit him. Great was the wonder of the Abbot that a lay man could utter words of such subtlety and devotion; but he bethought himself that through the fulness of Our Lady his words were full of the infused science and of devotion. "Fair son and brother!" said the Abbot, "God save thee, Who has filled thee thus with the fulness of the grace of Our Lady." That brother answered the Abbot: "Lord Abbot! If thou knowest aught wherein I may greatly love and honour Our Lady, I pray thee tell it me; for she is full of great grace and virtue, and therefore do I need fulness of understanding wherewith I may fully know her, that by the fulness of my knowledge my will may have such fulness that I may greatly love and praise her that is full of grace."

11. When the Abbot saw the plenteousness of grace, devotion and charity which was in the soul of that brother, and remembered that in his own soul there was less devotion than in that of this brother, he spake these words: "Ah! wherefore did I become Abbot and not a hermit, that I might have such fulness of devotion as has this brother?" The Abbot Blanquerna kneeled before the

brother of Gratia Plena, and prayed him that he would instruct and teach him, that he might have once more the devotion which he had had of old, the which he had lost by reason of the temporal cares of his office. This brother wept, and Blanquerna wept likewise, and each regarded the other with looks of love, yet neither could speak to the other, for that their love was too great; but each by signs made significance to the other concerning the image of Our Lady, and the Passion of her Son, and the sorrow which she bore while they tormented her Son and slew Him, making Him to hang upon the Cross whereon He suffered that all might see Him and mock Him.

12. Long did they weep, and were together for much time ere they could speak once more. And the Abbot remained kneeling, until the brother spake to him these words: "Full of grace was Our Lady when her Son departed this life. And that grace signifies the grace wherewith the sons of God are filled in this world when they suffer trials and death in honour of the Son of Our Lady Who is in glory, wherein is the fulness of grace of Our Lady." In this world lack we wholly fulness of grace. So the Abbot Blanquerna bewailed the sins of those that allow not fulness of grace to be in the world. And as Blanquerna wept he spake these words:

13. "Weeping, knowledge and love! Can ye have such power that to the remembrance of Our Lady who is full of grace ye may bring the lack of grace which is ours in this present life? Can it please her by your means to incline herself to pray her Son that He may be pleased to fill us with such grace that He may cause us to go and preach His honour to the unbelievers? And that Holy Church may recover that sacred land which the Saracens hold to our dishonour, by the which dishonour is signified ignorance, together with defect of charity and of remembrance of the Precious Blood which was shed for us? Is there naught which may aid you in this matter?"

" Brother! " said the Abbot, " Help thou me to weep and to pray, and let us weep more fervently and at greater length until the Queen whom thou lovest so greatly be pleased to help us, and give us in this world so much of her grace, that all things may be ordered to the honour of her Son." So for a long time the Abbot and this brother wept together; and, after their weeping was ended, they took leave courteously the one of the other, and the Abbot felt within his soul that the devotion which he had had of old had returned to him; wherefore the Abbot purposed to return ever and again to weep and to contemplate Our Lady in the chamber of Gratia Plena.

CHAPTER LXIII

DOMINUS TECUM

It came to pass one day that, as the Abbot Blanquerna held chapter, there came a farmer[1] to the chapter, saying that a certain peasant[2] had come to dig in one of the vineyards of his farm. This peasant farmer had said that the vineyard was his, and he threatened the brother grievously, and desired to turn him out of the vineyard. The Abbot asked counsel of the monks concerning that man of whom the farmer spake. Then an old monk spake to the Lord Abbot in these words: " For a long time there has been dispute between us and this man concerning the vineyard, and much harm has the monastery had thereof, for this man has spoken much evil concerning us in all the land; wherefore it is fitting that we go to the farm and turn him out of the vineyard, or that we commend the matter to the care of some knight who on our behalf will defend the vineyard from him."

[1] *granger*, the holder or owner of a *granja* (farm).

[2] *pagès*, labourer, peasant, rustic. Occasionally, as at certain places in this book, it can bear the meaning of " small farmer," but it is quite distinct from *granger*.

2. Deeply did the Abbot think upon the words which the monk spake, and in presence of all he said as follows: " A thing ill-beseeming is it that for the sake of possessions a religious should place himself in peril of death or kill another, and yet it is contrary to justice that a religious should permit himself to be deprived of that which by right is his; wherefore, according to charity and hope, it behoves that in this case a man have recourse to God and to the virtues, combating vices with virtues; for with such arms should every man do battle first of all, and especially a religious." When the Abbot had spoken these words, he rode forth, and took with him the Cellarer, and went to that place where the peasant was digging in the vineyard. The Abbot greeted the peasant, saying: " Dominus tecum " (The Lord be with thee). The peasant returned not the greeting of the Abbot, but continued to dig in the vineyard, and kept his arms beside him that he might be able to defend himself. Every time that the peasant struck with his spade the Abbot said: " Dominus tecum," but the peasant gave no sign that he had heard or seen the Abbot, but continued to dig in the vineyard.

3. The Abbot marvelled greatly that the peasant answered him not, and especially did he marvel because the virtue of the greeting was of no avail; so he perceived that it behoved him to dismount, and to kneel before the peasant, and greet him with devotion and humility, to the end that from this greeting might come virtue. The Abbot dismounted and kneeled before the peasant, raising his eyes and his thoughts and his hands, and spake these words:

4. " O Queen of Heaven and of earth! Within thee was God made man and yet was God; and in glory is the Lord within thee as God and as thy Son. In this world our Order is thine and is under thy protection. Now through this virtue whereby the Lord was in thee, I pray thee to mediate between this man and us, that through thee we may receive

virtue, whereby we may be servants of the virtue which was thine because the Lord was within thee."

5. The Cellarer reproved the Abbot sternly, saying that the whole monastery was disgraced by the honour which he did to the peasant; but the Abbot answered the Cellarer, saying that Christian humility was shown by the Son of God, Who desired to be wholly within the Virgin Saint Mary, as Man and as God, and to be tormented and despitefully used, and put to death upon the Cross; and the weapons of a monk, he said, are humility, charity, patience and prayer. With such devotion and humility did the Abbot continue to pray and repeat the words "Dominus tecum," and such great virtue did God set in the words which the Abbot spake, and in his devotion, that the peasant took knowledge of the injury which he did to the abbey, and through this knowledge there came to him contrition, charity and justice. Wherefore the peasant spake these words:

6. "Lord Abbot! What is it that has turned my mind to contrition, charity and justice? And who has driven avarice, wrath and injury from my mind?" The Abbot answered: "Through the will of God it came to pass that the angel Gabriel greeted Our Lady Saint Mary, and among other words said to Our Lady: 'Dominus tecum: the Lord is with thee.' And by the virtue of these words hope has given me confidence that the same words may give thee virtue whereby the Lord of heaven and earth and of all that is may be in thee and with thee, that the virtues may be in thy mind, and that through the virtues the vices may be displeasing to thee."

7. When the Abbot had spoken thus, the peasant said that these words "The Lord is with thee" had vanquished and overcome him, and that therefore he desired ever to be the servant of these words; so he prayed the Abbot to give him viands from the monastery wherewith he could live the life of a hermit upon a high hill near the abbey. The Abbot granted to the peasant that which he asked of

him, and made for him a cell in that high mountain whereon he desired to live, that he might contemplate the Lord and Our Lady in the words "The Lord is with thee." The Abbot gave to that place the name Dominus Tecum. He desired also to build a chapel in that hermitage, but the peasant desired it not, lest it should become an occasion of pilgrimages and vigils, and many persons should go there and impede his prayers and mortify his devotion.

8. When the peasant had taken up his abode in the hermitage of Dominus Tecum, the Abbot gave him a rule and manner wherein by means of these words "The Lord is with thee" he might contemplate God and Our Lady according to the form of these words following: "The Lord of the angels, and of all that is, performed in the person of Our Lady the greatest work which any creature may receive, namely when God was pleased to take within Our Lady human nature. In no creature can God perform a nobler work than this. God is Lord over Nature in Our Lady, and in all things wherein Nature has received its nature; but He exalted Nature in Our Lady more than in any other creature, wherefore the Lord was more truly within her and with her when the Angel spake to her these words, 'The Lord is with thee,' than with any other creature; and therefore we should all do reverence and honour to these words." After this wise and in many a manner beside did the Abbot give rule and doctrine to the hermit as to how he should contemplate God and Our Lady in these words "The Lord is with thee."

9. Long time abode the hermit in that place in penance and austerity of life, and in contemplation of God and of Our Lady. And abundance of deep devotion exalted his understanding, through the infused science,[1] that he might the better comprehend these things, than they are compre-

[1] The "infused" science is, of course, mystical theology, and is here contrasted with the "acquired" science, *i.e.* of theology in the usual sense of that word.

hended by the understanding of many monks who possess the acquired science, the which, through lack of devotion, may not be capable of such knowledge of the Divine Essence and of its operation. So great was the devotion of the hermit that many monks came to him to revive their devotion and knowledge, by reason of the holy life which he led, and by the devout and lofty matter of his speech concerning the words " The Lord is with thee."

CHAPTER LXIV

BENEDICTA TU IN MULIERIBUS

It was the custom of the Abbot Blanquerna to go often to visit the monk who had been Abbot before him, and likewise the Bishop who dwelt in that farm wherein was also the monk aforesaid. It happened one day that the Abbot was passing through a great forest, as he went to the farm wherein dwelt the monk and the Bishop. Upon the way was a fair fountain, beneath a lofty tree, in the shade whereof lay an armed knight who was going to seek adventure for the love of his lady. This knight had taken his helmet from his head by reason of the great heat. His horse was cropping the cool grass near the fountain; and the knight was singing a new song in the which he spake ill of troubadours who had spoken ill of love, and who had not praised above all ladies that lady whom the knight loved as his own.

2. The Abbot Blanquerna heard the song and comprehended the words thereof, and came to the place where the knight was singing. The Abbot dismounted, and took his seat near to the knight, and spake to him these words: " It is the nature of love that it causes that thing to be loved which is pleasing and agreeable to man. It appears to me, according to the significance of thy song, that thou art enamoured of some lady. Her dost thou praise above all

ladies else. I pray thee tell me, if there were another lady nobler and fairer and more beautiful than thine, wouldst thou love her more than that lady whom now thou lovest?" The knight left his singing, and answered the Abbot, saying these words:

3. "If fortune willed that there were any lady nobler and fairer than is she to whom love has bound me, then love would work wrong if it made me not to love her above all ladies else; for a lover who loves not the highest has defect of love, and love works defect against that lady who is the fairest if it gives her not a better and more fervent love than has any lady else of her worth and of her wealth." When the knight had spoken these words, the Abbot put to him these questions:

4. "Sir Knight! I pray thee tell me wherefore thou bearest arms." The knight answered: "To the end that I may defend my body against them that would harm me." The Abbot enquired of the knight if he had arms wherewith he could defend his lady against that lady who was loved by himself. The knight answered: "May love and beauty and valour assist me to prove that my lady is fairer and worthy of higher praise than any lady else." "Sir Knight!" said the Abbot, "After a nobler wise can my Lady be praised than can thine, and even so should she be praised, for her love and beauty and valour have greater favour; wherefore my Lady is worthier of praise than thine, and I am nobler in the love and service and praise of my Lady than art thou in that of thine."

5. Greatly was the knight displeased at the words of the Abbot, and he said that if the Abbot were also a knight he would slay him or take him captive because of the words that he spake, and that by force of arms he would compel him to own that his lady was fairer and worthier than any other. "Sir Knight!" said the Abbot. "Knowledge and reason are spiritual arms wherewith man conquers evil-doing and error. Wherefore if thou desirest to fight with

me using these arms, that we may see which lady is the fairer and more beautiful and worthy of the greater honour, thy reasons make me not to fear. Rather do I feel courage and strength within me whereby I may compel thee to own that my Lady is fairer than thine."

6. So between the Abbot and the knight there was a great dispute as to which of their ladies was the fairer. Both were of accord that each should praise his lady, that it might be seen of which of them could the greater praise be spoken. The Abbot desired that the knight should first praise that lady whom he loved. So the knight praised his lady, saying these words: "So fair and gentle is my lady that love has made me to overcome and vanquish many knights, and to honour my lady have I many times run into mortal danger; for her have I borne grievous hunger and thirst, heat and cold, and many trials have I suffered in my body to do her service. Wherefore, as all these things are greater and of greater worth than those wherewith thou servest thy lady, therefore, Sir Monk," said the knight, "is it signified that if thy lady were fairer and worthier than mine thou wouldst do, and wouldst have done, greater things, and have borne greater trials, in the love and service of thy lady, than those things which I have done and suffered in praise of mine." Many other words, the which words it would take long to relate, spake the knight to the Abbot in praise of his lady.

7. "Sir Knight!" said the Abbot. "Many things could I relate to thee truthfully in praise of my Lady; but one thing alone suffices for my Lady's praise, and this will prove that she is fairer and more beautiful than thine. Therefore against the things which thou hast said will I not speak, but will say alone in her praise: 'Blessed art thou among women.'" The knight desired that the Abbot should expound to him that article of praise aforesaid, so the Abbot expounded to him this thing which the angel Gabriel spake to Our Lady, in the words following:

8. " It was the will of the Son of God, and He was pleased to choose Our Lady Saint Mary above all other women, and to give her greater grace than that which is in any woman else; for God took of the Virgin Saint Mary human flesh when He became incarnate within her, and she, being a virgin, conceived by the grace of the Holy Spirit in her womb God and man. This Lady is Mother both of God and man. The God of Whom she is the Mother is greater than all the creatures; and the Son of Man of Whom she is Mother is greater than all the creatures likewise, because He is one Person with the Son of God Who of all creatures is Creator. This is she that is my Lady, and she is the Head of our Order; and this one article of praise suffices to vanquish any other praise soever which can be uttered concerning any woman."

9. Long did the knight reflect upon the praise which the Abbot had spoken concerning Our Lady Saint Mary; and through the light of grace and the merits of the Abbot, the knight reflected upon the vain and foolish love which he had borne to his lady, and how that through this love he was in mortal sin, and in peril of damnation, and how his lady had no power wherewith to defend him from the fire of hell, nor could give him as a reward the glory of heaven, nor could even lengthen his life. As the knight reflected thus, he sighed and wept and spake these words:

10. " How late, O love, art thou in filling this guilty sinner with love for that Lady who is the fairest![1] If I, O love, had known thee and loved thee, then had I been the servant and subject all the days of my life of that fairest Lady, whose servant is this monk that has done her honour in making her known to me as worthier than all women else. If in thee, O love, there were pity, or pardon, or gifts,[2] or patience, or charity or humility, couldst thou make me to be a servant of this fairest of women? Or

[1] Lit. " *la dona mellor.*"

[2] *ni perdó ni do:* a play upon words which occurs frequently in the book.

would death stay till I had done many things for love of her?" These words and many more did the knight utter with such great contrition and devotion that the Abbot was moved thereby to devotion and to tears.

11. "Sir Monk[1]!" said the knight, "Tell me if it be possible that the Lady whom thou lovest would suffer me to love her, and to strive for love of her with all my might, all the days of my life, in battles and combats, wherein I should ever be opposed to such as do her dishonour and deny her worth." The Abbot answered the knight, "The greater is the worth of the fairest of women, the more does she delight in a sinful man who suffers for her sake and becomes her servant and her lover; wherefore she is worthy to have honour above all ladies else." Great joy had the knight of this, and many tears did he shed, saying these words:

12. "No lettered man am I, nor am I versed in divers tongues, whereby through my words I may sing the praises of Our Lady to unbelievers; but with arms will I go and do honour to that Lady whom God has honoured above all women else. A new way will I make whereby Our Lady may be honoured. And this is that way, that I will go and do battle in the land of the Saracens against some knight who is no servant of Our Lady; and when I have overcome him, another will I overcome also." When the knight had spoken these words he took leave of the Abbot, and the Abbot gave him his blessing, and set for a name to that new rule which the knight had taken: "Benedicta tu in mulieribus."

13. Through the will of God it came to pass that this knight who had taken the service of "Benedicta tu" came to the country of a Saracen king. When he arrived there, he went, all armed, upon his steed, to the palace of the king, saying that he desired to speak with him. The king

[1] *Sènyer en monge!* The *en* is roughly the Catalan equivalent of "Mr". The mode of address is therefore quite deferential.

was pleased to give the knight admittance, and caused him to be brought before him. When the knight came before the king, he spake to him in these words: "The servant and the lover am I of a Lady who is worthier than all women else, and who through the grace of the Holy Spirit is Mother of God and Man. And with any man in thy Court who denies this honour to Our Lady will I here do battle, to the end that I may compel him to give due honour to Our Lady the Virgin Saint Mary, in whose service I am newly admitted knight."

14. The Saracen king said to the knight that he believed not that Our Lady was the Mother of God, but that he believed indeed that she was a holy woman and a virgin and the mother of a man that was a prophet; and that therefore he desired not that the knight should do battle, but rather that he should set before him arguments, since he denied to Our Lady that honour which the knight attributed to her. The knight answered the king and said that the greatest honour which Our Lady has is that of being the Mother of God; and that he would do battle with every man who forbade that such honour should be paid to Our Lady. But since he was unlettered and knew not the Scriptures, therefore he desired not to answer the king by argument, but rather would he do battle by force of arms with all the knights of his court, one after the other.

15. Great wrath had the king against this knight who challenged all his court, and he commanded that he should be delivered up to a cruel death. But a Saracen knight said to the king that if this knight were put to death, excepting in battle, it would appear that there was defect of chivalry in his court; and he prayed the king to allow him to do battle with the knight. It pleased the king and all his court that battle should be done between these two knights. When they were on the field of battle, the Christian knight had remembrance of his Lady and said: "Blessed art thou among women." And he made before his face the sign of

the Cross, and set spurs to his horse, and wounded the Saracen knight; and by force of arms overcame and slew him.

16. The king was moved with great wrath, and even so were all the rest. The king commanded that knight after knight should do battle with this Christian until they had vanquished him. So another knight entered the field, and all the day long they fought, yet neither of them vanquished the other. All that night the two combatants rested, and the king was arbiter in the battle, that it might not be said that by force of will the Christian knight was wronged therein. When the morrow came, both knights returned to the battle-field, and when the Christian knight was about to strike the Saracen with his sword the Saracen declared himself vanquished, and acknowledged that Our Lady was worthy to be lauded and praised according as the Christian praised her. In the presence of all he spake these words, and said that he would fain be of the rule and order of "Benedicta tu," and that he was prepared to do battle with any other Saracen knight who denied to Our Lady her due honour. Great was the wrath of the king, and he commanded that both knights should be taken and put to death. So they became martyrs for Our Lady, who honoured them with the glory of her Son, because for her sake they had suffered martyrdom. Even so is she ready to honour all those who in like manner will do her honour.

CHAPTER LXV

BENEDICTUS FRUCTUS VENTRIS TUI

When the Abbot had reached the farm wherein lived as contemplatives the Bishop and the monk, the Abbot related his adventure with the knight whom he had found by the fountain singing of love, and he recounted the words which this knight had spoken and the rule to the which he had bound him. Long did the Bishop think upon the history which the Abbot had related concerning the knight, and he had remembrance of those words in the Ave Maria which follow the words "Blessed art thou among women"; and when the Bishop had thought for a great space thereon he spake to the Abbot after this manner:

2. "I bless the Divine light of pity and grace which has enlightened that sinful man and bound him all the days of his life to be a servant of that blessed Fruit which was in the womb of Our Lady. Him do I adore, and bind myself to praise, with all the physical powers of my body, and with all the powers of my soul." Courteously and with great devotion the Bishop took leave of the Abbot and of the monk whose companion he had been in honouring Our Lady, and returned to his diocese. The canons and all the chapter and all the men of the city had wondrous joy that their Bishop had returned to them, for they had thought to have lost him.

3. Day by day the Bishop considered how he might find some manner wherein to honour the Fruit that Our Lady bare in her womb through the grace of the Holy Spirit. It came to pass one day that the Bishop held synod, and preached to all the clergy, asking of them counsel as to how he might greatly honour the Blessed Fruit of Our Lady. It chanced that there was in that synod a clerk who came from an isle beyond the sea, the which is called Majorca; and he said to the Bishop, in the presence of all, that that isle belonged to a noble and learned king, the which king of Majorca is called En Jacme.[1] That king is a man of noble customs, and has much devotion as to the manner wherein Jesus Christ may be honoured by preaching among the unbelievers; and to this end he has ordained that thirteen friars minor shall study Arabic in a monastery called Miramar,[2] established and set apart in

[1] *i.e.* James (for the prefix, see p. 253, above).
[2] See Introduction, pp. 17, 20, and p. 325, below.

a fitting place, and he himself has provided for their needs; and when they have learned the Arabic tongue they will be able to go, by leave of their General, to honour the Fruit of Our Lady, and in His honour suffer hunger and thirst, heat and cold, fears and tortures and death. And this establishment, he said, has been made in perpetuity.

4. Greatly did it please the Bishop and all the rest to hear of this establishment, and greatly did they praise the devotion of the king and all the friars who for the love of God desired to suffer martyrdom. After a few days the Bishop ordained and built in a fitting place, far from any town, a monastery right fair; and by the will of the Pope, and of the chapter of that diocese, the monastery was endowed, that within it thirteen persons might live and study, and learn divers sciences and divers tongues, that Holy Church might acquit its debt of honour to the Blessed Fruit of Our Lady. And to that monastery the Bishop gave the name Benedictus Fructus; and he resigned his bishopric, and, together with some canons and monks and laymen, established himself in that monastery to honour the Fruit of Our Lady, according to the rule and manner of the monastery of Miramar, the which is in the Island of Majorca.

CHAPTER LXVI

SANCTA MARIA, ORA PRO NOBIS

The monk that had aforetime been Abbot had a great yearning for the Bishop, who had of late been in his company. That monk had remembrance of these words in the Ave Maria: "Holy Mary, pray for us," and he desired to preach these words all the days of his life in honour of Our Lady. The monk considered how many are the preachers who preach the word of God in towns and churches, but that to the shepherds who wander through the woods and mountains no preachers are sent. Wherefore the monk spake to the Abbot Blanquerna these words:

2. "According to my knowledge there is a sore lack of preachers to those people that live and dwell[1] in the mountains and in the forests, and come not to church; therefore would I have a rule and office, whereby all the days of my life I may preach to these shepherds and speak to them of the words 'Holy Mary, pray for us'; for the shepherds have opportunity for thought and reflection, because they are all alone, and there is none to hinder them from thinking upon that which a man might say to them concerning the honour of Our Lady; and the greater is their thought, the more may devotion and love of Our Lady be increased in them."

3. The Abbot was right pleased at the devotion of the monk, and at the manner of life which he desired to lead from thenceforward in honour of Our Lady; and he returned to the monastery to see how he might make establishment, with the consent of the chapter, that ever thereafter it should be a custom that one man of that monastery should be a preacher to the shepherds, and that his office should bear the name "Ora pro nobis." That establishment gave pleasure to all the community; and the monk who had of old been Abbot took that office, and begged the Abbot for a rule and instruction whereby he should preach to the shepherds concerning the words: "Holy Mary, pray for us." So the Abbot gave this rule and instruction for the which the monk begged, in these words which follow:

4. "It is a thing most natural," said the Abbot, "that between the understanding and the will there should be strait agreement, since the understanding comprehends that which the will loves, and the will loves that which the understanding comprehends; wherefore that sermon is profitable wherein are shown forth such arguments as may be proved by the nature of understanding. Furthermore,

[1] *son e están.*

since shepherds are folk more likely to be led to understanding by means of argument than by authority, therefore they will the more readily love the honours of Our Lady if they have understanding thereof through reasons necessary and probable, than they would do if they had to believe them by authority."

5. "When the understanding has comprehended one of the arguments which a preacher has expounded, the understanding commits it to the memory, and understands in turn the remaining arguments of the preacher; and when the sermon is long, and the arguments therein are over-subtle, the memory cannot render to the understanding all that which the understanding has commended to it; whereof proceed ignorance and want of devotion in those that hear sermons. Wherefore, as this is so, it is a seemly ordinance that all such sermons as are made be brief."

6. "It is the nature of will to love that which is most pleasing to it. Wherefore, the better is the content of an argument, the more needful is it to pronounce it at the end, that the will may have desire for it, and through desire may come devotion to the words, and devotion may be turned into action; wherefore it is fitting that in a sermon the best word be kept till the end." Many things spake the Abbot which it is needful for a preacher to know, especially concerning good works and devout words.

7. When the Abbot had made exposition to the monk of Ora pro nobis, according to the manner aforesaid and in many another wise, concerning the method of his preaching, the Abbot made contemplation of Our Lady in presence of the monk, to the end that the monk might have rule and doctrine concerning the preaching of "Ora pro nobis." The Abbot therefore spake these words:

8. "Holy Mary! I adore and bless thy glorious Son, to Whom thou dost pray for us sinners. If thou hast greater desire to pray for us sinners than have we ourselves, it befits

us not to beg thee to pray for us; but, because we should not be worthy to be heard in thy prayers if we prayed not to thee and trusted not in thy prayers, therefore are we bound to pray to thee and to contemplate thee and thy honours, that we may do honour and reverence to thee, and that thou mayest have mind of us with pious remembrance, and look upon us with thine eyes of mercy, in these dark days wherein we live, having defect of devotion and charity; through the which defect we forget the Passion of thy Son, making not remembrance thereof as we ought, nor doing all that we might and ought to do in honour of thee and of thy Son; yet cease thou not to pray for us with all thy power. Wherefore, as this is so, do thou, O Queen of all kings and of all queens, lend us thine aid that we may honour thee in honouring thy Son in those places wherein He is despised, unloved, disbelieved and mocked by those men to whom He looks to do Him honour and defend Him as touching the faults which are attributed to Him by such as are in error and journey towards the eternal fires."

9. "O Queen! So soon as thou wert filled with the Holy Ghost and with the Son of God Whom thou didst conceive, thou wert bound to pray for us sinners; for the greater are thine honours, the more does it behove all men, both righteous and sinful, to trust in thee; and the more earnestly do we trust in thee, the more does justice make thee to have care for the healing of our diseases and the pardoning of our sins."

10. "Look down, O Queen, among us, and see how many men praise and adore thee, singing to thee, making remembrance of thee, and doing thee reverence. Where is thy justice, thy pity, thy charity and thy nobility if thou pray not for us? And if for us thou prayedst to thy glorious Son, and thy Son heard not thy prayers, where would be the love that He was wont to have toward thee, becoming incarnate within thee, and making remembrance of thee and

commending thee to Saint John when He hung upon the Cross and was near to death?"

11. "Beloved son!" said the Abbot to the monk, "According to the manner whereof thou hast heard, do thou go to preach among the shepherds, dwelling with them, and causing them to make contemplation of Our Lady; and return thou to us for certain festivals in every year. Have thou grace and blessing of God and of Our Lady. To honour Our Lady hast thou humbled thyself; and thou shalt indeed be exalted if thou makest her to be remembered and invoked and loved, for her prayers will make thee rise even to the glory which is without end." Then the monk took leave of the Abbot and of his companions, and went from them to those places wherein dwelt the shepherds.

12. The monk of Ora pro nobis went over mountains and plains and through forests, preaching to the shepherds concerning the honours of Our Lady, who prays both for righteous men and for sinners. It came to pass one day that the monk came to a great valley wherein were many herds of beasts. In that valley there was a cave, wherein a shepherd secretly held a woman whom he had carried off from her husband and with whom he dwelt in sin. The monk came by chance to that cave, in the which the shepherd and the woman were eating. Courteously did they welcome him and invited him to dine with them. "Sir!" said the shepherd, "Our meat is bread and water, and a little cheese and a few onions; may it please thee to eat with us of that which God has given us." The monk ate with the shepherd and drank of the water, as was his wont when he dined with the shepherds to whom he preached.

13. While they ate, the shepherd had to go to drive his sheep from a field of corn which they had entered, and the monk was left with the woman, of whom he enquired concerning her history; and the woman related to him

how that she was the wife of another shepherd, and was living with this shepherd in sin, and had repented her of the fault which she had committed against her husband; but for fear of her husband she dared not return to him, and the shepherd with whom she lived desired not to leave her, for the great love that he bore her. The shepherd returned, and they continued to eat together; and, when they had eaten, the monk made the sign of the Cross and blessed their table, and spake these words:

14. "Once on a time it came to pass that a shepherd lived in sin with a woman upon a high mountain. That woman prayed daily to Our Lady Saint Mary that she would deliver her from her sin. One night the shepherd slept; and he thought that he saw Our Lady Saint Mary, who wrote down the names of all those for whom she prayed to her Son, and wrote in her book the name of the woman with whom the shepherd lived. So the shepherd entreated Saint Mary that his name also might be written in that book. Saint Mary answered, and said that since he prayed not to her daily, he was not worthy that his name should be written therein."

15. "Sir!" said the shepherd to the monk: "Knowest thou if Our Lady would pray for me if I begged her daily so to do?" The monk answered and said that he would be surety to him that Our Lady would pray for him, provided only that he did no dishonour to her Son, to Whom all they that are in sin do dishonour, and all they that leave their sin do honour. As the monk spake these words, the shepherd had knowledge of the sin wherein he lived, and he spake to the monk as follows:

16. "I am in the sin of lust, and I would fain leave it, that I may honour the Son of Our Lady and that Our Lady may pray for me; but were I to leave this woman she would have no counsellor, neither dares she to return to her husband, wherefore I am compelled to live in sin." The

monk enquired of the woman if she trusted so much in the prayers of Our Lady that she would go with him to her husband. The woman answered, and said that she would indeed return to her husband, and accuse herself of her faults, that he might take vengeance upon her, and that she would trust in Our Lady to help her in the penitence which her husband would make her to suffer by reason of his vengeance.

17. So the monk and the woman journeyed to the house of the husband of that woman; and the shepherd, who remained in the valley, did penance continually, and gave adoration and praise to Our Lady daily. While the monk and the woman journeyed, they found, asleep, in the shade of a tree, the shepherd who was the husband of that woman, and who was going to seek his wife, with arms wherewith to slay the shepherd who had carried off his wife from him. So the monk and the woman kneeled before the sleeping shepherd, and the monk spake these words:

18. "Holy Mary, pray for us! Holy Mary! Fulfilled is thy prayer in this woman who is a sinner, and repents her of her sin; hadst thou not prayed for her, she would not have repented thereof. It behoves thee to bring it to pass that this shepherd may receive grace of thy Son, whereby he may pardon his wife. It behoves thee to reward the hope which we have placed in thee that thou wilt help us." When the monk had said these words, the woman, weeping and with great contrition of heart, spake as follows: "Guilty am I, and greatly have I sinned against my lord and master, who may use toward me justice or pardon. To all that he may do I am resigned. If it came to pass that my husband would pardon me, then should I desire to lead the life of a hermit, dwelling for ever alone, and doing penance for the sin which I have committed against him. If my husband strikes me or tortures me or throws me into captivity, he will act according to justice, and with patience will I bear my punishment. Thanks

will I give to the Queen of Heaven, and bless her Son, Whose will it is that in this world I suffer for my sins whereof indeed I am guilty." While the woman spake thus, she repeated often these words: "Holy Mary, pray for us," for she saw that these words would aid her in her necessities.

19. While the monk and the woman were on their knees before the sleeping shepherd, the shepherd dreamed that he was being tortured because he had killed a man, and that as his soul was about to leave his body, a demon very horrible to behold desired to take it; but Our Lady kept his soul within his body that the demon might not take it, and she prayed her Son to be pleased to pardon him for the death of the man whom he had wrongly killed. When the shepherd had dreamed thus, he heard, as it were in his dream, the words which his wife and the monk were repeating. At these words the shepherd awoke, and saw his wife, with the monk, who were kneeling before him, and adoring and invoking Our Lady with tears, as they spake the words aforesaid.

20. The shepherd marvelled greatly when he beheld his wife with the monk; and by the virtue of the words which they spake, and of the dream which he had dreamed, he was moved to forgiveness and to tears, and together with them he made prayer and praise to Our Lady. For a long time were they together weeping and in prayer; and, after they had prayed, the shepherd spake these words: "If lust moves the body to sin, how much the more ought remembrance of the Passion of Christ, and of the nobility of Our Lady, to move the will to pity and forgiveness! And he that repents and judges himself should not be punished twice. If I forgive not, I do wrong in asking for forgiveness. Not only do I pardon, but I would forfeit all that I have to give to any man that asked of me pardon. If Our Lady on my behalf asks pardon, it is right that I likewise should show pardon."

21. The woman kneeled before her husband, and kissed his hands and his feet, and her husband pardoned her, and commanded her to return to his house wherein she should remain in that peace which for so long she had enjoyed. "My lord!" said the woman. "Unworthy am I to be in company with thee; not only does it behove thee to pardon me, but likewise to bestow on me a gift, whereby I may be alone and in poverty live the life of a hermit, eating raw herbs and doing penance for the wrongs and the sins which I have committed against thee." So ordinance was made between these three, that the good woman should do penance in a cave, which was in a high mountain near to a spring, and that from time to time her husband should bring to her some pittance wherewith she might sustain her body, and that henceforth they should never know one another in carnal delight but should live each one in chastity. Very great was the devotion and the holy life of each, and whensoever the husband went to visit the woman, very great were the blessings which each bestowed upon the other, and the instruction which each of them gave to the other, that they might do honour therewith to God and to Our Lady.

22. In a meadow, near to a fair spring, there was a great company of shepherds who kept their flocks. The monk of Ora pro nobis came to that meadow, and greeted the shepherds, and said that he was a preacher to shepherds, and begged them that they would hear a sermon which he desired to preach to them. So the monk preached to the shepherds with examples,[1] that he might move them the more to devotion. So many pleasing sermons did the monk preach to the shepherds, that they thought daily upon that which he spake to them; and, thinking thereon, they grew to love and to honour God and to pray to Our Lady. For seven days did the monk remain with them in that place. On the eighth day he took leave of them, and went to

[1] See note, p. 189, above.

preach to other shepherds who dwelt in those regions. The good things and the praises whereby God was honoured by those shepherds to whom the monk preached, who may tell them? And the wondrous fame which the monk won in every land, who can relate it? And the shepherds who came to hear him, who can count them?

ENDED IS THE BOOK OF RELIGION

BEGINNETH THE THIRD BOOK WHICH IS OF PRELACY

CHAPTER LXVII

OF THE MANNER WHEREIN THE ABBOT BLANQUERNA WAS ELECTED BISHOP

When the Bishop had resigned his bishopric, and had set himself to study Arabic, the canons met in the chapter-house to make ordinance concerning the election of a pastor. One of the canons said that they ought to enquire of the Bishop as to which of them he thought should be Bishop in his stead, for since he had been Bishop and had renounced his see, desiring to die in honour of Jesus Christ, it was fitting that they should enquire of him and that he should have a vote in the chapter. All the canons found this counsel good. So he that was aforetime Bishop came to the chapter-house, and in the presence of all said that they should elect for their Bishop the Abbot Blanquerna, for he knew none that was so worthy of the office; yet he thought not that Blanquerna would desire to be Bishop. And if Blanquerna refused election, his counsel was that they should elect his successor according to the manner and art of election.

2. Greatly was the Archdeacon displeased at that which was said by him that was aforetime Bishop, and certain of the canons were displeased likewise, for they were canons secular, and feared that, if the Abbot Blanquerna were elected, he would cause them to become canons regular; but the greater number of the canons found it good that the Abbot Blanquerna should be Bishop; nevertheless they desired to make election by following the art of election. But the Archdeacon, together with certain of the canons, opposed the holding of an election according to the art. Wherefore the rest, who desired that Blanquerna should be Bishop, elected him to the office without the art; but

certain of the canons dissented, and elected the Archdeacon for their Bishop.

3. Great discord was there among the canons by reason of the discordance in the election which they had held. So two canons went to the Abbot Blanquerna, and said to him that he had been elected Bishop, and that he had received more votes than the Archdeacon; wherefore they prayed him, on behalf of all their companions, that he would accept the bishopric, and go to Rome, to the end that his election might be confirmed. The Abbot Blanquerna made excuses, saying that with the contemplative life it accorded not that a man should leave the life of religion to be a Bishop, and he said that he would in no wise accept the office. Greatly were these two canons displeased that the Abbot desired not to be Bishop, and the rest were displeased likewise, of those that had elected him Bishop. The Archdeacon went to Rome to seek his confirmation as Bishop; but the greater number of the canons sent against him an advocate, begging that their lord the Pope would make commandment that the Abbot Blanquerna should be Bishop.

4. When the Pope had heard either side, he spake these words: "Any semblance soever of simony is a thing to be shunned in an election, and opposition to it is a thing most fitting; wherefore it seems to us that the Abbot Blanquerna, who desires not to be Bishop, nor to pass from a cloistered life to a sphere of life more ample, is worthy to be elected Bishop." So the Holy Father willed that at all hazards Blanquerna should be Bishop, and sent to him the commandment that he should so become. Great was the displeasure of the Abbot and of all the community at the commandment of the Pope, and Blanquerna sent to the Pope two monks to excuse him, and to show the right which he had so to do; for (said they) if he that was aforetime Bishop could resign his diocese that he might choose a straiter life, it was evident that Blanquerna

could refuse election, since he had taken the habit of a monk, to the end that he might lead a life of greater contemplation.

5. So the monks went to Rome, and begged of their lord the Pope that he would not take from them the Abbot Blanquerna, for greatly would they be impoverished thereby, and great things had he done for the monastery, and most of all they made this prayer because he himself desired to be excused for the reasons aforesaid. But the Pope desired at all hazards that the Abbot Blanquerna should be Bishop, that he might do great things for his diocese even as he had done for the monastery; therefore the Pope was pleased to command him by his obedience that he should accept the office of Bishop. So the Abbot was compelled to leave his office, and to accept the office of Bishop. Greatly were all the monks displeased thereat, and great pleasure had the canons who had elected him.

CHAPTER LXVIII

OF THE MANNER WHEREIN BLANQUERNA ORDERED HIS DIOCESE

The Bishop was in chapter together with all his canons, and he spake these words: "It is your will, reverend sirs, that I be your pastor. As Abbot, I was in servitude, but now my servitude is greater, for with greater risk and peril does a pastor guard his well-fed sheep than his lean. Now since ye desire that I be your pastor, I beg of you aid and counsel, that ye may assist me in my pastoral office and in the guarding of my sheep. First of all I desire to know what is the income of the Cathedral Church, how many are the canons and the beneficed clergy of the diocese, and in what manner the income of the Cathedral is divided. Let all these things be set forth in writing, to the end that I may take counsel with myself, and see if there is aught as touching this church that can be bettered and ordered to the greater honour of God, and that good example likewise may be given to the lay folk, who oftentimes fall into sin through the evil example that they have of their pastor and of his companions."

2. In the presence of the Bishop and of all the canons, the writing for the which the Bishop asked was made, in the which writing it was found that the Bishop had within his diocese four and twenty canons, exception being made of the Sacrist and the Archdeacon, the Provost and the Master of the Schools.[1] Likewise were there thirteen chaplaincies,[2] and other offices also, according as is fitting in a Cathedral Church. Great was the income of the church, and the share of the Bishop amounted to three thousand pounds yearly.

3. Long did the Bishop think upon the estate of his diocese, and upon the manner wherein he could better it. It came to pass at Mass one day that the Gospel was sung wherein Jesus Christ makes promise of eight Beatitudes. When the Mass was ended, the Bishop held chapter, according to the custom which he had on one day in every week. When the Bishop was in chapter with all the canons, he spake to them these words: "Ye have heard, reverend sirs, in the Gospel, how that our Lord God Jesus Christ makes promise of eight Beatitudes. With your counsel and will, I should desire to make in this diocese a rule and an ordinance, according to the which these eight Beatitudes may be ours. First of all I begin with my income, whereof I will make three parts: the one shall be given for alms, the second shall go to make peace between those that are at enmity, the third shall be set aside for the expenses which are necessary for my needs and for those that are in my household."

[1] *cabiscol*, *i.e.* caput scholæ (in Castilian, *maestrescuela*).

[2] *capellanies* (Castilian, *capellanias*), canonical benefices to which certain obligations are attached.

4. The Archdeacon answered the Bishop, and said that dishonour would come to him and to all the clergy of the diocese, if he kept not in his house a large retinue, that he might have a great and honourable train, the which he could not keep with a third part of his income only. The Bishop answered that honour must not be desired save with intention to the service of God, and that to give alms is to do greater honour to God than to have an excessive retinue whereby a man may have vainglory; for the palace of a prelate is more honourable when at his gates there are many poor to whom alms are given, than when upon his table are many silver cups, and many persons dine with him, and many beasts are in his stables and many vestments in his wardrobes, and in his chests many pieces of gold.[1]

5. The Bishop desired also that division into three parts should be made in the number of the canons, and that one part should be set aside for the service of the eight Beatitudes, the second for the study of theology and canon law, and the third for the service of the Cathedral Church; and he desired that all these four-and-twenty canons and he himself and all the rest should be made regular. After this he desired that the priests who sang Mass and served the chaplaincies should, after Mass and the Hours, be set to study theology and law, and that they should take their food together in the refectory and sleep in the dormitory, to the end that, after the deaths of the canons, others should be chosen from among them, and the care of the parish churches should be given to them; and this ordinance he desired to be made for all time, and to be confirmed by the Pope, and likewise by the whole chapter.

6. Great was the strife that was between the Bishop and the Archdeacon, and certain of the canons who were of the same mind as the Archdeacon; but the Bishop said that he would not continue as their Bishop if they confirmed not that ordinance, and that he would send to the Holy

[1] For this sentiment, cf. p. 456 (§ 292), below.

Father to the end that he might confirm it; and if he would not confirm it, let him hold him excused from being Bishop, for he would not be the pastor of sheep whom he could not defend from the wolves. The Bishop sent to the Pope, by canons holy and devout, a report of the proceedings concerning this matter. Immediately the Pope replied in writing to the Bishop, desiring that all should be done according to his will; and saying that he rejoiced that he had confirmed him as Bishop, for he had great hope of the good that he would perform. When the messengers had returned from the court, the Bishop Blanquerna made ordinance concerning his diocese as he had said; and first he made ordinance concerning study, and afterward concerning the eight Beatitudes.

CHAPTER LXIX

OF POVERTY

When the Bishop was with the canons in chapter, he said to them that Jesus Christ promised the Kingdom of Heaven to the poor, wherefore he desired that one canon should be set aside for the office of poverty, the which canon should preach concerning poverty, and be at the head of the poor that were in that city, and that for the love of God he should give up the income of his canonry, and beg the wherewithal to live, and go poorly clad, and reprove them that were not poor in spirit. When the Bishop had set forth the details of this office, a certain canon, who was a man of holy life, rose upon his feet, and begged that he might have the office of poverty, promising to fulfil with all his power the conditions aforesaid, the which were fitting to the office.

2. The office was given to this canon, and the Bishop caused it to be proclaimed in all the churches that he was at the head of the poor, and that he would beg for them;

and he gave much pardon to any man who would give to the canon. So that canon gave up his rich vestments for the love of God, and all the beasts that he possessed, and all the livery of his household; and went about poorly clad, begging for the destitute poor, and for the poor that were sick, and for poor maidens that desired to marry, and for children that were orphans and needy, to all of whom he caused some trade to be taught whereby they might live.

3. It came to pass one day that the Canon of Poverty went to dine at the house of the Archdeacon. While the Archdeacon was eating delicate meats, served in divers fashions, the Canon of Poverty cried in a loud voice: "Let us flee from here! Let us flee! For the Archdeacon is devouring and wasting the possessions of the poor of Jesus Christ!" And, crying thus, the Canon went out from the house of the Archdeacon, and, as he cried, he went through the town and to the houses of the other canons, and many poor men went with him, who cried out likewise, using these same words that were uttered by the Canon. Great was the shame of the Archdeacon, and in many a man did the Canon awaken remorse by his reproof of him.

4. On another day it came to pass that the Canon of Poverty was dining with the Master of the Schools. While they ate, there entered into his courtyard many beasts laden with corn for him, for he was a mercenary man, and hoarded money wherewith to enrich a nephew of his whom he greatly loved. As soon as the Canon saw the beasts entering the courtyard, he rose from the table, and went through the streets, gathering together the poor; and, when he had gathered many poor folk together, he came to the palace of the Bishop, and cried "Justice! Justice!", and all the poor folk cried out the same thing with him. Great was the wonder of the Bishop at these cries, and greatly marvelled all the rest. The Bishop and his canons went out to the gate, where they found the poor, who with

their advocate the Canon cried ever: "Justice! Justice!" The Bishop enquired of the Canon wherefore he thus cried, and the Canon spake to the Bishop these words:

5. "My Lord Bishop! It is written that all that remains to thy clergy over and above their necessities belongs to the poor. Now the Master has made storage of much corn, and desires to sell it, to the end that he may buy a castle for his nephew. I ask therefore that the money which he will receive for the corn may be given to me, for it belongs to these poor folk whom thou hast commended to me; and his nephew is not a cleric, neither has he himself a mouth or a belly which has need of so much corn: I demand therefore that justice may be done." The Bishop sent for the Master and enquired concerning the truth of that which the Canon of Poverty had said; and he found that it was even as he had said. So the Master had shame and confusion, and the Bishop gave sentence that all that corn should be given to the poor; and if the nephew of the Master desired to be treated as poor, that he should have a share likewise, even as the others of the poor.

6. The Canon of Poverty preached in every place in praise of poverty and in condemnation of riches. One day it came to pass that a very wealthy and honourable burgess of that city had invited him to dine. Before they ate, the Canon prayed the burgess to show him all his house. So the burgess led him through all the rooms of his house, and the Canon saw that there was no room nor any chamber that had lack of aught; for the house was very fair and wondrously fashioned. In every room was all that pertained to its office; for in the chambers there were many beds and rich coverings, and in the hall were many weapons and many benches, in the stables many beasts, in the kitchen many utensils, in the courtyard many hens and geese, and much wood, and in the garden many trees. In the granaries was much corn, and in the pantry much bread and wheat; in the armoury were many silver cups, in the

wardrobes many vestments, and in the chests many pieces of gold. The burgess and his wife and his children and all his retinue had abundance of clothing and of all that they needed. When the Canon had seen all these things, he said that neither here nor there was there a place, neither in any room, wherein he could see poverty; wherefore he desired not to dine with the burgess, since he was a servant of Wealth, the which was contrary to Poverty who was his Lady.

7. The Canon desired therefore to leave the house of the burgess and to go and dine elsewhere. But the burgess said to him that he had a secret room in his house, the which he had not yet seen, and he desired that he should see it. So the burgess led the Canon to that room, which was poorly furnished. In that room the Canon dined that day with the burgess and with his wife secretly, and they ate meagrely. And the burgess showed him a poor bed wherein he and his wife lay, and he showed him the hair shirts which they wore, and he showed him a book wherein was made note of the alms which he did secretly. In another secret room was the crucifix before the which the burgess and his wife were oft-times to be found in prayer and in contemplation, praying to God and speaking to one another concerning Him. Greatly did the Canon marvel concerning the lives of the burgess and his wife; and he enquired of the burgess wherefore he kept his retinue and his house with so great abundance of clothing and of victuals, and wherefore he had it apparelled with all things. The burgess answered, and said that the greater was the number of the things in his house the poorer was he in spirit; for the greater was the abundance and the riches of others, the oftener did he see and despise them, wherefore was he the poorer in spirit. Greatly was the Canon pleased at the lives of the burgess and his wife, and he praised and blessed God, Who had given him so worthy a companion in the service of Poverty.

CHAPTER LXX

OF MEEKNESS

THE Bishop Blanquerna gave the office of meekness to a certain Canon, the which Canon was to preach meekness and to be himself meek, that his sermons might have the greater truth. The remaining offices he divided among the remaining canons whom he set apart for the service of the Beatitudes, and for his own he kept the office of peace. It came to pass one day that the overseer of the Archdeacon had bought meat and hens and partridges; and the Canon of Poverty, going with a great company of poor folk through the streets, met the overseer of the Archdeacon, who passed with two men that were laden with flesh. The Canon and the poor folk cried out: "Thieves, thieves! See, the Archdeacon is taking meat from the poor of Jesus Christ!" Great scandal and wrath had the overseer thereat, and more wrathful still was the Archdeacon when the overseer told him of it. So great was his wrath that he desired to strike the Canon of Poverty, but the Canon of Meekness reminded him how that Our Lord Jesus Christ was meek upon the Cross, whereon He suffered Himself to be nailed, and tortured, and wounded, and put to death, albeit He had done no sin. Wherefore, since the Archdeacon had sinned, how great should be his patience, for the Canon of Poverty accused him according to justice, and reproved him for the harm which he did to the poor, who had been commended to the Canon of Poverty, through the will of the Bishop and of all the chapter. So devoutly and with such humble words did the Canon of Meekness speak in this wise to the Archdeacon that the Archdeacon took knowledge of his sins, and had patience, and refrained from wrath and ill-will, and begged forgiveness of the Canon of Poverty.

2. In that city there was a lady who greatly loved her husband, but the husband was given to luﬆ, and this lady was impatient of his sins, to wit, his sins of unfaithfulness to her. It came to pass one day that she was going with certain other ladies to church, and on the way she met the Canon of Meekness, who was preaching meekness and patience, saying these words: "Strong is the meek and simple man over the man that is wrathful and impatient and proud; for meekness does battle with the aid of charity, juﬆice, prudence and fortitude, and wrath and impatience do battle using things that are contrary to these virtues aforesaid." Long did the lady think upon the words which the Canon preached, and she thought that she would endeavour to correct her husband for his vices and his luﬆ with words that were simple and humble, and with meekness and patience. Wherefore this lady spake meek and humble words to her husband, the which words seemed good to him; and the more her husband sinned, the more did she increase the consciousness of his sin within him, through the which he was remorseful, and thence came there to him chaﬆity, juﬆice and shame, which agree with consciousness of sin, and together with fortitude they overcame the luﬆ that was in his mind.

3. In the chief square of the city preached the Canon of Meekness, and a man that was there reproached another for theft, and the other excused himself with great wrath and many threats, and in such wise did he excuse himself that it would have appeared by his words that he was God, and that he could neither go aﬆray nor commit sin; and the more he excused himself, the greater grew and increased the wrath in him that had accused him, and the greater was his suspicion concerning him, since wrath and suspicion are ever in accord, and men that sin excuse themselves more vehemently in their words than do they that have no sin. Now while the two disputed thus, the Canon, who was preaching, spake these words: "Wrongly was

Jesus Christ accused when they said that He was possessed and had a devil, and humbly and devoutly and with few words did He answer, saying that He was neither possessed nor yet had a devil. Wherefore, he that excuses himself more vehemently than did Jesus Christ would make it to appear by his words that he can neither go astray nor commit sin."

4. While the Canon spake these words a slate fell from a roof and struck the Canon on the head and wounded him sorely; and the Canon had patience, and bore the wound in peace, and spake words that were humble and devout. While they led the Canon to the surgeon two men began to quarrel, and the one endeavoured to strike the other with a knife, and he struck the Canon of Meekness in the arm, and wounded him sorely; and the Canon with meekness begged for him the pardon of God, and praised and blessed God, Whose will it was that he should have patience and speak words of meekness. Greatly did the words of the Canon edify all them that were with him, and especially him that excused himself so vehemently concerning the charge of theft.

5. After some time the Canon was healed of his wounds. Now the Prince of that land disendowed the Church, and did to it many wrongs; for that Prince was not a good Christian, neither desired he to obey the Bishop Blanquerna as concerning that which he commanded him by virtue of his office. To the Pope came knowledge of the wrong which that Prince did to the Church, and the Holy Father sent a message to the Bishop that the Prince should be excommunicated and forbidden the offices of the Church. But all feared to forbid them to him, because they knew that he was a wicked and cruel man, and they had fear of death; wherefore they were afraid to forbid them to him. One day the Bishop was in chapter with the canons, and the canons who held the offices of the eight Beatitudes were present. There was discussion among them which of the

eight by virtue of his office should go to the Prince with the message of the Pope, and it was decided by the chapter that the Canon of Meekness should have that office, because of the meekness of Jesus Christ, Who was their Pastor, Whose advocates are all the pastors of this world; and because this must needs be done with meekness of speech and contrition of heart, therefore was it decreed that the Canon of Meekness should bear this message to the Prince.

6. When the Canon was brought before the Prince, he spake these words: "Our Lord Jesus Christ said that the meek should possess the earth. Since I am meek, it is decreed that I should be sent to thee to tell thee that thou art forbidden the offices of the Church by reason of the wrong that thou doest her. Meekness has vanquished me and makes me to be in peril of death. If there is within thee fortitude, justice, humility and patience, meekness will make my words to be pleasing to thee; but if within thee there is wrath, disobedience and wrong, then will my words of humility combat thy words of pride."

7. Greatly did this message displease the Prince, and he commanded that the Canon should be stripped and bound and scourged before him, and afterwards delivered to a cruel death. While the Canon was being bound and scourged, he prayed to God for the Prince, and for them that scourged him, and he praised God, Who made him to bear punishment for the sins which he had committed in this world. The more violent were his scourging and his torture, the more of piety was in his looks, and the more devoutly did he speak, using these words: "Lord Jesus Christ! Thou hast created me in Thy likeness and hast taken a human nature which is like unto my nature. In like manner as Thou didst will to be tormented, dost Thou make me to be tormented, to the end that I may be more like unto Thee: I cannot reward Thee for the gifts which Thou desirest to give me. I bless Thee, O Lord, for that Thou desirest to honour me; if I were wrathful

with them that torment me I should not be meek nor like unto Thee."

8. Greatly marvelled the Prince at the words which the Canon spake. Wherefore he commanded that he should no more be scourged nor harmed, and spake these words: "Not long is it since the clergy were proud and spake evil. Whence comes it that thou dost speak such devout and humble words? Can the time have come when humility and devotion have agreement within you clergy, and when we that are laymen may take example from you? I beg and conjure you by God to speak to me concerning the estate of the Bishop and of thy companions; for there is in thee some new virtue, that in such a case as this they have sent to me a man like thyself."

9. So the Canon related to him the history of the Bishop Blanquerna, and how he was aforetime Abbot, and how he had been elected Bishop, and how he had ordered his diocese, and how he himself was one of the eight companions that by their lives were to give example of the eight Beatitudes that Jesus Christ promised to the Apostles and to such as followed them. Then the Divine Light warmed the heart of the Prince with heavenly love, and he spake these words: "It behoves not that such a Bishop or his companions should be disobeyed in aught." So the Prince and the Canon of Meekness went to the Bishop Blanquerna, and the Prince begged forgiveness and made satisfaction, and took leave of the Bishop and of the chapter with their grace and blessing.

CHAPTER LXXI

OF TEARS

The Bishop Blanquerna gave a rule to the Canon of Tears whereby he was to weep and suffer all those things for the which tears are fitting, and he gave him an art and a rule whereby his heart might be moved to love God so greatly, that it should bring tears to his eyes and make them to weep. It came to pass one day that this Canon passed by a slaughter-house, and he saw therein the Canon of Meekness, who was gazing at the lambs which he saw the slaughterers bind and slay,[1] and he observed that they lamented not but received their death in peace. The Canon of Tears enquired of the Canon of Meekness wherefore he was in that place, and he answered him, saying that he was there to behold the slaughter of the lambs, and to remember thereby his Lord Jesus Christ, Who suffered Himself to be bound and slain as meekly as did the lambs, that He might save sinners. When the Canon of Tears had heard these words, he said that it behoved him to weep for the death of his Lord Jesus Christ. So for a great space these two canons were in tears and had devotion together, and oftentimes did they come to that place to weep together, for the comfort which they had from weeping, and for the profit which they brought to many men in that place, the which men had contrition for their sins and wept for the Passion of Jesus Christ.

2. The Canon of Tears passed by the Synagogue of the Jews, and saw many Jews entering therein that they might pray to God; so he sat at the door of the Synagogue. The Canon remembered how that the Jews had been the cause of the Passion of Jesus Christ, and how they dishonoured Him in the world, and believed not in Him but maligned Him daily. While the Canon thought upon these things, and on the damnation whither the Jews through ignorance go, he wept right bitterly, saying these words: "Ah, Charity and Devotion! How is it that ye go not to honour our Lord among these people who think that they honour Him, yet do Him dishonour? Ah, Pity! How is it that thou hast not mercy upon these people who daily through ignorance journey towards the fire that is everlasting?"

[1] To this day the custom of killing lambs on Good Friday remains in Majorca.

Many other words spake the Canon, and long did he weep in that place, and many times came he to weep in that place, to the end that Divine grace might enlighten those that had strayed, and give devotion to Christians, that by the virtue of God they might have greater diligence than now they have in enlightening the unbelievers.

3. A certain worthy lady had a husband whom she greatly loved, and he had been in captivity, and with a large sum of money had been redeemed. This lady sold all her possessions and those of her husband that she might pay the ransom, and, since this sufficed not, she went through the chief squares begging. The Canon of Tears found her one day in the principal square of the city. As she begged she wept, and related to a great company of notable citizens the story of the captivity of her husband and the torment which he suffered in prison. Together with her she led four small children. All the citizens had pity upon this lady, giving her money, and consoling her in her tribulation. When the lady had spoken and received alms, the Canon of Tears, weeping, spake these words: " This lady weeps for her husband, and has pity for the torment which he suffers in prison. Her children have come to poverty, wherefore she goes with them begging. All her power does this lady put forth to ransom her husband. But who is he that puts forth all his power in honouring his Creator, Redeemer,[1] Benefactor, and the Lord of all things that are? That Lord is more greatly to be loved than is the husband of this lady: yet that place is in captivity wherein He was conceived and born and crucified, for the Saracens hold it in their power. Which of you will assist me to weep for the ignorance of all such as put not forth their whole power to honour their Lord?" The Canon wept, and the people that were present began to count their money and to speak of their merchandise, whereat the tears of the Canon began to be increased.

[1] Lit. *recreador.*

4. At the entrance to the city were certain women of a brothel. It came to pass one day that the Canon of Tears passed by that place, and saw a great company of these women; so he seated himself beside them and began to say these words: " I will weep for the sins of these women who sell themselves to devils for money. The whole world is not so great in value as one soul, yet each of these women gives her soul to the devil for a single piece of money. It behoves me to weep that the Prince of this land forbids not these women to be in this place and cause men to sin. Mine eyes shed tears because in this city there is none whose business it is to see that these poor women live not by this office." While the Canon wept thus, the women wept, together with the Canon, and excused themselves, alleging their poverty. So the Canon and the women were all in tears, and they that passed along the street had pity upon them. While they wept thus, a rich burgess who had no children entered the city riding upon his palfrey, and his wife and his retinue accompanied him; and he heard the words of the Canon and of the women, and through the merits of the Canon God was pleased to inspire the burgess and his wife with Divine grace, so that they received these women as their daughters and took them to their home; and the burgess established a hostel wherein should live all of these women that desired to forsake the sin of lust; and the burgess and his wife brought them up to be servants, or in some other trade whereby they might gain their livelihood. Furthermore the burgess treated with the Prince and with the governors of the city, so that never thereafter were such women suffered to be on any of the roads which are at the entrance of the city, to the end that men and women who entered and left the city should have no bad example from them.

5. At Eastertide, and upon Easter Day, the Canon of Tears desired to have some rest from the weeping to which he had given himself by reason of the Sacred Passion of

his Lord. So he went to the church wherein the Bishop Blanquerna was to preach; and as he was at the entrance thereof, he saw many women entering the church, the which women were arrayed in noble garments. They had dyed their eyebrows and their hair; and on their faces were colours of white and scarlet, that they might be looked upon by men, who should have desire for them in respect of the pleasures of lust. Young men nobly arrayed and with garlands upon their heads entered the church also, and they looked rather upon the women than at the Altar or the Cross, wherein is represented the Passion of the Son of God. When the Canon had seen all these things, he seated himself at the door of the church, and wept for the sins of these people and their neglect of the Passion of the Son of God.

6. While the Canon wept thus, the Bishop Blanquerna came to the church, where he found the Canon weeping, and enquired of him wherefore he wept. Then the Canon made answer in these words: "The Son of God had remembrance of the people whom He had lost, and came to take human flesh and suffer Passion, that He might redeem His people, and now His Passion is forgotten, and there is none that is joyful for His Resurrection. Yet they have remembrance of lust. Women and men bearing the signs of lust come to this church that they may behold us weeping; and I must console myself with tears, for my tears are all my consolation, and the thoughts which their sins awaken within me are my despair.

7. Greatly was the Bishop pleased at the tears of the Canon, and he sat beside him, and they both wept for a great space, and all the people that were in the church knew the reason of their tears, and those men and women that bore the signs of lust were in great shame and confusion thereat. Then the Bishop preached, and said that thenceforward he desired that men and women should not be together in a church wherein there were no means to

prevent them from looking upon each other; and he gave as an example the temples of the Saracens and the Jews, saying that if they have this ordinance, albeit they live in error, how much the more should the Christians who follow the true religion have it, and look to it that no dishonour be done to the Holy Sacrifice of the Altar, since this is worthy of such great honour."

8. Daily went the Canon to the church to weep for sinners, and daily went he through the streets and wept whensoever he had occasion thereof; and he endeavoured to weep whensoever he perceived that God was not loved, neither known nor obeyed, that the people might have contrition and knowledge thereof, and beg of God forgiveness and devotion. The good which he did, and the evil which came to an end through that which he did, who can recount it? Of a truth, they that now take their ease will have no more rest, if they once desire to resemble him.

CHAPTER LXXII

OF AFFLICTION

THE Canon of Affliction prayed daily concerning fasts and vigils and affliction, saying that Jesus Christ promises to all them that will suffer hunger and thirst for love of Him that they shall be filled. It came to pass one day that a waggoner was eating bread and onions while his mule ate oats. That waggoner was pale and thin, and his mule was fat. The Canon demanded of the waggoner why he thought more of his mule than of his own person; and the waggoner said that the mule could not draw her loads without sufficient oats, but that he himself could live upon bread and onions. When the waggoner had said these words, the Canon spake as follows in the presence of many men:

2. "To fast and to eat poor food through avarice is none occasion of the bliss which God promises in the Gospel;

neither does it accord with justice that a man should satiate an ass and starve his own body through avarice."

3. It came to pass one day that the Canon of Affliction was preaching in the chief square of the city and the Archdeacon passed through the square upon his horse, for he was going to take recreation in a castle[1] that belonged to him; and in his retinue there were barrels of wine, and hens which had already been killed that they might be very tender for their dinner; new white bread was there likewise, with sauces and sweetmeats. The Archdeacon was very fat and a great eater. Then in presence of them all the Canon enquired of the Archdeacon which satiety was of greater profit to the soul, whether the satiety of temporal viands or satiety of the grace which God promises to all them that for love of Him will suffer hunger and thirst and affliction. The Archdeacon had no reply ready, wherefore he went from him without making any answer.

4. The Canon left the city, and went into another city to preach affliction; and at the fork of two roads he met two monks who were disputing the one with the other, for one of them desired to follow the one road and the other to follow the other road. The one had devotion to go and preach in a certain village,[2] but the other excused himself because the village was far away, and upon the road he would have hunger and thirst; wherefore, to avoid hunger and thirst, he desired to follow the other road. When the Canon of Affliction had learned the reason of their dispute, he reproved that brother very sternly who feared to suffer hunger and thirst to preach the word of God; for if Jesus Christ feared not hunger and thirst and death that He might save His people, how much the less should any man

[1] This word (*castell*) can mean: (1) a castle, (2) the inhabitants of a castle, (3) a small town or village built around a castle and depending upon it, (4) the inhabitants of such a town or village. The present paragraph and the next illustrate two of these meanings. [2] *castell.*

excuse himself from suffering hunger and thirst that he might honour and preach the word of God!

5. When the Canon had gone so far that he came to the gate of the city whither he was going, he found a man who had given to a poor person a piece of money, that God might hold him excused for having broken his fast on one day in Lent. The Canon and that man disputed together for a great space of time as to whether that piece of money excused him or not from his fast; the man alleged his reasons, saying that greater good resulted from the piece of money than from his fast, wherefore the alms that he did excused him therefrom. The Canon said the alms were not in that case given according to justice; for if a man had sinned through superfluity of gluttony, it behoved him that he should be punished for his sin by hunger, the which hunger he had not through giving the piece of money. So the Canon reproved the man very straitly and vanquished him in argument.

6. When the Canon entered the city, he found a great multitude of poor folk who were going through the streets, begging alms for the love of God. All the poor folk came towards the Canon, and the Canon went about with them to the houses of wealthy men, crying, "Hunger, hunger!" It came to pass one day that a rich merchant commanded that they should give the Canon and the poor folk to eat until they were filled. When the Canon and the poor folk had eaten, they cried more loudly than before, "Hunger, hunger!" Great was the wonder of the merchant, and he supposed that they had not eaten enough, and commanded them to be given more. "Sir!" said the Canon, "We have eaten and drunk sufficiently by the grace of God and by thy favour; but we cry concerning hunger, that thou and others may hunger and thirst for the love of God, that ye may be satisfied with the blessing of salvation."

7. The Canon endeavoured, in so far as he was able, to have hunger and thirst that he might punish himself for

his sins, and give doctrine to the people whereby they might suffer afflictions and have remembrance of the hunger which Jesus Christ suffered in the desert and the thirst which He endured upon the Cross. And the Canon had not alone the office of preaching concerning bodily hunger, but also that of the hunger of the spirit, that the people might have hunger for justice, charity and the other virtues, and that they might be filled therewith and so lead good lives.

CHAPTER LXXIII

OF MERCY

The Canon of Mercy preached daily concerning mercy. It came to pass one day that according to the decree of justice a certain man was to suffer death. That man had a wife and five children, who lived upon the evil gains which that man had won at his trade. When the King commanded that justice should be done to him, the woman came to the Canon who served in the office of Mercy and begged him to intercede for her and for her children with the King, that he might have mercy upon her husband, and that she and her children might have the wherewithal to live. So the Canon went to the King, and spake to him these words:

2. "Sire! Mercy and justice are sisters. Wherefore, if thou hast been chosen king to the end that thou mayest serve justice, it behoves thee, if ever thou hast been inclined to sin, to be the servant of mercy, that thou mayest be pardoned, and that there may be fulfilled in thee that word which Jesus Christ spake in the Gospel that they who themselves have mercy shall receive mercy. If thou art not sometimes merciful, thou wilt not be forgiven; and as I am an advocate of mercy, therefore in the presence of justice I beg of thee that thou have mercy upon this woman and restore her husband to her." Long did the

King consider the words which the Canon of Mercy spake to him, but he had fear lest if he obeyed his words he should act against justice, wherefore he spake these words:

3. "It behoves me to honour justice; and if I forgive, I fear lest I dishonour justice; if I forgive not, I fear lest Justice be aggrieved because I obey not Mercy her sister. Therefore do I think very deeply, and I know not what to choose. The Canon answered and said that the greater likeness to God a man had in his works the better, the nobler and the more worthily accustomed was he. Wherefore, since God sometimes pardoned and sometimes condemned, and because a prince was set in the country to represent God and to do His offices, therefore was it lawful and right that an earthly lord should likewise sometimes pardon and sometimes condemn. So many good reasons did the Canon allege before the King, and so piously did he beg him to have mercy, that the King pardoned the man that was condemned to death, and said to the Canon that it behoved him not to disobey any man who was so truly a servant of mercy and who entreated him so piously as he himself had done.

4. So fervently did the Canon serve in his office, that he came many times to the place wherein the court was held, to reason and to plead for the poor, without receiving reward, and he was an advocate for the poor and the orphans and the widows who had none other to help them. The Canon was a notable clerk, and learned in the law, and he reproved those advocates that falsely conducted their lawsuits; and all the advocates feared him, and through their fear of him they ceased to act falsely and to practise deception in the lawsuits wherein they pleaded. It came to pass one day that a peasant[1] had suffered great wrong by reason of a field which a neighbour was endeavouring to take from him. This peasant had come to

[1] *pagès.* See note, p. 245, above.

the court many times, and the judge had refused to hear him. The peasant went to the palace of the King to tell him of the wrong which had been done to him, but he could not come in a fashion nor at a time at the which he could speak with the King; for sometimes the King was hunting, at other times he was privately in his bed-chamber, at other times he was eating or sleeping or taking recreation. So the peasant went to the Canon of Mercy, and begged for his aid, and related his necessities to the Canon, telling him how he could not gain speech with the King. The Canon was in court, discussing a plea with a poor woman, and he cried aloud so that all they that were in the court could hear him, and he said: "Is there none in this court who has hope of mercy?" Many were the men and women that answered saying that they hoped in mercy. Then the Canon spake to them, and begged them that they would assist him to honour mercy, and he went with them to the gate of the palace of the King, and in a loud voice they all cried together, "Mercy, mercy!"

5. Great was the wonder of the King at these cries, and greatly marvelled all the rest; and he came to the gate, and enquired of the Canon wherefore he and his companions cried thus. "Sire!" said the Canon, "Our Lord Jesus Christ gave Himself up to death because He had mercy, and thou dost give thyself wholly to hunting, eating, sleeping and taking recreation, and none other mercy hast thou, save only this. Wherefore men that have need of justice may not see thee nor speak with thee." Great was the shame of the King at the words which the Canon spake to him, and he made ordinance that a man should stand at the gate of the palace to hear all those that came to him through the defects of the Court of Justice, and that he should make representation to the King, that the judge and the other officials should be punished if they had not administered justice according to the office which pertained to them.

6. It came to pass one day in presence of the Canon that a peasant,[1] at the beginning of the winter season in the which man is accuſtomed to sow, loſt one of his oxen, so that there remained to him but one, and he gathered together money enough to go to the market to buy another ox. In the market was a draper[2] to whom the peasant owed money, and he made complaint in the court concerning the peasant. So the court gave sentence that the peasant should pay the money. The peasant cried to the Canon of Mercy that he would help him, and that time should be given him wherein he could pay, and that he should be permitted to buy the ox, that he might not lose his sowing, and that his wife and children should have the wherewithal to live for that year. For long did he beg the Canon of Mercy, that he would plead for him with the judge or with the draper, but they would not lengthen the time of grace that the debt might be paid. The Canon of Mercy had himself naught wherewith to help the peasant, for he had given up all the income of his canonry for the love of God; so he commanded the peasant to bring the ox that remained to him. The peasant brought the ox, and the Canon and the peasant together led the ox through the market and through all the town, crying aloud and enquiring if there were any man in that town who would give himself in exchange for that ox. For long did they walk and cry, but they found no man who would give himself in exchange for the ox. While the Canon and the peasant led the ox through the town, they met the King, who was returning from Mass, and the Canon enquired of the King if he would give himself to the peasant in exchange for the ox. Great marvel had the King at these words which the Canon of Mercy spake to him, and he enquired of the Canon what was signified by his words.

7. "Sire!" said the Canon, "God gives Himself to such as give themselves to Him, and in so much as God

[1] *pagès.*

[2] See note, p. 86, above.

is of greater worth than those to whom He gives Himself, He works superabundance of mercy ; wherefore greater is the mercy which God gives in Himself when He gives Himself to those whom He pardons and who give themselves to Him, than would be the mercy which thou wouldst do in thyself to this peasant if he gave thee the ox and thou didst give thyself to him in exchange." Right pleasing to the King and to all those that heard were the words which the Canon spake concerning the mercy of God, and he gave them great hope of mercy, and commanded that the money which the Court had exacted from the peasant should be returned to him, and he himself paid the draper on behalf of him, and caused the thing to be written down concerning the draper, to the end that if it should chance that he begged mercy from the King, the King would use justice in respect to him. Thereafter the King made ordinance that no man for any debt soever should be dispossessed of oxen whereof he had need in his daily calling.

8. Day by day went the Canon through the city, and took note of them that offended and did wrong to mercy, and wrote down their names, and went to the Canon of Humility that he might cause them to have conscience thereof, and to the Canon of Tears he gave their names that he might bewail their sins, and that the Canon of Affliction might fast because of them and make prayer. In this manner did the Canon work night and day in the service of Mercy; and all the eight canons who were officers of the eight Beatitudes came together in one place, and assisted each other to honour the Beatitudes wherein God should be honoured. The good and the sound discipline which came from their work in that city, who can tell it? And the good example which other cities had therefrom, who is he that may reckon it?

CHAPTER LXXIV

OF PURITY

THE Canon of Purity preached daily concerning cleanness of heart, because all they that have purity of conscience shall in the next life see God, according as Jesus Christ has promised in the Gospel. That Canon went through the city, and took note of those that were in sin and those that were in penitence; and to those that were in sin he preached and gave many similitudes whereby he made them to be conscious of their sins. It came to pass one day that before a great multitude of people he put forth this parable, speaking to them as follows:

2. "In a certain country there lived a man who had in his belly a great serpent, which devoured him and ate his entrails, and in his hand this man had a precious stone which was very pleasant to look upon, so that in looking upon it he found some recreation from the thoughts that he had concerning the serpent which tormented him and destroyed him without his being able to defend himself. While this man was in that state, a physician came to him, saying that he would cast the serpent from his belly if he would give him that precious stone. But the man loved the precious stone so greatly that he would not give it to the physician; and the serpent caused the death of that man in the presence of the physician, and the physician carried away the stone. The serpent signifies that consciousness of sin which causes the soul grief for its sins, and by the stone are signified worldly riches, which are won with great labour and are pleasant to possess. And the death of the man signifies how that the riches remain to them that live, and how the soul of him that possesses them through evil-doing loses them and goes to the fire which is everlasting. Wherefore, as this is so, more foolish is he that dies in sin, having knowledge thereof, than was

the man that would not give the precious stone to the physician."

3. While the Canon spake these words, a certain man wept very bitterly in his presence, saying: "That serpent is in my belly, and destroys my heart, and the stone which the physician asks of me is in my hands, and death comes in company with the devil, who desires to take from me the stone and likewise to carry away my soul." The Canon begged the man secretly that he would expound to him that which was signified by his words. So the man told him that he was in sin, and had knowledge thereof, yet confessed not himself, neither forsook his sin; for he had been in this sin and had not made his confession. Straitly did the Canon reprove that man because he forsook not his sin, and most of all because he confessed it not. "Sir!" said the man. "So great is my fear that confession will take from me the stone that I will not confess; and when I desire to confess, I think that I shall not forsake my sins, therefore do I despise confession, the which is of no avail if a man confess not with intention to forsake his sins." Great argument was made between the Canon and that man, as to whether the man should confess himself or not, seeing that it was not in his will to forsake his sin. While they thus strove, came the Canon of Mercy, whom they appointed as judge, and he gave sentence that mercy was the more proper to men that confessed their sins, albeit they desired not to forsake them, than to those that confessed not themselves at all; and this was so because mercy and consciousness of sin and confession accord each with the other against obstinacy and cruelty and despair.

4. Before them all there passed a lady right nobly clad, and upon her features she had set divers colours that she might be looked upon pleasantly with respect to the pleasures of lust. Then the Canon of Purity spake before them all, in such manner that the lady heard it, and asked which thing was capable of being greater, whether purity

of body or impurity of soul. A learned man, who was in the presence of the Canon, answered and said that even as the soul was a cleaner and purer creature than the body, the more therefore could it be soiled through an unruly will and through unclean remembrance, which should have remembrance of uncleanness to the end that the will might love it. Right pleased was the Canon with that which the wise man had truthfully said, and he begged him to become his companion in the service of purity. While they spake together thus there passed before them a pig which had wallowed in a quagmire of filth, and the Canon said, in the presence of all, that that pig was less unclean than the woman who had colours upon her features. Now in the place wherein they spake, there was a foolish man who was a kinsman of that lady, and he reproved the Canon very sternly, and menaced him; but the Canon answered and said that to keep silence concerning the truth is a thing that is as contrary to purity of heart, as it is to speak against knowledge. Wherefore he asked for sentence as to which of the two had erred.

5. The Canon went daily to the houses of the clergy, that he might know which of them were of honest life; and the names of these he wrote down, and made mention thereof to the Bishop and to the Canons, to the end that if there came a case of election or of a gift of benefice, it might be known to whom the gift should be made. And many laymen he watched, and made search concerning their sins and wrong-doings, and evil customs and habits, and all this likewise he wrote down. He likewise asked for aid in destroying evil customs and furthering customs that were good; and by night he went through the streets, crying loudly, and blowing upon a horn that men might hear him. And he spake these words: "Day is over, night is come; let every man before he lie down to sleep enquire of his conscience if this day he have done aught that is against cleanness of heart and against his conscience;

and on the morrow let him seek forgiveness and do penance. For if it is a thing most foul to look upon carrion and those unclean parts of the person which nature commands us to cover, how much the more foul is it to remember, understand and love sin and guilt, whereby the soul may no more see God but will see itself for ever in hell, and behold only the demons, which are things most horrible to the sight."

CHAPTER LXXV

OF PEACE

THE Bishop Blanquerna desired to take himself the office of peacemaker, for they that have it will be called the sons of God; and therefore the Bishop desired to take upon himself that office, and to spend the third part of his income in reconciling and making peace between those that were at war and strife. It happened one day that the Bishop was returning from Vespers, to the which he went daily in the Cathedral Church, wherein also he sang Mass daily for the greater honour of his diocese. As he was coming from Vespers, there came to him a great multitude of Jews, making complaint concerning the Christians, who on the eve of the Passover had stoned and wounded two of their number. Long did the Bishop think upon the complaints which the Jews had made concerning the Christians, and he reflected that if Christians and Jews held one belief, the ill-will and strife that was among them would cease; wherefore the Bishop went every Sabbath to the Synagogue to preach and hold discussion with the Jews, to the end that they might become Christians, and praise and bless Jesus Christ, and be at peace with the Christians. Many Jews were baptized and embraced the Holy Roman Faith; and the Bishop, with the third part of his income which he gave up for the love of God, made them many alms; and he appointed for them an advocate, who should provide for all such as became Christians, until they had some office and manner wherein they might live by the fruits of their labours.

2. In the precincts of the city were two knights who had a castle which their father had left to them, and they were at discord concerning the division thereof, and made contention about a vineyard; wherefore there was great strife between these knights, and each desired mortal injury to the other, and there was none that could make peace between them. So one day the Bishop Blanquerna invited one of them to his house, and gave him a horse and begged him to sell to him his part in the vineyard; and this he sold to him for a thousand *morabatins*. On the next day the Bishop invited the other knight to his house, and gave him a horse, and bought his part of the vineyard for a thousand *morabatins*. Thus the Bishop bought it twice, since each knight had the intent to sell the entire vineyard, for each held it to be his own. When the Bishop had entered into possession of the vineyard, he went there, and begged the two brothers to help him to divide it into two equal parts. When the two knights and the Bishop had divided the vineyard, the Bishop gave one part thereof to one knight, and the other part he gave to the other, and so made concord and peace between them.

3. In that city wherein Blanquerna was Bishop there lived a burgess that was honoured both for his lineage and his riches; but he was held in dishonour because he was bound to the sin of lust. That burgess was in great discord with his wife and his kinsfolk, because he had left his wife for a vile woman whom he greatly loved. The Bishop could in no wise bring it to pass that the burgess should leave this wicked woman with whom he lived. So one day secretly the Bishop sent her a message begging her to leave the burgess, and this he commanded by reason of his office. But the woman answered him, saying that she was poor, and unless the burgess or some other person were to assist

her from his wealth, she had not the wherewithal to live. The Bishop made request to the woman with words so devout and humble that she promised him to take a husband and to be no longer with the burgess. Then the Bishop gave five hundred *morabatins* as a dowry to the woman and bestowed upon her a husband; and the burgess, through the good example that the Bishop had given to him, and because the woman desired not to return to her sin, began once more to love his wife, and there was peace between him and his kinsfolk, and the ill-will that was aforetime between them ceased.

4. The devil one day put forth his strength, and brought it to pass that a draper in that city slew a merchant, to whom he owed much money for cloth that he had bought of him. This merchant had two sons. The one was a grown man, and he made an outcry concerning the death of his father; and there were great factions in the city on the one side and on the other. No man could make peace between them, and the notables of the city went to the Bishop Blanquerna, praying him that, as he had the office of peacemaker, he would make peace between the two parties, in so far as he was able. So the Bishop went to the house of the man that cried out for vengeance upon his father, and he begged him to give him charge of his brother, who was still at school, that he might make of him a canon so soon as he was of age. With great pleasure did this man give up his brother, and the Bishop invited him to his house many times weekly, that he might grow in friendship towards him; and he made him his bailiff; and whensoever the brother who was at school was in his presence, the Bishop gave signs of his great love for this brother, that he might have the greater love from his bailiff. When the Bishop had brought it to pass that his bailiff both loved him and feared him,—for love and fear accord the one with the other,—the Bishop made a great feast, to the which came both these two factions in the

city. When they had eaten and feasted for a great space, the Bishop, in the presence of them all, presented the brother with a benefice that was very rich; and he kneeled to his bailiff, and, holding a cross in his hand, begged him that, for the honour of the Cross, he would pardon the draper, who repented very deeply of the murder which he had committed. All the notables and the canons and the other persons who were in that place kneeled likewise when they saw that the Bishop kneeled. So the draper was pardoned, and concord and friendship were made between the two factions, and an alliance was made between them by matrimony, in the which the Bishop gave jewels and money from that part of his income which he had set aside for the making of peace between all men.

5. Every day, after divers manners, did the Bishop make peace between men, and sent gifts and invitations to the notables of the city, both these and those, and he did them much honour, to the end that all might love him, and, through their love, obey him. And whensoever there was strife in the city, straightway the Bishop was enabled to make peace, by reason of the love and favour which he had among all the people. The Bishop preached daily concerning peace, and said that war and strife are the occasion of all evil, but peace is the occasion of all good; wherefore Jesus Christ preached peace daily for so long as He was among us. Great was the good which the Bishop did, and all the people praised and blessed God Who had given them so good a pastor, and through the merits of that Bishop God blessed that city.

CHAPTER LXXVI

OF PERSECUTION

The Canon of Persecution considered the greatness of the burden that was entrusted to him by reason of his office, that he might use justice. It happened one day that he passed before a tavern, wherein had gathered together a great company of gamblers and of gluttons and of loose-living men, who were drinking in the tavern and singing and dancing and playing instruments of music. The Canon entered the tavern and bought wine, and danced with the gamblers, and recited these verses concerning Our Lady:

To thee, My Lady Mary, holy Maid,
I dedicate my will, which is aflame
With love so fierce that cannot be allayed,
Nor aught desires or loves beside thy fame.
All my desires are more effectual made
Than any such as on thee are not stayed,
Of men that love not, Mother of love, thy name:
Who loves thee not, no other love may claim.

Since all my love thy power has now obeyed
My knowledge and remembrance canst thou claim
For once my love before thy feet is laid
The rest are naught to me. Do thou inflame
With love our threefold powers,[1] O blessed Maid,
That we[2] may go to Syria unafraid
The souls of unbelievers fierce to tame
And give to Christians peace in Jesus' Name.

How many boast that if occasion came,
Right gladly they would die by sword or flame!
But oh, how few will go on God's Crusade
For when they think on Death they are dismayed!

2. When he had recited these verses, he begged all the company to be seated and to drink with him, and to relate such things as should be agreeable. While the Canon was among these folk, the men that passed along the street scoffed and reproved him because he was in the company of men so vile; but the Canon did all in his power that he might be loved by those that were in his company, and they all had great delight therein, and made him to be their chief, and listened to the words which he spake to them

[1] Memory, understanding and will.
[2] The reference is apparently to the clergy in general.

concerning Jesus Christ and the Apostles and the despising of this world. With such gentle words did he entertain them, and so often in every week did he resort to their company, that many of these men were converted thereby to good customs and habits, which they forsook not for the derision of the people.

3. The Canon went daily through the streets of that city, taking note of those that worked at their trades therein, namely, the drapers, shoe makers, furriers, blacksmiths, butchers and those that followed other trades; and, when he knew that any of them acted falsely in his profession, he reproached him immediately, and reproved him in such manner that he made the thing known to all those that were in the streets; wherefore all that traded in that city had both fear and respect for him, and many of them had ill-will towards him; but for fear of him all these men ceased from acting craftily in their business.

4. It came to pass one day that in the quarter of the drapers, while the drapers had gone to dine, the Canon came with a great multitude of loose-living men[1]; and climbing up to the shutters which the drapers place over their doors that there may be darkness in the shops, to the end that none may see clearly the quality of their cloth, they cut and tore in pieces and destroyed all those shutters and all the blinds which prevent men from seeing the cloth which is shown to them. When the drapers returned from dining, they found the Canon and his companions at this work of destruction in their shops. Great was the strife between them, and on either side were evil words spoken; and the Canon and his companions cried, "Justice! Justice!" Then the drapers went to the Court and made complaint concerning the Canon and his companions, The bailiff and the judge of the city reproved and reproached the Canon and his companions very severely, and blamed the Canon because he went about in the com-

[1] Lit. *ab gran re de tafurs e d arlots.*

pany of men so vile. Now in the Court was the Canon of Mercy, who had come to support the argument of his comrade, and he spake these words: "The Canon of Persecution labours for the sake of justice, the which justice he demands; and he commands that the light of the sun, which God gives for the eyes, wherewith it is His will that men may see, be not taken from the shops by the false drapers who deceive those men that buy cloth of them. These gamblers and harlots conceal not their vices, but make them manifest to all; the drapers conceal that which justice commands shall be shown; wherefore the drapers are viler people than the gamblers, inasmuch as they are the more opposed to justice." When the Canon of Mercy had spoken these words, the gamblers and the Canon of Persecution cried in a loud voice: "Wrong, wrong is in the King, who in his Court has not a bailiff or a judge that is a lover and a server of justice." Even to the King went the Canon and his comrades, crying, "Wrong! wrong!" And they made complaint against the judge and the bailiff and the drapers, and the King made an ordinance that from that time forward there should be nothing placed before any shop in the quarters of the drapers which should keep the light from those that desired in that place to buy cloth.

5. A certain knight died in that city, and, as they bore him to the church for burial, his wife and his kinsfolk, clothed in black, accompanied the body, and wept very bitterly and made great ado, tearing their hair and plucking at their faces and their clothing. Upon a great horse fully apparelled there rode a squire in armour, weeping and wailing for the death of his lord, and bearing his arms reversed. The Canon of Persecution met the body, and he perceived that, in respect of those that wept, the will of our Lord God was dishonoured, since it was He that had desired that the knight should pass from this world. The Canon saw that he must needs strive for the sake of

justice, and he went to the Canon of Poverty and to the Canon of Tears, begging them to help him to cause the honour to be done which it behoves man to pay to the will of God. So all these three canons went to the Prince and to the Bishop, and laid these words before them:

6. " Lords ! " said the Canon of Persecution, " In both of you is represented the Divine dominion. I beg you, then, to give me sentence, whether these persons that weep for the knight whom God has willed to slay do not dishonour to the will of God; and if just sentence be given that God is offended by them, I beg that satisfaction be made, to the end that no persons henceforward may accompany a corpse weeping or giving signs of sadness concerning that which is willed by the Divine Will, nor through their tears impede the Divine Office of the Mass." After this spake the Canon of Tears, saying that it is meet to weep that there may result therefrom contrition and devotion. " But," said he, " they that follow this corpse weep through vainglory and hypocrisy, wherefore their tears are opposed to the will of God, and for this cause I cry out upon them for that they do dishonour to the office which is commended to me in weeping for an unlawful cause." The Canon of Poverty spake likewise, and said that the money which was spent upon garments of mourning was stolen from the poor, and from the soul of the man deceased, and that therefore he desired to recover it, and that thenceforward that which would have been spent upon garments of mourning should be given to the poor, and that no man for the death of another should be garbed in mourning. The Prince and the Bishop took counsel with the notables of the city concerning the words which were spoken to them by the three canons, and they desired that constitution according to the will of the canons should be made for all time in that city upon the matters aforesaid.

7. At that time, after the feast of the Nativity of our Lord Jesus Christ, it came to pass that the Archdeacon

desired to sing his first Mass.[1] Great was the concourse and the assembly of many persons who had come from distant lands to do honour to the Archdeacon. When the Archdeacon had entered the church with great pomp and pride, and was about to begin the Mass, the Canon of Persecution cried in a loud voice, saying: " How simple was Jesus Christ, Who in His great humility desired to be born in the lowliest poverty! And behold, the Archdeacon prepares great pomp and solemnity for his Mass, and in this wise with pride and vainglory endeavours to be like to Jesus Christ! "

8. When the Canon cried out thus, the people rebuked him and threatened him; but none the less the Canon continued to cry for so long as he might concerning the folly which the Archdeacon committed, saying that it was a thing ill-beseeming that any man who had within him the devil of vainglory should sing Mass. Wherefore the Canon of Tears wept likewise for the dishonour which was done to the Mass, and the Bishop preached, that he might make peace between humility and the Archdeacon. And the Canon of Purity rebuked the Bishop who gave the Archdeacon permission to begin with pride that office which is the noblest and the holiest and the humblest that may be; and he rebuked the King who had come to the Mass, which was dishonoured by all such as had come to it.

9. In the month of April there was a great lack of rain in that country whither the Canon of Persecution had gone to preach; and the Bishop, with many of the clergy, and many religious men, made procession in honour of God, that He might give rain, for otherwise the wheat would be destroyed. The Canon, in the likeness of a fool, which he had oftentimes been accustomed to take, went through the town speaking certain foolish words, to the end that thereby

[1] *Missa Novella, i.e.* the first Mass to be sung by him after his ordination to the priesthood. The Archdeacon would not necessarily be a priest at the time of his appointment to his office.

he might inspire men to good works. After this wise went the Canon, and all men thought that he was a fool, and he placed himself in the centre of the procession and spake these words loudly that all might hear him: "Honoured is God by many clerks and many that are religious, to the end that He may give rain for the wheat; but few are the clerks or the religious who will go to honour God among the Saracens and the Jews and the unbelievers by whom the name of God is dishonoured and unknown. And if in this place there are many religious and many clerks who will pray to God for rain, how comes it that there are not so many, even in all the world, who will go to unbelievers to preach the Trinity and Incarnation and Passion of the Son of God?" Loudly did the Canon cry out these words, and for none would he be silent, and two clerks struck him and beat him sorely by reason of the words which he spake; and the more they beat him the more did he call upon justice to aid him for that he served her.

10. After the procession it came to pass that a thief was being led out to be hanged. The Canon enquired of those that led him wherefore they were about to hang him, and they answered and said that that man was a great gambler and a great thief; and he enquired of the man if that which they spake were true, and he answered that he had been a thief in that he cheated at dicing. Whereupon the Canon said that the King, rather than the thief, should be hanged, and upon a gibbet that was higher. All they that were in the household of the King were greatly displeased because this fool spake such evil words of the King. So they hanged the thief, and afterwards led the fool to the King with his hands bound, and repeated to him the words which he had spoken. The King desired to know the reason for the which he had spoken them, and he answered that it was because of justice, whose servant he was; for, since the King forbade not dicing in his land, that man, who would have been righteous and true but for the game

of dice, had become a thief. And when a Prince who is the occasion of wrong-doing hangs them that do that which he allows, he himself should be hanged rather than they that do wrong through him. For a great space did the King consider the words which the fool had spoken, and he said that the fool had changed his likeness and had taken the likeness of a fool that thereby he might make others wise; so he commanded that honour should be done to him, and that from thenceforward an ordinance and custom should be made that in that country there should be no more games of dice.

11. It came to pass one day that the Canon was leaving the city and going to another city, and he found upon the way a great multitude of men who came from Santiago and were clothed after the likeness of the Apostles. The Canon enquired of them of what Order they were, and they answered him saying that they were of the Order of the Apostles; and the Canon replied that his office and the name of their Order agreed the one with the other. The friars who named themselves of the Order of the Apostles begged him to expound to them the agreement whereof he spake, and the Canon said that one that is an Apostle should be persecuted unrighteously; wherefore, if they desired to be in the Order of the Apostles, it behoved them to preach the word of God in the cities and the towns and the castles and the villages through the which they would pass, and to reproach men for sins which they saw committed, and fear neither trials nor death, but go to preach the Catholic Faith to unbelievers, that they might be more like to the Apostles thereby. Even so went the Canon through every land, and he reproved all such as did not their duty in their office, and he was persecuted and tormented many times by those whom he reproved, but through his merits God did much good in all those countries where the Canon journeyed and sojourned, for, as the trials and the persecutions of the Canon were increased, so like-

wise God increased in the people through the merits of the Canon His virtues and His grace.

CHAPTER LXXVII

OF QUODLIBETS

ACCORDING to his custom the Bishop Blanquerna commanded that there should be a quodlibetal disputation, to the end that if a clerk or lay man saw any thing that might be bettered or made a custom, it should be propounded after the manner of questioning, that he might cause it to be done. It came to pass one day that while the Bishop was in chapter, having ordered a quodlibetal disputation, a lay man propounded this question: "Whether the Bishop, after he has risen in the morning, should go to recreation before he hear Mass." Many arguments were raised upon either side, but the Bishop resolved the question, saying that if lay men have the custom and rule to go first to Mass before they take recreation or do other business soever, how much more should clerks, who live by the patrimony of Holy Church, hear Mass or sing it before they do other business or go to take recreation! And if they do not this, then do they give to lay men bad example.

2. Many questions were propounded before the Bishop, and all of them he resolved and brought to an end; and then there were put to him ten questions, which are as follows:

¶ It is a question if Christians are to blame for the ignorance of unbelievers who know not of the Holy Catholic Faith.

¶ It is a question which have the greater power and opportunity: whether Catholics, who are in the way of truth, to convert unbelievers to the true way of life, or unbelievers, to drive Catholics from the truth and bring them into error.

¶ It is a question if Christians are to blame because the Saracens hold the Holy Land beyond the sea, wherein Jesus Christ was conceived and born and crucified.

¶ It is a question if the articles of the Christian Faith may be understood through necessary reasons.

¶ It is a question whether the Faith is of less or greater worth if the articles may be understood.

¶ It is a question what is the chiefest reason for the which man was created.

¶ It is a question if visitation should be made to bishops and archbishops, to the end that they may be deprived of their sees if they use their office ill.

¶ It is a question which is the greater sin, that the bishop should give the possessions of Holy Church to his kinsfolk, or that a Christian who has been a Jew should retain his possessions.

¶ It is a question if man should give the possessions of Holy Church to make peace between Christian princes and kings.

¶ It is a question which is the noblest work that man can undertake to honour God.

3. With great wonder did the Bishop marvel at the ten questions aforesaid, for they were of very great profundity, and much was spoken thereof upon the one hand and upon the other. The Bishop desired not to determine these ten questions, but went to the Court of Rome, that he might propound them before the Pope and the Cardinals and that they might determine and resolve them, and that the works should be done which accorded with the solution and determination thereof; and if it came to pass that they would not do this, that he should reprove and blame them before all men, fearing not to suffer trials or death.

4. The Bishop went to Rome to the Consistory, and before the Pope and the Cardinals he propounded these ten questions aforementioned, saying these words: " Error is in the world. There is defect of love and of devotion,

and valour is exiled from us according as is recounted in the Book of Religion.[1] Wherefore I ask that these ten questions be resolved and determined for me, and that in the solution and determination thereof satisfaction be made to justice, to the end that truth may cast out error from the world and charity and devotion may be increased." Greatly did the questions please the Holy Apostolic Father and the Cardinals and all the rest in the Court, and they enquired concerning the holy life of the Bishop whom they heard speaking many good words. While the Pope and the Cardinals made discussion concerning the manner wherein they should answer and determine the questions, it came to pass by the will of God that the Pope died, and the solution of the questions was deferred.

[1] See Chap. XLVIII, above.

ENDED IS THE THIRD BOOK

BEGINNETH THE FOURTH BOOK, WHICH IS OF THE APOSTOLIC ESTATE

CHAPTER LXXVIII

OF THE MANNER WHEREIN THE BISHOP BLANQUERNA BECAME POPE

RIGHT grieved was the Bishop Blanquerna at the death of the Pope, for many reasons, and especially by reason of the questions which he had propounded. Now while the Cardinals treated concerning the election of the next Pope, the Bishop went to a Cardinal and enquired of him if the election would be long delayed, begging him to bring it to pass that an answer might be given to the ten questions which he had propounded; for great was his desire to know the opinions of the Cardinals concerning the determination of the questions. The Cardinal answered the Bishop, and said that he believed that in a short time they would elect a Pope, since it was a thing ill-beseeming that the Papacy should go for long unfilled, and that he for his part would answer one of the ten questions, in a sense not determinate, but according to his own opinion; and he said that if the articles could be understood by necessary reasons, the faith would have less worth, because men would have less merit in believing it.

2. The Bishop answered and said that there are two manners of demonstration: the one is when a thing is demonstrated in such a way that no contradiction can be given thereto, as when it is said that a quadrangle has more angles than a triangle; in the other manner contradiction can be made, as when a cause is proved by the effect; and the sphere of faith is that wherein a demonstration can be contradicted. Wherefore he understood it not to be true that the articles could thus be demonstrated without contradiction, according to the former manner of demonstration, for if after the former manner they could be

demonstrated, it would be a thing impossible that the articles should be a matter of faith; but he asked whether the articles could be understood or no according to the second manner of demonstration; and he meant by demonstration that which could not be destroyed by necessary reasons, and by its contrary that which could be destroyed by necessary reasons. And he said that if the articles could be disproved by necessary reasons, he understood it to be proved by necessary reasons that faith will be the nobler and the greater and the more meritorious thereby, and understanding and charity will have the nobler disposition, according as it is signified in the first book of the *Demonstrations Concerning the Articles*.[1] And if it were not so, it would follow that faith and understanding worked mutual destruction the one to the other; and this is impossible, according to the conditions of the trees which are mentioned in the book which is called *Of the Gentile and of the Three Wise Men*.[2]

3. Greatly was the Cardinal pleased by the answer of the Bishop, and when he was in the Consistory with the Cardinals his companions, he extolled very highly the learning of the Bishop by reason of the reply which he had made to him. While the Cardinal thus praised the Bishop Blanquerna, it came to pass that the cleric who had aforetime ruled the diocese whereof Blanquerna was Bishop came to the Court with two brothers in religion and with a lay man; all four had learned Arabic right well, and they came to the Court to beg for a blessing, and for letters wherewith they might be sent to some other land to preach therein, and to convert the inhabitants thereof, and to suffer martyrdom, that God thereby might be praised. While they were in the Consistory with the Cardinals, and were

[1] Another of Lull's works.

[2] See p. 114. This book has not been translated into English as a whole, but some extracts, together with a summary of the book which explains fully the reference to the "trees," will be found in *Bulletin of Spanish Studies*, Vol. II, No. 7, June, 1925.

making their petition, the Bishop Blanquerna came among them. Right hearty was the welcome which he had of them; and the Cardinals made enquiry concerning Blanquerna, and they spake much good of him, and recounted the great good which he had done in the abbey and in his diocese, according to the manner which we have already related.

4. It came to pass one day that, while a certain Cardinal was dining, there came to his Court a jester[1] right fairly clothed and adorned: he was a man of pleasing speech and fair to look upon, and he sang and played instruments of music very cunningly. That jester was called the Jester of Valour, and was the same whom Blanquerna had met in the forest, when he likewise met Valour and the Emperor, according as is related in the chapter concerning Valour.[2] When the Cardinal had dined, the Jester sang songs and couplets which the Emperor had made concerning Our Lady Saint Mary and concerning Valour, and he brought forth his instruments of music, playing thereon the dances and the songs which the Emperor had composed in honour of Our Lady. Right pleasing was it to hear and to listen to the Jester and his instruments; and the Cardinal enquired of him concerning his welfare and his history.

5. "Lord!" said the Jester, "By the working of God it came to pass that my lord the Emperor and I encountered a holy man, Blanquerna by name, the which man was journeying through a great forest in search of a place wherein to make his hermitage and to adore and contemplate God all the days of his life. In that forest lived Valour, who made complaint concerning those that have changed her name, and persecute her in the world; wherefore the Emperor has appointed divers jesters who shall go through the world and be advocates of Valour, and among others he has sent me to this Court that I may sing the praise of Valour and reproach all such as are opposed

[1] *juglar*. See note, p. 175, above. [2] See p. 175, above.

to her, and praise Disvalour in her stead." Very pleasing to the Cardinal and to all that were of his Court were the words and the arguments of the Jester; and the Cardinal ordered that he should be given a fair cup of silver wherefrom he himself was wont to drink; but the Jester would not take it, and spake these words:

6. "Commandment has been made to me by the Emperor, my lord, and in my person upon the Holy Gospels have I sworn, that I will take naught of any man save only of the Emperor, my lord, who gives me wages every year which suffice abundantly for my wants; wherefore I hold myself excused from taking thy gift. And since through taking gifts a jester is corrupted and bound to praise those that should be blamed, and to blame those that should be praised, and since by such false praise and blame Valour is dishonoured, therefore the Lord Emperor would desire that I should take no gift of thee, nor that any other jester soever of his Court should dare to take any gift."

7. "Fair friend!" said the Cardinal. "Wouldst thou know the man whom thou callest Blanquerna if thou shouldst see him?" "Lord!" said the Jester, "Well indeed should I know him if I were to see him; but I think not that I could see him in this place, for I think that in places uninhabited and in deserts he has made his habitation; and in such a place does my lord the Emperor purpose to be his companion, when he has ordered his Empire, and when his son is fully grown that he may be able to reign in his stead." So the Cardinal sent for the Bishop Blanquerna that he should go to him, and the Jester of Valour saw him and knew him, and right great joy had he at seeing him; but he marvelled greatly that he was so nobly clad and wore upon his finger a golden ring. The Bishop enquired concerning the Emperor, and related to the Jester his own history, which the Jester desired to know that he might reprove him if his devotion which he had aforetime for the life of a hermit had become cold.

8. Great joy had they the one of the other, and the Jester prayed the Bishop that he would assist him in that Court to uphold Valour for so long as he was there, and the Bishop made him this promise. On the next morning after Mass, the Jester went to the Consistory wherein were the Cardinals awaiting each other to the end that they might treat concerning the election. Then the Jester spake these words: "Valour has greater hope of them that are greatest and most honoured in this world than she has of other men, and they who because of her have the most honour do her the most dishonour; wherefore they have the greater sin and blame, and thereby they shall have the greater punishment in the world to come, by reason of the greater dishonour which in this world they do to Valour, than they whom Valour has less greatly honoured in this world."

9. Each of the Cardinals considered very deeply the words which the Jester spake; and the Cardinal related to his companions that which the Jester had spoken concerning Blanquerna. By reason of these words which the Cardinal spake to them concerning him, and of others which they had already heard of him, it became the will of the Cardinals that the Bishop Blanquerna should be created Pope, and they all said and desired that he should be Pope. So they said the *Veni Creator Spiritus* and the *Te Deum Laudamus*, and they desired that Blanquerna should take his seat in the Apostolic Chair. But Blanquerna desired it not, and spake these words:

10. "It is bruited through all the world that the Pope with his companions could order the whole world if he so desired; and since the world is in such discord and disorder, therefore is it a dreadful thing to be Pope, and great sin is to be attributed to the Pope if he use not his power in ordering the world, and if his will follow not all the power which God has given to the Papacy for the ordering of the world. Wherefore, as I am unworthy to have power so great, because I have defect of knowledge and will, there-

fore apostolical power so great and so noble should not be committed to one of knowledge and will so weak; for the which cause I refuse the apostolical power, and I demand that answer be made to me concerning the questions which I have propounded in this Court."

11. The more vehemently did the Bishop Blanquerna excuse himself and refuse the office of Pope, the more was the will of the Cardinals kindled and inflamed in their desire that he should become Pope, for it is a condition of election that he who excuses himself the more vehemently, and refuses an office, should the rather be elected, provided that he fulfil the other conditions which make a man worthy to be elected. While they spake thus and Blanquerna desired in no wise to be Pope, a certain Cardinal who himself desired to be Pope said that he would speak privately with his companions, and he spake to them these words: "Many a time does it chance that men through craft and skill make others to beg and force them to take that which they desire to have; and it seems to me that the Bishop Blanquerna causes himself to be begged to accept the office of Pope to the end that we may have the greater desire to create him Pope. And if he have such will, by reason of that same will he is unworthy to be Pope."

12. Much thought did the Cardinals give to that which this Cardinal had spoken; but because in the words of Blanquerna there was signified neither craft nor skill, and because of the good reputation which he had, and because this Cardinal himself desired to be Pope, as they already knew by certain presumptions, therefore knew they that the craft and skill were in the words of the Cardinal, and they desired that at all hazards Blanquerna should be Pope; but Blanquerna would not consent, until a Cardinal said to him that if he were Pope he could ordain that which he desired should be done concerning the solution of the questions aforesaid. Wherefore the Bishop Blanquerna, with great fear, and trusting that God would aid him, and

with intent to produce much fruit and utility through his ordering of that which the questions signified, gave consent, and accepted the apostolical office, and spake these words:

13. "Both knowledge and will do I lack whereby I may be fitted to receive the apostolic power. If by you I am elected Pope, I beg of you aid that through our united will and knowledge we may use the power that is given to me and cause God to be known and loved, and His people to have happiness through Him. If this ye do not, then do ye do sin and wrong to me." All the Cardinals gave him promise most cordially that they would aid him with their whole will according to the freedom of power and the knowledge which God had given to them, and according to the way wherein God had bound their wills to serve Him. So it came to pass that the Bishop Blanquerna was created Pope.

CHAPTER LXXIX

OF THE ORDINANCE WHICH THE POPE BLANQUERNA MADE IN HIS COURT

According as we have related, Blanquerna was elected Pope: Blessed be God because of it! Now Blanquerna the Pope, before he would ordain aught in his Court, delayed for a time that he might see what was the estate thereof, and each day he wrote, in certain tablets which he carried, those things that were to be ameliorated in his Court. It chanced one day that the Pope was at his window, and he saw a Cardinal approaching with a very numerous retinue, which belonged to his house, of men full nobly clad and mounted; and in this retinue was a great multitude of men who were of the kinsfolk of the Cardinal. Immediately following him the Pope Blanquerna saw another Cardinal with a small retinue, less nobly clad and adorned. Long did the Pope consider that which he had seen in the two Cardinals; and when he was in the Consistory he spake these words to the Cardinal who had come with the smaller retinue and humbly clad:

2. "I desire to know wherefore thou hast not come to my Court with so great a retinue and with vestments so noble as this other Cardinal who came before thee, since thou shouldst honour my Court as greatly as this other, seeing that thou hast the same income as he." "Lord!" answered the Cardinal, "I spend upon my retinue and upon my alms all the income which I receive from my office, and I have sworn that I will take naught for the service of any man; and since my income suffices not for a greater retinue, therefore have I not been able to bring one with me." Then the Pope enquired of the other Cardinal wherefore he had come with a company so great and so nobly clad, and the Cardinal answered and said that it was to honour his Court. The Pope commanded enquiry to be made concerning his life, and he found that that Cardinal took money for the service of men, and had broken the sacrament and the promises that he had made when he was elected Cardinal; and the men who gave to him, that he might prosper their affairs, accompanied him whensoever he came to the Court; and for this reason he brought a greater retinue than the others.

3. It came to pass one day that the Pope invited all the Cardinals to visit him, and held a great Court on that day. When they had eaten, there came into the Court a man with shaven head and clothed in the garb of a fool. In the one hand he carried a sparrowhawk, and in the other hand a cord to the which was tied a dog which he led. This man greeted the Lord Pope and the Cardinals and all the Court on behalf of the Lord Emperor, and he spake these words: "I am Ramón the Fool, and I come to this Court by the commandment of the Emperor that I may exercise my profession and seek my companions." When he had spoken these words, he gave the sparrowhawk food, and afterwards

made it come to his hand two or three times. After this he struck and beat the sparrowhawk with the cord to the which his dog was tied, and again he cried to it that it should come to his hand; but the sparrowhawk, because the Fool had struck it and put it from him, escaped and flew out of the palace of the Pope, and became wild. When Ramón the Fool had lost his sparrowhawk, he struck the dog very severely two or three times; and whensoever he called it the dog returned willingly to him.

4. "Ramón the Fool!" said the Pope, "Who art thou, and wherefore sayest thou that thou hast come to this Court to seek thy companions? And what is the significance of that which thou hast done in our presence with the sparrowhawk and with the dog?" "Lord!" said Ramón the Fool, "I was aforetime in the Court of the Emperor, and I learned to be a fool, to the end that I might gather together money; and the Emperor has spoken to me so often of the Passion of Jesus Christ and of the nobility of God, that I desire to be a fool that I may give honour and glory to Him, and I will have no art nor device in my words by reason of the greatness of my love. And since thy Court has greater honour than any Court beside, by reason of the Passion of my Beloved and of His Incarnation, therefore do I think to find in thy Court many companions who are of my office. The sparrowhawk signifies the men who assist not to sustain the honour and governance of thy Court without money or rewards; and when a man prays them and gives them naught they become disheartened, afflicted and slothful[1]; wherefore they escape from among men and become wild. The dog signifies those men that are so greatly inflamed and kindled with love for the honour and the governance of the Court, to the end that God may therein be honoured, that without satisfaction being given them by any man for the trials which they bear, they suffer

[1] Lit. "their hearts are struck with sloth and with affliction": the sense is slightly strained so that the similitude may be adhered to.

these trials and anxieties by reason of men that desire to gain advancement in the Court, and they are pleasing to all men and agreeable."

5. When Ramón the Fool had thus exercised his office, and had answered the Pope, the Jester of Valour sang and played instruments of music very sweetly in honour of Valour. After this he spake these words: "To honour a great lord, honour is done to his horse, which is given a fair saddle and harness; and if in his mind that lord have love for the virtues and hatred for the vices, therein is Valour honoured, both in his mind and in his harness; and if that lord is honoured who loves vice and hates virtue, then is Valour dishonoured and her enemy is honoured, even he who loves the dishonour of Valour." "Jester of Valour!" said the Pope. "What is this that thy words signify?" "They signify," he answered, "the questions which thou hast made to thy two Cardinals: the one honours Valour with wrong, perjury and vainglory; but the other honours her with justice, truth, humility and fortitude."

6. When the Jester had spoken the words aforesaid, the Pope wept and said: "Ah! Canon of Tears, I would that thou wert in this Court, to help me weep for the dishonour that is done herein to Valour, through the which dishonour that honour which it beseems my Lord to have is no more." Bitterly wept the Pope, saying that if the dishonour which Valour received in the Court were not cast therefrom, and Valour were not honoured in its stead, all the Cardinals would sin against Valour, and greatest of all would be the sin of the Pope their lord, to whom the Cardinals promised that with all their knowledge and will they would help him to maintain the power which they had in honouring Valour. Excepting only the Chamberlain, all the Cardinals said to the Pope that they were prepared to agree together, and to make ordinance of all things, to the end that Valour might be restored to the honour which was aforetime hers.

7. Weeping, and with great devotion, and remembering the heavy burden which had been laid upon him, namely that he should honour the Son of God, the Pope spake these words: "Fifteen are ye Cardinals that have been given to me as companions that I may be preserved and aided as Vicar[1] upon earth of Jesus Christ. Let us divide into fifteen parts the *Gloria in Excelsis Deo;* and let the first part be assigned to me, because through the dignity of my office I am the first among you. To each of you Cardinals let there likewise be given a part according to the antiquity and dignity of his office, and let each part follow the other according to its order; and let each part be an office, which each one of you shall hold himself bound to honour and maintain in the Court, that Jesus Christ may be honoured in the Court, and that through it He may be honoured in all countries of the world." All the Cardinals held that which the Pope said to be good; so the Pope took the words "Gloria in Excelsis Deo"; and the Cardinal who was senior in the Court took "Et in terra pax hominibus bonæ voluntatis"; and after this the Cardinals took the other parts according to their order and turn, and to each part was assigned its proper office, and each Cardinal was named after that part of the *Gloria in Excelsis Deo* which came to him in order.

8. When the Pope and the Cardinals had made the ordinance aforesaid, they ordained that each of the Cardinals should have an equal income to be spent upon his necessities, and that each should have a certain number of persons and of beasts according as befits justice, temperance and humility; and that beside their expenses they should have in equal fashion a certain allowance over and above their incomes to devote to expenses extraordinary, and that this should satisfy them entirely, and that they should be allowed to take no gift, unless it were of viands, and that that

[1] *procurador:* this word is generally translated "representative," and occasionally, when the context gives it this meaning, "advocate."

Cardinal who should take a gift of any man should lose his office; and if he resigned it not, that the Pope and the Cardinals should live upon bread and water every Friday until he had resigned it. This ordinance was confirmed by the Pope and by the Cardinals, and promise and sacrament were made concerning it, and officers and spies were appointed who should keep watch, lest any Cardinal should sin against the ordinance aforesaid; and to these spies were assigned others who should spy out if they used their office well, and, if they did not so, they should lose their office and nevermore have preferment. Right well was ordinance made concerning the establishment aforesaid, for it was very needful that it should be kept, that the Cardinals might have none occasion of dissension nor of pride against each other, by reason of a difference in power, and that the people who came to the Court should not return despoiled, neither in poverty, neither with evil example, nor should they speak ill of the Pope and of his companions, but rather they should have the greater devotion to praise and serve God by reason of the holy life, fraternity and charity of the Pope and of his companions.

9. After the ordinances and establishment aforesaid had been made, it was ordained that from the possessions of Holy Church and from the superfluity which remained to bishops and archbishops and other prelates, after expending the possessions of Holy Church, should be made the offices which the Cardinals had taken of the *Gloria in Excelsis Deo*, and that one of the Cardinals should be appointed to answer for the expenses of all these offices, and that all the bishops, archbishops and prelates and their subjects should furnish that Cardinal with the wherewithal to provide for these offices.

10. It was ordained by the Pope and the Cardinals that once in every week the Pope should hold chapter with the Cardinals only, and that each should make accusation concerning the others, even as is done by monks, and that each

Cardinal should ask pardon for his sins in presence of the rest. The establishment was ordained by them likewise that each Cardinal should hold chapter upon one day in the week with his officers. Afterwards it was ordered that one Cardinal should hold chapter with the scriveners upon one day in the week, and then another, and the same with the judges and the advocates according to rotation.

11. Another establishment was ordained by the Pope and the Cardinals, which was very needful, to wit, that throughout the world they should have representatives who should send them letters or messengers reporting the condition of every country, to the end that if any irregularity or change were there, or there were need of any amelioration, they should be able to treat immediately concerning that which was good for the betterment of those countries. After this manner did the Pope Blanquerna order and direct his Court. And all the good and favourable ordinances which he made in his Court can no man recount. And the merit which he will have thereby, who may tell it?

CHAPTER LXXX

GLORIA IN EXCELSIS DEO

The Pope Blanquerna went into the Consistory with the Cardinals to the end that through their good works glory might be given to God in the Heavens[1]; and the Pope said to the Cardinals that he prayed them that they would assist him to use his office to the glory of God, in such wise that they might be able to bring men back to the first intent of the offices and the sciences, namely, that glory might be given to God; for the world has come to such a sinful state, that there is scarce any man who has his intent directed toward that thing for the which he was created, nor for the which he holds the office which is his. While the Pope

[1] *en los cels.*

spake thus with the Cardinals, a Saracen messenger came before him and the Cardinals, and presented to him a letter from the Soldan of Babylon. In that letter were written many things, and among them the Soldan said to the Pope that he marvelled greatly concerning him, and concerning all the kings and princes of the Christians, that in conquering the Holy Land beyond the seas they acted according to the manner of the prophet Mahomet, who held by force of arms the lands which he conquered. He marvelled that the Pope and the Christians worked not after the manner of Jesus Christ and of the Apostles, who through preaching and through martyrdom converted the world, and that they followed not the manner of those who preceded them in conquering other countries; for this cause, he said, God willed not that they should possess the Holy Land beyond the seas. These letters the Saracen brought to the Holy Apostolic Father, and like letters brought he to the kings and princes of the Christians. Deeply thought the Pope and the Cardinals upon the words which the Soldan had written to them; and Ramón the Fool spake these words: "Faith sent Hope to Contrition, that she might send her Devotion and Pardon, to the end that they might honour her in those places wherein her Beloved is dishonoured." The Jester of Valour said that Valour is brought to great dishonour in those places wherein the Son of God and the Apostles did her more grace and honour than in any place which is in the world. After these words there entered the Court a messenger bringing the news that two unbelievers had been suborned to slay a Christian king, and that they had now themselves been delivered up to a cruel death. When he had spoken these words, the Jester of Valour said: "Of what avail are the humility and charity of Jesus Christ which He had himself towards His people, when He willed to suffer Passion of them, if unbelievers, who are in error, have greater devotion in dying for their master than have Christians in honouring their superior?" The

Fool saw two Cardinals speaking, and he supposed that they spake of his Beloved, but they spake of the election of two bishops who had been elected after a contest; wherefore the Fool said to the Cardinals that the most pleasant words are those that are between the Lover and the Beloved.

2. The Pope was marvellously moved to ordain how that example might be given of the faith of Holy Church and how the devotion to the honour of God which aforetime existed might return; so he sent messengers throughout divers lands to the superiors of religious houses and to the Masters of the Temple and of the Hospital that they should come to speak with him concerning the making of ordinances whereby glory should be given to God. When all these had come, and were before the Pope and the Cardinals, Ramón the Fool spake thus: "The Lover and the Beloved met, and kept silence with their tongues; and their eyes, wherewith they made signs of love, were in tears; and the love of the one spake with the love of the other." "This story," said the Jester of Valour, "has relation to that which has been reported to the Holy Father and the Cardinals concerning the Soldan and the assassins; and if naught that is useful follows therefrom, great wrong is done to Valour, and the most honourable of creatures, who die for love, are not loved; albeit it is of greater valour that lovers should speak the one to the other than that mouths should eat." The Fool said: "A certain man wrote, and in a book he wrote the names of lovers and loved, and a man that was a lover enquired of him if in that book he had written the name of his beloved; and he that wrote said to him: "Hast thou eaten food that was cooked with the fire of love? And hast thou washed thine hands with the tears of thine eyes? And art thou inebriated and become as a fool through the love which thou hast drunk? Hast thou ever been in peril that thou mightest honour thy beloved? Hast thou the materials of love wherewith a man may make ink for thy beloved to write? If all these things

be not so, then is thy beloved not worthy to be written of in this book."

3. After these words, the Pope and the Cardinals and the religious, to honour the glory of God, ordained that to all monks that had learning there should be assigned friars to teach divers languages, and that throughout the world there should be builded divers houses, which for their needs should be sufficiently provided and endowed, according to the manner of the monastery of Miramar, which is in the Island of Majorca. Right good seemed this ordinance to the Pope and to all the rest, and the Pope sent messengers through all the lands of the unbelievers to bring back certain of them to learn their language and that they at Rome might learn the tongues of these unbelievers, and that certain men should return with them to preach to the others in these lands, and that to those unbelievers that learned Latin, and gained a knowledge of the Holy Catholic Faith, should be given money and garments and palfreys, that they might praise the Christians, who when they had returned to their own lands would continue to assist and maintain them.

4. Of the whole world the Pope made twelve parts, and appointed to represent him twelve men, who should go each one throughout his part and learn of its estate, to the end that the Pope might know the estate of the whole world. It came to pass that those who went to the unbelievers brought from Alexandria and from Georgia and from India and Greece Christians who were monks, that they might dwell among us, and that their will might be united with the will of our monks, and that during this union and relationship they might be instructed in divers manners concerning certain errors against the faith, and should then go and instruct those that were in their country. Wherefore the Pope sent also some of our monks to the monks aforesaid, and ordered that each year they should send to him a certain number of their friars, that they

might dwell with us, and, while they dwelt among us, learn our language.

5. " Beloved sons ! " said the Pope to the monks : " Jews and Saracens are among us who believe in error, and disbelieve and despise the Holy Faith whereby we are bound to honour the glory of God. I desire and ask that to these Jews and Saracens who are in the lands of the Christians there be assigned certain persons to teach them Latin and to expound the Scriptures, and that within a certain time they shall learn these, and if they have not done so, that there shall follow punishment; and while they learn let them be provided for from the possessions of Holy Church; and after they have learned let them be made free men and honoured above all others, and then will they convert their fellows and be the better fitted to understand the truth and to convert these others."

6. When the Pope had spoken these words, the Chamberlain said that, if the Pope made this establishment, the Jews and the Saracens that are among the Christians would take flight to other lands and the income of Holy Church would be diminished. But Ramón the Fool said to the Chamberlain: " Once on a time a man loved a woman, and said to her that he loved her more than any woman beside, and the woman enquired of him wherefore he loved her more than any other woman, and he replied that it was because she was fairer than any. The woman made sign with her hand in a certain direction, saying that in that direction there was a woman that was fairer; and when the man turned and looked in that direction the woman said that if there were another woman that was fairer, he would love her more, and this signified that his love to her was not perfect." The Jester of Valour said that if there were another thing better than God the Chamberlain would love it more than God; so there was question among them which thing was the more contrary to the glory of God and to Valour, whether the diminution of the income of Holy

Church or the dishonour which the Jews and the Saracens show to the glory of God and to Valour.

7. As the Pope desired, even so was it ordained. After this the Pope enquired of the Masters of the Temple and of the Hospital what part they would take in honouring the glory of God, and both these Masters answered and said that they were already in the Holy Land beyond the seas to defend that land and to give example of the Catholic Faith. The Jester enquired of Ramón the Fool if the love which he had to his Beloved was growing in proportion as his Beloved gave him greater pleasures. The Fool answered: "If I could love Him more, it would follow that I should love Him less if He diminished the pleasures which He gives me." And he said likewise that, since he could not do other than love his Beloved, neither could he increase the love which he bore to Him; but the trials which he suffered grew daily, and the greater they were, the more were the joys increased which he had in loving his Beloved." The Holy Apostolic Father said to the two Masters that from that which was signified by the aforesaid words, it followed that to honour the glory of God both the Masters should make ordinance whereby an Order should be created, that the Jester of Valour should not cry out upon the dishonour which is done to Valour by disputes concerning that wherein there would be agreement if they made an Order. He said furthermore that they should use their houses and masterships to make schools and places of study, wherein their knights should learn certain brief arguments, by means of the *Brief Art of finding Truth*[1]; that they might prove the articles of the Holy Faith and give counsel to Masters, princes and prelates through the art aforesaid; and that they might learn divers languages, and go to kings and princes of the unbelievers that one knight might challenge another to maintain, by feats of arms or by learning, the honour and truth which beseem the valour

[1] See pp. 114, 332.

that is in the Holy Catholic Faith. The ordinance aforementioned was granted to the Pope by the two Masters and by all the friars of their Order, and Ramón the Fool spake these words: "Humility conquered Pride, and the Lover said to his Beloved: 'If Thou, Beloved, wert to die, I should go to weep upon Thy tomb.' And the Beloved answered: 'Weep before the Cross, which is My monument.' The Lover wept bitterly, and said that through over much weeping the sight of his eyes was blinded and knowledge became clear to the eyes of his understanding. Wherefore the Order did all that it could to honour the glory of God."

8. According to the manner aforesaid, the Holy Apostolic Father made ordinance concerning the ordinance of the glory of God, and he appointed officers and ministers, and representatives to see that this order was carried out; and he endeavoured daily with all his power to bring it to pass that benefit might come from the ordinance aforementioned. It came to pass one day that Ramón the Fool and the Jester of Valour brought ink and paper before the Pope, and said that they desired to send in writing the aforementioned ordinance to the Soldan and the Caliph of Bagdad, that they might see if they had subjects as noble as those of the Pope, or could make as fair an ordinance as the Pope had made to do honour to the glory of God in the Heavens and cause Valour to return to the world.

9. It came to pass one day that the Cardinal of Domine Deus sent to a certain country to spy out the government of the Bishop and all the princes of that country. While this spy was in that land, commandment came from the Pope to the Bishop that he should provide yearly for fifty Tartars and ten friars whom the Pope sent to that diocese, that the Tartars might teach their language to the friars and the friars teach theirs to the Tartars, according as it was ordained in the Court; and that the Bishop should found a monastery without the city where they should live,

and that endowment should be given to it in perpetuity. Greatly was the Bishop displeased at the commandment which the Pope had given him, bewailing the expense thereof; and he spake ill of the Pope and of the Cardinals in the presence of the prince of that country. But the Prince rebuked the Bishop sternly, and said that never before had he heard of any Pope or any Cardinals who had to such extent and to the best of their power made ordinances whereby the glory of God was so greatly honoured, and that he himself, to honour the glory of God, and to follow the good example which the Pope and the Cardinals gave him, desired to have a share in the expenses which the students would incur, and to bear the moiety of the cost of the monastery. The King praised the ordinance of the Pope and of the Cardinals greatly, and said that it seemed to him that the time had come wherein God desired that His servants should do Him great honour, and that those that had strayed should be converted.

10. So soon as the spy had heard the words which the Prince and the Bishop had uttered, he reported in writing to his lord the Cardinal those very words that he had heard, and he wrote likewise that, according to the knowledge which he had gained, the Bishop had bought a castle for a nephew of his for twenty thousand pounds. These letters were read in the Consistory before the Pope and the Cardinals, and the Cardinal to whom the letter had come wrote down the name of the king, to the end that, if an expedition were set on foot,[1] or an occasion occurred wherein the Church might show any favour to a king, it should be shown to that king. The Pope sent his messenger to the King, and gave him thanks, and commanded that the castle should be his, and that he should

[1] The context does not make it clear whether a royal expedition is meant, which the Pope might aid either materially or spiritually, or a papal expedition, which a secular prince might be chosen to command. Possibly the writer has either case in mind.

give ten thousand pounds for the building of the monastery; and he sent to the chapter of that diocese commanding that, if the Bishop desired not to hold his office and contribute that which he commanded him to give, they should elect another in his place, and that the Bishop who had spoken ill of him should have only the income of a canon. The Fool said to the Beloved: "Pay me and give me my recompense for the time that I have served Thee." The Beloved increased in his Lover his love for Him and the grief which he had suffered for the sake of love, and He said to him: "Behold the Pope and the Cardinals who honour the glory of their Lord." And the Jester sent letters by Devotion to comfort Valour, who wept for the dishonour which for long her enemies had done to her Lord.

11. Throughout all the world went forth the fame of the holy life of the Pope and the great good which he did, and daily was valour increased and dishonour diminished. The good which came from the ordinance which the Pope had established illumined the whole world, and brought devotion to them that heard the ordinance recounted; and throughout all the world was sent in writing an account of the process of the making thereof. It chanced one day that the Pope had sent to a Saracen king a knight who was also a priest, and of the Order of Science and Chivalry. This knight by force of arms vanquished ten knights one after the other on different days, and after this he vanquished all the wise men of that land by his arguments, and proved to all that the Holy Catholic Faith was true. By messengers of such singular talent, and by many more, did the ordinance aforementioned, which was established by the Holy Apostolic Father, illumine the world.

12. It came to pass that of the fifty Tartars who learned our language and gained understanding of our faith, thirty were converted, and the Pope sent them with five friars to the Court of the Khan. These thirty, together with the

five friars who had learned the language of the Tartars, came before the great Khan, and preached the faith of the Christians, and converted many people in his Court, and they turned the great Khan from the error wherein he lived and made him to doubt it; and after a time, by process of this doubt, he came to everlasting life.

13. In a certain land there were studying ten Jews and ten Saracens together with ten friars of religion; and when they had learned our holy law and our letters, the half of them were converted to our law, and they preached our law to other Jews, and to Saracens our holy Christian faith, in the presence of many that had not yet been converted, and thus did they daily and continually. And because the Papal Court did all that was in its power, and through the continuance of the disputation, and because truth has power over falsehood, God gave grace to all the Jews and Saracens of that country so that they were converted and baptized, and preached to others the Holy Faith. Wherefore the good and the honour which, through the Pope Blanquerna, was done to the Christian Faith, can in no wise be recounted.

CHAPTER LXXXI

ET IN TERRA PAX HOMINIBUS BONÆ VOLUNTATIS

THE Cardinal who served the office of "Et in terra pax hominibus bonæ voluntatis" sent his spies throughout the city of Rome to spy out if any man was in strife with any other; and the same thing did he throughout divers countries; and daily did he treat concerning peace even so much as he could. It came to pass one day that a spy whom he had sent through the city of Rome told him that in that city were a Christian and a Jew who disputed daily concerning their laws, and that they had great strife the one with the other while they disputed, and that each bore the other ill-will because of it. The Cardinal went to that place wherein they disputed, and reasoned with them, saying these words:

2. "It is the nature of understanding that it comprehends more clearly when a man is joyful and glad than when he is angered, for anger disturbs the understanding, wherefore the understanding may not comprehend that which it would have comprehended if the man had not been angered. Another property has understanding in its comprehension, to wit, that a man affirms to be possible anything which the will desires that the understanding shall comprehend; for if, before the understanding comprehend it, he affirm that impossibility is therein, the understanding will not be prepared to comprehend the possibility or impossibility which is to be understood therein. Another property yet has the understanding when it soars aloft in comprehension of any matter, namely, that the will may love equally that which it affirms or denies, before the understanding comprehend it; for when the will is inclined to the one side before the understanding has comprehension thereof, the understanding is impeded from comprehension. All these manners and many more are needful to the understanding that it may comprehend; and if it may not comprehend through all of them, it behoves a man to have recourse to the *Brief Art of finding Truth*, which is an art whereby the understanding may soar aloft in comprehension, even as the voice, through the art of music, soars aloft in song." After this manner the Cardinal gave instruction to the two wise men who were disputing together, and through the humility which he caused to come to them, they became friends the one of the other, disputing and agreeing with each other in love and conceding to each other the truth. The Cardinal left them, and gave them his benediction, and said to them that they should send each other gifts, that there might be occasion of friendship between them, through the which friendship they would have understanding the more easily the one of the other.

3. At that time it came to pass that two Christian kings, of great nobility and power, had had long strife and dispute between themselves, and had attacked each other in battle. The Cardinal went to the two kings with letters from the Pope that he might make peace between them, and bare many jewels and much money that he might give jewels to them both, and many gifts to their counsellors. With all his power the Cardinal endeavoured to make peace between these two kings, and since they had continued for long in their lawsuit and there had been no peace between them, therefore was each king so incensed against the other that the Cardinal could not make peace, nor even a truce. Wherefore the Cardinal wrote to the Pope in these words:

4. " There was war between God and the human race when Adam had sinned and all had strayed from the peace and blessing of God. And because this strife was very grievous, it beseemed God in His own person to come and make peace and concord between God and His creatures; wherefore came the person of the Son to take flesh within Our Lady Saint Mary, and He suffered death upon the Cross when He was grown to be a man." These letters were read in the presence of the Pope and of the Cardinals, and Ramón the Fool related this story: " A certain lady had great strife with her husband. But a fair son was born to them, and because of the son whom each one loved, they had peace and concord for all the time of their lives." The Jester of Valour said that humility, charity and peace were sisters of Valour.

5. Long did the Pope consider that which was signified by the words aforesaid, and by virtue of his will to work that which was good he understood the significance of the words. The Pope went with four Cardinals to the two kings, who dwelt far from Rome, and to each of them he gave gifts and jewels, and he held a great Court of prelates and princes and barons, and this Court he held at great

cost. Before the Pope spake concerning the making of peace between the two kings, he said in the presence of all that he had come to that land to set on foot an expedition against the enemies of the Cross, and he desired and prayed that both the kings would take part in the expedition, and that one of them would go against the Saracens that are in the East, and the other against those that are in the West; and, when they had conquered them, that they would unite, and the one would come to the other that both might conquer the Saracens that are in the South. The Pope gave great indulgences and ordered a Crusade, and from the possessions of Holy Church he made great gifts to the two kings and to other barons, and he placed their lands under his own protection and command. So pleasing was this ordinance to the two kings, and so great mind had they to do deeds of arms, that both agreed to entrust their claims to the power of the Pope; and they joined the expedition and set aside the matter which had been at dispute between them, that no harm might come to their expedition by reason thereof.

6. The two kings set on foot a very great expedition, and with them went many friars who had learned Arabic, as messengers to the Saracens, that they might convert them ere the two kings slew them and their souls went to everlasting fire. The Pope returned to Rome, and did all that was in his power for the success of the expedition. The Cardinal who had the office of peace-maker remained for a long time in the land of the two kings that he might set the people at peace with each other. It came to pass one day that, as he was riding in the city, he passed through the chief square, wherein two drapers were disputing the one with the other, because each had envy of the other concerning his gains, thinking that the other took his gains from him. The Cardinal purchased their two shops, which belonged to a burgess of the city, and had two others made, the one far from the other, and gave the one shop to the

one draper and the other to the other; and of the two shops which he had bought he had two houses made; in each he put a man who dwelt there as a recluse and lived upon alms, and preached peace, and spake good words to the people that dwelt in that square, and to others that passed through the streets.

7. It came to pass that a spy of the Cardinal passed through the square, and saw that both the recluses were at strife, and spake evil words, having each one envy of the other. When the Cardinal knew this, he took one recluse from that place, and put him in another place far from that from the which he had taken him, and from the house whence he had taken him he made a place wherein should be men to whom the recluse should speak words concerning peace and God; and a like place made he for the other recluse. Great was the good which both the recluses did in that city, and very good was this establishment, since in public places, wherein so much evil is done, there should be men to mortify these evils through the example which they give of good living, and through devout words, and the reading of books of prayer and devotion.

8. The Cardinal went into another city which was situate between the territory of an archbishop and a king, and they disputed concerning the boundaries of the city, for the which cause there was great strife between them. The Cardinal could not make them to agree, for he could not cast out the avarice which was deep rooted in the soul of either. So the Cardinal went to Rome and prayed the Pope that he would make peace between the archbishop and the king. Immediately the Pope went to that city wherein was the strife. He called the king and the archbishop and made them a great feast and banquet. On the same day the Pope preached concerning peace, saying how Jesus Christ preached peace daily. Before they went to dine, the Pope desired that the king would expound to him the cause of his strife with the archbishop. The king showed the Pope

the boundaries which, as he said, marked out his dominion, and the Pope said to the king that he had understood that the dominion of the king extended farther, and he desired that the king would take some of that which pertained to the Church; for greater was the worth of the peace which would follow therefrom than was the income of the land of the archbishop. When the king saw that the Pope desired to give him more of the city than he asked of him, he said to the Pope: "Lord! Come thou and take thy part of my dominion whereof for a long time I have deprived the Church." And the king desired to assign to the Church more than the archbishop asked. Great strife and dispute was there before the Pope and the king could be made to agree; for each desired to give up to the other his right; wherefore the question was put into the power of two men who knew the truth concerning the boundaries, and their will was followed; so peace and friendship were made between the king and the archbishop.

9. In a city wherein sojourned the Cardinal who went seeking peace, was an old man who had a young wife. So deeply did he love her that he had great jealousy because of her, the which jealousy vexed him greatly; his wife likewise and all his household were greatly vexed because of it. It came to pass one day that this man was in the square, and the Cardinal passed by, and all the people said: "Behold the Cardinal who goes in search of peace." This good man wondered within himself if the Cardinal could give him peace likewise, and bring him out of the trouble wherein jealousy had set him. When the Cardinal went to his lodging, the jealous man recounted to him secretly his estate, and begged him to give him counsel as to how he could have peace. The Cardinal spake many good words to this man, and asked him to come daily to speak with him for a space; and the Cardinal spake in secret with the wife of the man, counselling her not to embroider her garments nor to set colours in her face nor to give in her

person any signs of lust, and to do all honour to her husband and to have patience when he spake sternly. When the Cardinal had instructed the lady without the knowledge of her husband, he preached daily concerning God and holiness of life, speaking evil of lust and praising chastity; and wheresoever he preached he took with him always this good man who was jealous; and when he was in his house the Cardinal invited him to come and read with him from Holy Scripture. For a long time the Cardinal remained in that city that he might bring peace to that man. So the jealousy which he had aforetime remained no longer in him, for the words which the Cardinal had spoken concerning God, and the good life of his lady, weaned him from the custom of thinking upon such things as make a man to be jealous.

10. The Cardinal went to another city to find out if there were any trouble therein. It came to pass one day that, according to his custom, the Cardinal sent to four notable men of the city, that they might watch and see if in that city there were need to set any man at peace with any other. Among these four notables was a man of honoured lineage who had been very wealthy, and he was in great trial night and day, casting in his mind for means whereby he might maintain the estate of honour which he had begun to maintain and had for a long time kept; wherefore that good man besought counsel of the Cardinal, relating to him the trouble which his thoughts had given him. That man had no wife and he had five sons. The Cardinal counselled him that he should enter a religious order that he might have no more fear of coming to poverty and shame; and he commended one of his sons to the Prince of that land, and another to the Bishop that he might become a clerk; another of them he took himself, that he might bring him up and give him a benefice, and the two that remained were well provided for by the possessions of their father; and the father entered a religious order, and

had peace all the days of his life, fleeing from the world and from the vainglory wherein he had lived aforetime.

11. While the Cardinal was in that city there came a message from Rome by means of a spy whom he kept there, that he should go to Rome to make peace between the two advocates of two princes who were sorely at strife with each other. The Cardinal went to Rome, and secretly sent a message to one of them, making him swear to keep secret that which he should tell him. After the Cardinal had made him swear this, he said that in his name he would send gifts and jewels to the other man with whom he was at strife; and since this man was avaricious and would think that he had sent him the jewels, his wrath would be restrained. And he counselled him that, if his adversary gave him thanks for aught that he had given him, he should make it to appear that it was indeed he that had sent it to him. In like manner spake the Cardinal with the other man; and sent jewels often to either, in such wise that each thought that the one was sending them to the other. By reason of the jewels which the Cardinal sent, each greeted the other and did kindnesses to the other; and though the Cardinal said no more, they both became friends and pleasing the one to the other. After this manner and in many another wise did the Cardinal set men at peace, that they might have good will and that peace might be made on earth, and this peace be to them occasion of the life of salvation. Great was the good that the Cardinal did, and whensoever there was any strife in the land, men had recourse to the Cardinal that he might make peace among them.

12. In the courts wherein lawsuits were tried and disputes settled, the Cardinal had advocates to make peace among those that came to law, and he himself came oftentimes to the court to make peace between them. The Cardinal secretly employed likewise devout and good women to whom he gave rule and doctrine as to how they might make peace between women that were at strife.

The great good which the Cardinal did in setting men at peace with each other was so pleasing to God and to all men that, through the merit of the Cardinal, God gave peace and blessing to the lands whither the Cardinal went and wherein he lived.

CHAPTER LXXXII

LAUDAMUS TE

THE Cardinal of Laudamus Te took the office of praise; and in the Court of Rome and through all Christian lands he sent his representatives to praise God, and he, in his own person, went many times throughout these lands to give praise to God for the work which He has in Himself,—that is to say, in His Divine Persons,—and for the work which He has in the creatures. It came to pass once that the Cardinal was praising God in a city wherein dwelt a lady who had two sons: the one son was a clerk, and the other a layman, and this lady and her sons praised God; and there was question in that city which of the three praised God the more fervently. On either side there were persons who made argument, and recounted the praise which each gave to God according to the manner following:

2. The good lady, who was the mother of the two sons aforementioned, had brought up her sons to praise God, and since the death of her husband she was accustomed to go to other women and to reprove them for those things wherein they erred, and to praise God in their presence as well as she might. By reason of the reproofs which this lady made to others concerning the garments which they wore, and the painting of their faces, and their evil customs, many a woman embraced good customs in that city. And all feared this lady, because she reproved them so straitly, and knew and spied out their secrets and their faults.

3. The clerk was a priest, and he loved poverty, and sang Mass daily, and when it was the hour to dine he went to the house of some man to beg him to give him meat on that day, for the which favour he would sing Mass on the morrow for the welfare of his soul. Oftentimes came this clerk to eat and to beg alms with the poor at the gates of religious houses and of the palace of the Bishop; and he went to the clergy, reproving them for the faults which he saw in them, and feared not to speak the truth to any clerk whom he saw despising honesty and holiness of life: wherefore as he reproved them he praised God, and as he praised God he reproved them. That clerk was accustomed to go daily through the streets of the city, and on the way, whensoever he encountered clerks whom he saw to be in sin, he reproved them; afterwards he went to the churches, wherein he remained in prayer and contemplation, praising God, and reproving the clerks in any church, when he saw them do aught that was wrong. And the same thing did he in all the churches.

4. The other brother, who was a layman, went through the streets of the city, and when he found any layman who sinned in respect of his clothing, or his walking, or his speaking, or in anything soever, he reproved him incontinently, fearing no calumny neither harm to his person; and when he had reproved them he praised and blessed God in the presence of those whom he had reproved. And for the boldness which he had in reproving those who erred, and in praising God, all the men in that city feared him, and most of all was he feared by such as sinned.

5. Great was the good which that man did in the city, and great likewise was the good that was done by the lady and the clerk; wherefore there was question among the ladies and the clerks and the laymen of that city which of the three praised God the best; and on behalf of each there were those that maintained that that one praised God the best. Each of the three parties came before the Cardinal,

and put to him the question. And the Cardinal was greatly pleased, and brought the question to Rome that the Pope might solve it, and that in the city of Rome also there might be ladies and clerks and laymen who in like manner should praise God, and that the Pope might make establishment that for all time in the city of Rome there might be these three offices.

6. When the Cardinal had come to Rome and had laid this question before the Pope and the Cardinals, Ramón the Fool came before them, and he brought fire and wood and flour and water, and a sieve, and he said that he desired to make a loaf compounded of hope, charity, justice, chastity and humility, that he might give it to eat to those in whom was despondency, cruelty, wrong, lust and pride. After these words, the Jester of Valour said to the Cardinal who had put the question, that he besought him to apprise Ramón the Fool thereof, for in praise of God and to reprove the vices of the Court of Rome Ramón the Sage had taken the office of fool. Greatly was the Cardinal pleased, and even so were all the rest, that Ramón the Fool should be apprised of that question.

7. While the Pope and the Cardinals debated the solution of the question, a courier brought to the Jester of Valour a letter from the Emperor, instructing him to request the Pope and the Cardinals upon his behalf to judge which of these four persons following praised God the most truly, the which persons praised Him in the manner related in these words:

8. In a certain monastery there was a brother who was a man of holy life and a notable clerk. That brother had devotion in praising God in those works which God has in Himself, to wit, in the generation of the Son by the Father, and in the procession of the Holy Spirit from the Father and the Son. This brother had given himself up wholly to praising the Trinity, saying that in all these things praise should be given to the noblest work which exists; and

since the noblest work of any is the generation of God and the procession of God, in the which generation and procession there is infinity and eternity of goodness, power, wisdom, love and perfection, therefore the friar had no intent to praise God save in His Holy Trinity and Unity. That friar praised God in word and thought, according to the manner aforesaid, and with respect to the creatures, and to the work which God has in the creatures, he endeavoured with all his power to prove to Christians that concerning the which he praised God, and, from the praises which he spake and proved, there resulted devotion and charity in those to whom the friar praised God, and from this devotion and charity followed many good works and many evils ceased.

9. There was a bishop who had devotion in praising God in His Incarnation; for the noblest work which the Creator can perform in the creature is to unite the creature with Himself, that they may be one person only. And through the great devotion which the bishop had in praising God as touching the noblest work that God can have in the creature, the bishop had devotion to go and praise Him among the unbelievers, that by means of his praise he might convert them and suffer martyrdom. That bishop went to the land of the Saracens to praise the Holy Incarnation and Passion of the Son of God, and he did much good in that land, and suffered martyrdom in praise of God.

10. In that city wherein the bishop was martyred, there was a philosopher who was a very great master in philosophy, and through the words which he heard the bishop speak concerning the Incarnation of God he became a Christian, and had devotion to praise God in those lands wherein He is unknown, and whose inhabitants adore and believe in idols. That philosopher went to those countries to praise God, and to prove that God is, and is one only, the which God is the First Cause and Sovereign Good.

He praised God likewise in the good which He performs in creatures who by their goodness give significance of the goodness of the Creator. While the philosopher, by means of the creatures, proved God to exist, and to be wholly good, the people of that city slew him, and he became a martyr in praise of God, Whom he praised as Lord of all creatures.

11. After the death of the philosopher, a Christian knight came to that city wherein the philosopher had been martyred in praise of God. In that city God worked many miracles through the death of the philosopher, by the which miracles many people were converted. That knight came to the city to challenge in single combat any man who should say that God existed not, or that God was the sun or the moon or the other creatures which idolaters set in the likeness of God. With a great company of knights of that land the knight did battle, and conquered many, and at the last an archer wounded him with an arrow which cleft his heart, and the knight became a martyr, having praised God in the office of arms.

12. After this letter had been read, the Pope and the Cardinals praised and blessed God for the praise which was given to Him in the persons of the four men above mentioned; and many were the arguments that were put before the Court on the one side and the other; and the stronger was the argument between the partisans of each of the four in judging which of them had praised God best, the more was devotion increased in the people who heard the arguments. So the Cardinal of Laudamus Te said to the Pope that he should defer for a long time the solution of the question aforementioned, and that men should be chosen in his Court, who should make argument daily upon either side, and that all the arguments should be set down in writing; for if one suit had lasted for twenty years in the court of two kings who made dispute concerning their empire, how much the more should sentence be de-

ferred concerning the question aforementioned, to the end that devotion and good example might be the more increased in that Court, by the which devotion and example many should praise God and suffer martyrdom in His praise!

13. That which the Cardinal demanded was granted to him by the Pope and the other Cardinals, and endowment was made of advocates from the possessions of Holy Church, the which advocates were to make arguments upon either side all the days of their life. It came to pass one day that the advocate who made argument concerning the bishop who died in praise of the Incarnation of God put forward in his plea two arguments, namely, that God can be the better praised with respect to justice and mercy in a clerk that is a sinner, than in any other man; for since the clerk holds the office of Jesus Christ, he is the greater sinner, when he sins, than another man, wherefore God can manifest greater justice in punishing him or greater mercy in pardoning him his sins. And since this greater demonstration of praise is given in the Incarnation of the Son of God and in the Sacrifice of the Altar and in the Passion of Jesus Christ, therefore the advocate thought it to be proved that the bishop praised God more than all the rest. Arguments of like kind were put forward by the other advocates, and many notable arguments and questions were made in the plea aforesaid, from the which there followed much good in the Court.

14. While the aforementioned suit was being conducted daily in the Court, Ramón the Fool made question to the Pope, and the Cardinals, as to how and why it could be that the Popes who had been poor in temporal possessions had been praised more greatly than the Popes who were richer, after they had acquired the Empire of Rome. The Pope answered and said to Ramón the Fool that it was a light matter to solve this question.

CHAPTER LXXXIII

BENEDICIMUS TE

THE Cardinal of Benedicimus Te came before the Pope and the Cardinals with a great company of men to whom he had commended divers offices wherein God might be blessed; they were to go through many lands to bless God, to the end that God might bless those lands by reason of the blessing of His Name therein. These men were to go through the streets crying out and saying: "Blessed be God Who has created the trees, beasts, birds, men, metals, elements, skies, stars, angels and all other creatures; and blessed be God Who is the Orderer of the world, in that He has created divers offices therein: clerks, knights, religious, prelates, princes, labourers, merchants, blacksmiths, carpenters, drapers, shoe-makers, furriers, butchers, fishermen and men of all other offices." These men have promised to cry out and bless God for that He was pleased to become incarnate, and to die, and to work miracles, and to create Paradise and Hell, and for that He will make the good and the evil to rise again, sentencing the good to everlasting glory and the evil to eternal punishment. Furthermore, these men were to cry aloud and bless God in His Essence and in His Trinity and in His Virtues and in all things soever wherein is significance of His nobility.

2. When the Cardinal had related to the Pope and the other Cardinals the ordinance which he had established that the name of God might be blessed, he prayed the Pope to grant great indulgences to those that would hold this office, and to cause the clerks to give them to eat, for so long as they were in any land whither they had gone to bless the name of God. The Pope and the Cardinals were greatly pleased at that which this Cardinal had ordained, and the Pope commanded all the bishops that each one should provide for these men for so long as they were in

his diocese, and he gave them great indulgences and sent them away thus privileged, to go to divers dioceses by two and two. So they praised and blessed God in marvellous wise, crying aloud night and day concerning the Name and the virtue of God. And for the blessing which they gave to God, God blessed their words, and granted devotion to many people, who by reason thereof lived holy lives.

3. The Cardinal went through the city of Rome, bearing much money, which he gave to the poor that they might bless God; and as he went through the streets he cried to the people that they should bless God. It came to pass one day that a crier, who was wont to go about crying wine, considered the great devotion of the Cardinal, and through the Divine will the crier had devotion to be a crier of the name of God; and he came to the Cardinal, and with his license took the office of crying that the name of God should be blessed; and the Cardinal gave him a daily wage of five *sous* whereon he should live, and buy nuts and fruit to give to the children who followed him, crying also that the Name of God should be praised and blessed, and saying: "Blessed be God, praised be God, adored be God, obeyed be God, and may the work and virtue of God be ever praised and served." That crier went daily through Rome with many children, and they cried and blessed God and His virtue. As the crier and the children cried out and blessed God, many men that were sinners had remembrance and understanding and love of God, mortifying the vices and nurturing the virtues in their minds, and righteous men exalted their devotion in loving and serving God.

4. It came to pass in the city through the which went two of these men who cried out and blessed God, that a certain learned merchant had lost his wife, and he desired to bless God after the manner wherein he might the most effectually bless Him; so he sold all that he had, and spent the money upon a palfrey and upon a goblet of gold; and

he rode upon the palfrey, bearing the goblet before him, and he cried out through all the town that he would give that palfrey and that goblet to the man who would best instruct him to bless God. When the merchant went thus through the city crying aloud, there were many men in the city who had great desire to possess the palfrey, and the goblet of gold, which was very precious, and they thought of many and divers manners of blessing God; wherefore there was question among them which of these was the best way of blessing God.

¶ In a certain election a Canon received many votes that he might be made a bishop, and he blessed God that he was not a bishop; and the Bishop who was elected blessed God because He had charged him with so great and perilous a task and with an office so honoured and useful. Wherefore it is a question which gave the greater benediction to God.

¶ It is a question which gave the greater blessing to God: whether a certain man whose goods God increased, giving him wealth and honour in this world so that he blessed God for it; or one who blessed God because he was ill and dishonoured, and whose temporal possessions God had taken from him.

¶ A certain man wounded another mortally, though this man had done no wrong, and the wounded man blessed God and had patience; and the man that wounded him likewise had patience, and praised and blessed God, and judged himself to be guilty, while he suffered his lawful punishment.

¶ There was a man who praised and blessed God when he saw lepers, and beasts, and men that were sinners, because God had made him neither a leper nor a beast, but had made him a man. Another man blessed God because He had given him grace to live without mortal sin. Wherefore it is a question which of these blessed God the more truly.

¶ Between a man and a woman there was question which blessed God the more: whether the man because God had not made him a woman, or the woman because she was not a man, and was in greater submission in this world than is a man.

¶ There was a question likewise between a Christian and a Saracen, which of them praised God the more truly according to his law.

¶ A like question was made between a woman and her son, for the son blessed God because He had given him a good mother and the mother blessed God because He had given her a good son.

¶ A certain king blessed God because He had given him a noble people; and the people blessed God because He had given them a worthy king. Wherefore there was question which of them blessed God the more truly.

These questions and many more were given in writing to the merchant, to the end that he might bestow the palfrey and the goblet on him who had brought the question which signified which one among all these persons blessed God the most truly.

5. When the merchant had received the questions aforementioned, he rode upon his palfrey with the questions and the goblet of gold in his hand, and came to Rome, to the Cardinal whose office was to bless God, and he prayed him that he would solve the questions above-mentioned, that he might make choice of the manner wherein he could the most effectually bless God, and give the goblet and the palfrey to him that had brought the best question. The Cardinal went with the merchant to the Consistory before the Pope and the Cardinals, to solve this question; but agreement was made by the Pope and the Cardinals that the questions should be debated for a long time in the Court that they might not be forgotten, and that through remembering them many men might have example and devotion in praising and blessing God, and that the use

and custom of blessing God might be increased, and the office of the Cardinal have the greater utility; wherefore there was made an establishment that at the gate of the Cathedral of Rome should be set a palfrey of marble, and a man riding thereon who should hold in his hand a goblet, and that on the pedestal should be inscribed these questions aforesaid, together with the reason for the which the merchant had come to Rome.

6. It came to pass one day that the Cardinal rode through the city to see if he could hear any man blessing God, and he passed before a tavern wherein were many riotous men and idlers who played at dice, and one of them cursed and blasphemed God, saying many foul and evil words concerning Jesus Christ and Our Lady Saint Mary because of a game which he had lost at dice. The Cardinal dismounted from his palfrey, and gave it to this ribald man who blasphemed God, to the end that he might bless Him and never blaspheme Him more, and he went to the Pope and to the Cardinals, saying to them these words: " One day a certain friar was at Mass, which a Master in theology was singing, and he considered this Master, who for a long time through his words had given reason whereby God could be blessed by His disciples. Wherefore," said the Cardinal, " I am in very great wrath when I think that for a game of dice there are many riotous men and knaves who curse and blaspheme God and Our Lady and the saints in glory. I ask that satisfaction be made to me for the injury and wrong which is being done to me by dicing, and hindering the office which is commended to me. If satisfaction be not made to me and to my office by such as have power, they will be opposed to the blessing of God, and agree together in having malediction of Him." So vehement were the words that the Cardinal spake to the Pope and his companions that he made their minds to be in contrition and in thought, and they took knowledge of the power which they had, which was superior to their will. And the

Jester of Valour said: "What is the worth of a lover who forbids not that dishonour be done to his Beloved?" And Ramón the Fool said that the lover was tormented by his Beloved, of the which lover they enquired while they tormented him if it was time to rest; and he answered saying that, provided his Beloved knew, it was time for him to rest in the trials which he suffered for his Beloved.

7. While they spake thus there entered a Legate who recounted how he had fulfilled his commandment in excommunicating a prince who had disendowed the Church; and the Cardinal of Benedicimus Te enquired of the Pope which thing ought the more straitly to be spoken against: whether that for the which men blasphemed and dishonoured God, or the disendowment, by that prince, of one bishopric only.

8. Blanquerna the Pope was riding one day through the city of Rome and he saw a great company of ribald men in a tavern, who cried out saying: "Blessed be the Name of God." The Pope enquired how it came to pass that these ribald men blessed God in that place or how God could be blessed by such people. "Lord!" said a knight who was of the city of Rome: "There is a ribald man to whom the Cardinal of Benedicimus Te gave a palfrey, and he has made a custom of speaking these words concerning God whensoever he is with his fellows; and so devout are the words which he speaks to them that many a time he makes them to weep through the words which he speaks concerning God and His Passion, and in their poverty he comforts them and makes them to have patience; and when he has brought them to such devotion he makes them to cry out and to bless the name of God; and all the ribald men and the harlots of this city have made this man their lord and their chief; and this man is of such good customs that he gives great devotion to the people by his words and his good works." Greatly did the Pope rejoice at the words which he heard concerning this man, and he said that

though his name might be vile, his life was holy and glorious. So the Pope caused this man to come to him, and he enquired of him how he could make God to be blessed by people so vile as are ribald men and harlots, especially when they were in taverns. "Lord!" said the ribald man: "In that place wherein the name of God is dishonoured the most often, and by those people that bless Him least, should man put forth his greatest power that the name of God may be praised therein and blessed." The Pope thought deeply upon the words which this ribald man had spoken to him, and he said that it was a thing very needful that the name of God should be blessed among those people that are unbelievers, who do no honour to the name of God.

9. When the Pope had spoken these words there came to him a knight, saying to him: "Lord! I have been a man of arms, and all my life have I spent in slaying and destroying men that I might have of all men fame and renown in battle. If it please thee, I would have this office all the days of my life, that I may go among men who are brought near to death, whether by justice or by sickness, and that I may speak to them words of God, to the end that I may make satisfaction to God for my sins, and that those that die may be the more confirmed in the faith and mercy of God because of me, and that, as they die, they will bless and praise the name of God, and that after their deaths I may bring consolation to their kinsfolk." The Pope granted this office to the knight, and when he went to his palace he made a book wherein was the doctrine that he gave to the knight, and the words which he should speak to dying men, and to those who have need of consolation. The knight learned this book, wherein were written the words convenient for his office, and he went throughout the city of Rome spying out those that were near to death; and he spake to them words so devout that they were confirmed in their faith because of them; and he made them

to have such consciousness of their sins that he caused them to make restitution for the injuries and the wrongs which they had done, and made them to despise this world and to desire the world to come, so that they blessed and praised God as they died. And so many good words were spoken by this knight, that the kinsfolk of the men that died had consolation and patience because of them, and praised and blessed the justice and mercy of God. So great was the good that the knight did in that city, that when any man was near to death or had need of consolation, they sent a message always to this knight, and he brought with him his book, and read and expounded the doctrine which the Pope Blanquerna had given him.

CHAPTER LXXXIV

ADORAMUS TE

THE Cardinal of Adoramus Te was in great thought as to how he might bring it to pass that God should be more perfectly adored by His people, and he reflected that he might go to live alone for some time with a holy hermit who dwelt upon a high mountain, and that in that place he might consider the manner wherein he could bring it to pass that God should be contemplated and adored, according as is beseeming, and according as He has commanded His people. While the Cardinal went to the hermit and considered that which he so greatly desired, it chanced that he passed along a road wherein was a church which a poor man served by providing lights for worship, and wherein he caused Mass to be sung by begging for alms which men gave him. In that church there was a very great crucifix, right nobly sculptured and enchased. And there had entered a pilgrim, who was destroying the crucifix and knocking it to pieces with stones, and the good man who served the church was forbidding him with all his power. While these two men thus strove, the Cardinal passed by and entered the church, and marvelled greatly at the pilgrim who was thus stoning the crucifix, and enquired of the pilgrim wherefore he dishonoured the figure which is represented by the image of Jesus Christ. " Sir! " said the pilgrim: " It was formerly the custom for people to adore idols, and in this present time there are many men who adore idols, and the Saracens and the Jews reproach us who are Christians because we adore images, for an image sculptured and enchased is more like in figure to an idol than is an image which is unadorned. Wherefore to signify that unadorned images are more seemly than those that are enchased, I have made it a custom to destroy every graven image upon an altar, for its likeness to an idol."

2. While the Cardinal and the pilgrim held this converse there entered a man who came from foreign lands, and he kneeled before the Altar and adored and prayed to God very earnestly. The Cardinal considered that God had set some virtue in this man, by reason of the which he adored God so devoutly, and he desired to know of this man the manner wherein he adored God. " Sir! " said that man: " It is almost a custom among the men that are in this world that they adore God to the end that He may give them glory and not punishment; and many a time do they adore Him to the end that He may give them temporal possessions according to their need. Wherefore as it is a wrongful thing to adore God the rather in respect of the things of man, than for the goodness which is in God, therefore do I go to the Pope that he may give me his benediction, and I desire to cry aloud in all the squares and streets of cities and towns that men should adore God chiefly and above all because He is good, and worthy, that through His very goodness and perfection men should adore Him and bring Him love and do Him reverence and honour."

3. The Cardinal marvelled and rejoiced greatly, and with this man who desired to cry aloud concerning the best manner wherein man may adore God, he returned to the

city of Rome to make representation to the Pope concerning these two men according as has been said above. As they went all three along the road speaking of the manner wherein man should adore God, they met an old Jew who was going to the Court and was very wearied by reason of the long journey which he had made. His face and his features gave significance of great trouble and sorrow. The Cardinal enquired of the Jew wherefore he went so sadly and pensively. "Sir!" said the Jew: "For a long time I have been in grievous thought, from the which I cannot escape, and that thought so greatly torments my soul, that I have scarce any pleasure in aught that I hear or see." The Cardinal desired to know at all costs the thought wherein the Jew had entered, and the Jew spake to him of his trouble according to these words. "Sir!" said the Jew: "In the beginning, as it pleased God,—Blessed be His Name!—He honoured the people of the Jews above all other peoples. Twice were we in captivity: the first captivity was of four hundred years and the second of seventy years. In these two captivities were we because we committed many sins; yet after the punishment which we suffered in captivity, we recovered the liberty which we had had aforetime. But now, though we neither slay prophets nor adore idols, and live our life in this world with great trials, we have been in captivity more than one thousand and two hundred years and we know not why; wherefore I have great fear that we have been guilty of the death of the Christ, and that for this reason we are in captivity. Therefore go I as a man in exile throughout many lands to enquire if any man can show and make clear to me that we are in captivity because we adore not Jesus Christ Whom we have crucified."

4. When the Jew had ended his words, the Cardinal put to him this question: "There was debate between three wise men which of the three adored God most perfectly. The one had the office whereby he went over hill and dale

and adored God in herbs, plants, beasts, birds, and men, and in all the creatures. The second wise man adored God in that which He did in the works which He performed above nature, even as also in the miracles which He did, and in the creation of the world from nothing, and in the raising of the dead, and in everything that nature cannot perform. The third wise man adored God in those things which God is and in those things which God works in Himself, through Himself, and of Himself, and in that which God works in Himself with respect to the creatures. And it was a question which of these three adored God the most perfectly; and if there should be another who adored God according to the three manners aforementioned, there would be question likewise if he adored Him more perfectly than any of the three sages aforementioned." "Sir!" said the Jew: "He that adores God for that which God works in Himself is he that adores Him the most perfectly, rather than he that adores Him for that which He does in others; and he that adores God according to the three manners aforementioned adores Him more perfectly than he that adores Him in one manner only." The Cardinal answered and said "that he had rightly judged: and they that praise God for the works which He shows in the things of nature are the philosophers of olden time, and they that adore God in His miracles and in the works which they believe Him to do above nature are the Jews; but now the time has come wherein the Jews believe no more in miracles, and adore not God, for they believe not that which He does above nature to show forth His power; but the Christians believe that God performs in Himself a greater work than nature can either do or receive, in that the Father Who is God has engendered the Son Who is God, and from these proceeds the Holy Spirit Who is God, and yet together they are no more than one God. And God the Son has united with Himself the human nature of Christ, with Whom He is no more than one Person; and since this

Christ was crucified and slain by you Jews, when He came among you to take His human nature, and suffered death to save you, and since ye adore Him not, therefore has He punished you by delivering you into the captivity of the Christians, and of the Saracens also, signifying thereby that in every wise ye are unworthy to be free, wherefore He has made you to be subjected to the faithful and the unfaithful alike." Deeply did the Jew consider the words which the Cardinal had spoken, and through the questions and the arguments which he had made, he perceived the truth and became a Christian, and received the office that he should go into the synagogues of the Jews to adore God in the presence of all according to the three manners aforesaid; and the Pope gave him the privilege of that office.

5. As the Cardinal was before the Pope, and ordained his officers who were to help him in the fulfilment of his office, there came before the Pope an ancient and reverend Saracen, and on behalf of the Saracen king he presented to the Pope a letter, in the which the Saracen king prayed him that he would send to him to say if that which a certain Christian had related to him of the Holy Catholic Faith was true. This Christian, he said, had turned him from the faith of Mahomet which he had aforetime held, but since the Christian had told him that the Catholic Faith could not be proved by arguments, therefore he desired not to be a Christian, for he would not leave one faith for another, but he said that through understanding he would fain leave the faith of Mahomet and hold the Catholic Faith, providing that the Pope would send to him to say if it could be proved, and if this were so he would become a Christian and adore Jesus Christ as God, and make over all his domain to the Church of Rome, to the end that all that dwelt therein should adore Jesus Christ.

6. When these letters had been read in presence of the Pope and the Cardinals, there entered a Gentile[1] who came

[1] *i.e.* a heathen. Cf. p. 311, above.

from a southern land which lies within the regions of the desert, and from a city which is called Gana. In that land there were many kings and princes who adored idols and likewise adored the sun and the stars and the birds and the beasts. The people of that land are very many, and they are black, and have no law. It came to pass one day that a man from that country considered that it was beseeming that there should be adored some one thing only, which should be nobler than any of those to which they did adoration in that land, and in honour of that thing the nature whereof he knew not, he went through every land crying out that man should seek and make enquiry concerning this thing which alone should be adored. For so long did that man continue in this office, and so diligently did he serve therein, that he moved the people in that land to devotion, and they had a desire to have knowledge of that thing which above all others should be adored; wherefore they held a Court, and came together, and ordained that messengers should be sent through divers lands to enquire what that thing could be which was worthy of adoration above all things else; and one of the messengers was this man who came to the Pope. Straightway the Pope sent for the articles of the faith and the books whereby it is shown that these articles may be proved. He sent also for the friars that had learned Arabic, the which friars went to the Saracen king, who had sent these letters to the Pope, and by the grace of God they converted the Saracen king and a great multitude of people; and with the messengers of the Pope they went to those countries through the which the Gentile had passed, and they proclaimed and showed by necessary reasons that God was sovereign over all things, and that He it was Whom all the people of these lands should adore; and they destroyed the idols wherein they had been wont to believe. So agreement and friendship was made between these people and the Catholics; and by the friendship and converse which the Catholics had with them, many of these people in a brief space of time received baptism.

7. Upon a certain feast day the Pope made a procession with a great company of prelates and religious and other clerks. Many were the songs and praises which were made to our Lord God therein. The Cardinal of Adoramus Te walked in that procession, and he reflected how that there were many lands in the world wherein were numbers of people who praised not God neither adored Him, and he desired very earnestly that God should be adored in all these lands. While the Cardinal considered thus it chanced that he passed before a great company of silversmiths and shopkeepers, who had in their shops very many cups and basins, jugs, dishes, and bowls of gold and silver and many other precious things, to wit, rings, purses, girdles and precious stones. The Cardinal commanded four squires to seize all these cups and jewels and to throw them into the street and to say that he had commanded them to do this. The squires performed his commandment, and the men who owned these precious things were greatly scandalised thereat, and it seemed that all the procession would be disturbed because the Cardinal had commanded his squires to act in this wise, and because there was like to be strife between them and the men who owned these precious things.

8. After this adventure there came another, namely, that the Cardinal of Adoramus Te saw a lady who followed the procession, the which lady was richly adorned with gold and silver and precious stones, and her face shone with the colours which she had placed thereon, even as images shine when man has placed varnish upon them. The Cardinal kneeled before the lady and made as though he would adore her, saying that she was like to an idol and for this reason he kneeled to her. Great was the shame of that lady and of all the others that were with her. When the Pope had ended the procession and had sung Mass, he

desired to know for what reason the Cardinal had disturbed the procession and had kneeled before the lady; and the Cardinal related to him how that great devotion had come to him as he had reflected how many lands there were wherein God was not adored, and that the cups of gold and silver and the other precious things wherewith prelates adorn their tables and fill their chests impeded this office[1]; wherefore he had commanded that these precious things should be destroyed. So the Pope made establishment from thenceforward that none of these jewels should be in any city or place wherein he was, lest they should be an occasion to the unworthy will of any prelate. After this he made establishment likewise that no woman that was dressed and adorned after the manner of idols should walk in his procession nor be in any church wherein he sang Mass.

CHAPTER LXXXV

GLORIFICAMUS TE

THE Cardinal to whom the Pope had commended the office of Glorificamus Te said to the Pope that he desired to take the office whereby he should honour in this world the will of God against those who do it dishonour. Wherefore the Cardinal related this story: " There was a king who had gone with a great company of his retainers into a fair forest to take recreation. In this forest he dallied and feasted and had great delight. It came to pass that there was evil weather in that place wherein the king dwelt, with cold and snow and rain, and the king remained in his tent and took many sauces and strong wines and wore much clothing, so that neither the cold nor the evil weather in that place could harm his person; but among his people and his servants it caused death and destruction, for they

[1] V: "impeded the office of Adoramus Te."

could not defend themselves from the evil weather." When the Cardinal had ended this story, he expounded it in these words: "The king is the Pope, and his barons and knights are the Cardinals and the prelates of Holy Mother Church, who send not to far countries friars, religious and worthy men to learn divers languages and to have converse with the people of these lands, that they may understand them and preach to them without interpreters; and since such a custom would be agreeable to the will of God, all they that could and should follow it, that the will of God may be done in this world, and do not so, are opposed to the will of God. They that die are the Christians in these lands, for they dwell among the Saracens and the Tartars, to whom they are subject, and these are ignorant of the faith and the preachers thereof. And to the Christians in these lands, through the captivity wherein they have perforce to dwell, is done much wrong as to their persons, and as to their wives and daughters; wherefore they oftentimes have no more belief in the Holy Catholic Faith, but renounce it, and take the faith of those among whom they live in opposition to the will of God."

2. When the Pope had heard these words, he made ordinance concerning those Orders that follow after learning, that even as the prince who goes to war with another prince is accustomed to set armed outposts on the boundaries of his domains, even so there should be established monasteries in the domains of those Christians who mingle with unbelievers, and that, whatsoever language these people speak, the monks shall learn that language, and mingle with them and preach to them. These things the Pope ordained, that with all his power he might cause the will of God to be done.

3. The Cardinal had great will to honour the will of God, that he might glorify God in honouring His will, and he appointed officers, who in their divers offices should aid him to honour the will of God. It came to pass one day

that the Cardinal went through the city of Rome, and passed through a square wherein were many people, and he enquired of the men who were going to and fro in the square why their will made them to go here and there thus diligently; and each one answered that the will that caused them thus diligently to go was that which they had with respect to their temporal business. Wherefore the Cardinal ordered that a man should stand in that square and cry aloud to the people that they should direct their intent to the service of God in their conduct of the business of this world, and that they should conduct this business with intent to serve God, that in all their works the will of God should be honoured rather than the will that loves temporal business. So that man stood in the square and cried aloud according as the Cardinal had ordered him. Many were the men who, through that which they heard, directed their will to the service of the will of God.

4. The Cardinal appointed another officer who should go through the streets crying aloud how men ought to obey the will of God in believing the fourteen articles, and in performing that which they were commanded to perform by the ten commandments; and that they should glorify the will of God because He has been pleased to create the world, and to become incarnate and to give the world to men. And this officer was to say to every man that he ought to glorify the will of God Who had made him a man and a Christian; for had He not so willed, God had not created the world, nor taken our nature, nor given the world to man, and those that He has made men He might rather have made beasts. When the Cardinal had instructed the officer who should perform this office aforementioned, that man enquired of the Cardinal on what he should live; and the Cardinal said that if a jester[1] lived on that which was given to him, and knew not how to do more than tell the people where there is good wine, how much the more

[1] *juglar.*

should he find a livelihood if he served the will of God by repeating the words aforesaid!

5. Another office likewise was established by the Cardinal, which is very needful to the end that the will of God may be honoured, to wit, that a man should go to all clerks and religious, and that in the streets and the churches and in whatsoever place he might find them, he should call to their minds how they ought to obey the will of God, Who commanded them in the Gospels to go through all the world preaching to every creature. This officer was appointed by the Cardinal. It came to pass one day that this officer found two clerks in a certain street, to whom he said that which the Cardinal had commanded him to say; and they answered him that if God desired that a man should go to preach to the unbelievers He would give him the will to go; and the officer was greatly scandalised by that which the two clerks had said, and he answered that God had commanded them when He spake to the Apostles in the person of Holy Church; and since God, in willing to become man, and to die for all those that are in Holy Church, had so straitly charged each one to do this for love of Him, none should wait for God to compel his free will, without the which he would be unworthy to preach the will of God. So there was a great dispute between the two clerks, and they came for judgment to the Court of the Pope.

6. The Cardinal asked one of his squires, who had served him for a long time, if he desired to serve the will of God by going from door to door, begging for the love of God. When men gave to him for the love of God, he would glorify His will, and when he was refused that which he desired for the love of God, then would he have grief in his soul and weep, because those that give not for the will of God, and give for their own will, are not loved by the will of God. That squire took this office, and went with the poor, begging for the love of God, that he might

have knowledge of those that honour the will of God and of those that prize the will of God less than the alms which are asked of them by men, which they refuse to those that beg for the love of God. This squire performed his office ever very well, and when he had begged from door to door for the meat whereof he had need on that day, he went to the church and remained therein for the rest of the day contemplating the will of God.

7. A certain philosopher came to the Cardinal and spake to him these words: "Lord! It is a custom among us to deny that which is contrary to the course of nature. But, though I have had this custom, I desire to change it and to take an office wherein I may go to philosophers and great masters, saying that if a miraculous work is a thing ill-beseeming to nature, how much the more ill-beseeming is it to the Lord of nature that He should not do that which pertains to His will and is superior to the work of nature!" Right well pleasing was this office to the Cardinal, and the philosopher did much good therein, proving many things to be true which are contrary to the course of nature, that God may not be contrary to His own will in perfection, justice, infinity, power, wisdom, mercy and humility. These officers and many more did the Cardinal appoint, to the end that in the honour which they did to the will of God He might be glorified by men, and that they likewise through the will of God might be glorified in the glory of God.

CHAPTER LXXXVI

GRATIAS AGIMUS TIBI PROPTER MAGNAM GLORIAM TUAM

THE Cardinal of Gratias Agimus Tibi, who had received the office of honouring the wisdom of God, came one day before the Pope and his companions, and spake these words: "It is a natural thing that even as the human understanding is the better directed to understand God, even so is the will the more prepared to love God, and to cease from loving sin; wherefore I ask for an office wherein I may bring it to pass that the human understanding may be exalted to understand God, that God may be known and loved by His people, and that His people may give Him thanks and bless His glory." The Pope and the Cardinals gave him the office for the which he asked.

2. While they spake thus, a student[1] entered the presence of the Pope and said that through increase of the sciences, in theology and in natural science and in law and in medicine, there were increased the diversity of opinions in each one of the sciences aforementioned; and the reason of this was that authors and masters made works upon the sciences wherein the opinions of some differed from the opinions of others. Wherefore the student said to the Pope and the Cardinals that all the sciences aforementioned should be reduced by man to their brief and necessary elements, and that they should reason thereupon by method, to the end that, if there arose any error or false opinion, a man should be able, by following this method, to direct himself in the elements of each of the sciences, and to destroy false opinions that are contrary to the sciences aforementioned.

3. Right pleased was the Cardinal of Gratias Agimus Tibi at that which the student had said, and he confirmed it and counselled that his petition should be granted. After these words there came before the Pope a master in canon and civil law, and he said that the glosses of the writings concerning the science of law were so numerous that the human understanding was brought to confusion by them, and that therefore he could not judge clearly of facts nor could the disciples who learned that science be taught the elements thereof; wherefore he counselled that that science should be reduced to a method, and to its briefest elements, according to necessity and reason, and that to this method

[1] *artista, i.e.* student qualified in the Faculty of Arts.

should be reduced the entire science of law. In like manner, on divers occasions, a master in theology and another in natural science and another in medicine made petition to the Pope and the Cardinals, that of each science the brief and necessary elements might be set forth according to method, to the end that there should be no confusion concerning any science through the increase of writings upon it, and that when the time of Anti-Christ came they should be the better prepared to destroy his false beliefs.

4. When the master aforementioned had spoken thus, the Cardinal said that he was right glad at these words, and that this matter concerned his office, the which he had taken to honour the wisdom of God; wherefore he desired that his office should be concerning that business. After these words rose a wise religious, and said in the presence of all that he desired an office in virtue whereof he should go to the Saracens, Jews, Tartars and all unbelievers, to expound the articles of the Holy Catholic Faith; for many a man that was an unbeliever feared to enter the Roman Faith because he understood not the manner wherein Christians believe the articles, for unbelievers think that Christians hold a belief other than that which in fact they hold, and therefore they fear to become Christians.

5. Before the Pope and the Cardinals could give any answer to the masters who desired the offices aforesaid, there came before the Pope two sages, the one of whom was a Latin and the other a Greek, and they spake to the Pope and the Cardinals these words: "Lord! In the *Book of the Holy Spirit*[1] there is made a disputation between a Latin and a Greek before a Saracen sage who enquires of them which thing is true concerning the person of the Holy Spirit, whether He proceeds from the Father and from the Son or whether He proceeds from the Father alone. Each of the two sages proves his opinion, according to his power,

[1] Like the other books mentioned in *Blanquerna*, this is by Lull himself.

by ten arguments, and the Saracen is in perplexity, knowing not to which of the beliefs he will incline; wherefore have we journeyed throughout the land of Greece, and likewise through a great part of the land of the Latins, and we have put the questions to sages in whatsoever place we have visited, to the end that they may seek out the truth, and decide which belief the Saracen ought to have held." Right pleased were the Pope and the Cardinals at that which the two sages said, and the Pope committed the answer thereto to the Cardinal who had taken the office of honouring the wisdom of God. With these sages there was a Christian who went among the Saracens and the Jews to enquire of the Gentile which of the three laws he had taken, according as is related in the *Book of the Gentile and of the three Wise Men*.

6. The Cardinal had many men to assist him in serving his office, and he sent them throughout the world to enquire of divers masters how they used the sciences which they taught; and when he found that any master used ill the science which he taught, he punished him and deprived him of his office; and this resulted in much good, for all the masters feared him, through the which fear their disciples were the better grounded in the sciences which they learned of them, because their masters taught them more diligently and with fewer words. It happened once that the Cardinal went to a city wherein was made much study of the sciences. At the entrance to the city he found the two sons of the king who was lord of that city, who caused his sons to be taught to bear arms and to practise fencing. The Cardinal enquired of the masters of the two children if the king caused them to be taught the science of letters, and the masters answered him that he did not, but that he caused them to be taught to ride, and to bear arms. "Foolish is the king," said the Cardinal, "who teaches his sons the rather to slay men, than to know if men should be slain." When he had spoken these words the Cardinal

went to the king and reproved him straitly because he caused not his sons to be taught laws and sciences, according as was the custom heretofore with kings and princes, who caused their sons to be taught sciences that they might know how to rule their people. The king was greatly pleased at that which the Cardinal spake, and was obedient to his counsel.

7. So great was the will of the Cardinal to increase wisdom and to direct it aright that he went to the general chapters of the religious orders wherein the sciences were studied, and there he directed and ordained how, in honour of the wisdom of God, the sciences should be increasingly studied by all men, to the end that they might know and love God. It came to pass that the son of a certain Count went to Bologna to study law; and the Cardinal, who went also to Bologna, where there was to be a general chapter of the Preachers, met with the son of the Count, and spake to him so many good words on the road, that he taught him to love the science of theology, which is more needful to a clerk than the science of law; wherefore the son of that Count returned to Paris and learned theology, in the which he became a master.

8. The Cardinal went one day to the school of the Preachers to hear the lesson in theology, and on the way he found a great school of law wherein were many disciples clothed in ecclesiastical habits. He went on farther and found another school which was full of decretalists, who likewise wore the ecclesiastical habit; and the Cardinal commanded the disciples of law that since the science of law was secular they should study in secular habit, that dishonour might not be done to the honour which the science of canon law should have above that of civil law; and he made this commandment especially, that simony might not have its beginning in lawyers, who, after studying the science of law, become decretalists, to the end that they may be able to rise to some prelacy.

9. After this ordinance was made, the Cardinal entered the school of the Preachers, wherein a master in theology was delivering a lecture, and in that school there was scarce any disciple who was not a religious; wherefore the Cardinal cried in a loud voice that to wisdom was being done great dishonour by those that love science that is lucrative rather than science that is of merit only, or that which demonstrates Divine wisdom. Wherefore the Cardinal made a commandment that once in every week, in each of the schools of law, Friars Preachers and Friars Minor should preach, and that they should speak therein of the great harm which is done to theology by those that are beneficed from the possessions of Holy Church, and study the science of laws, or learn more of law than of theology. After this manner, and in many another wise, the Cardinal endeavoured to do honour to wisdom to the end that by wisdom men should have knowledge how that every man is bound to give thanks to God for the possessions which He has given to him, to the which thanks ignorance is a thing opposed.

CHAPTER LXXXVII

DOMINE DEUS REX CŒLESTIS, DEUS PATER OMNIPOTENS

In the Consistory was the Cardinal of Domine Deus, and he said, in presence of the Pope and of the Cardinals, that he desired to have the office of honouring the power of God, Who suffered dishonour in this world through many men who dishonoured Him after divers manners. It came to pass one day that the Pope desired to send his messengers to a land called Georgia, whereof a Christian king is lord; and the Pope sent to that king, begging him to send him certain religious from among the people of his land, that they might teach their language and their letters to Latin friars, and that they might learn Latin, and together with the Latin friars return to their own land to preach the holy faith and doctrine of Rome. When the Pope Blanquerna ordained these things, the Chamberlain said that it would be a matter of great peril to cause these persons to be sent, and to learn their language, and to teach our Latin to them, and that this was a thing which required convenient place and time and great expense.

2. Greatly was the Cardinal displeased at that which the Chamberlain had said, and he related this story: "Once on a time it came to pass that a certain man named Jofa was going along a road, and he came to a river, on the bank whereof was a great multitude of men who were gazing at a man who had drowned himself in the water. He enquired of them why that man had not gone up higher, to the source of the river, where he might have crossed to the other side. A man answered: "But how long a time he would have taken to do this, seeing that it is five days' journey to the source of the stream!" Jofa answered: "But how much longer will he take to come to life again and rise from this place!" In these words did the Cardinal sternly reprove the Chamberlain, saying that the power of man through long practice can direct and bring to an end all that which the Pope desires to ordain concerning the religious of Georgia; but no power can bring back the damned in hell to a state of salvation, since they have passed from this present life. The Cardinal had a squire who had served him for long that he might gain a better promotion. It came to pass one day that the squire was very grievously sick of a fever. The Cardinal was greatly troubled at his sickness, and the squire begged him that he would heal him and take from him the fever which so severely tormented him. The Cardinal answered that he had no power to take the fever from him, for that power was from God alone, Whose power did all that it desired with the power of nature. The squire recovered from his malady, and he took the office of honouring the power of God in every land,

crying aloud and saying that the power of God is superior to the power of nature, and that therefore God was able to make the first man, and to rise from the dead, and cause a woman that was a virgin to conceive and bring forth a child, through His Divine power; and that the power of the stars and of the heavenly bodies is vanquished and overcome, or given leave to work, by the Sovereign Power only. Right worthy was the office which was taken by the squire; for oftentimes Catholics were confirmed thereby in their faith, and the unbelievers were vanquished and overcome in their belief that a virgin could not conceive or bring forth a child, and a man could not rise from the dead; whereas the power of God in these things is as effectual as in the creating of the world from naught, the which creation is superior to the power of nature.

3. "Lord!" said the Cardinal to the Pope: "I would fain know which has the greater power, whether truth or falsehood." The Pope answered and said that truth has greater power than falsehood, because truth has greater aid of God and accords with being, and falsehood has no aid of God and accords not with being. Wherefore after these words the Cardinal asked the Pope how it came to pass that falsehood could have such power in the world that there should be more men who are idolaters and believe in idols than there are of men that believe in God. And the Pope answered that this thing came not to pass that falsehood might have power over truth, but through defect of devotion and charity, which desires not that the truth be shown forth; wherefore even as darkness comes through defect of light, even so come error and falsehood from the defect of those that dare not to say or to preach the truth.

4. In a certain province it came to pass that the devout and blessed men who went to preach the word of God to unbelievers were refused a hearing, and banished from the country. And the Cardinal had recourse to the secular arm, and treated with the Christian princes, and with the Pope,

to the end that by force of arms they should fight and conquer all such as allow not holy Christian men to enter their countries and preach therein the word of God, and that the Church should make no truce with any unbeliever who suffered not the Christians to show forth in his land the truth of the Catholic Faith. So great was the power of the Christians that the unbelievers of that land suffered that they should preach to them, and that there should be a truce between them for so long as they suffered the Christians to preach and to convert the unbelievers in their land.

5. It came to pass that a very powerful Saracen king desired not that Christian monks should enter his country to preach therein, and two friars whom the Saracens had banished from their land came to the Cardinal of Domine Deus saying that they could not remain in that land because the Saracens desired it not. But the Cardinal said that they had dishonoured the power of the will, which is stronger and nobler than the power of the body, and therefore he made complaint to the Pope, saying these words: "Lord Pope! The power of the will makes men to fast and weep and labour to honour and praise the power of God, and God has bound and submitted the power of the body to the power of the spirit. Wherefore, if the king defends himself with bodily power against the power of our souls, it is seemly that his power should be vanquished and overcome, through loving and honouring greatly the Passion of God, and through the shedding of tears and of blood, and by means of holy men who shall go both secretly and openly among the unbelievers, that through long continuance the power of the body may be vanquished by the power of the spirit, in significance that the power of God vanquishes spiritually the sensual and the intellectual power that is in creatures, according as is represented in the Sacred Host."

6. So fervent and devout was this Cardinal in honouring the power of God, that he established divers offices to

honour the power of God. To one man he gave the office that he should go through the world preaching and crying aloud that man should not trust in the power of riches, neither in friends nor wisdom nor youth, nor omens nor fates nor divinations, nor in any other power soever whereby man loses the grace of the Divine power. Another office gave the Cardinal to one who should cry out that the power of God was so great that it could do all things, and that no sin could result therefrom. Another officer cried that God could do no sin, because sin and lack of power are things which agree with each other, and are contrary to power, and to the virtues, which agree together likewise. Another officer cried that God exhausted not His power in respect of His creatures, for He had power to do many things more than He did. Another cried that God in His Trinity did all that was in His power. Many other officers were there who honoured the power of God, and all had rule and doctrine whereby they were to bless and honour the power of God; and among the other officers was one whose duty it was to show by means of nature how man could mortify within himself the vices, and strengthen the virtues, and weep for his sins. Another office was held by a man who carried the branch of a tree and a bird, and led a dog, and he cried that there was no man who could create a leaf of that branch, neither a feather of that bird, neither a hair of that dog, neither a nail of his own hand.

7. So great was the fame of the Cardinal and of his officers in honouring the power of God, that whensoever a man had defect of power, straightway he went for succour and for counsel to the Cardinal and to his officers. And the same thing came to pass with the Cardinal who served the will of God, and with the Cardinal who served the wisdom of God; so that whensoever a man had defect of will or of knowledge or of power, incontinently he had recourse to the Cardinals above-mentioned.

CHAPTER LXXXVIII

DOMINE FILI UNIGENITE JESU CHRISTE

GREAT was the devotion which a certain Cardinal had to the Person of the Son of God, Who united with Himself human nature, and through the devotion which he had to the Son of God he spake to the Pope and to the Cardinals these words: " A thing most manifest is it, O Holy Father and Pope, that thou, with all of us that are Cardinals, hast received honour, through the Son of God, above all other Christians in this world; wherefore it is meet and right and our bounden duty to send messengers throughout all the world who shall report to us the condition of every land, according to the manner wherein the Son of God is honoured in the world by some, and dishonoured and despised by others; and that this thing may be accomplished, I ask for this office, and for the wherewithal to provide for my messengers, whom I will send through the whole world, that they may report to me the condition wherein they find it, and this will I myself report to you, to the end that ye may make ordinance how the Son of God may be loved and praised through all the world, and His virtue be showed forth, with all that He did in this world for love of us." Right pleased were the Pope and all the Cardinals at this office which the Cardinal of Domine Fili demanded, and all that he asked was granted to him; and herein was the prefiguration fulfilled that the emperors of Rome, who were the lords of the world, had messengers who reported to them the condition of the world, wherein it was figured that the Pope, the Vicar of God and lord of Rome, would know the estate of every land, that it might be subject to the Holy Catholic Faith.

2. The Cardinal divided the world into twelve provinces, and sent forth twelve messengers who should go through the whole world to learn the estate thereof. It came to

pass that one of the messengers of the Cardinal journeyed southwards, and found a caravan of six thousand camels, laden with salt, leaving a town by name Tibalbert, and going to that country wherein is the source of the river Damiata. So many people did this messenger find here, that in fifteen days all the salt was sold; and these men are all black, and adore idols, and they are men of genial temper, who hold justice very dear, and slay every man whom they discover in falsehood, and hold all that they have in common. In that land is an island in the middle of a great lake; and on that island there lives a dragon to whom the people of that land do sacrifice, adoring it as a god. The messenger went through these countries to enquire concerning the customs of the people, and to estimate the number thereof. And the people marvelled greatly at the messenger, because he was a white man and a Christian; for never before had they heard of any Christian coming to that land. The messenger sent news in writing to the Cardinal by a squire of all the things aforesaid, and many beside, and the Cardinal related them to the Pope and to his companions. Great was the displeasure of the Pope and of the Cardinals when they heard of the dragon that was adored as a god, and they debated how they might destroy the error wherein these people lived.

3. Another messenger journeyed northward, beyond the mountains, where he heard and saw Latin peoples, who related to him that in those parts there were many men of divers beliefs, and that the devil kept them in error by means of certain illusions and deceptions. For there was one land, Gotlandia by name, where at the end of every five years there appeared a white bear, as a sign that that year there would be abundance of fish, whereon these people live. There was another land wherein by enchantment the trees were made to speak. Another land is there, near to Bohemia,[1] where there is a hoopoe in a wood, and

[1] P. *Boemia*. The other versions have *Bocinia*.

if any man cuts a branch from a tree in that wood, straightway come lightning and thunder from the heavens and set in peril of death every man who is in that wood. In another land every man thinks that he has a god in his field, and another in his stable and another in his garden. In another land, near to Dacia, are men who live on naught save the beasts which they hunt, and they go in chase of the beasts and kill them, and when they have killed one of them they remain in that place till they have eaten it, and then seek another. All this news, and much beside, the messenger from beyond the mountains sent in writing to the Cardinal; and ordinance was made by the Pope and the Cardinals that holy and devout men should be sent to those peoples, to learn their languages and preach to them by example and custom, and by metaphor and similitude, until their sensual natures were so ordered that the virtue of the similitudes worked upon the powers of the soul, and that thereby their intellectual natures were illumined by the Holy Catholic Faith.

4. To Barbery there went a messenger of the Cardinal who found many knaves and harlots, who preached to the Saracens from the Koran and spake to them of the bliss of Paradise; and so devout were the words which they preached, that almost all they that listened to them wept. Great was the marvel of the messenger at the devotion which the people had to those words, when he reflected that that which they preached was error; and he found that the people wept because of the fair manner of speech which they had, and because they related the lives of many men who died for their devotion. He found also a book *Of the Lover*[1] *and the Beloved*, wherein was recounted how devout men made songs of God and of love, and how through the love of God they forsook the world and went through the

[1] Lit. *amic*; and this, in general, is the original of the word here translated "lover." Sometimes, however, we find the word *amant*, which is also thus translated, there being no real distinction.

world enduring poverty. The messenger found also that, in the courts wherein lawsuits were held, the disputes of the questions which each had against the other were briefly ended. All these things and many beside the messenger reported to the Cardinal, and one translated the *Book of the Lover and the Beloved*,[1] and brought it to pass that, through devotion of word, sermons should be made more pleasing to the people, and likewise that, following the custom of the Saracens, lawsuits and disputes which are conducted by Christians should be shortened.

5. There went a messenger to Turkey, and he found there four friars who had learned the language of the Turks, and the Turks forbade them to preach in their land; and the messenger reported this in writing to the Cardinal, and messengers were chosen whom the Pope sent with many gifts to the ruler of the Tartars who had subjected Turkey to his overlordship. The Pope requested the ruler of the Tartars, by his messengers, that he would suffer the four friars to preach the honour of the Son of God throughout all Turkey, and the ruler suffered it by reason of the prayers and the gifts which the Pope sent to him; so the Turks no longer dared to forbid the friars to preach from thenceforward.

6. Across the seas there went a messenger who sent to the Cardinal to say that two assassins had slain a certain prince and had been put to death; and the Cardinal went to preach to the religious who were learning divers tongues, and he exhorted them to desire death for Jesus Christ, since there were men living in error who desired to die that their kinsfolk might have liberty; wherefore establishment was made that once in every week these things should be preached, to the end that with greater affection[2] they might learn and desire to die.

[1] While this passage must not be taken as proving the *Book of the Lover and the Beloved* to be a translation, it suggests, together with another passage (p. 410, below), that that book was written under strong Oriental influence.

[2] P has "affliction."

7. According to this manner aforesaid, ordinance was made that the messengers should go through all the world. After another wise went many other men, who took the office of relating examples[1] and good words to the people, that they might oftentimes have remembrance of the Son of God and of the Passion which He suffered for our sakes. These messengers went through the towns and cities and villages,[2] and visited the rulers and governors, to whom they related good examples.[3] It came to pass one day that a certain one of these men went to a carpenter who was planing a log of wood, and related to him how he had heard that a certain tree had been so strong that it had borne a greater weight than the whole world. The carpenter wondered at this saying, and through his wonder he conceived devotion when the messenger expounded to him that saying,—namely, that this tree is the Cross whereon the Son of God was nailed, for He has taken from His people who serve Him a greater weight than that of all the world. And by the devotion which the carpenter conceived, he became a man of good life, and left a certain deadly sin wherein he had lived.

8. It came to pass one day that one of the messengers departed from a town and went to a castle,[4] and on the way he found a great multitude of pilgrims who were going to Santiago, so he fell in company with them, and went with them as far as Santiago; and as they journeyed along the road he related to them examples[3] and devout words, and recounted the histories of the Old Testament and of the New, and described to them the events which are in the lives of the Popes and the Emperors, according as is written in the chronicles. So great was the pleasure which the pilgrims had in his good words, that the greater devotion came to them in their pilgrimage, and in their journeying and their trials they had the less suffering; wherefore many

[1] *exemplis*. See note, p. 189, above.
[2] *castells*. See p. 286, above.
[3] *exemplis*. See note, p. 189, above.
[4] Or "village" (*castell*).

other men took that same office, to the end that they might beguile the way of the pilgrims and set them in devotion.

9. Very great was the good which resulted from this office of the Cardinal, the which Cardinal kept the Pope and the other Cardinals greatly pleased with the reports and news which came to him daily from divers parts of the world. It came to pass one day that a certain man, with intent to gather much money, feigned that he was a messenger and a relator of news commissioned by the Cardinal, and he went with the pilgrims, who gave to him freely and showed him much kindness. But that man was not well instructed in relating such things as he recounted, and the Cardinal came to know it, and commanded that the man should be taken and put into prison, because he had taken this office without his license; and he ordered that none of his relators should take aught from any pilgrim, and if he had need of aught, that he should be aided by the bishop of the country wherein he was, and that each relator should bear the seal of the Cardinal.

CHAPTER LXXXIX

DOMINE DEUS AGNUS DEI FILIUS PATRIS

The Pope was in Consistory one day with the Cardinals, and he spake to them in these words: "It is a thing most certain that the orders of religion which are among us are ruled and governed by chapter, wherein they make ordinance yearly how their order may be well preserved in religion and in holy life; wherefore it is a needful thing that we secular clergy make ordinance of a chapter likewise, after such manner that our life may be pleasing both to God and to man; for unless we hold chapter, both general and special, we cannot be perfectly ordered in this world. Wherefore, as this is so, I pray each of my companions that he help me to discuss how we may ordain among us general and provincial chapters." Greatly did the words of the Pope please the Cardinals, and together with the Pope they made ordinance of a chapter after this manner:

2. First, it was ordained that every bishop should hold chapter once in each year, and that he should appoint in his diocese inquisitors, and that denunciation should be made in chapter if any clerk were deserving of punishment for any faults that he had committed during the year. After this, establishment was made that once in every year each archbishop should hold chapter with his bishops, and that he likewise should appoint inquisitors over them who should accuse them in chapter, that they might be punished by the archbishops. It was ordained also by the Pope and the Cardinals that the world should be divided into four parts, and that the archbishops from one of these parts should come together in one place, and those of the second part in another, and even so with the rest; and that four cardinals should hold chapter with them every year, each cardinal going to one of the parts of the world, and that the cardinals should make inquisition concerning the archbishops. After this ordinance it was ordained that the Pope should hold chapter with the four cardinals once in every year, and appoint inquisitors over them, and punish them if they had committed any fault against their rule. Likewise establishment was made that there should be inquisitors set over the Pope, and that once in every year there should be a chapter, and that he likewise should be punished if he had committed any fault during the year. After this, it was ordained that in every five years should be held a general chapter, to the which should come the archbishops with two auxiliaries appointed by the bishops of their archdioceses. And it was ordained likewise that in every ten years there should be held a council to the which should come all bishops and archbishops and abbots.

3. When they had made ordinance concerning the manner wherein the chapters should be held, the Pope said to the Cardinals: "Which of you desires to have the office of being inquisitor in chief, beneath the which inquisitor shall be set all the others, the inquisitor in chief being director of the chapter?" When the Pope had said these words, a certain Cardinal answered that he desired to take that office, to serve therein Domine Deus Agnus Dei Filius Patris, and the Pope granted him that office for so long as he used it well. And straightway they made a book wherein was written the manner and the rule whereby the Cardinal should proceed in his office, and how he should hold chapter.

4. The Pope sent immediately to the prelates in every land, and he held a council wherein was established the ordinance aforementioned; and the Cardinal ordained and established spies who should be watchful and make enquiry secretly as to whether the prelates followed the establishment aforementioned or no, and if the things came to the knowledge of the chapter when the Cardinal caused inquisition to be made, and if the spies of the clerks against the prelates, or of the prelates against the clerks, or of one prelate against another, agreed with the spies of the Cardinal. Great was the good and the utility which resulted from the establishment aforementioned; and the princes and the barons had such good example thereby that in their courts they likewise established inquisitors and made ordinance whereby justice and peace should be preserved.

5. There were certain particular matters whereof inquisition was to be made, namely: vainglory, pride, avarice, simony, lust, injustice, infidelity, gluttony and certain other things like to these. It came to pass one day that a bishop had made inquisition in his diocese, and had taken money, and accused not the wrongdoers neither punished them; and the inquisitors of the archbishop dis-

covered that the bishop had pardoned those faults by reason of the money which he had taken. When the archbishop held chapter, these inquisitors accused the bishop, and the bishop secretly gave money to the archbishop also, wherefore the archbishop punished him not. But the inquisitors of the Cardinal learned this thing and accused the archbishop when he came to the chapter, and the Cardinal who held chapter punished the archbishop and the bishop, and deprived each of his office.

CHAPTER XC

QUI TOLLIS PECCATA MUNDI, MISERERE NOBIS

A CERTAIN Cardinal considered for a great space of time how he might take some office wherein to serve Jesus Christ, Who takes away the sins of the world. As he rode through the city of Rome, considering what office he might have, he saw the two advocates of two princes, who disputed feloniously the one with the other, and spake evil words. So the Cardinal perceived that in the Court of Rome there was need for an advocate who should be set over all other advocates, and be feared by them all; wherefore he went to the Pope and spake to him these words:

2. "Lord Pope! Thou knowest that in thy Court there are many advocates from divers lands, and that these are contrary to those, and that for this cause there arise among them disputes and strife. Now, if it please thee, I would fain take this office of advocate, to be the occasion whereby the advocates should be governed in their profession, and be punished, if they be unruly, according as justice requires." The Pope was right pleased to give this office to the Cardinal, and he made him to be lord over all the advocates. The Cardinal had beneath him certain other advocates who were advocates in the court in general,—that is to say, of those that had no advocate in the court;

and they were recompensed with the possessions of Holy Church, for it was provided that they should take naught else of any man.

3. It came to pass one day that a suit which was being heard between a bishop and one of his canons was to be determined, and ere sentence was given one of the two advocates died, and the suit was impeded, wherefore the other advocate had recourse to the Cardinal, and he appointed an advocate, who should represent the side which had been served by the advocate who had died. So the sentence was given, and there was dispute in the court whether the sentence was valid in law, or no. Judgment was given in the court that the sentence was valid, because the Pope had made establishment that the Cardinal should appoint a sufficiently qualified advocate and that this advocate should take naught of any man.

4. Again it came to pass that the advocate of an archbishop made petition against the canons of his chapter, but they had no advocate in the court, and the Cardinal gave one of his advocates to plead on behalf of the chapter, and he sent to the chapter to advise them of that which the advocate of the archbishop had put forward against the canons of that archbishop; and that advocate filled their place in the court until the canons had sent to the court their own advocate.

5. The Cardinal had an advocate among the rest who was to be ever at the gate of the palace of the Pope, to be the advocate of those that have no money to give to the doorkeepers, and this advocate was to represent to the Pope that which was needful on their behalf. It happened one day that the advocate was at the gate of the palace, and a poor clerk, from whom a bishop had wrongfully taken his benefice, desired to have audience of the Pope, and the gatekeepers forbade him to enter, but they allowed the bishop to enter, who had taken from the clerk his benefice. Wherefore the advocate of the poor presented that clerk to

the Cardinal, and the Cardinal carried his defence against the bishop before the Pope.

6. "Holy Father and Pope!" said the Cardinal, "The dead are forgotten, and have no advocates who may plead that their will may be done as concerning the testaments which they have made; wherefore I desire to have leave of thee to be their advocate." The Pope desired that the Cardinal should be advocate for the dead; and the Cardinal appointed advocates and sent them throughout the world to the divers parts thereof to enquire if there were any man in those parts who made complaint of living men that had not fulfilled the will of the dead; wherefore each of the advocates of the Cardinal made inquisition concerning the bishop and the archbishop of that land, as to whether or no they had obliged the executors, who should carry out the testaments of the dead, to do their duty; and if any bishop or archbishop were negligent or partial in this matter, accusation was made to the Cardinal thereof, and the Cardinal punished him according as seemed to him good.

7. In a town which is called Montpellier, in the which was written this *Book of Evast and Blanquerna*, there was a great Chapter General of Preachers. In this Chapter were assembled bishops and other prelates and friars of all Christian lands, and they read letters in the Chapter concerning divers things, and recounted the deaths of friars from all Christian lands who had died that year. After these words there rose a layman who was the advocate of the unbelievers when they embrace the Holy Catholic Faith, and he said in the presence of all that if mention were made of the deaths of the friars whose souls live in Paradise, how much the more should remembrance be made of the deaths of the unbelievers who die in the sin of ignorance, and lose eternal life, and die in everlasting fire. And he begged that instruction should be given to them through the which these words should be fulfilled in

them,—namely, that Jesus Christ has taken away the sin of the world through His Incarnation and Passion. It came to the knowledge of the Cardinal who was advocate of the dead that this layman had spoken in the Chapter according to the manner aforesaid; wherefore establishment was made that, in all chapters general of religious brothers, memorial should be made of the unbelievers who have died in the sin of ignorance; and that the Cardinal should send his advocates to each of these chapters, with their letters, to the end that the Holy Catholic Faith may be preached in all the world.

CHAPTER XCI

QUI TOLLIS PECCATA MUNDI, SUSCIPE DEPRECATIONEM NOSTRAM

Now the Pope and all the Cardinals, with the exception of five Cardinals only, had taken divers offices, the which offices were named according to the *Gloria in Excelsis Deo;* wherefore the Pope said to those five Cardinals that, according to the constitution of the Court of Rome, they should seek offices wherewith should be completed the number of the rubrics of the *Gloria in Excelsis Deo.* So one of these Cardinals rode through the city of Rome to seek what office he might take which should bear the name of Qui tollis peccata mundi. As he rode through the city of Rome and passed by the Court, he saw a man who wept and spake these words: "Alas, thou wretched one! How great dishonour is done to the Holy Catholic Faith! For the Jew who denies and mocks and believes not in the Son of God, our Lord Jesus Christ, Who is the foundation of Holy Church, finds reasoners and advocates to uphold him in his suit against thee, and thou hast no man who may defend thee nor uphold thy right against him; wherefore thou wilt of necessity become poor, and be compelled to go with thy wife and children from door to door begging for the love of God."

2. Great marvel had the Cardinal at the words which that man spake, and he enquired of him wherefore he wept, and he spake these words. "Lord!" said that man: "A certain Jew, by reason of his great wealth, wrongs me, and demands of me more money than I possess; and for a long time have we been at law together, and because I cannot give so great a recompense to the judge and to my advocate as can he, therefore can I not have justice in the Court. And I have great shame because through lack of money my righteous cause is lost in the court of Rome, to the which court Jews are more opposed through their beliefs, and their evil will, than are other men."

3. Great was the wonder of the Cardinal, and greatly was he displeased in his mind when he had heard the words that that man spake to him, and he began to think deeply. While the Cardinal was yet in thought, a certain bishop, who had an income of twenty thousand marks of silver, entered Rome, and passed through a square wherein the Cardinal was, and the people that were in the square with him said: "Yonder is the bishop who has an income of twenty thousand marks of silver, and has purchased an annuity for his brother for thirty thousand marks of silver." When the Cardinal had heard these words, he heaved a great sigh and said within himself: "Alas, poor in mind and in devotion and charity! To whom has God committed His place in the world? How ill are the possessions of Holy Church divided!"

4. When the Cardinal had reflected for a great space of time, he came before the Pope and the Cardinals, and put to them this question, saying as follows: "It came to pass once that Understanding was called upon to give judgment. Understanding had two sisters: the one was Memory, and the other was Will. And between these two sisters there was a dispute as to which of the two should accompany

Understanding. Will made allegations against Memory, saying that, by her own virtue, Understanding is diligent in seeking out truth, and in desiring to judge according to right; yet, by overmuch remembrance, Understanding is oftentimes impeded in his comprehension; wherefore it seemed to Will that she herself should accompany Understanding ere he gave judgment. On the other side Memory alleged against Will that by overmuch desire Understanding is corrupted and inclined towards ignorance; wherefore it behoved rather that Memory and Understanding should be in agreement, than that Understanding and Will should be so; and in this manner, according to natural right, it was reasonable that Memory rather than Will should accompany Understanding." When the Cardinal had put forward these reasons upon either side, he prayed the Pope and the Cardinals that they would give judgment upon this matter.

5. The dispute was long, wherefore deliberation and counsel were needful that the true solution might be found. The Pope and the Cardinals, when they had reviewed the arguments upon either side, and had sought the just solution, gave sentence that in the first place Memory should go with Understanding, to the end that at the beginning Will should not incline Understanding to take one side, and that between either side there should be equality; and that Will should go after, to the end that the equality of Memory and Understanding should be preserved. Right pleasing to the Cardinal was the sentence which the Pope and the Cardinals had given, and he spake these words:

6. "According to the nature of the three powers of the soul, it is ordained in law that a judge be granted, with whom first of all there company understanding and memory, and that the two advocates who conduct the case, the one against the other, should first of all have with them memory and will. But through the giving of gifts and bribes, will takes the place of memory in the judge,

and the advocates, through the taking of gifts, have ever more of will and less of remembrance; through the which decrease of remembrance their understanding is led away from comprehension; and for this reason lawsuits are prolonged, and oftentimes false sentences are given, and disputes and strifes and wars and deaths and crimes are engendered in great number. Now, to the end that all the evils aforesaid may cease, it would be a seemlier thing to give to ten judges and to twenty advocates, from the possessions of Holy Church, such income that they should be ever in the court of Rome, and take naught else from any man, than it is to give to this bishop an income of twenty thousand marks of silver, for he has purchased for his brother an annuity of thirty thousand marks of silver, the which thirty thousand marks are alienated from the affairs of Holy Church." Right pleasing to the Pope and to the Cardinals was that which the Cardinal had said, and establishment and ordinance were made that ten judges and twenty advocates should be ever in attendance at the court, and that the Pope should recompense them sufficiently from the wealth of Holy Church, in such manner that they should take naught else of any man, and that, if they took aught else, they should lose their benefices; and by this ordinance the lawsuits in the court were greatly shortened, and many constitutions were made to expedite them.

7. Throughout every land went fame concerning the ordinances aforementioned, and many men came to plead at the court that their cases might be the more speedily concluded. So great was the number of those that came to the ten judges and the twenty advocates, that they sufficed not for all the cases which came to the court, and they had recourse to the Cardinal who was set over the office of the judges and of the advocates, and they said that they could not endure so much work; wherefore the Cardinal presented their petition to the Pope and to the

Cardinals, saying how they were occupied above measure with the multitude of their cases. So the Pope and the Cardinals ordained that in each diocese there should be judges and advocates, who should judge and argue for the poor in their disputes, and that these should be paid from the possessions of Holy Church, and that they should take naught of any man for giving sentence or pleading for them.

CHAPTER XCII

QUI SEDES AD DEXTERAM PATRIS, MISERERE NOBIS

It came to pass that upon a day of high festival in the city of Rome a deacon had sung the Gospel wherein Jesus Christ says that it is better to enter Paradise with one eye and with one foot, than to go with two eyes and two feet into hell. The deacon considered long upon that comparison, and by the grace of the Holy Spirit there came to him the will to go through the world making comparisons to all men, that he might lead them into the life of salvation. This deacon went to the Pope and to the Cardinals, and begged for the office of comparisons. The Pope said that he would give that office to a Cardinal, and that this Cardinal should have beneath him many officers who should go through the whole world making comparisons, and that this office should be called Qui sedes ad dexteram Patris, miserere nobis. When the Pope had spoken these words, there rose a Cardinal who took the office aforementioned. That Cardinal ordained that a book should be written, wherein should be kept the comparisons which his disciples would propound to all men. It came to pass one day that a king came to the court, and made complaint to the Pope concerning a king that had disinherited him, and cast him out from his kingdom albeit he had done him no wrong. When he had ended his complaints, the king wept and made semblance of great sorrow, saying these words: "For long have I been in the world honoured; now have I become poor and despised by men because of a king that is proud and a wrongdoer, who, through his great power and avarice, has taken from me my dominions." While the king wept thus and despaired, the Cardinal of the offices aforementioned enquired of the king which thing was the more pleasing to him, whether justice or wrongdoing. The king answered "Justice." The Cardinal said to him that it was better to be disinherited, and to be just and patient, than to be a king that was unjust and miserly and proud; wherefore he acted against justice if he wept at that for the which he should rather rejoice, for it was he who had disinherited him that should weep because he was proud and an evildoer. After this comparison the Cardinal made another, namely, that for one that has patience and humility it is of more advantage to be loved by God than it is harmful to be blamed by men. Deeply did the king consider these words which the Cardinal had spoken, and he spake as follows: "If I have possessed with my body in this world the kingdom which has now been taken from me, henceforward may my soul possess patience, hope, humility, justice and charity, praising and resigning itself to the will of God." Greatly were the Pope and the Cardinals pleased at that which the king had said, and from the possessions of Holy Church they made for him honourable provision, and debated how that whereof he had been deprived might be restored to him.

2. To that Court there came a Bishop who was accused by his chapter. That Bishop was a man both just and of holy life, and, because he used justice with his clergy, they desired to depose him and to have over them a lord who should be consenting to their sins. That Bishop went to the Cardinal, and asked counsel of him which was better, whether to allow himself to be accused without excusing himself, and to have patience, humility and poverty, or to excuse himself, and to permit his chapter to accuse him

and to bring the accusation into court according as was allowed by justice. The Cardinal and the Bishop spake for a great space of time concerning the matter aforementioned, and they debated according to which of the two manners aforesaid the Bishop could use the greater perfection and the more virtues; and they found that to the Bishop it was of greater advantage that he should not make excuse for himself, for from this course would follow greater patience and virtue and humility; but that, with respect to justice and charity, it was well that he should excuse himself and that the truth should be made manifest, to the end that justice should not lose its right in his chapter. Wherefore the Cardinal said to the Bishop that he could make choice of which course he desired to follow, for in either case he could act virtuously and in such wise as would be pleasing to God.

3. To a certain city there came a man who made comparisons, and he went through the streets crying aloud: "Which thing is the more needful, whether to bring up a son in good customs, or to make him heir to great riches? Or which thing is better, whether to restore wealth ill-gotten and to leave one's children poor and enter into Paradise, or to leave one's children wealthy and make no satisfaction for wrong-doing and enter into hell?" While this man went crying aloud in this wise through the streets, he passed by the house of a usurer, who thought deeply upon the words that were spoken by this man, and so often did he hear these words cried aloud that his conscience vanquished his sensual nature and ever fortified him in charity; so he undid the wrongs which he had done, and brought up his children in good habits.

4. Death, who spares neither young nor old, slew the son of an honoured citizen of Rome. That citizen had none other sons save one, neither hoped to have any again, and by reason of the death of his son he was moved to very great sorrow and wrath. It came to the ears of the Cardinal

that that citizen was in great despair, so he went to him, and made a comparison before him in these words: "Beloved son! Which thing is of greater utility to a man, whether to praise God for the good things which He has given in this world, or to praise Him for the good things which He takes from him?" "Lord!" answered that citizen: "The one kind of praise has respect to gratitude, and the other to patience; and since patience gives suffering without fault, there belongs thereto greater virtue than to gratitude, which gives pleasure without passion." "Happy son!" said the Cardinal: "Thou hast given a right judgment, and therein hast thou judged that thou thyself must have patience; for God has satisfied thee in two manners: namely, by giving thee occasion of gratitude, for this thou hadst in praising God for giving to thee thy son; and likewise, by giving thee patience, when He called him from this life to the next. Now if thy son had not died, thou hadst after one manner lost the merit which is prepared for thee, to be to thee an occasion of great happiness."

5. There went a man through the city of Rome, crying aloud: "Which thing has the greater worth, whether to sell cheaply and speak the truth, or to lie and sell dearly?" As he cried aloud these words, there passed through the square a great number of women. Among these was a great lady who was wondrously adorned and garbed, and greatly made up in her features with colours and other adornings. And that man cried aloud, enquiring which thing was of the greater worth, whether a fair lady who showed herself to be enamoured of lust, or a lady that was ugly but gave semblance of chastity. This man went before all these women crying aloud in the words aforesaid. With that lady there went squires who followed her, and she commanded that the man should be beaten and scourged, because of the words which he spake. So the squires beat the crier of comparisons and he had not

patience thereat, but made complaint to the Cardinal of the wrong which was done to him. The Cardinal reproved him straitly because he had made complaint, and deprived him of his office, and in his place set another who was a lover of patience.

6. To a certain city there went a crier who cried aloud enquiring which of these two things had the greater worth: whether "Little-care-I" or "What-will-men-say." As he passed through the principal square crying aloud in this wise, the men who were therein besought him that he would expound to them these words which he cried aloud. So he said that "What-will-men-say" was the reproach which men have when they do aught against the vanities of this world, and "Little-care-I" was the despising of this reproach because it is contrary to virtue and to the honour of God and the contempt of this world. Then a certain wise man spake to this crier and said that Sir What-will-men-say has a greater number of followers, but that Sir Little-care-I has nobler followers.

7. It came to pass on a certain occasion that two friars who had learned Arabic went to the country of the Saracens to preach the Incarnation and the Passion of the Son of God; and in one of these friars devotion and charity grew cold, so he returned and left his companion, for death made him to fear, and he longed for the dainty meats which he had been wont to enjoy, and the honours which he was accustomed to have among the people. As he returned, he met at the entrance to a certain city a crier who cried aloud, and asked which was of the greater worth, whether death that came through wrong-doing or death that came through martyrdom; and which of these manners of death accorded better with the seven virtues or was more contrary to the seven deadly sins; and through which of these manners of death is man more fitted to wear the crimson vestments which the Son of God took in human nature. While this man cried thus aloud, the friar, who had re-

turned from his journey, was seated beside a fair woman and had temptation of carnal pleasure; and the crier made comparison, asking which thing had the greater merit, whether to go among the unbelievers in peril of death, mortifying the fear of death through strength of mind, or remaining among faithful Christians and striving against temporal pleasures. Long did this religious think upon the words which the crier spake, and he returned to his companion, and had contrition for the weakness of mind into the which his want of devotion had led him.

8. Another time it came to pass that that crier cried aloud in the palace of the king, asking which thing was of the greater worth, whether to be merely a simple knight or to be king. Then he went to the palace of the bishop, and cried out asking which thing was of the greater worth, whether to be only a parish priest or to be bishop. After this he went to an abbey, and cried aloud enquiring which was of the greater worth, whether to be a cloistered monk or an abbot. Then he went before the Pope, crying aloud and asking which thing was of the greater worth, whether that the tithe of Holy Church should for ever be assigned to the government of the world, or that the bishops should have superfluity to spend on vanities. In all these manners and in many more cried the officers that were appointed to make comparisons. And very great was the good which they did, for daily they awakened in the minds of men devotion, conscience, diligence and the other virtues.

CHAPTER XCIII

QUONIAM TU SOLUS SANCTUS

The Pope Blanquerna was with his Cardinals one day, and they considered if they could do aught whereby there should be profit in the exaltation of the Catholic Faith. While they were together, there entered a Cardinal who had preached to a great multitude of people, and the Pope enquired of the Cardinal if he had seen any man weeping during his sermon. The Cardinal answered that he had not, but that he had seen many men sleeping while he preached to them. The Pope said to the Cardinals how great a marvel it was that men had so little devotion to sermons, and he enquired wherefore the Saracens, who are in error, weep during sermons. A scrivener in Arabic of the Pope answered that he had been born and brought up in a country beyond the seas, and that he was of the number of those Christians that were of heathen birth, and he said that among the Saracens they preach of devotion and of considerations upon the glory of Paradise and the pains of hell; for the which reason they have devotion to sermons, and they weep by reason of the devotion which they have.

2. After these words the Cardinal said that it was very natural, and that it was a thing of utility to preach and to prove by natural reasons the manner wherein virtues and vices are contrary, and how one virtue agrees with another, and one vice with another, and in what manner a man may mortify a vice with a virtue, or with two, and how with one virtue a man can revive another virtue; and this manner is in the *Brief Art of Finding Truth*. Wherefore natural art and devotion and consideration and brevity of sermons accord with preaching, that men may ever have devotion and may not be wearied.

3. When the Cardinal had spoken these words, the Pope and the Cardinals made ordinance that as many sermons should be preached as there are days in the year, and that in these should be contained all the best matter which is most meet to be preached, and that they should be of seemly length, and understandable by the people, for through ignorance the minds of men are oftentimes without devotion; these three hundred and sixty-five sermons were to be general and to be preached one after another in every year. After this the Pope made ordinance that men that

were devout and of holy life should go daily through the streets of the cities and of the towns, telling aloud their reflections upon Hell and its pains, and upon the glory of Heaven, that men might have daily in remembrance the pains of Hell and the glory of Paradise. When all these things had been ordained, the Pope committed this office to a Cardinal who should be the officer of Quoniam Tu Solus Sanctus through the work of preaching and of telling aloud these reflections.

4. The Cardinal who was beneficed with the office aforementioned appointed advocates and officers who should go through every land crying aloud concerning the pains of Hell and the glories of Paradise and the death of this world, according as is recounted in the *Book of Doctrine for Boys*,[1] the which book was written by a certain man for his beloved son. After this he made ordinance with religious, and with those that have the office of preaching, as to the manner wherein they should preach; and if in this office of preaching there were any excesses, how these might be corrected; and how through preaching the will might soar so high that God should be fervently loved and served through the fortifying and exalting of great devotion.

CHAPTER XCIV

TU SOLUS DOMINUS

It came to pass that a messenger from the Cardinal of Quoniam Tu Solus Sanctus sent a message to him that through the diversity of languages preaching was impeded, and that the criers of reflections could not cause men to have devotion concerning Paradise nor fear of the pains and torment of Hell. When this Cardinal had received the messenger, he made representation of this matter to the Pope, to the end that ordinance might be made whereby

[1] See note, p. 39, above.

preachers and criers of reflections should have greater freedom in the use of their offices.

2. While the Cardinal was presenting to the Pope the letters which his messenger had sent to him, it came to pass that a messenger of the Cardinal of Tu Solus Dominus came before the Pope, to whom he related that he had found great strife in the world among men, because these men were of divers nations and of divers tongues; through the which diversity of tongues men made war with each other; and through this war and this diversity of tongues there was diversity likewise of beliefs, and there were created opposing sects. Long did the Pope consider the two messages aforementioned, and he gathered all the Cardinals together, enquiring of them what counsel might be taken to destroy the diversity of languages, or by means of what language all men in religion might be brought together, that they might have understanding, and love one another, and agree in the service of God.

3. A Cardinal answered: "Lord Pope! With respect to that which thou dost ask, it is a needful thing that thou and thy court be pleasing to Christian princes and beloved by them, and that ye make them and their subjects to agree as touching their customs, to the end that the best customs may be chosen, and that in every province there may be a city wherein Latin is spoken by all; for Latin is the most general tongue, and in Latin are many words that are found in every language, and in Latin are all our books. After these things are done it behoves thee to set apart men and women to go to that city to learn Latin, to return to their own lands and to teach it to their children so soon as they begin to speak; and thus by long continuance wilt thou be able to bring it to pass that in the world there shall be one language, one belief and one faith, when one Pope after another shall have devoted himself to this matter aforementioned, according as is fitting for the accomplishment of so great a business as this that thou hast begun."

4. When the Cardinal had ended his words, the Chamberlain said to him that that which he had counselled would be too grievous a thing to accomplish, and that in order to bring it to pass there would be need of great expenditure. While the Chamberlain spake these words, a certain man that had been elected to a bishopric entered the presence of the Pope, having come to the Court to be confirmed. The diocese to the which he was elected had a yearly income of fifteen thousand silver marks. To this bishop-elect there came a messenger from the Cardinal of Domine Fili, who related that in every place where he had been he had heard it said that all the evil and error which were in the world came through fault and defect of the Pope and the Cardinals, who might well take counsel whereby the world should be well ordered, but had no diligence or care about this matter; and it was said that through the evil example which they and their officers gave to the people, the world was in strife and in error.

5. After the messenger had spoken these words, the Pope enquired of the Chamberlain which thing was better, whether to give effect to the proposal aforementioned and assign to it five thousand marks from the income of the said diocese, or to confirm the bishop and cause the Pope and his Cardinals to have evil fame. The Chamberlain answered and said that it would be better to give effect to the proposal aforementioned, that man might be more certain of its accomplishment. The Pope enquired of the Chamberlain whether through the power of God and of Holy Church it were possible that that business might wholly or partially be brought to fulfilment, and the Chamberlain, in shame and confusion, was compelled to allow that the intention of the Pope might be fulfilled.

6. "Companions and lords, friends, beloved sons!" said the Pope to the Cardinals: "That the Passion of Jesus Christ may be honoured, I require you to aid me in bringing it to pass that all the languages which exist

be reduced to one language only; for if there be no more languages than one, men will grow to understand each other, and through understanding they will love each other more, and adopt the more readily the same customs wherein they will agree. And by this proceeding our preachers will go, alike with greater ardour and greater prudence, to the unbelievers, and these will the sooner have understanding concerning the truth of eternal life; and through this business the whole world may come to good estate, whereby they that have erred may be brought to conversion." Right pleased were the Cardinals at that which the Pope besought of them, and each one offered himself to undertake his share of the task with all the powers of his understanding and will; and the Pope and the Cardinals made establishment concerning that ordinance, and commended that office to a Cardinal who should serve it and have for his expenditure sufficient money to maintain it.

CHAPTER XCV

TU SOLUS ALTISSIMUS, JESU CHRISTE, CUM SANCTO SPIRITU IN GLORIA DEI PATRIS. AMEN

THE Pope Blanquerna considered how he might bring peace and concord to the communities that are in great discord because they agree not in being obedient to one prince only who may rule them in peace and justice. While the Pope considered thus, two friars learned in Arabic, who could not pass to a certain city wherein they desired to preach the Gospel, sent letters to the Pope telling him how that they were impeded, and saying that they could not go securely along the roads, and they begged the Pope that he would write to the prince of that land to give them escort, wherewith they might go to that city where they desired to be. When the Pope had received the letter, he called the Cardinals, and spake to them these words:

2. " Agreement was made among us that for so long as the *Gloria in Excelsis Deo* should last, and be sung in Holy Church, there should be assigned to each clause a Cardinal to serve its office. Wherefore it is a thing most needful that messengers be ordained who shall go to princes throughout the world, and treat concerning the manner wherein our friars may go through all the world to preach the Word of God, and that princes may have from us letters and prayers and thanks, that they may be favourable to our friars through love of us. Likewise, it is necessary that we send messengers continually to the communes, and that we treat of peace throughout Lombardy and Tuscany and Venice, and that we treat likewise concerning the keeping of justice and charity between one commune and another. Wherefore I commit this office to the Cardinal who as yet has received none."

3. Right pleasing to the Cardinal was this office of sending messengers, the which had been given to him by the Pope, and he sent his messengers through all the provinces, and commanded enquiry to be made as to which lands were best suited to the friars and to other men who had learned divers tongues, that by these roads they might go from one land to another. When the Cardinal had ordained all these things, the Pope sent his messengers bearing gifts from him to the princes of those lands, that they might cause the roads to be made safe for those that were sent by the Pope.

4. Along these roads the Cardinal erected hostels and bridges and churches and other buildings, to the end that men might travel the more securely along these roads, and that, through the mingling of people from one country and another there might be charity and concord, and the Holy Roman Faith might be preached in the lands of pagans and of unbelievers. Great were the sums of money that the

Chamberlain gave to the Cardinal to the end that he might accomplish the task aforementioned, wherefore he said to the Pope that he should gather together treasure from the possessions of Holy Church which might suffice for the officers of the *Gloria in Excelsis Deo;* and the Pope made ordinance that the officers aforementioned should have all that was needful to them; and, through the example that Holy Church had of the officers of *Gloria in Excelsis Deo,* the income of the Church was greater than was the expenditure which they disbursed in their offices.

5. "Holy Father!" said the Cardinal to the Pope. "How may we order our messengers that they may bring peace to the communes?" The Pope answered and said to him that the messengers should go throughout the communes, and keep watch and see which commune did wrong to another; and the Pope made ordinance how that once in every year each power[1] should come to a safe place whither all the other powers should come likewise, and that, after the manner of a chapter, they should hold discussion in all friendship and make correction each of the other, and that they that refused to abide by the decisions of the definitors of the chapter should be fined. Wherefore, by reason of the ordinance which the Pope made in the manner aforementioned, the communes grew in peace and in concord.

6. It came to pass one day that two messengers from the king of India came to the Pope, beseeching him to give them students to learn their language. So the Pope sent immediately to the Cardinal of Tu Solus Altissimus, and commanded him to procure that which the king of India besought of him; for the procuring thereof accorded with his office. The Cardinal made treaty, and procured that which the Pope commanded him. Great was the benefit and good was the example that resulted from the office of the Cardinal. And because the Pope and the Cardinals

[1] *potestat:* "authority," in the modern concrete sense.

did their utmost to serve in the offices which they had taken upon themselves, God gave to them blessing, and to their works fulfilment, and made them to be pleasing to men.

ENDED IS THE BOOK OF GLORIA IN EXCELSIS DEO

BEGINNETH THE FIFTH BOOK, WHICH IS OF THE LIFE OF THE HERMIT

CHAPTER XCVI

OF THE MANNER WHEREIN BLANQUERNA RENOUNCED THE PAPACY

Blanquerna the Pope grew old, and he remembered the desire which he had had aforetime to lead the life of a hermit; so he went secretly into the Consistory with all the Cardinals, to whom he spake these words: "Through the Divine blessing the Papacy and the Court of Rome are in right good estate, and by the ordinance thereof there results wondrous good example to the Catholic Faith. Wherefore, by reason of the grace which God has given to the Court, and that He may maintain it in the state wherein it now is, it would be well that we should appoint an officer to devote himself daily to prayer and to lead the contemplative life, praying God therein to maintain the estate of the Court, to the profit of the Court and to His own honour." Each of the Cardinals held this to be very good, and they sought out a man that was holy and devout and of great perfection, that his prayers might be the more pleasing to God.

2. When the Pope had learned the will of the Cardinals, he kneeled before them all, praying them to grant that he should renounce the Papacy, and that this office of prayer should be given to him. All the Cardinals kneeled before the Pope, and strove with him every one, saying that it was a thing ill-beseeming that he should renounce the apostolical dignity, the more so because, if he renounced it, there would be the danger that the Court should no longer be in the same estate wherein it was by the grace of God and through the life of Blanquerna. The Pope Blanquerna answered that the Cardinals had come to such great perfection through the offices of *Gloria in Excelsis Deo*, that thenceforward this goodly estate might not be destroyed,

especially if another Pope were elected by the rule and art according to the which the Abbess Natana was elected. For so long did the Pope kneel and weep before the Cardinals, and with such great devotion and affection did he beg of them indulgence, that all the Cardinals obeyed his commandment.

3. When Blanquerna was freed from the Papacy and felt himself at liberty to go and serve God in the life of a hermit, who can tell the joy and the gladness that was his? As Blanquerna thought and joyed thereon, he spake to the Cardinals these words: "My lords! For a long time have I desired to be the servant and contemplator of God in the life of a hermit, to the end that in my mind there may be naught but God alone. To-morrow after Mass I go to seek my hermitage, wherefore I must take my leave, and beg for grace and blessing of you, my lords, who will be in my memory all the days of my life, and likewise in my prayers; and I heartily thank God and you that ye have assisted me so well to hold the Papacy for a great space of time."

4. Right displeased were the Cardinals when they heard that the Pope desired to go into the forest and become a hermit, and they prayed him to stay and live in the city of Rome or in some other city, whichever was the more pleasing to him, and to remain in that city in contemplation and prayer. But the blessed Pope Blanquerna consented not to their prayers, so greatly kindled was his soul by virtue of the Divine inspiration; and on the morrow after Mass he desired to go to his hermitage and to take leave of his companions.

5. "Lord Blanquerna!" said the Cardinals. "For a great space of time have we been obedient to thee every one and have fulfilled thy commandments. Thou art old and worn, and hast need of good viands and a place wherein thou mayest have corporal sustenance, to the end that thou mayest the better labour in the spiritual and contemplative

life; wherefore we pray thee that thou remain for such time among us, until we have sought thee out a convenient hermitage, and prepared it in such wise that thou mayest dwell therein, and sing and celebrate the Divine office; and until we also, with thy counsel, shall have elected a Pope who will give us grace and blessing when thou takest leave of us, for we shall have great sorrow at thy departure." With such great devotion, and with words so reasonable, did the Cardinals beg this of Blanquerna, that he had perforce to obey their prayers.

6. While Blanquerna was with the Cardinals in the city of Rome, the Cardinals sent messengers through the forests and over the high mountains, that they should seek out a convenient place wherein Blanquerna might dwell; and they made ready a place upon a high mountain wherein was the church of a hermitage, near to a fountain, that Blanquerna might dwell there, and they made ordinance that a certain monastery which was at the foot of the mountain should provide for the necessities of Blanquerna all the days of his life. And during this time wherein the Cardinals sought a place for Blanquerna to dwell, they elected as Pope the Cardinal of Laudamus Te, the which Cardinal was made Pope according as the art whereby he was elected made plain to the Cardinals; and to this Pope was committed the office of Gloria in Excelsis Deo, the which Blanquerna had aforetime held; and the office of that Cardinal was committed to a Cardinal newly elected and set in the place of the Cardinal of Laudamus Te.

CHAPTER XCVII

OF THE LEAVE WHICH BLANQUERNA TOOK OF THE POPE AND OF THE CARDINALS

Blanquerna rose early, and secretly sang the Mass of the Holy Spirit. After this the Pope sang a solemn Mass, and preached, and related the good things and the ordinances which Blanquerna had established in the Court, and how he had renounced the Papacy, and was going to do penance upon a high mountain, and how he desired to be in company of the trees and of the birds and of the beasts, and to contemplate the God of glory. Such good matter had the Pope to speak of Blanquerna the hermit, and with such great devotion did he speak of him, that the Cardinals and the people of Rome who were present at the sermon could not refrain from weeping, and all lamented that Blanquerna was to leave them, the more so because he was an old man and desired to torment his body, in solitude, with austerity of life.

2. While the Pope preached, all the people wept, and a hermit who was upon the walls of Rome spake these words to the Pope: "Lord and Apostolic Father! There is a great company of hermits in the city of Rome, who dwell near the walls[1] and live alone, and oftentimes it comes to pass that we have temptations, and know not how to contemplate, neither to weep for our sins. Now since Blanquerna has appointed many officers to serve God and to order the world, I pray Blanquerna, on behalf of all the hermits of Rome, that he remain with us and be our master and our visitor, and that this be his office; through the which office he will advantage both himself and us, and will be able to continue in the life of a hermit."

3. The Pope and the Cardinals begged Blanquerna to remain, and to take upon him this office whereof the hermit spake, for great good would follow therefrom, especially through the good example which he would give to all men. But Blanquerna made excuse for himself, and said that in no wise would he remain among men; and he took leave of all of them together, praying, supplicating and beseeching pardon, and begging that, if he had committed any fault against them, they would forgive him and pray for

[1] *en los murs.* Some authorities prefer to read "on the walls," others, "in the mountains" (*munts*), presupposing an error in the text.

him to the God of glory. When Blanquerna had ended his words, the hermit begged for himself the office which he had desired that Blanquerna should take, and the Pope granted it to him with his grace and his benediction.

4. Blanquerna took the humble clothing which accords with the life of a hermit, and made upon himself the sign whereby is signified our redemption, and kissed the feet and the hands of the Pope, and commended him to God with tears. The Pope kissed him, and commanded that two Cardinals should follow him to the hermitage wherein he was to dwell, and that if in that place there were aught to be prepared which he needed, these two Cardinals should follow him and make it ready for him immediately. The Cardinals followed Blanquerna, and all the people followed him likewise so far as the entrance of the city. Blanquerna prayed the Cardinals that they would return, and all the people with them, and that they would remain within the city; but the Cardinals would not remain, and went with him even to the cell wherein his habitation had been prepared.

5. Near to that habitation was a fountain wondrous fair, and an ancient church, and a cell that was very comely. Further, about a mile from that church there was a house wherein dwelt a man who would serve Blanquerna and prepare his food, that Blanquerna might the better have contemplation. This man was a deacon whom Blanquerna greatly loved, and who desired not to leave him, and in company with this deacon Blanquerna desired to remain that he might assist him daily in the Divine office. When Blanquerna was in his hermitage, and had prepared it in such a manner as beseems the life of a hermit, the Cardinals took leave of Blanquerna very courteously, and, commending themselves to his prayers, they returned to Rome.

CHAPTER XCVIII

OF THE LIFE WHICH BLANQUERNA LED IN HIS HERMITAGE

Blanquerna rose daily at midnight, and opened the windows of his cell, that he might behold the heavens and the stars, and began his prayer as devoutly as he might, to the end that his whole soul should be with God, and his eyes in weeping and tears. When Blanquerna had remained in contemplation and tears for a long time, even to the hour of Matins, he entered the church and rang for Matins, and the deacon came to assist him to say Matins. After dawn he sang Mass. When he had sung Mass, Blanquerna spake certain words of God to the deacon, to the end that he might cause him to love God, and they spake both together of God and of His works, and wept together through the great devotion which they had to the words which they spake. After these words the deacon entered the garden, and worked in divers manners, and Blanquerna left the church and took recreation in his soul from the work which his body had done, and he looked upon the mountains and the plains that he might have recreation therein.

2. So soon as Blanquerna felt himself refreshed, he betook himself again straightway to prayer and contemplation, or read in the books of Divine Scripture, and in the *Book of Contemplation*,[1] and thus he remained until the hour of terce. After this they said terce, sext and none, and after terce the deacon went away to prepare for Blanquerna certain herbs and vegetables. Blanquerna likewise laboured in the garden, or at some other business, that he might not become slothful, and that his body might have the greater health, and between sext and none he went to dine. After he had dined he went back alone to the church

[1] The reference is to Lull's large work of that name, not to the brief *Art of Contemplation* which follows the *Book of the Lover and the Beloved* in the present volume.

to give thanks therein to God. When he had ended his prayer, he remained yet an hour, and went to take recreation in the garden, and by the fountain, and visited all those places wherein he could best make glad his soul. After this he slept, to the end that he might the better endure the labours of the night. When he had slept, he washed his hands and his face, and remained alone until it was the hour to ring for vespers, to the which came the deacon; and when they had ended vespers they said compline, and the deacon departed, and Blanquerna entered into the consideration of those things which were the most pleasing to him, and might best prepare him to enter upon his prayers.

3. After the sun had set, Blanquerna mounted the high ground which was above his cell and remained in prayer until prime, gazing upon the heavens and the stars with tearful eyes and devotion of heart, and meditating upon the honours of God and upon the sins which men commit in this world against Him. In such great affection and fervour was Blanquerna in his contemplation, from the set of the sun even until prime, that when he had lain down and fallen asleep, he thought that he was with God even as he had made his prayer.[1]

4. In this life and in this happy state Blanquerna remained until the people of those parts conceived a great devotion to the virtues of the altar of the Holy Trinity which was in that church; and through the devotion which they had, there came to that place men and women, who disturbed Blanquerna in his prayer and contemplation. And lest the people should lose the devotion which they had to that place, he feared to tell them that they should not come there, wherefore Blanquerna changed his

[1] Part of this passage will be found quoted in the popular edition of the *Book of the Lover and the Beloved* (S.P.C.K., 1923). The divergences which will be found to exist between the two renderings are due to the fact that the earlier translation was made principally from V.

cell, and went to a hill which was a mile distant from the church, and another mile from the place where the deacon lived; and in that place he remained and dwelt, and would not go to the church at any time when the people were there, neither desired that any man or any woman should come to that cell wherein he had taken up his abode.

5. Even so lived Blanquerna, and remained in the estate of a hermit, considering that never had he led so pleasant a life, nor ever had been so well prepared for the exaltation of his soul to God. So holy was the life wherein Blanquerna dwelt that he blessed God for it, and directed in that selfsame way all such as had devotion to the virtues of the place wherein was the church. And, through the holy life of Blanquerna, the Pope and the Cardinals and their officers stood likewise the better in the grace of God.

CHAPTER XCIX

OF THE MANNER WHEREIN THE HERMIT BLANQUERNA MADE THE "BOOK OF THE LOVER AND THE BELOVED"

It came to pass one day that the hermit who was in Rome, according as we have related above, went to visit the other hermits and recluses who were in Rome, and found that in certain things they had many temptations, because they knew not how to live in the manner which best beseemed their state. So he bethought himself that he would go to Blanquerna the hermit, and beg him to make a book which should treat of the life of the hermit, and that by means of that book he should learn and be enabled to keep the other hermits in contemplation and devotion. When Blanquerna was at prayer one day, that hermit came to his cell, and begged him to write the book aforementioned. Long did Blanquerna think in what manner he would make the book and what should be the matter of it.

2. While Blanquerna thought in this wise it came to his will that he would give himself fervently to the adoration and contemplation of God, to the end that in prayer God should show him the manner wherein he should make the book and likewise the matter of it. While Blanquerna wept and adored, and God caused his soul to rise to the supreme height of its strength in contemplation of Him, Blanquerna felt himself carried away in spirit through the great fervour and devotion which he had, and he considered that the strength of love knows no bounds when the Lover has very fervent love to his Beloved. Wherefore it came to the will of Blanquerna that he should make a book of the Lover and the Beloved, the which Lover should be a faithful and devout Christian and the Beloved should be God.

3. While Blanquerna considered after this manner, he remembered how that once when he was Pope a Saracen related to him that the Saracens have certain religious men, and that among others are certain men called Sufis, who are the most prized among them, and these men have words of love and brief examples which give to men great devotion; and these are words which demand exposition, and by the exposition thereof the understanding soars aloft, and the will likewise soars, and is increased in devotion. When Blanquerna had considered after this wise, he purposed to make the book according to the manner aforementioned, and he commanded the hermit to return to Rome, saying that in a short time he would send to him by the deacon the *Book of the Lover and the Beloved*, whereby for evermore fervour and devotion would be increased in the hermits, for it would seek to inspire them with the love of God.

OF THE "BOOK OF THE LOVER AND THE BELOVED"

PROLOGUE

BLANQUERNA was in prayer, and considered the manner wherein to contemplate God and His virtues, and when he had ended his prayer, he wrote down the manner wherein he had contemplated God: and this he did daily, and brought new arguments to his prayer, to the end that after many and divers manners he should compose the *Book of the Lover and the Beloved*, and that these manners should be brief, and that in a short space of time the soul should learn to reflect in many ways. And with the blessing of God Blanquerna began the book, the which book he divided into as many verses as there are days in the year; and each verse suffices for the contemplation of God in one day according to the *Art of the Book of Contemplation.*

BEGIN THE MORAL METAPHORS

1. The Lover asked his Beloved if there remained in Him anything still to be loved. And the Beloved answered that he had still to love that by which his own love could be increased.

2. Long and perilous are the paths whereby the Lover seeks his Beloved. They are peopled by considerations, sighs and tears. They are lit up by love.

3. Many lovers came together to love One only, their Beloved, who made them all to abound in love. And each one had the Beloved for his possession, and his thoughts of Him were very pleasant, making him to suffer pain which brought delight.

4. The Lover wept and said: "How long shall it be till the darkness of the world is past, that the paths to hell may be no more? When comes the hour wherein water, that flows downwards, shall change its nature and mount upwards? When shall the innocent be more in number than the guilty?"

5. "Ah! When shall the Lover with joy lay down his life for the Beloved? And when shall the Beloved see the Lover grow faint for love of Him?"

6. Said the Lover to the Beloved: "Thou that fillest the sun with splendour, fill my heart with love." And the Beloved answered: "Hadst thou not fulness of love, thine eyes had not shed those tears, neither hadst thou come to this place to see Him that loves thee."

7. The Beloved made trial of His Lover to see if his love for Him were perfect, and He asked him how the presence of the Beloved differed from His absence. The Lover answered: "As knowledge and remembrance differ from ignorance and oblivion."

8. The Beloved asked the Lover: "Hast thou remembrance of aught wherewith I have rewarded thee, that thou

wouldst love Me thus?" "Yea," replied the Lover, "for I distinguish not between the trials that Thou sendest me and the joys."

9. "Say, O Lover!" asked the Beloved, "If I double thy trials, wilt thou still be patient?" "Yea," answered the Lover, "so that Thou double also my love."

10. Said the Beloved to the Lover: "Knowest thou yet what love meaneth?" The Lover answered: "If I knew not the meaning of love, I should know the meaning of trial, grief and sorrow."

11. They asked the Lover: "Why answerest thou not thy Beloved when He calleth thee?" He replied: "I brave great perils that I may come to Him, and I speak to Him begging His graces."

12. "Foolish Lover! Why dost thou weary thy body, cast away thy wealth and leave the joys of this world, and go about as an outcast among the people?" "To do honour to the honours of my Beloved," he replied, "for He is hated[1] and dishonoured by more men than honour and love Him."

13. "Say, Fool of Love! Which can be the better seen, the Beloved in the Lover, or the Lover in the Beloved?" The Lover answered, and said: "By love can the Beloved be seen, and the Lover by sighs and tears, by trials and by grief."

14. The Lover sought for one who should tell his Beloved how great trials he was enduring for love of Him, and how he was like to die. And he found his Beloved, Who was reading in a book wherein were written all the griefs which love made him to suffer for his Beloved, and the joy which he had of his love.

[1] *desamat*, lit. "unloved." See note, p. 148, above. This word, which occurs with particular frequency in the *Book of the Lover and the Beloved*, implies rather indifference than hate.

15. Our Lady presented her Son to the Lover, that he might kiss His feet, and that he might write in his book, concerning the virtues of Our Lady.

16. "Say, thou bird that singest! Hast thou placed thyself in the care of my Beloved, that He may guard thee from indifference, and increase in thee thy love?" The bird replied: "And who makes me to sing but the Lord of love, Who holds indifference[1] to be sin?"

17. Between fear and hope has Love made her home. She lives on thought, and dies of forgetfulness, the foundations whereof are the delights of this world.

18. There was a contention between the eyes and the memory of the Lover, for the eyes said that it was better to behold the Beloved than to remember Him. But Memory said that remembrance brings tears to the eyes, and makes the heart to burn with love.

19. The Lover enquired of Understanding and Will which of them was the nearer to his Beloved. And the two ran, and Understanding came nearer to the Beloved than did Will.

20. There was strife between the Lover and the Beloved, and another lover saw it and wept, till peace and concord were made between the Beloved and the Lover.

21. Sighs and Tears came to be judged by the Beloved, and asked Him which of them loved Him the more deeply. And the Beloved gave judgment that sighs were nearer to love, and tears to the eyes.

22. The Lover came to drink of the fountain which gives love to him that has none, and his griefs redoubled. And the Beloved came to drink of that fountain, that the love of one whose griefs were doubled might be doubled also.

[1] *desamor.* See preceding note.

23. The Lover was sick and thought on the Beloved, Who fed him on His merits, quenched his thirst with love, made him to rest in patience, clothed him with humility, and as medicine gave him truth.

24. They asked the Lover where his Beloved was. And he answered: "See Him for yourselves in a nobler house than all the nobility of creation; but see Him too in my love, my griefs and my tears."

25. They said to the Lover: "Whither goest thou?" He answered: "I come from my Beloved." "Whence comest thou?" "I go to my Beloved." "When wilt thou return?" "I shall be with my Beloved." "How long wilt thou be with thy Beloved?" "For as long as my thoughts remain on Him."

26. The birds hymned the dawn, and the Lover,[1] who is the dawn, awakened. And the birds ended their song, and the Lover died in the dawn for his Beloved.

27. The bird sang in the garden[2] of the Beloved. The Lover came, and he said to the bird: "If we understand not one another in speech, we may make ourselves understood by love; for in thy song I see my Beloved before mine eyes."

28. The Lover was fain to sleep, for he had laboured much in seeking his Beloved; and he feared lest he should forget Him. And he wept, that he might not fall asleep, and his Beloved be absent from his remembrance.

29. The Lover and the Beloved met, and the Beloved said to the Lover: "Thou needest not to speak to Me. Sign to Me only with thine eyes, for they are words to My heart,—that I may give thee that which thou dost ask."

[1] All the texts read here "Lover," though we should have expected "Beloved." We must either suppose therefore that in this verse Christ is the Lover and God the Father is the Beloved, or we may read "Beloved," and assume an error on the part of the author, copied by later MSS.

[2] *verger:* more properly "orchard."

30. The Lover was disobedient to his Beloved; and the Lover wept. And the Beloved came in the vesture of His Lover, and died, that His Lover might regain what he had lost. So He gave him a greater gift than that which he had lost.

31. The Beloved filled His Lover with love, and grieved not for his tribulations, for they would but make him love the more deeply; and the greater were the Lover's tribulations, the greater was his delight and joy.

32. The Lover said: "The secrets of my Beloved torture me, for my deeds reveal them, and my mouth keeps silence and reveals them to none."

33. This is Love's contract: the Lover must be long-suffering, patient, humble, fearful, diligent, trustful; he must be ready to face great dangers for the honour of his Beloved. And his Beloved is pledged to be true and free, merciful and just with His lover.

34. The Lover set forth over hill and plain in search of true devotion, and to see if his Beloved were well served. But in every place he found that devotion was sorely lacking. So he delved into the earth to see if there he could find more perfect devotion, which was lacking above ground.

35. "O bird that singest of love, ask thou of my Beloved, Who has taken me to be His servant, wherefore He tortures me with love." The bird replied: "If Love made thee not to bear trials, wherewith couldst thou show thy love for Him?"

36. Pensively the Lover trod the paths of his Beloved. Now he stumbled and fell among the thorns; but they were to him as flowers, and as a bed of love.

37. They asked the Lover: "Wouldst thou change for another thy Beloved?" He answered and said: "Why, what other is better or nobler than the sovereign and eternal

Good? For He is infinite in greatness and power and wisdom and love and perfection."

38. The Lover wept, and sang of his Beloved, and said: "Swifter is love in the heart of the lover than is the splendour of the lightning to the eye, or the thunder to the ear. The tears of love gather more swiftly than the waves of the sea; and sighing is more proper to love than is whiteness to snow."

39. They asked the Lover: "Wherein is the glory of thy Beloved?" He answered: "He is Glory itself." They asked him: "Wherein lies His power?" He answered: "He is Power itself." "And wherein lies His wisdom?" "He is Wisdom itself." "And wherefore is He to be loved?" "Because He is Love itself."

40. The Lover rose early and went to seek his Beloved. He found travellers on the road, and he asked if they had seen his Beloved. They answered him: "When did the eyes of thy mind lose sight of thy Beloved?" The Lover answered and said: "Even when my Beloved is no longer in my thoughts, He is never absent from the eyes of my body, for all things that I see picture to me my Beloved."

41. With eyes of thought and grief, sighs and tears, the Lover gazed upon his Beloved; and with eyes of grace, justice and pity, mercy and bounty, the Beloved gazed upon His Lover. And the bird sang of that Countenance so full of delight, whereof we have already spoken.

42. The keys of the doors of love are gilded with meditations, sighs and tears; the cord which binds them is woven of conscience, contrition, devotion and satisfaction; the door is kept by justice and mercy.

43. The Lover beat upon the door of his Beloved with blows of love and hope. The Beloved heard the blows of His Lover, with humility, pity, charity and patience. Deity

and Humanity opened the doors, and the Lover went in to his Beloved.

44. Propriety and Community met, and joined together, that there might be love and benevolence between Lover and Beloved.

45. There are two fires that nurture the love of the Lover: the one is made of pleasures, desires and thoughts: the other is compounded of fear and grief, of weeping and of tears.

46. The Lover longed for solitude,[1] and went away to live alone, that he might have the companionship of his Beloved, for amid many people he was lonely.

47. The Lover was all alone, in the shade of a fair tree. Men passed by that place, and asked him why he was alone. And the Lover answered: "I am alone, now that I have seen you and heard you; until now, I was in the company of my Beloved."

48. By signs of love, the Lover held converse with the Beloved; by means of fear, and of weeping and tears and thoughts, the Lover recounted his griefs to the Beloved.

49. The Lover feared lest his Beloved should fail him in his greatest need; and the Beloved took love from His Lover. Then the Lover had contrition and repentance of heart; and the Beloved restored hope and charity to the heart of the Lover, and to his eyes weeping and tears, that love might return to him.

50. Whether Lover and Beloved are near or far is all one; for their love mingles as water mingles with wine. They are linked as heat with light; they agree and are united as Essence and Being.

51. Said the Lover to his Beloved: "In Thee are both my healing and my grief: the more surely Thou healest

[1] So D (*solitat*); the other versions have *soliditat*.

me, the greater grows my grief; and the more I languish, the more dost Thou give me health." The Beloved answered: " Thy love is a seal and an impress whereby thou dost show forth My honour before men."

52. The Lover saw himself taken and bound, wounded and killed, for the love of his Beloved; and they that tortured him asked him: " Where is thy Beloved ? " He answered: " See Him here in the increase of my love, and the strength which it gives me to bear my torments."

53. Said the Lover to the Beloved: " I have never fled from Thee, nor ceased to love Thee, since I knew Thee, for I was ever in Thee, by Thee and with Thee whithersoever I went." The Beloved answered: " Nor since thou hast known Me and loved Me have I once forgotten thee; never once have I deceived or failed thee."

54. As one that was a fool went the Lover through a city, singing of his Beloved; and men asked him if he had lost his wits. " My Beloved," he answered, " has taken my will, and I myself have yielded up to Him my understanding; so that there is left in me naught but memory, wherewith I remember my Beloved."

55. The Beloved said: " It would be a miracle against love that the Lover should fall asleep and forget his Beloved." The Lover answered: " It would be a miracle likewise against love if the Beloved awakened him not, since He has desired him."

56. The heart of the Lover soared to the heights of the Beloved, so that he might not be impeded from loving Him in this abyss, the world. And when he reached his Beloved he contemplated Him with sweetness and delight. But the Beloved led him down again to this world that he might contemplate Him in tribulations and griefs.

57. They asked the Lover: " Wherein is all thy wealth ? " He answered: " In the poverty which I bear for my Be-

loved." "And where is thy repose?" "In the afflictions of love." "Who is thy physician?" "The trust that I have in my Beloved." "And who is thy master?" "The signs which in all creatures I see of my Beloved."

58. The bird sang upon a branch in leaf and flower, and the breeze stirred the leaves, and bore away the scent of the flowers. "What means the trembling of the leaves, and the scent of the flowers?" asked the Lover of the bird. The bird answered: "The trembling of the leaves signifies obedience, and the scent of the flowers, suffering and adversity."

59. The Lover went in desire of his Beloved, and he met two friends, who greeted and embraced and kissed each other, with love and with tears. And the Lover swooned, so strongly did these two lovers call to his memory his Beloved.

60. The Lover thought on death, and was afraid, till he remembered his Beloved. Then in a loud voice he cried to those that were near him: "Ah, sirs! Have love, that ye may fear neither death nor danger, in doing honour to my Beloved."

61. They asked the Lover where his love first began. He answered: "It began in the glories of my Beloved; and from that beginning I was led to love my neighbour even as myself, and to cease to love[1] deception and falsehood."

62. "Say, Fool of Love! If thy Beloved no longer cared for thee, what wouldst thou do?" "I should love Him still," he replied. "Else must I die; seeing that to cease to love is death and love is life."

63. They asked the Lover what he meant by perseverance. "It is both happiness and sorrow," he answered,

[1] *desamar.*

"in the Lover who ever loves, honours and serves his Beloved with fortitude, patience and hope."

64. The Lover desired his Beloved to recompense him for the time that he had served Him. And the Beloved reckoned the thoughts and tears and longings and perils and trials which His Lover had borne for love of Him; and the Beloved added to the account eternal bliss, and gave Himself for a recompense to His Lover.

65. They asked the Lover what he meant by happiness. "It is sorrow," he replied, "borne for Love."

66. "Say, O Fool! What meanest thou by sorrow?" "It is the remembrance of the dishonour that is done to my Beloved, Who is worthy of all honour."

67. The Lover was gazing on a Place where he had seen his Beloved. And he said: "Ah, place that recallest the blessed haunts[1] of my Beloved! Thou wilt tell my Beloved that I suffer trials and sorrows for His sake." And that Place made answer: "When thy Beloved hung upon me, He bore for thy love greater trials and sorrows than all other trials and sorrows that Love could give to its servants."

68. Said the Lover to his Beloved: "Thou art all, and through all, and in all, and with all. I would give Thee all of myself that I may have all of Thee, and Thou all of me." The Beloved answered: "Thou canst not have Me wholly unless thou art wholly Mine." And the Lover said: "Let me be wholly Thine and be Thou wholly mine." The Beloved answered: "What then will thy son have, and thy brother and thy father?" The Lover replied: "Thou, O my Beloved! art so great a Whole, that Thou canst abound, and be wholly of each one who gives himself wholly to Thee."

69. The Lover extended and prolonged his thoughts of the greatness and everlastingness of his Beloved, and he

[1] Lit. *custumes:* "ways."

found in Him neither beginning, nor mean, nor end. And the Beloved said: " What measurest thou, O Fool ? " The Lover answered: " I measure the lesser with the greater, defect with fulness, and beginning with infinity and eternity, to the end that humility, patience, charity and hope may be planted the more firmly in my remembrance."

70. The paths of love are both long and short. For love is clear, bright and pure, subtle yet simple, strong, diligent, brilliant, and abounding both in fresh thoughts and in old memories.

71. They asked the Lover: " What are the fruits of love ? " He answered: " They are pleasures, thoughts, desires, longings, sighs, trials, perils, torments and griefs. And without these fruits Love's servants have no part in her."

72. Many persons were with the Lover, who made complaint of his Beloved that He increased not his love, and of Love, that it gave him trials and sorrows. The Beloved made reply that the trials and sorrows whereof he accused Love were the increase of love itself.

73. " Say, O Fool ! Why dost thou not speak, and what is this for the which thou art thoughtful and perplexed ? " The Lover answered: " It is for the beauties of my Beloved, and the likeness between the joys and the sorrows which are brought to me and given me by Love."

74. " Say, O Fool ! Which thing was in being first, thy heart or thy love ? " He answered and said: " Both my heart and love came into being together; for were it not so, the heart had not been made for love, nor love for reflection."

75. They asked the Fool: " Wherein had thy love its birth: in the secrets of the Beloved, or in the revelation of them to men ? " He answered: " Love in its fulness makes no such distinction as this; for secretly the Lover keeps

hidden the secrets of his Beloved; secretly also he reveals them, and yet when they are revealed he keeps them secret still."

76. The secrets of love, unrevealed, cause anguish and grief; revelation of love brings fervour and fear. And for this cause the Lover must ever have sorrow.

77. Love called his lovers, and bade them ask of him the most desirable and pleasing gifts. And they asked of Love that he would clothe and adorn them with his own garments, that they might be the more acceptable to the Beloved.

78. The Lover cried aloud to all men, and said: "Love bids you ever love: in walking and sitting, in waking and sleeping, in speech and in silence, in buying and selling, in weeping and laughing, in joy and in sorrow, in gain and in loss—in whatsoever you do, ye must love, for this is Love's commandment."

79. "Say, O Fool! When came Love first to thee?" "In that time," he replied, "when my heart was enriched and filled with thoughts and desires, sighs and griefs, and my eyes abounded in weeping and in tears." "And what did Love bring thee?" "The wondrous ways of my Beloved, His honours and His exceeding worth."[1] "How came these things?" "Through memory and understanding." "Wherewith didst thou receive them?" "With charity and hope." "Wherewith dost thou guard them?" "With justice, prudence, fortitude and temperance."

80. The Beloved sang, and said: "Little knows the Lover of love, if he be ashamed to praise his Beloved, or if he fear to do Him honour in those places wherein He is most grievously dishonoured; and little knows he of love who is impatient of tribulations; and he who loses trust in his Beloved makes no agreement between love and hope."

[1] *valors.* See note, p. 175, above.

81. The Lover sent letters to his Beloved, asking Him if there were others who would help him to suffer and bear the grievous cares which he endured for love of Him. And the Beloved replied to the Lover: "There is naught in Me that can fail or wrong thee."

82. They asked the Beloved concerning the love of His Lover. He answered: "It is a mingling of joy and sorrow, of fervour and fear."

83. They asked the Lover concerning the love of his Beloved. He answered: "It is the inflowing of infinite goodness, eternity, power, wisdom, charity and perfection. This is that which flows to the Lover from the Beloved."

84. "Say, O Fool! What meanest thou by a marvel?" He answered: "It is a marvel to love things absent more than things present; and to love things visible and things corruptible more than things invisible and incorruptible."

85. The Lover went to seek his Beloved, and he found a man that was dying without love. And he said: "How great a sadness is it that any man should die without love!" So the Lover said to him that was dying: "Say, wherefore dost thou die without love?" And he answered: "Because I have lived without love."

86. The Lover asked his Beloved: "Which thing is greater—loving, or love itself?" The Beloved answered: "In creatures, love is the tree, the fruit whereof is loving; and the flowers and the leaves are trials and griefs. And in God, love and loving are one and the same thing, without either griefs or trials."

87. The Lover was in grief and sorrow, through overmuch thought. And therefore he begged his Beloved to send him a book, wherein he might see Him in His virtues, that his sorrow might thereby be relieved. So the Beloved sent that book to His Lover, and his trials and griefs were doubled.

88. Sick with love was the Lover, and a physician came in to see him who multiplied his sorrows and his thoughts. And in that same hour the Lover was healed.

89. Love went apart with the Lover, and they had great joy of the Beloved; and the Beloved revealed himself to them. The Lover wept, and afterwards was in rapture, and Love swooned thereat. But the Beloved brought life to His Lover by bringing to his memory His virtues.

90. The Lover said to the Beloved: "By many ways dost Thou come to my heart, and revealest Thyself to my sight. And by many names do I name Thee. But the love whereby Thou dost quicken me and mortify me is one, and one alone."

91. The Beloved revealed Himself to His Lover, clothed in new and scarlet robes. He stretched out His Arms to embrace him; He inclined His Head to kiss him; and He remained on high that he might ever seek Him.

92. The Beloved was absent from His Lover, and the Lover sought his Beloved with his memory and understanding, that he might love Him. The Lover found his Beloved, and he asked Him whither He had been. "In the absence of thy remembrance," answered the Beloved, "and in the ignorance of thy understanding."

93. "Say, O Fool! Hast thou shame when men see thee weep for thy Beloved?" "Shame apart from sin," answered the Lover, "signifies defect of love in one who knows not how to love."

94. The Beloved planted in the heart of the Lover sighs and longings, virtues and love. The Lover watered the seed with his tears.

95. In the body of the Lover the Beloved planted trials, tribulations and griefs. And the Lover tended his body with hope and devotion, patience and consolations.

96. The Beloved made a great feast, held a court of many honourable barons, sent many invitations and gave great gifts. To this court came the Lover, and the Beloved said to him: "Who called thee to come to this court?" The Lover answered: "Need and love compelled me to come, that I might behold Thy adornments and Thy wonders."

97. They asked the Lover: "Whence art thou?" He answered: "From love." "To whom dost thou belong?" "I belong to love." "Who gave thee birth?" "Love." "Where wast thou born?" "In love." "Who brought thee up?" "Love." "How dost thou live?" "By love." "What is thy name?" "Love." "Whence comest thou?" "From love." "Whither goest thou?" "To love." "Where dwellest thou?" "In love." "Hast thou aught but love?" "Yea," he answered, "I have faults; and I have sins against my Beloved." "Is there pardon in thy Beloved?" "Yea," answered the Lover, "in my Beloved there is mercy and justice, and therefore am I lodged between fear and hope."

98. The Beloved left the Lover, and the Lover sought Him in his thoughts, and enquired for Him of men in the language of love.

99. The Lover found his Beloved, who was despised among the people, and he told the Beloved what great wrong was done to His honour. The Beloved answered him, and said: "Lo, I suffer this dishonour for lack of fervent and devoted lovers." The Lover wept, and his sorrows were increased, but the Beloved comforted him, by revealing to him His wonders.

100. The light of the Beloved's abode came to illumine the dwelling of the Lover, to cast out its darkness, and to fill it with joys and griefs and thoughts. And the Lover cast out all things from his dwelling, that the Beloved might be lodged there.

101. They asked the Lover what sign his Beloved bore upon His banner. He answered: " The sign of One dead." They asked him why He bore such a sign. He answered: " Because He once died and was crucified, and because they that glory in being His lovers must follow in His steps."

102. The Beloved came to lodge in the dwelling of His Lover, and the steward demanded of Him the reckoning. But the Lover said: " My Beloved is to be lodged freely."[1]

103. Memory and Will set forth together, and climbed into the mountain of the Beloved, that understanding might be exalted and love for the Beloved increased.

104. Every day sighs and tears are messengers between the Lover and the Beloved, that between them there may be solace and companionship and friendship and goodwill.

105. The Lover yearned for his Beloved, and sent to Him his thoughts, that they might bring him back from his Beloved the bliss which for so long had been his.

106. The Beloved gave to His Lover the gift of tears, sighs, griefs, thoughts and sorrows, with the which gift the Lover served his Beloved.

107. The Lover begged his Beloved to give him riches, peace and honour in this world; and the Beloved revealed His Countenance to the memory and understanding of the Lover, and gave Himself as an Aim to his will.

108. They asked the Lover: " Wherein consists honour?" He answered: " In comprehending and loving my Beloved." And they asked him also: " Wherein lies dishonour?" He answered: " In forgetting and ceasing to love Him."

109. " Tormented was I by love, O Beloved, until I cried that Thou wast present in my torments; and then

[1] V reads: " My Beloved is to be lodged freely,—yea, with a gift,—for long ago He paid the price of all men."

did love ease my griefs, and Thou as a guerdon didst increase my love, and love doubled my torments."

110. In the path of love the Lover found another who was silent, and who with tears, grief, and drawn features made accusation and reproach against Love. And Love made excuse with loyalty, hope, patience, devotion, fortitude, temperance and happiness; and he blamed the Lover who cried out upon Love, for that he had given him gifts so noble as these.

111. The Lover sang and said: "Ah, what great affliction is love! Ah, what great happiness it is to love my Beloved, Who loves His lovers with infinite and eternal love, perfect and complete in everything!"

112. The Lover went into a far country thinking to find therein his Beloved, and in the way there met him two lions. The Lover was afraid, even to death, for he desired to live and serve his Beloved. So he sent Memory to his Beloved, that Love might be present at his passing, for with Love he could better endure death. And while the Lover had remembrance of his Beloved, the two lions came to him humbly, licked the tears from his eyes, and caressed his hands and feet. So the Lover went on his way in peace to seek his Beloved.

113. The Lover journeyed over hill and dale, but he could find no way of escape from the imprisonment in which Love had for so long enthralled his body and his thoughts and all his desires and joys.

114. While the Lover went toiling in this wise, he found a hermit who was sleeping near to a fair spring. The Lover wakened the hermit, and asked him if in his dreams he had seen the Beloved. The hermit answered that his own thoughts likewise, whether he was sleeping or waking, were held captive in the prison of Love. The Lover joyed greatly that he had found a fellow-prisoner; and they both wept, for the Beloved has few such lovers as these.

115. Naught is there in the Beloved wherein the Lover has not care and sorrow, nor has the Lover aught in himself wherein the Beloved joys not and has no part. And therefore is the love of the Beloved ever in action, while that of the Lover is in grief and suffering.[1]

116. A bird was singing upon a branch: "I will give a fresh thought to the lover who will give me two." The bird gave that fresh thought to the Lover, and the Lover gave two to the bird, that its afflictions might be assuaged; and the Lover felt his griefs increased.

117. The Lover and the Beloved met together, and their caresses, embraces and kisses, their weeping and tears, bore witness to their meeting. Then the Beloved asked the Lover concerning his state, and the Lover was speechless before his Beloved.

118. The Lover and the Beloved strove, and their love made peace between them. Which of them, think you,[2] bore the stronger love toward the other?

119. The Lover loved all those that feared his Beloved, and he feared all those that feared Him not. And there arose this question: Which thing was greater in the Lover, whether love or fear?

120. The Lover made haste[3] to follow his Beloved, and he passed along a road where there was a fierce lion which killed all that passed by it carelessly and without devotion.

121. The Lover said: "He that fears not my Beloved must fear all things, and that he that fears Him may be bold and fervent in all things beside."

122. They asked the Lover: "What meanest thou by occasion?" He answered: "It is to have pleasure in

[1] *passió.* The reference is to the Aristotelian category. Cf. *acció,* above.
[2] *e fo questió,* translated in § 119 "and there arose this question." The translation of this phrase, which occurs frequently, is varied to avoid monotony.
[3] *jurtar,* an obscure word. Cf. modern Majorcan *juitar,* to strive.

penance, understanding in knowledge, hope in patience, health in abstinence, consolation in remembrance, love in diligence, loyalty in shame, riches in poverty, peace in obedience, strife in malevolence."

123. Love shone through the cloud which had come between the Lover and the Beloved, and made it to be as bright and resplendent as is the moon by night, as the day-star at dawn, as the sun at midday, and as the understanding in the will; and through that bright cloud the Lover and the Beloved held converse.

124. They asked the Lover: "What is the greatest darkness?" He answered: "The absence of my Beloved." "And what is the greatest light?" "The presence of my Beloved."

125. The sign of the Beloved is seen in the Lover, who for love's sake is in tribulations, sighs and tears, and thoughts, and is held in contempt of the people.

126. The Lover wrote these words: "My Beloved delighteth because I raise my thoughts to Him, and for Him my eyes weep, and without grief I have neither life nor feeling, neither can I see nor hear nor smell."

127. "Ah, Understanding and Will! Cry out[1] and awaken the watchdogs that sleep, forgetting my Beloved. Weep, O eyes! Sigh, O heart! And, Memory, forget not the dishonour which is done to my Beloved by those whom He has so greatly honoured."

128. The enmity that is between men and my Beloved increases. My Beloved promises gifts and rewards, and threatens with justice and wisdom. And Memory and Will despise both His threats and His promises.

129. The Beloved drew near to the Lover, to comfort and console him for the griefs which he suffered and the tears which he shed. And the nearer came the Beloved to

[1] *ladrats:* "bark."

the Lover, the more he grieved and wept, crying out upon the dishonour which was done to his Beloved.

130. With the pen of love, with the water of his tears, and on paper of suffering, the Lover wrote letters to his Beloved. And in these he told how devotion tarried, how love was dying, and how sin and error were increasing the number of His enemies.

131. The Lover and the Beloved were bound in love with the bonds of memory, understanding, and will, that they might never be parted; and the cord wherewith these two loves were bound was woven of thoughts and griefs, sighs and tears.

132. The Lover lay in the bed of love: his sheets were of joys, his coverlet was of griefs, his pillow of tears. And none knew if the fabric of the pillow was that of the sheets or of the coverlet.

133. The Beloved clothed His Lover in vest, coat and mantle, and gave him a helmet of love. His body He clothed with thoughts, his feet with tribulations, and his head with a garland of tears.

134. The Beloved adjured His Lover not to forget Him. The Lover answered that he could not forget Him because he could not do otherwise than know Him.

135. The Beloved said to His Lover: "Thou shalt praise and defend Me in those places where men most fear to praise Me." The Lover answered: "Provide me then with love." The Beloved answered: "For love of thee I became incarnate, and endured the pains of death."

136. The Lover said to his Wellbeloved: "Show me the way wherein I may make Thee to be known and loved and praised among men." The Beloved filled His Lover with devotion, patience, charity, tribulations, thoughts, sighs and tears. And to the heart of the Lover came boldness to praise his Beloved; and in his mouth were praises

of his Beloved; and in his will was contempt of the reproaches of men who judge falsely.

137. The Lover spake to the people in these words: "He that truly remembers my Beloved, in remembering Him forgets all things around; and he that forgets all things in remembering my Beloved, is defended by Him from all things, and receives a part in all things."

138. They asked the Lover: "Whereof is Love born, whereon does it live, and wherefore does it die?" The Lover answered: "Love is born of remembrance, it lives on understanding, and it dies through forgetfulness."

139. The Lover forgot all that was beneath the high heavens that his understanding might soar the higher towards a knowledge of the Beloved, Whom his will desired to contemplate and to preach.

140. The Lover went out to do battle for the honour of his Beloved, and took with him faith, hope, charity, justice, prudence, fortitude and temperance wherewith to vanquish the enemies of his Beloved. And the Lover had been vanquished had the Beloved not helped him to make known His greatness.

141. The Lover desired to attain to the farthest goal of his love for the Beloved; and other objects blocked his path. For this cause his longing desires and thoughts gave the Lover sorrow and grief.

142. The Lover was glad, and rejoiced in the greatness of his Beloved. But afterwards the Lover was sad because of overmuch thought and reflection. And he knew not which he felt the more deeply—whether the joys or the sorrows.

143. The Lover was sent by his Beloved as a messenger to Christian princes and to unbelievers, to teach them an *Art* and *Elements*,[1] whereby to know and love the Beloved.

[1] References to certain works of Lull himself.

144. If thou seest a lover clothed in noble raiment, honoured through vainglory, sated with food and sleep, know thou that in that man thou seest damnation and torment. And if thou seest a lover poorly clothed, despised by men, pale and thin with fast and vigil, know thou that in that man thou lookest upon salvation and everlasting weal.

145. The Lover made complaint, and his heart cried out for the heat of love that was within him. The Lover died, and the Beloved wept, and gave him the comfort of patience[1] and hope and reward.

146. The Lover wept for that which he had lost; and none could comfort him, for his losses could not be regained.

147. God has created the night that the Lover may keep vigil, and think upon the glories of his Beloved: and the Lover thought that it had been created for the rest and sleep of those that were wearied with loving.

148. Men mocked and reproved the Lover, because he went about as a fool for love's sake. And the Lover despised their reproaches, and himself reproved them, because they loved not his Beloved.

149. The Lover said: "I am clothed in vile raiment; but love clothes my heart with thoughts of delight, and my body with tears, griefs and sufferings."

150. The Beloved sang, and said: "Those that praise Me devote themselves to the praise of My valour,[2] and the enemies of My honour torment them and have them in contempt. Therefore have I sent to my Lover that he may weep and lament the dishonour which I have suffered, and his laments and tears are born of My love."

[1] P: "consolation and patience."

[2] *i.e.* "worth." See note, p. 175, above.

151. The Lover made oath to the Beloved that for love of Him he endured and loved trials and sufferings, and he begged the Beloved that He would love him and have compassion on his trials and sufferings.[1] The Beloved made oath that it was the nature and property of His love to love all them that loved Him, and to have pity on such as endured trials for love of Him. The Lover was glad, and rejoiced in the nature and essential property of his Beloved.

152. The Beloved silenced His Lover, and the Lover took comfort in gazing upon his Beloved.

153. The Lover wept and called upon his Beloved, until the Beloved descended from the supreme heights of Heaven; and He came to earth to weep and grieve and die for the sake of love, and to teach men to know and love and praise His honours.

154. The Lover reproached Christian people, because in their letters they put not first the name of his Beloved, Jesus Christ, to do Him the same honour that the Saracens do Mahomet, who was a knave and no true man, when they honour him by naming him in their letters first of all.

155. The Lover met a squire who walked pensively, and was pale, thin, and poorly clothed; and he greeted the Lover and said: "Now God guide thee, that thou mayest find thy Beloved!" And the Lover asked him how he had recognised him; and the squire said: "Some there are of Love's secrets that reveal others, and therefore between lovers is there recognition."

156. The glories, honours and good works of the Beloved are the riches and the treasure of the Lover. And the treasures of the Beloved are the thoughts, desires, torments, tears and griefs wherewith the Lover ever honours and loves his Beloved.

[1] P, D: that He would have his trials and suffering(s) in remembrance.

157. Great companies and hosts of lovers have assembled themselves together; they bear the banner of love, whereon is the figure and the sign of their Beloved. And they will have with them none that has not love, lest their Beloved should be dishonoured.

158. Men that show their folly by heaping up riches move the Lover to be a fool for love; and the shame that the Lover has of men at going among them as a fool makes him to be esteemed and loved. Which of the two emotions, think ye, is the greater occasion of love?

159. Love made the Lover to be sad through excess of thought; the Beloved sang, and the Lover rejoiced to hear Him. Which of these two occasions, think ye, gave to the Lover the greater increase of love?

160. In the secrets of the Lover are revealed the secrets of the Beloved, and in the secrets of the Beloved are revealed the secrets of the Lover. Which of these two secrets, think ye, is the greater occasion of revelation?

161. They asked the Fool by what signs his Beloved might be known. He answered and said: " By mercy and pity, which are essentially in His Will, without change soever."

162. Such was the love which the Lover had to the Beloved, that he desired the good of all above the good of each,[1] and for his Beloved to be everywhere known and praised, and desired.

163. Love and Indifference met in a garden,[2] where the Lover and the Beloved were talking in secret. And Love asked Indifference for what intent he had come to that place. " That the Lover may cease to love," he replied, " and the Beloved to be honoured." The words of Indiffer-

[1] There is here a play upon words, which may be brought out by translating: " Through the particular love which the Lover had to his Beloved, he desired the general good above the particular, that his Beloved might be generally known and praised and desired."

[2] *verger*.

ence were greatly displeasing to the Beloved and the Lover, and their love was increased, that it might vanquish and destroy Indifference.

164. "Say, O Fool! In which thing dost thou take the greater pleasure—whether in loving or in hating?" "In loving," he replied, "for I have only hated to the end that I may love."

165. "Say, O Lover! Which thing dost thou strive to understand the better—whether truth or falsehood?" He answered: "Truth." "And wherefore so?" "Because I understand falsehood that I may the better understand truth."

166. The Lover perceived that he was loved by his Beloved, and he enquired of Him if His love and His mercy were one and the same thing. The Beloved affirmed that in His Essence there was no distinction between His love and His mercy. Therefore said the Lover: "Why, then, does Thy love torment me, and why does not Thy mercy heal me of my griefs?" And the Beloved answered: "It is mercy that gives thee these griefs, that thou mayest the more perfectly honour therewith My love."

167. The Lover desired to go into a far country to do honour to his Beloved, and he wished to disguise himself that he might not be taken captive on the way; but he could not hide the tears in his eyes, nor his pale and drawn face, nor the plaints and thoughts and sighs, the sorrow and the griefs of his heart. And so he was taken captive on the journey and delivered to the tormentors by the enemies of his Beloved.

168. Imprisoned was the Lover in the prison of Love. Thoughts, desires and memories held and enchained him lest he should flee to his Beloved. Griefs tormented him; patience and hope consoled him. And the Lover would have died, but the Beloved revealed to him His Presence, and the Lover revived.

169. The Lover met his Beloved, and he knew Him and wept. The Beloved reproved him, because he wept not until he knew Him. "Wherein didst thou know Me," He asked, "since thine eyes were not already wet with tears?" The Lover answered: "In my memory, understanding and will, whereby, so soon as the eyes of my body saw Thee, my love was increased."

170. "What meanest thou by love?" said the Beloved. And the Lover answered: "It is to bear upon the heart of the Lover the features and the words of the Beloved. It is the yearning that is in the heart of the Lover, with desire and tears."

171. "Love is the mingling of boldness and fear, that comes through great fervour. It is the desire for the Beloved as the end of the will. It is that which makes the Lover like to die when he hears one sing of the beauties of the Beloved. It is that wherein I die daily, and wherein for ever is my will."

172. Devotion and Yearning sent thoughts as messengers to the heart of the Lover, to bring tears to his eyes, which for long had wept but now would weep no more.

173. Said the Lover: "O ye that love, if ye will have fire, come light your lanterns at my heart; if water, come to my eyes, whence flow the tears in streams; if thoughts of love, come gather them from my meditations."

174. It happened one day that the Lover was meditating on the great love which he had for his Beloved, and the great trials and perils into the which this love for so long had led him, and he fell to considering how that his reward would be great. And as he thus discoursed with himself, he remembered that his Beloved had recompensed him already, since He had kindled within him a love for His Presence, and through that very love had given him his griefs.

175. The Lover was wiping away the tears which for Love's sake he had shed, lest he should reveal the sufferings which his Beloved sent him. But the Beloved said: "Why wouldst thou hide from others these marks of thy love? For I have given them to thee that others may love My valour also."

176. "Say, thou that for love's sake goest as a fool! For how long wilt thou be a slave, and forced to weep and suffer trials and griefs?" He answered: "Till my Beloved shall separate body and soul in me."

177. "Say, O Fool, hast thou riches?" He answered: "I have my Beloved." "Hast thou towns, castles or cities, provinces or duchies?" He answered: "I have love, thoughts, tears, desires, trials, griefs, which are better than empires or kingdoms."

178. They asked the Lover wherein he recognised the decrees of his Beloved. He answered: "In that He allots to His lovers equality of joys and griefs."

179. "Say, O Fool! Which of these knows the more of love—he that has joys thereof or he that has trials and griefs?" He answered: "There can be no knowledge of love without both the one and the other."

180. They asked the Lover: "Wherefore wilt thou not defend thyself from the sins and the false crimes whereof men accuse thee?" He answered and said: "I have to defend my Beloved, whom men falsely accuse; man may indeed be full of deceit and error, and is scarce worthy to be defended."

181. "Say, O Fool! Wherefore defendest thou Love when it thus tries and torments thy body and thy heart?" He answered: "Because it increases my merits and my happiness."

182. The Lover made complaint of his Beloved, because He caused Love so grievously to torment him. And the

Beloved made reply[1] by increasing his trials and perils, thoughts and tears.

183. " Say, O Fool! Wherefore makest thou excuse for the guilty? " He answered: " That I may not be like to those that accuse the innocent with the guilty."

184. The Beloved raised the understanding of the Lover that he might comprehend His greatness, and incline his memory to recall his own shortcomings, and that his will might hate them, and soar aloft to love the perfections of the Beloved.

185. The Lover sang of his Beloved and said: " So great is my will to love Thee, that all things that once I hated are now, through love of Thee, a greater happiness and joy to me than those that once I loved without loving Thee."

186. The Lover went through a great city, and asked if there were any with whom he might speak of his Beloved as he desired. And they showed him a poor man who was weeping for love, and who sought a companion with whom to speak of love.

187. Thoughtful and perplexed was the Lover, as he wondered how his trials could have their source in the glory of his Beloved, Who has such great felicity in Himself.[2]

188. The thoughts of the Lover were between forgetfulness of his torments and remembrance of his joys; for the joys of love drive the memory of sorrow away, and the tortures of love recall the happiness which it brings.

189. They asked the Lover: " Will thy Beloved ever take away thy love? " He answered: " No, not while memory has power to remember, nor understanding to comprehend the glory of my Beloved."

[1] *escusava s.*

[2] Some versions add: And then he thought of the sun, which, though it is so high, strikes the weak eyes of us men that are here below.

190. "Say, O Fool! What is the greatest comparison and similitude of all that can be made?" He answered: "That of Lover with Beloved." They asked him: "For what reason?" He replied: "For the love that they have each one."

191. They asked the Beloved: "Hast Thou never had pity?" He answered: "If I had not had pity, my Lover had never learned to love Me, nor had I tormented him with sighs and tears, with trials and with griefs."

192. The Lover was in a vast forest, seeking his Beloved. He found there Truth and Falsehood, who were disputing of his Beloved, for Truth praised Him and Falsehood accused Him. Wherefore the Lover cried out to Love that he would come to the aid of Truth.

193. There came the temptation to the Lover to leave his Beloved, that memory might awaken and find the Presence of the Beloved once more; for in this wise he would remember Him more deeply than he had remembered Him aforetime, and the understanding would soar the higher in comprehending Him, and the will in loving Him.

194. One day the Lover ceased to remember his Beloved, and on the next day he remembered that he had forgotten Him. On the day when it came to the Lover that he had forgotten his Beloved, he was in sorrow and pain, and yet in glory and bliss,—the one for his forgetfulness, and the other for his remembrance.

195. So earnestly did the Lover desire that his Beloved should be praised and honoured, that he doubted if he could remember Him enough; and so strongly did he abhor the dishonour paid to his Beloved, that he doubted if he could abhor it enough. And for this cause the Lover was speechless and perplexed between his love and fear of his Beloved.

196. The Lover was like to die of joy, and he lived by grief. And his joys and torments were mingled and united, and became one and the same thing in the will of the Lover. And for this cause the Lover was like to be living and dying at one and the same time.

197. For one hour only the Lover would fain have forgotten his Beloved, and known Him not, that his grief might have some rest. But such oblivion and ignorance had themselves made him to suffer; therefore he had patience, and lifted up his understanding and his memory, in contemplation of his Beloved.

198. So great was the love of the Lover to his Beloved that he believed all things that He revealed to him. And so earnestly did he desire to understand Him that he strove to understand by unanswerable reasons all things that were said of Him. And therefore was the love of the Lover for ever between belief and understanding.

199. They asked the Lover: "What thing is farthest from thy heart?" He answered: "Indifference." "And why so?" "Because nearest to my heart is love, which is the contrary of indifference."

200. "Say, O Fool! Hast thou envy?" He answered: "Yea, whensoever I forget the bounty and the riches of my Beloved."

201. "Say, O Lover! Hast thou riches?" "Yea," he replied, "I have love." "Hast thou poverty?" "Yea, I have love." "How then is this?" "I am poor," he replied, "because my love is no greater, and because it fills so few others with love that they may exalt the honour of my Beloved."

202. "Say, O Lover! Where is thy power?" He answered: "In the power of my Beloved." "Wherewith dost thou strive against thine enemies?" "With the strength of my Beloved." "Wherein dost thou

find consolation?" "In the eternal treasures of my Beloved."

203. "Say, O Fool! Which lovest thou the more—whether the mercy of thy Beloved or His justice?" He answered: "So greatly do I love and fear justice that I find it not in my will to love anything more than the justice of my Beloved."

204. Sins and merits were striving among themselves in the conscience and the will of the Lover. Justice and remembrance increased his remorse, but mercy and hope increased the assurance of pardon in the will of the Beloved; wherefore in the penitence of the Lover merits conquered sins and wrongs.

205. The Lover affirmed that all was perfection in his Beloved, and denied that in Him was any fault at all. Which of these two, think you, is the greater,—whether that which he affirmed or denied?

206. There was an eclipse in the heavens and darkness over all the earth. And it recalled to the Lover that his sins had long ago banished his Beloved from his will, wherefore the darkness had banished the light from his understanding. This is that light whereby the Beloved reveals Himself to His lovers.

207. Love came to the Lover, who asked him: "What wilt thou?" And Love replied: "I have come to thee that I may nurture and direct thy life, so that at thy death thou shalt be able to vanquish thy mortal enemies."

208. When the Lover forgot his Beloved, Love fell sick; and the Lover himself fell sick when he gave himself to over-much thinking, and his Beloved gave him trials, longings and griefs.

209. The Lover found a man who was dying without love. And the Lover wept that a man should die without love, for the dishonour which it brought to his Beloved.

So he asked that man: " Why doſt thou die without love? " And he answered: " Because no man will give me knowledge of love, and none has taught me to be a lover." So the Lover sighed and wept, and said: " Ah, devotion! When wilt thou be greater, that sin may grow less, and that my Beloved may have many fervent and ardent lovers who will praise Him and never shrink from extolling His honours? "

210. The Lover tempted Love to see if he would remain in his mind though he remembered not his Beloved; and his heart ceased to think and his eyes to weep. So his love vanished, and the Lover was perplexed and speechless. And he asked all men if they had seen Love.

211. Love and loving, Lover and Beloved are so ſtraitly united in the Beloved that they are one actuality in Essence. And Lover and Beloved are entities diſtinct, which agree without contrariety or diversity of essence. Wherefore the Beloved is to be loved above all other objects of affection.

212. " Say, O Fool! Wherefore haſt thou so great love? " He answered: " Because long and perilous is the journey which I make in search of my Beloved, and I muſt seek Him bearing a great burden and journey with all speed. And none of these things can be accomplished without great love."

213. The Lover watched and faſted, wept, gave alms, and travelled afar that the Will of the Beloved might be moved to inspire His subjects with love to honour His Name.[1]

214. If love suffices not in the Lover to move his Beloved to pity and pardon, the love of the Beloved suffices to give to His creatures grace and benediction.

[1] Some versions add: But the Lover considered that water does not by nature grow hot, nor mount on high, unless it be first heated. Therefore he prayed the Beloved that He would deign first to warm him in his journeys, alms and vigils with the heat of love, that he might accomplish his desires.

215. "Say, O Fool! How canst thou be most like to thy Beloved?" He answered: "By comprehending and loving with all my power the virtues of my Beloved."

216. They asked the Lover if his Beloved had defect of aught. "Yea," he answered, "of those who will love and praise Him, and extol His valour."

217. The Beloved chastened the heart of His Lover with rods of love, to make him love the tree whence He plucks the rods wherewith He chastens His lovers. And this is that tree whereon He suffered grief and dishonour and death, that He might bring back to love of Him those lovers whom He had lost.

218. The Lover met his Beloved, and saw Him to be very noble and powerful and worthy of all honour. And he cried: "How strange a thing it is that so few among men know and love and honour Thee as Thou deservest!" And the Beloved answered him and said: "Greatly has man grieved Me; for I created him to know Me, love Me, and honour Me, and yet, of every thousand, but a hundred fear and love Me; and ninety of these hundred fear Me lest I should condemn them to Hell, and ten love Me that I may grant them Glory; hardly is there one who loves Me for My goodness and nobility." When the Lover heard these words, he wept bitterly for the dishonour paid to his Beloved; and he said: "Ah, Beloved, how much hast Thou given to man and how greatly hast Thou honoured him! Why then has man thus forgotten Thee?"

219. The Lover was praising his Beloved, and he said that He had transcended place, because He is in a place where place is not. And therefore, when they asked the Lover where his Beloved was, he replied: "He is, but none knows where." Yet he knew that his Beloved was in his remembrance.

220. The Beloved with His merits bought a slave, and made him to suffer griefs and thoughts, sighs and tears.

And He asked him: "What wilt thou eat and drink?" The slave replied: "That which Thou wilt." "Wherein wilt thou be clothed?" "In that which Thou desirest." "Hast thou then no remnant of self-will?" asked the Beloved. He answered: "A subject and a slave has none other will than to obey his Lord and his Beloved."

221. The Beloved enquired of His Lover if he had patience. He answered: "All things please me, and therefore I need not to have patience, for he that has no dominion over his will cannot be impatient."

222. Love gave himself to whom he would; and since he gave himself to few and inspired few with fervent love, being not constrained, therefore the Lover cried out on Love, and accused him before the Beloved. But Love made his defence and said: "I strive not against free will, for I desire my lovers to have great merit and great glory."

223. There was great strife and discord between the Lover and Love, because the Lover was wearied at the trials which Love made him to bear. And they debated whether Love or the Lover was to blame. So they came to be judged of the Beloved; and He chastened the Lover with griefs and rewarded him with increase of love.

224. There was a contention whether Love had more of thought than of patience. And the Lover resolved the contention, saying that Love is engendered in thought and nourished with patience.

225. The Lover has for neighbours the virtues of the Beloved; and the neighbours of the Beloved are the thoughts of His Lover, and the trials and the tears which he bears for the sake of Love.

226. The will of the Lover desired to soar on high, that he might greatly love his Beloved; so he commanded the understanding to soar as high as it might; and even so did the understanding command the memory, so that all three

mounted to the contemplation of the Beloved in His honours.

227. The will of the Lover left him and gave itself up to the Beloved. And the Beloved gave it into the captivity of the Lover, that he might love and serve Him.

228. The Lover said: "O let not my Beloved think that I have left Him to love another, for my love has united me wholly to One, and to One alone." The Beloved answered and said: "Let not My Lover think that I am loved and served by him alone; for I have many lovers who have loved Me more fervently and for longer than he."

229. Said the Lover to his Beloved: "O my Beloved, that art worthy of all love, Thou hast taught and accustomed mine eyes to see and mine ears to hear of Thy honours. And these have accustomed my heart to thoughts which have brought tears to my eyes and to my body grief." The Beloved answered the Lover: "Had I not taught and guided thee so, thy name had not been written in the book of those who shall come to eternal blessing, whose names are wiped out from the book of such as shall go to eternal woe."

230. In the heart of the Lover are gathered the perfections of the Beloved, increasing his thoughts and trials, so that he had altogether died if the Beloved had increased in him any further the thoughts of His greatness.

231. The Beloved came to sojourn in the hostelry of the Lover; and His Lover made Him a bed of thoughts, and there served Him sighs and tears; and the Beloved paid His reckoning with memories.

232. Love put trials and joys together into the thoughts of the Lover, and the joys made complaint of that union and accused Love before the Beloved. But when He had parted them from the torments which Love gives to his lovers, behold, they vanished and were gone.

233. The marks of the love which the Lover has to his Beloved are, in the beginning, tears; in the continuance, tribulations; and, in the end, death. And with these marks does the Lover preach before the lovers of his Beloved.

234. The Lover went into solitude; and his heart was accompanied by thoughts, his eyes by tears, and his body by afflictions and fasts. But when the Lover returned to the companionship of men, these things aforementioned forsook him, and the Lover remained quite alone in the company of many people.

235. Love is an ocean; its waves are troubled by the winds; it has no port or shore. The Lover perished in this ocean, and with him perished his torments, and the work of his fulfilment began.

236. " Say, O Fool! What is love?" He answered: Love is a working together of theory and practice towards one end, to the which in like manner moves the fulness of the will of the Lover, that men may honour and serve his Beloved." Think you now that the Lover's will accords truly with this end when he longs to be with his Beloved?

237. They asked the Lover: " Who is thy Beloved?" He answered: " He that makes me to love, desire, faint, sigh, weep, endure reproaches, suffer and die."

238. They asked the Beloved: " Who is Thy Lover?" He answered: " He that fears naught so that he may honour and praise My Name, and renounces all things to obey My commandments and counsels."

239. " Say, O Fool! Which is the heavier and more grievous burden—the trials of love, or the trials of such as love not?" And he answered: " Go, enquire of those that do penance for the love of their Beloved, and of those that do penance from fear of the pains of hell."

240. The Lover slept, and Love died, for he had naught whereon to live. The Lover wakened, and Love revived in the thoughts which the Lover sent to his Beloved.

241. The Lover said: " The infused science comes from the will, devotion and prayer; and acquired science comes from study and understanding." Which of the two, then, think you, is the more proper and more pleasing to the Lover, and which possesses he the more perfectly?

242. " Say, O Fool! Whence hast thou thy needs?" He answered: " From thoughts, from longing, from adoration, from trials and from perseverance." " And whence hast thou all these things?" He answered: " From love." " And whence hast thou love?" " From my Beloved." " And whence hast thou thy Beloved?" " From Himself alone."

243. " Say, O Fool! Wilt thou be free of all things?" He answered: " Yea, save only of my Beloved." " Wilt thou be a prisoner?" " Yea, of sighs and thoughts, of trials, perils, exiles, tears, that I may serve my Beloved, for to praise His exceeding valour was I created."

244. Love tormented the Lover, for the which cause he wept and made complaint. His Beloved called him to come to Him, and be healed; and the nearer came the Lover to his Beloved, the more grievously did love torment him, for he felt the greater love; but the more he felt of love, the greater was his joy, and the more perfectly did the Beloved heal him of his troubles.

245. Love fell sick, and the Lover tended him with patience, perseverance, obedience and hope. Love grew well, and the Lover fell sick; and he was healed by his Beloved, Who made him to remember His virtues and His honours.

246. " Say, O Fool! What is solitude?" He answered: " It is solace and companionship between Lover

and Beloved." "And what are solace and companionship?" "Solitude in the heart of the Lover, when he remembers naught save only his Beloved."

247. They asked the Lover: "In which is there greater peril, whether in trials borne for love's sake or in pleasures?" The Lover took counsel with his Beloved, and answered: "The perils that come through afflictions are the perils of impatience; and those that come through pleasures are the perils of ignorance."

248. The Beloved gave Love his freedom, and allowed men to take him to themselves as much as they would; but scarce one was found who would take him. And for this cause the Lover wept, and was sad at the dishonour which is paid to Love in this world by the ungrateful among men and by false lovers.

249. Love destroyed all that was in the heart of his faithful Lover that he might live and have free course therein; and the Lover would have died had he not had remembrance of his Beloved.

250. The Lover had two thoughts: the one was of the Essence and the Virtues of his Beloved, whereon he thought daily, and the other was of the works of his Beloved. Which of these, thinkest thou, was the more excellent and the more pleasing to the Beloved?

251. The Lover died, by reason of his exceeding great love. The Beloved buried him in his country, wherein the Lover rose again. From which, thinkest thou, received the Lover the greater blessing, whether from his death or from his resurrection?

252. In the prison-house of the Beloved were evils, perils, griefs, dishonours and trials, that the Lover might not be impeded from praising the honours of his Beloved, and filling with love those men that hold Him in contempt.

253. One day the Lover was in presence of many men whom his Beloved had in this world too greatly honoured, because they dishonoured Him in their thoughts. These men despised the Beloved and mocked His servants. The Lover wept, tare his hair, struck his face and rent his clothing. And he cried in a loud voice: "Was ever so great a sin committed as to despise my Beloved?"

254. "Say, O Fool! Wouldst thou fain die?" He answered: "Yea, to the pleasures of this world and the thoughts of the unhappy sinners who forget and dishonour my Beloved; in whose thoughts I would have no part nor lot, since my Beloved has no part in them."

255. "If thou speakest truth, O Fool, thou wilt be beaten by men, mocked, reproved, tormented and killed." He answered: "From these words it follows that if I spake falsehoods I should be praised, loved, served and honoured by men, and cast out by lovers of my Beloved."

256. False flatterers were speaking ill of the Lover one day in the presence of his Beloved. The Lover was patient, and the Beloved shewed His justice, wisdom and power. And the Lover preferred to be blamed and reproved in this wise, than to be one of those that falsely accused him.

257. The Beloved planted many seeds in the heart of His Lover, but one of them only took life and put forth leaf and gave flower and fruit. And it is a question if from this single fruit there may come forth divers seeds.

258. Far above Love is the Beloved; far beneath it is the Lover; and Love, which lies between these two, makes the Beloved to descend to the Lover, and the Lover to rise toward the Beloved. And this ascending and descending are the beginning and the life of that love whereby the Lover suffers and the Beloved is served.

259. On the right side of Love stands the Beloved, and on the left side is the Lover; and thus he cannot reach the Beloved unless he pass through Love.

260. Before Love stands the Beloved, and beyond the Beloved is the Lover; so that the Lover cannot reach Love unless his thoughts and desires have first passed through the Beloved.

261. The Beloved made for His Lover Two like unto Himself to be equally beloved in honour and valour. And the Lover conceived equal love for all Three, albeit love is one only in significance of the essential unity of One in Three.

262. The Beloved clothed Himself in the raiment of His Lover, that he might be His companion in glory for ever. So the Lover desired to wear crimson garments daily, that his dress might be more like to the dress of his Beloved.

263. "Say, O Fool! What did thy Beloved before the world was?" He answered: "My Beloved was,—because of His Nature and His divers properties, eternal, personal and infinite, wherein are Lover and Beloved."

264. The Lover wept and was sad, when he saw how the unbelievers were losing his Beloved through ignorance; but he rejoiced in the justice of his Beloved, Who punishes those that know Him and are disobedient to Him. Which, think you, was greater, whether his sorrow or his joy? And was his joy greater when he saw his Beloved honoured than his sorrow at seeing Him despised?

265. The Lover contemplated his Beloved in the greatest diversity and harmony of virtues; and in the greatest contrariety of virtues and vices; and again in His Being and perfection, which have greater harmony between themselves than non-existence and imperfection.

266. The diversity and harmony which the Lover found in the Beloved revealed to him His secrets, to wit, His

plurality and unity, to the greater concordance of essence without contrariety.

267. They said to the Lover: " If corruption, which is contrary to being, in that it is opposed to generation, which is the contrary of non-existence, were eternally corrupting and corrupted, it would be impossible that non-existence or end should harmonise with corruption or the corrupted." By these words the Lover saw in his Beloved eternal generation.

268. If that which increases the love of the Lover for his Beloved were falseness, that which diminished this love would be truth. And if this were so, it would follow that there would be defect of the great and the true in the Beloved, and that there would be in Him harmony with the false and the mean.

269. The Lover praised his Beloved, and said that if in Him were the greatest degree of perfection and the greatest possible freedom from imperfection, his Beloved must be simple and pure actuality in essence and in operation. And while the Lover praised his Beloved thus, there was revealed to him the Trinity of his Beloved.

270. In the numbers i and iii the Lover found greater harmony than between any others, because by these numbers every bodily form passed from non-existence to existence. And by considering this harmony of number, the Lover came to the contemplation of the Unity and the Trinity of his Beloved.

271. The Lover extolled the power, the wisdom and the will of his Beloved, Who had created all things, save only sin; and yet, but for His power and wisdom and will, had sin not existed. But neither the power, the wisdom nor the will of the Beloved are an occasion of sin.

272. The Lover praised and loved his Beloved, for He had created him and given him all things; and he praised

and loved Him too because it pleased Him to take his form and nature. And it may be asked: "Which praise and which love had more of perfection?"

273. Love tempted the Lover concerning wisdom, and asked him whether the Beloved showed the greater love in taking his nature, or in redeeming him. And the Lover was perplexed, and replied at last that the Redemption was necessary to put away unhappiness, and the Incarnation to bestow happiness and bliss. And this reply provoked the question again: "Wherein was the greater love?"

274. The Lover went from door to door asking alms, to keep in mind the love of his Beloved for His servants, and to practise humility, poverty and patience, which are virtues well-pleasing to the Beloved.

275. They asked pardon of the Lover, for the love of his Beloved; and the Lover not only pardoned them but gave them himself and his possessions.

276. With tears in his eyes the Lover described the Passion and the pains which his Beloved bore for love of him; and with sad and heavy thoughts he wrote down the words which he had related; and by mercy and hope he was comforted.

277. Love and the Beloved came to see the Lover, who slept. The Beloved cried out to His Lover, and Love wakened him; and the Lover was obedient to Love and made answer to his Beloved.

278. The Beloved taught His Lover how to love; and Love instructed him in perils[1]; and Patience, to bear afflictions for the love of Him to whom he had given himself to be a servant.

279. The Beloved asked men if they had seen His Lover, and they asked Him: "What are the qualities of Thy

[1] *a perillar*, "in the undergoing of perils." D has *a parlar*, "in speech."

Lover?" And the Beloved said: "My Lover is ardent yet fearful; rich and yet poor; joyful, sad and pensive; and every day he grieves because of his love."

280. They asked the Lover: "Wilt thou sell thy desire?" He answered: "I have sold it already to my Beloved, for such a price as would buy the whole world."

281. "Preach, thou, O Fool, and speak concerning thy Beloved; weep and fast." So the Lover renounced the world, and went forth with love to seek his Beloved, and praised Him in those places wherein He was dishonoured.

282. The Lover builded and made a fair city wherein his Beloved might dwell; of love, thoughts, tears, complaints and griefs he builded it; with joy, hope and devotion he adorned it; and with faith, justice, prudence, fortitude and temperance he furnished it.

283. The Lover drank of love at the fountain of his Beloved, and there the Beloved washed the feet of His Lover, though many a time he had forgotten and despised His honours, and the world had suffered thereby.

284. "Say, O Fool! What is sin?" He answered: "It is intention directed and turned away from the final Intention and Reason, for the which all things have been created by my Beloved."

285. The Lover saw that the world is a thing created, since eternity is more in harmony with his Beloved, who is Infinite Essence in greatness and in all perfection, than with the world, which is a finite quantity; and therefore in the justice of his Beloved the Lover saw that His eternity must have been before time and finite quantities were.

286. The Lover defended his Beloved against those who said that the world is eternal, saying that the justice of his Beloved would not be perfect, if He restored not to every soul its own body, and for this no place or material order

would suffice; nor, if the world were eternal, could it be ordered for one end only; and yet, if it were not so ordered, there would be wanting in his Beloved perfection of wisdom and will.

287. " Say, O Fool! Wherein hast thou knowledge that the Catholic Faith is true, and that the beliefs of the Jews and Saracens are falsehood and error?" He answered: " In the ten conditions of the *Book of the Gentile and the Three Wise Men*."[1]

288. " Say, O Fool! Wherein is the beginning of wisdom?" He answered: " In faith and devotion, which are a ladder whereby understanding may rise to a comprehension of the secrets of my Beloved." " And wherein have faith and devotion their beginning?" He answered: " In my Beloved, Who illumines faith and kindles devotion."

289. They asked the Lover: " Which thing is greater—whether the possible or the impossible?" He answered: " The possible is greater in the creature, and the impossible in my Beloved, since possibility and power are in agreement, and impossibility and actuality."

290. " Say, O Fool! Which thing is the greater—whether difference or harmony?" He answered: " Save in my Beloved, difference is greater in plurality, and harmony in unity; but in my Beloved they are equal in difference and in unity."

291. " Say, O Lover, what is valour?" He answered: " It is the opposite of that which this world holds to be valour, and which false and vainglorious lovers desire; for they go after valour, and in truth have it not,[2] being persecutors of true valour."

[1] See p. 366, above.

[2] *qui volen valer havents desvalor.* This theme is expounded in Chap. XLVIII, above.

292. "Say, O Fool! Hast thou seen one without his reason?" He answered: "I have seen a Bishop who had many cups on his table, and many plates and knives of silver, and in his chamber had many garments and a great bed, and in his coffers great wealth—and at the gates of his palace but few poor."

293. "Knowest thou, O Fool, what is evil?" He answered: "Evil thoughts." "And what is loyalty?" "It is fear of my Beloved, born of charity and of shame, which men reproach." "And what is honour?" He answered: "It is to think upon my Beloved, to desire Him and to praise His honours."

294. The trials and tribulations that the Lover endured for love's sake made him weary and inclined towards impatience; and the Beloved reproved him with His honours and His promises, saying that he whom either trouble or happiness affected knew but little of love. So the Lover was contrite and wept, and he begged his Beloved to restore his love again.

295. "Say, O Fool! What is love?" He answered: "Love is that which throws the free into bondage, and to those that are in bonds gives liberty." And who can say whether love is nearer to liberty or to bondage?

296. The Beloved called His Lover, and he answered Him, saying: "What wilt Thou, O Beloved, Thou that art the sight of my eyes, thought of my thoughts, love of my love and fulness of my perfections,—yea, and the source of my beginnings?"

297. "O Beloved," said the Lover, "I come to Thee, and I walk in Thee, for Thou dost call me. I go to make contemplation in contemplation, with contemplation of Thy contemplation. In Thy virtue am I, and with Thy virtue I come to Thy virtue, whence I take virtue. And I greet Thee with Thy greeting which is my greeting in Thy

greeting, by the which I hope for eternal greeting in blessing of Thy blessing, wherein I am blessed in my blessing."

298. " High art Thou, O Beloved, in Thy heights, to the which Thou dost exalt my will, which is exalted in Thy exaltation with Thy height. And this exalts in my remembrance my understanding, which is exalted in Thy exaltation, that it may know Thy honours, and that the will may have thereof exaltation of love and the memory may have high remembrance."

299. " O Beloved, Thou art the glory of my glory, and with Thy glory in Thy glory, dost Thou give glory to my glory, the which has glory of Thy glory. And by this Thy glory both trials and griefs are in equal measure glory to me, for they come to me to honour Thy glory with the joys and the thoughts that come to me from Thy glory."

300. " O Beloved! In the prison-house of love dost Thou hold me enthralled by Thy love, the which has enamoured me of itself, through itself and in itself; for Thou art naught else save love, wherein Thou makest me to be alone, with Thy love and Thy honours for my only company. For Thou alone art in myself alone, who am alone with my thoughts, because Thy uniqueness[1] in virtues makes me to praise and honour its valour without fear of them that know Thee not and have Thee not alone in their love."

301. " Solace of all solace, Beloved, art Thou; for in Thee I solace my thoughts with Thy solace which is solace and comfort of my griefs and my tribulations, which are caused by Thy solace, when Thou solacest not the ignorant with Thy solace, and fillest not more with love those that know Thy solace that they may honour Thy honours."

302. The Lover made complaint to his Lord concerning his Beloved, and to his Beloved concerning his Lord. And

[1] The play upon words would require " *alone*ness."

the Lord and the Beloved said: "Who is this that makes division in Us, that are One only?" The Lover answered and said: "It is pity, which belongs to the Lord, and tribulation, which comes through the Beloved."

303. The Lover was in peril in the great ocean of love, and he trusted in his Beloved, Who came to him with troubles, thoughts, tears and weeping, sighs and griefs; for the ocean was of love, and of honour that is due to His honours.

304. The Lover rejoiced in the Being of his Beloved, for (said he) "from His Being is all other Being derived, and by It sustained, and constrained and bound to honour and serve the Being of my Beloved. By no being can He be condemned or destroyed, or made less or greater." "What is the Being of thy Beloved?" He answered: "It is a bright ray throughout all things, even as the sun which shines over all the world. For if it withdraw its brightness, it leaves all things in darkness, and when it shines forth it brings the day. Even more so is my Beloved."

305. "O Beloved, in Thy greatness dost Thou make my desires, my thoughts and my afflictions great; for so great art Thou that all things which have remembrance and understanding and joy of Thee are great; and Thy greatness makes all things small which are contrary to Thy honours and commandments."

306. "In Eternity my Beloved has beginning, and has had beginning and will have beginning, and in Eternity He has no beginning neither has had nor will have beginning. And these beginnings are no contradiction in my Beloved, because He is eternal, and has in Himself Unity and Trinity."

307. "My Beloved is one, and in His unity my thoughts and my love are united in one will; the unity of my Beloved is the source of all unities and all pluralities; and the

plurality that is in my Beloved is the source of all pluralities and unities."

308. " Sovereign Good is the good of my Beloved, Who is Good of my good. For my Beloved is Good without other good; for, were He not so, my good were of another Sovereign Good. And since this is not so, let all my good, therefore, hereafter in this life, be to the honour of the Sovereign Good, for even so beseems it."

309. " Thou knowest my sinfulness, O Beloved; be Thou merciful, then, and pardon. Thy knowledge is greater than mine; yet even I know Thy pardon and love, since Thou hast made me to have contrition and grief, and the desire to suffer death that Thy Name may be thereby exalted."

310. " Thy power, O Beloved, can save me through Thy goodness, mercy and pardon, yet it can condemn me through Thy justice, and my failures and imperfections. But let Thy power be perfected in me, for it is wholly perfection, whether it bring salvation or eternal punishment."

311. " O Beloved, Truth visits my contrite heart, and draws water from mine eyes, whensoe'er my will loves her; and since Thy truth, O Beloved, is sovereign, it exalts my will, that it may do honour to Thy honours, and bears it down, that it may hate my sins."

312. " Never was aught true that was not in my Beloved, and false is that which is not in my Beloved, and false will be that which will not be in my Beloved. Wherefore all that will be, or was, or is, must needs be true if my Beloved is therein; and false is that which is in truth, if my Beloved is not therein, without any contradiction following therefrom."

313. The Beloved created, and the Lover destroyed. The Beloved judged, and the Lover wept. Then the Be-

loved redeemed him, and again the Lover had glory. The Beloved finished His work, and the Lover remained for ever in the companionship of his Beloved.

× 314. By verdant paths of feeling, imagination, understanding and will, the Lover went in search of his Beloved. And in those paths the Lover endured perils and griefs for the sake of his Beloved, that he might exalt his will and understanding to his Beloved, Who wills that His lovers may comprehend and love Him exceedingly.

315. The perfection of the Beloved moved His Lover to be, and his own shortcomings moved him to be no more. Which of these two forces, think you, has by nature the greater power over the Lover?

316. "Thou hast placed me, O Beloved, between my evil and Thy good. On Thy part may there be pity, mercy, patience, humility, pardon, restoration and help; on mine let there be contrition, perseverance and remembrance with sighs and weeping and tears for Thy sacred Passion."

317. "O Beloved, Thou that makest me to love! If Thou aidest me not, why didst Thou will to create me? And why didst Thou endure such grief for my sake and bear Thy so grievous Passion? Since Thou didst help me thus to rise, Beloved, help me also to descend to the remembrance and hatred of my faults and sins, that my thoughts may the better rise again to desire, honour and praise Thy valour."

318. "My will, O Beloved, hast Thou made free to love Thy honour or despise Thy valour, that in my will my love to Thee may be increased.

319. "In granting me this liberty, O Beloved, hast Thou put my will into danger. Remember, then, Thy Lover in this danger, who places in servitude his free will, praises Thy honour, and increases in his body grief and tears."

320. "O Beloved! Never from Thee came fault nor sin to Thy Lover, nor can Thy Lover attain to perfection but through Thy grace and pardon.[1] Then, since the Lover has Thee in such possession, do Thou remember him in his tribulations and perils."

321. "O Beloved, Who in one Name, Jesus Christ, art named both God and Man, by that Name my will must needs adore Thee as God and Man. And if Thou, Beloved, hast so greatly honoured Thy Lover, through none of his merits, who names Thee thus, and wills Thee to be thus named, wherefore honourest Thou not so many ignorant men, who knowingly have been less guilty of dishonouring Thy Name, Jesus Christ, than has this Thy Lover?"

322. The Lover wept, and he spake to his Beloved in these words: "O Beloved, never wert Thou sparing or aught but liberal to Thy Lover, in giving him being, in redeeming him and in granting him many creatures to serve him. Then wherefore, O Beloved, Thou who art sovereign liberality, shouldst Thou be sparing to Thy Lover of tears, thoughts, griefs, wisdom and love that he may do honour to Thy Name? So then, O Beloved, Thy Lover asks of Thee long life, that he may receive of Thee many of the gifts aforesaid."

323. "O Beloved, if Thou dost help just men against their mortal enemies, help to increase my thoughts and desires for Thy honour. And if Thou dost help sinners to lead just lives, help Thy Lover that he may sacrifice his will to Thy praise, and his body for a testimony of love in the path of martyrdom."

324. "My Beloved makes no difference between humility, humble and humbled, for all these are humility in pure actuality." Wherefore the Lover reproves Pride, for he desires to raise to the heights of his Beloved those

[1] *do e perdó*. See p. 252, above.

whom He has so greatly honoured in this world, but whom Pride has clothed with hypocrisy, vainglory and vanities.

325. Humility has humbled the Beloved to the depths of the Lover, through the contrition, and likewise through the devotion, of the Lover. And it is a question, in which of these two manners the Beloved has humbled Himself the more.

326. The Beloved had mercy upon His Lover, because of His perfect love, and because of His Lover's needs. Which of these two reasons, think you, moved the Beloved the more strongly to forgive the sins of His Lover?

327. Our Lady and the angels and saints in glory prayed to my Beloved. And when she remembered the errors wherein the world lies through ignorance, she remembered also the great justice of my Beloved, and the great ignorance of His lovers.

328. The Lover lifted up the powers of his soul, and mounted the ladder of humanity to glory in the Divine Nature; and by the Divine Nature the powers of his soul descended, to glory in the human nature of his Beloved.

329. The straiter are the paths whereby the Lover journeys to his Beloved, the vaster is his love; and the straiter his love, the broader are the paths. So that however it be the Lover receives love, trials and griefs, joys and consolations from his Beloved.

330. Love comes from love, thoughts come from griefs, and tears from griefs likewise; and love leads to love, as thoughts lead to tears and griefs to sighs. And the Beloved watches His Lover, who bears all these afflictions for His love.

331. The desires of the Lover and his memories of the nobility of his Beloved kept vigils and went on journeys and pilgrimages. And they brought to the Lover graces which

lit up his understanding with splendour, whereby his will increased in love.

332. With his imagination the Lover formed and pictured the Countenance of his Beloved in bodily wise, and with his understanding he beautified It in spiritual things; and with his will he worshipped It in all creatures.

333. The Lover purchased a day of tears with another day of thoughts; and he sold a day of love for a day of tribulations; and both his thoughts and his love were increased.

334. The Lover was in a far country, and he forgot his Beloved, but was sad at the absence of his lord, his wife, his children and his friends. But soon the memory of his Beloved returned to him, that he might be comforted, and that his exile might cause him neither yearning nor sorrow.

335. The Lover heard the words of his Beloved; his understanding beheld Him in them; his will had pleasure in that which he heard; and his memory recalled the virtues and the promises of his Beloved.

336. The Lover heard men speak evil of his Beloved, and in this evil-speaking his understanding perceived the justice and patience of his Beloved; for His justice would punish the evil-speakers, while His patience would await their contrition and repentance. In which of these two, think you, did the Lover believe more earnestly?

337. The Lover fell sick, and made his testament with the counsel of his Beloved. His sins and faults he bequeathed to contrition and penance; worldly pleasures to contempt. To his eyes he left tears; to his heart sighs and love; to his understanding the graces of his Beloved, and to his memory the Passion which his Beloved endured for love of him. And to his activity he bequeathed the guidance of unbelievers, who go to their doom through ignorance.

338. The scent of flowers brought to the Lover's mind the evil stench of riches and meanness, of lasciviousness, of ignorance and pride. The taste of sweet things recalled to him the bitterness of temporal possessions and of entering and quitting this world. The enjoyment of earthly pleasures made him feel how quickly this world passes, and how the delights which are here so pleasant are the occasion of eternal torments.

339. The Lover endured hunger and thirst, heat and cold, poverty and nakedness, sickness and tribulation; and he would have died had he not had remembrance of his Beloved, Who healed him with hope and memory, with the renunciation of this world and contempt for the revilings of men.

340. The Lover made his bed between trials and joys: in joys he lay down to sleep and in trials he awakened. Which of these two, think you, is more proper to the bed of the Lover?

341. In anger the Lover lay down to sleep, for he feared the revilings of men; in patience he awakened, remembering the praises of his Beloved. Of which, think you, had the Lover the greater shame—whether of his Beloved or of men?

342. The Lover thought upon death, and he was afraid, until he remembered the city of his Beloved, to the which city love and death are the gates and the entrance.

343. The Lover made complaint to his Beloved concerning the temptations which came to him daily to afflict his thoughts. And the Beloved made answer, saying that temptations are an occasion whereby man may have recourse to memory, making remembrance of God and loving His honours and perfections.

344. The Lover lost a jewel which he greatly prized, and was sorely distressed, until his Beloved put to him this

question: " Which thing profiteth thee the more, whether the jewel that thou hadst or thy patience in all the works of thy Beloved? "

345. The Lover fell asleep as he thought upon the trials and the hindrances which he met in serving his Beloved; and he feared lest through those hindrances his works might be lost. But the Beloved sent consciousness to him, and he awakened to the merits and powers of his Beloved.

346. The Lover had to make long journeys over roads that were rough and hard; and the time came when he should set out, carrying the heavy burden that Love makes his lovers to bear. So the Lover unburdened his soul of the cares and pleasures of this world, that his body might bear the weight with more ease, and his soul journey along those roads in company with its Beloved.

347. Before the Lover, one day, they spake ill of the Beloved, and the Lover made no reply neither defended his Beloved. Which, think you, was the more to be blamed, the men who spake ill of the Beloved, or the Lover who was silent and defended Him not?

348. As the Lover contemplated his Beloved, his understanding conceived subtleties and his will was kindled with love. In which of the two, think you, grew his memory more fruitful in thinking on his Beloved?

349. With fervour and fear the Lover journeyed abroad to honour his Beloved. Fervour bore him along and fear preserved him from danger. And while the Lover was journeying thus, he found sighs and tears, which brought him greetings from his Beloved. Through which of these four companions, think you, received the Lover the greatest consolation in his Beloved?

350. The Lover gazed upon himself that he might be a mirror wherein to behold his Beloved; and he gazed upon his Beloved, as in a mirror wherein he might have know-

ledge of himself. Which of these two mirrors, think you, was the nearer to his understanding?

351. Theology and Philosophy, Medicine and Law met the Lover, who enquired of them if they had seen his Beloved. The first wept, the second was doubtful, but the other two were glad. What, think you, was the meaning of each of these happenings to the Lover that was seeking his Beloved?

352. Full of tears and anguish the Lover went in search of his Beloved, by the paths of the senses and likewise by intellectual roads. Into which of these two ways, think you, did he enter first, as he went after his Beloved? And in which of them did the Beloved reveal Himself to him the more openly?

353. At the Day of Judgment the Beloved will cause all that men have given Him in this world to be placed on one side, and on the other side all that they have given to the world. Thus shall it be clearly seen how truly[1] they have loved Him, and which of their two gifts is the greater and nobler.

354. The will of the Lover was enamoured of itself, and the understanding asked: "Is it more like the Beloved to love oneself or to love the Beloved? For the Beloved is worthier of love than anything beside." With what answer, think you, could the will make reply to the understanding most truly?

355. "Say, O Fool! What is the greatest and noblest love to be found in the creature?" He answered: "That which is one with the Creator." "And wherefore so?" "Because there is naught wherewith the Creator can make nobler a creature."

356. One day the Lover was at prayer, and he perceived that his eyes wept not; and to the end that he might weep

[1] *com coralment*, lit. "how much from their heart," hence "how truly," "how sincerely."

he bade his thoughts to think upon wealth, and women, and sons, and meats, and vainglory. And his understanding found that each of the things aforesaid has more men as servants than has his Beloved. And thereupon were his eyes wet with tears, and his soul was in sorrow and pain.

357. The Lover was walking pensively, thinking on his Beloved, and he found on the way many people and great multitudes who asked him for news. And the Lover, who was rejoicing in his Beloved, gave them not that which they asked of him, and said that he could not reply to their words without departing far from his Beloved.

358. Behind and before was the Lover vested in love,[1] and he went seeking his Beloved. Love said to him: "Whither goest thou, O Lover?" He answered: "I go to my Beloved, that thou mayest be increased."

359. "Say, O Fool! What is Religion?" He answered: "Purity of thought, and longing for death whereby the Beloved may be honoured, and renouncing the world, that naught may hinder one from contemplating Him and speaking truth concerning His honours."

360. "Say, O Fool! What are trials, plaints, sighs, tears, afflictions, perils in a Lover?" He answered: "The joys of the Beloved." "And why are they so?" "That He may be the more deeply loved by reason of them, and the Lover be the more bounteously rewarded."

361. They asked the Lover: "Wherein is love the greater, in the Lover that lives or in the Lover that dies?" He answered: "In the Lover that dies." "And wherefore?" "Because in one that lives for love it may yet be greater, but in one that dies for love it can be no greater."

362. Two lovers met: the one revealed his Beloved, and the other comprehended Him. And it was disputed which of those two was nearer to his Beloved; and in the solution

[1] Or "Within and without was the Lover covered with love."

the Lover took knowledge of the demonstration of the Trinity.

363. "Say, O Fool! Wherefore speakest thou with such subtlety?" He answered: "That I may raise my understanding to the height of the nobility of my Beloved, and that thereby more men may honour, love and serve Him."

364. The Lover drank deeply of the wine of memory, understanding and love for the Beloved. And that wine the Beloved made bitter with His tears, and with the weeping of His Lover.

365. Love heated and inflamed the Lover with remembrance of his Beloved; and the Beloved cooled his ardour, with weeping and tears and forgetfulness of the delights of this world, and the renunciation of vain honours. So his love grew, when he remembered for Whom he suffered griefs and afflictions, and for whom the men of the world bore trials and persecutions.

366. "Say, O Fool! What is this world?" He answered: "It is the prison-house of them that love and serve my Beloved." "And who is he that imprisons them?" He answered: "Conscience, love, fear, renunciation and contrition, and the companionship of wilful men;[1] and the labour that knows no reward, wherein lies punishment."

Because Blanquerna had to compose the book of the *Art of Contemplation*, therefore desired he to end the *Book of the Lover and the Beloved*, the which is now ended, to the glory and praise of our Lord God.

[1] Some versions end thus: "And who is he that frees them?" "Mercy, pity and justice." "And where are they then sent?" "To eternal bliss, and the joyful company of true lovers, where they shall laud, bless and glorify the Beloved everlastingly, to whom be ever given praise, honour and glory throughout all the world."

BEGINNETH THE ART OF CONTEMPLATION

PROLOGUE

So high and excellent is our Sovereign Good, and so low is man through his guilt and sins, that oftentimes it befalls a hermit or a holy man to be greatly impeded in lifting up his soul to contemplate God; and, since an art or method in this business is of great help therein, Blanquerna fell to considering how he might make an Art of Contemplation which should lead him to have devotion in his heart, and in his eyes weeping and tears, and make his will and understanding the higher rise to the contemplation of God in His honours and His wonders.

2. When Blanquerna the hermit had considered thus, he made by art a Book of Contemplation, the which he divided into twelve parts, namely these: Divine Virtues, Essence, Unity, Trinity, Incarnation, *Pater Noster*, *Ave Maria*, Commandments, *Miserere mei Deus*, Sacraments, Virtues, Vices.

3. The art of this book is that the Divine virtues should first be contemplated in relation to each other, and that then they should be contemplated with the other parts of the book, the soul of the contemplative being fixed upon the Divine virtues in his memory, understanding and will; and also that he should learn to unite in his soul the Divine virtues and the other parts of the book, to the honour and glory of the Divine virtues, which are these: Goodness, Greatness, Eternity, Power, Wisdom, Love, Virtue, Truth, Glory, Perfection, Justice, Liberality, Mercy, Humility, Dominion, Patience.

4. These virtues may be contemplated in divers manners, one of which is to contemplate one with another, or one with two or three or more. A second manner is that whereby man may contemplate these virtues in their relation with Essence or Unity or Trinity or Incarnation, and

so with the other parts of this book. Another manner is that whereby with these virtues is contemplated Essence or Unity or Trinity or Incarnation. Another manner is in the words of the *Pater Noster* and the *Ave Maria*, etc. A man may contemplate God and His works with all the sixteen virtues or with any of them, according as he would make his contemplation long or short, and as the matter of the contemplation befits certain virtues rather than others.

5. The conditions of this art are that a man should be suitably disposed toward contemplation and in a fitting place, for by repletion, or with overmuch grieving, or in a place wherein is bustle and noise or excess of heat or cold, his contemplation may be hindered. And the chief condition of all in this art is that a man be not impeded by temporal cares in his memory, understanding or will, when he enters upon contemplation.

6. Seeing that we are occupied in treating of other books, we will but briefly relate the way and manner wherein Blanquerna followed the art of contemplation. And with the first part of the book we will first begin.

CHAPTER I

OF THE MANNER WHEREIN BLANQUERNA CONTEMPLATED THE VIRTUES OF GOD

BLANQUERNA rose at midnight and gazed upon the heavens and the stars, and cast out all things from his thoughts, and fixed them upon the virtues of God. For he was fain to contemplate the goodness of God in all the sixteen virtues, and the sixteen virtues in the goodness of God; for the which cause, falling on his knees, and raising his hands to the heavens and his thoughts to God, he spake these words with his lips and pondered them in his soul with all the powers of his memory, understanding and will:

2. "O Sovereign Good, Thou that art infinitely great in eternity, power, wisdom, love, virtue, truth, glory, perfection, justice, liberality, mercy, humility, dominion, patience! I adore Thee as I remember, comprehend, love and speak of Thee and of all these virtues herein named, which are one thing with Thyself, as Thou art one with them, one very Essence without difference soever."

3. "O Sovereign Good, that art so great, Sovereign Greatness, that art so good! Wert Thou not eternal, Thou wert not so great a good that my soul could fill its memory with remembrance of Thee, nor its understanding with understanding of Thee, nor its will with love of Thee. But since Thou art infinite and eternal Good, Thou canst fill my whole soul and every soul with infused grace and blessing, that memory, understanding and love may be given to Thee, O infinite and eternal Sovereign Good."

4. Through the power which Blanquerna remembered in Sovereign Goodness, he gained power and strength to raise his consideration above the firmament, and considered a greatness so exceeding great that it had infinite power of movement, like unto a flash of light shining in the six common directions—to wit, above and below, before and behind, to left and to right; and finding no limit, nor beginning nor end. As Blanquerna thus considered, he marvelled greatly, the more so when to the consideration of this goodness he joined that of eternity, which has neither beginning nor end. And while Blanquerna was wholly absorbed in this consideration, he remembered how great a good is that of Divine power, which can be so great and so everlasting, and whose knowledge and will are infinite and eternal, as are its virtue, truth, glory, perfection, justice, liberality, mercy, humility, dominion and patience.

5. As Blanquerna pursued his contemplation in this wise, his heart began to burn within him, and his eyes to weep, at the great joy which he had in remembering, understanding and loving such noble virtues in Sovereign Goodness.

But ere he could perfectly weep, his understanding descended to the level of the imagination, and he fell to thinking and doubting how it could be that, before the world was, God should have justice, liberality, mercy, humility, dominion; and, through the alliance of understanding and imagination, doubt chilled the warmth of his heart and the tears in his eyes grew fewer. So Blanquerna parted understanding and imagination and exalted the former above the latter, remembering how the Sovereign Good is infinite in all perfection, and how for this cause, through His own virtue and glory, He may have and can have to so great a degree of perfection all the virtues above named before the world was as well as now that the world is; only that, while the world was not, there was lacking any person who might receive from the Sovereign Good the grace and the influence of these above-named virtues.

6. Greatly now joyed the will of Blanquerna because his understanding had cast down the imagination which impeded its working and had soared aloft, leaving the imagination behind, to comprehend the infinite power of God, which in justice, liberality, and the like, must needs have been before the world was; for, were this not so, it would follow that in Sovereign Goodness there was defect of greatness, power, eternity and virtue. And since it is impossible that in God is any defect at all, for that cause the will set the heart of Blanquerna so fiercely on fire that his eyes were abundantly filled with tears.

7. While Blanquerna contemplated and wept, his memory, understanding and will conversed mentally with each other within his soul, and they found great delight in the virtues of God, as these words show: "Memory," said Understanding, "what remembrance hast thou of the goodness, wisdom and love of God? And thou, O Will, what dost thou love in them?" Memory answered and said: "When I consider in my remembrance how great a good it is to know oneself to be greater and nobler in know-

ledge and will than any beside, I feel not so high nor so great as when I remember the Sovereign Good, Who is infinite in knowledge and will. And when I consider eternity, power, virtue, truth, and the rest, then I do feel myself to be magnified and exalted as I think upon these things." With these words and many others did Memory reply to Understanding; and Will replied in like manner, saying that she felt not so great nor high when she loved the Sovereign Good because He is more loving and wise than any beside, as when she loved Him because of His infinite and eternal wisdom and love. After these words, Understanding said to Memory and Will that her own state was like to theirs in the contemplation of the Sovereign Good.

8. Memory, Understanding and Will agreed among themselves that they would contemplate the Sovereign Good in His virtue, truth and glory. Memory recalled the virtue of the infinite Good, His virtue being infinite in truth and glory. Understanding comprehended that which Memory recalled, and Will loved that which Memory recalled and Understanding comprehended. Once again Memory turned to remembrance, and recalled the infinite truth of Sovereign Good, in the which truth are virtue and glory. And Understanding comprehended infinite glory, which is in virtue and truth, and our glorious Sovereign Good; and Will loved this wholly and in the unity of one actuality, in one and the same perfection.

9. Blanquerna enquired of his Understanding: "If the Sovereign Good give me salvation, what wilt thou thereby comprehend?" Understanding answered: "I shall comprehend the mercy and humility and liberality of God." "And thou, O Memory, if He condemn me, what wilt thou remember?" He answered: "I shall remember the justice and dominion and perfection and power of God." "And thou, O Will, what wilt thou love?" He answered: "I will love that which Memory recalls, so that I be in a

place where I may love it; for the virtues which are in the Sovereign Good are worthy in themselves to be loved."

10. After these words, Blanquerna remembered his sins, and comprehended how great a good it is that in God there is patience; for were there no patience in God, so soon as man sinned he would be punished and cast out from this world. And therefore he enquired of his Will: "What thanks shall I render to the patience of God which has thus borne with me?" Will answered and said that he should love justice in his Sovereign Good, even were it possible that his Understanding should know that he was to be punished by damnation for his sins. Blanquerna was greatly pleased at the answer which Will had made; and with his mouth and with the three powers of his soul he praised and blessed patience in the Sovereign Good through all the Divine virtues.

11. In this wise did Blanquerna contemplate the Divine virtues, from midnight until the hour when he should ring for matins, and he gave thanks to God because He had humbled him by guiding him in his contemplation. And as he was about to cease from contemplation and to ring for matins, he began to bethink himself that he had not contemplated the patience of God as highly as the other virtues, because he had contemplated it in relation to himself, as has been declared above. Therefore it behoved him to turn once more to contemplation, and he said that he adored and contemplated the patience of God in that it was one self-same thing with Sovereign goodness and with all the other virtues, without difference soever. Wherefore Understanding greatly marvelled how patience could be one thing in essence with the remaining virtues. But Memory recalled that in God the virtues have no diversity the one from the other, but that, since their operations in the creatures are diverse, they themselves appear diverse, even as the reflection of a person appears when he looks into two mirrors, of which one is crooked and the other

straight, yet the reflection itself is one, in each of the mirrors, without diversity soever.

CHAPTER II

OF THE MANNER IN WHICH BLANQUERNA CONTEMPLATED BY THREE AND THREE THE VIRTUES OF GOD

"DIVINE Goodness," said Blanquerna, "Thou that art of infinite greatness in eternity, Thou art the good whence springs all good beside; from Thy great good comes all that is good both great and small, and from Thy eternity comes all that abides. Wherefore in all wherein Thou art goodness and greatness, and eternity, I adore Thee, call upon Thee, and love Thee above all that I can understand and remember. And I pray Thee to make great and abiding that good which Thou hast granted me, that I may praise and serve Thee with all that pertains to Thy honour."

2. "Eternal Greatness in power! Far greater art Thou than I can remember or comprehend or love. My power rises to Thee, that Thou mayest make it great and abiding, that I may remember, comprehend and love Thy power which is infinite and eternal, from whose influence we trust there may fall upon us grace and blessing, whence we ourselves may become great and may abide even unto eternity."

3. "Eternity, Thou that hast power of knowledge without end or beginning! Thou hast given me a beginning and created me that I may abide without end. Thou hast power to save or to damn me. That which Thou wilt do with me and with others, Thy knowledge eternally knows and Thy power can accomplish. For in Thy eternity is no movement or change. No power have I to know how Thou wilt judge me, for my power and knowledge have a beginning. So, then, may it please Thee, that whatsoever Thou wilt do with me, my power and knowledge and abidingness in this world may be to Thy glory and to the praise of Thine honour."

4. "Power, that hast all knowledge and will in thyself! Knowledge, that hast all power and will in thyself! Will, that hast all power and knowledge in thyself! Take all my knowledge and power—for already hast Thou taken all my will—that they may love and serve Thee. Thou, O Power, canst know and will, inasmuch as Thou art without increase or diminution or any change soever. Thou, O Knowledge, dost know even as Thou dost will. And Thou, O Will, dost will even as Thou dost will in will, power, and knowledge. Wherefore, since thus it is, and naught can make it otherwise or different, may grace come to my power from this great influence, that I may ever have power, knowledge and will to honour Thy power,—to my knowledge that I may honour Thy knowledge,—and to my will that I may honour Thy love."

5. "Wisdom Divine! In Thee are virtue and love. Thou knowest Thyself to be love above all other love, and virtue above all other virtue: Thou knowest Thyself to be wisdom greater than all wisdom beside. Wherefore if my knowledge perceive that my will has small virtue in loving Thy Will, Thy knowledge must needs know that Thy love is greater in loving me, than is my love in loving Thee. And if Thou knewest not this, Thy knowledge could not know how much greater virtue there is in Thy love and Thy will than in mine, nor could my knowledge and will have the virtue wherewith to contemplate God in perfection." While Blanquerna pursued this contemplation, he bethought himself that if God knew that His will loved sin, He would have no virtue wherewith to love Himself. And thus Blanquerna comprehended that, if he ceased to love God, he would have no virtue wherewith he might cease to love sin. So Blanquerna wept abundantly, when he remembered his sin and guilt at such times as he had sinned.

6. "Love Divine! Thy virtue is more real than that of any love beside, and Thy Truth is more real than all truth

beside. For if the virtue of the sun be real in giving light, and the virtue of fire in giving warmth, far more real is Thy virtue in loving. For between the sun and its splendour there is a difference, and between fire and its heat. But between Thy love and virtue and truth there is no essential difference; and all that Thy love disposes in truth, It does with infinite virtue in love and in truth; whereas all that is done by things beside is done with virtue finite in quantity and time. Wherefore, since this is so, to Thee, O love, O virtue, O truth, I bind and submit myself all the days of my life, that I may honour Thy graces, and proclaim to unbelievers, and to Christians who have lost their devotion, the truth of Thy virtue and Thy truth and Thy love."

7. Virtue, Truth and Glory met in the thoughts of Blanquerna, when he contemplated his Beloved. Blanquerna considered to which of these three he would give the greatest honour in his thoughts and will; but since he could conceive in them no difference soever, he gave them equal honour in remembering, comprehending and desiring his Beloved. And he said: "I adore Thee, O Virtue, that hast created me; I adore Thee, O Truth, that shalt judge me; I adore Thee, O Glory, wherein I hope to be glorified in Virtue and Truth, which will never cease to give glory without end."

8. Blanquerna enquired of the Truth of his Beloved: "If in Thee glory and perfection were not that which Thou art, what then wouldst Thou be?" And Understanding answered Blanquerna: "What but falsehood, or a truth like to that of thine, or naught at all, or that in which there would be affliction everlasting?" And Blanquerna said: "And if truth were not, what then would glory be?" And Memory answered: "It would be naught."[1] "And if perfection were not, what would glory be?" "It would be that which is naught, or nothingness."

[1] Lit. *defalliment*, defect; here total defect, complete loss. non-existence.

9. Blanquerna fell to considering colour, and comprehended the difference that is between white and red, and the contrariety that is between white and black. He considered the glory, perfection and justice of his Beloved, and herein he could comprehend neither difference nor contrariety. He considered whiteness, and could comprehend therein neither difference nor contrariety. He considered glory, and comprehended perfection and justice. He considered perfection, and comprehended justice and glory. He considered justice, and comprehended glory and perfection. Great marvel had Blanquerna as he considered thus, and in that consideration did he exalt his memory and understanding and will to the contemplation of his Beloved. He desired His glory, and his eyes were filled with tears; and he wept, for he feared the justice of his Beloved.

10. Memory, Understanding and Will endeavoured in Blanquerna to soar to the Beloved. Memory desired to soar that she might think upon perfection; Understanding, that he might comprehend justice; and Will, that she might love liberality. And none of these three powers could rise above any other, for each had need of the three virtues of the Beloved, signifying that the three virtues in the Beloved are one and the same.

11. "Justice," said Blanquerna, "what thing desirest thou in my will?" Memory answered for Justice: "I desire therein contrition and fear; I desire tears in thine eyes, in thy heart sighs, and in thy body afflictions." "And thou, Liberality, what desirest thou in my will?" Understanding answered for Liberality: "I desire to possess it wholly, for love, for repentance and for the despising of the vanities of this world." "And thou, Mercy, what desirest thou of my memory and understanding?" Will answered for Mercy: "I desire thy memory wholly, for remembrance of the gifts of Mercy and her pardon,[1] and

[1] *son do e son perdó,* lit. "its giving and forgiving." See note, p. 252, above.

thine understanding wholly for comprehension of the same, and these yet more for the contemplation of Mercy herself." So Blanquerna gave himself wholly to that which the virtues of his Beloved desired of him.

12. Blanquerna adored and contemplated, in his Beloved, liberality, mercy and humility, and he found them greater and nobler than when he contemplated them in himself. Wherefore he said to Understanding that in his Beloved he could not wholly comprehend liberality, mercy and humility; and to Will he said that the mercy of his Beloved had so great liberality that he might take therefrom as much humility as he would, and have therefrom as much mercy and liberality as was needful for his salvation.

13. Blanquerna perceived that he was in peril of thinking the dominion of his Beloved to be greater than His mercy and humility, because His dominion is over all men, while His mercy and humility illumine not those that believe not the Catholic Faith. But the Beloved awakened the memory of Blanquerna, and brought to his mind that mercy made the Son of God to humble Himself by taking our flesh, and dying, as to His Manhood, upon the Cross. And this He did that His dominion might be revealed and proclaimed throughout all the world by those unto whom God has humbled Himself in the Holy Sacrifice, and whom He has so greatly honoured; and His mercy waits for them to make satisfaction for mortal sins, so many and so grievous, displeasing both to God and man.

14. Blanquerna said that in this world it befits not a prince to have dominion without humility and patience, signifying that it befits not that there should be dominion without humility and patience in God. Wherefore Blanquerna, as prince and lord of his memory, understanding and will, humbled himself, though a prince, to have patience, that he might contemplate humility, dominion and patience in his Beloved, from Whom he holds his principality in fief, to give account thereof to his Beloved.

15. So Blanquerna ended his prayer; and, on the day following, he returned to it after another manner, to wit, that he left patience and fell to considering dominion, taking the virtues by three and three that he might follow a new manner. And on the day following he considered the virtues by four and four, by five and five, or by two and two, uniting them with Greatness or Eternity, and so with the other virtues. And in every such combination of one virtue with another appeared new argument and diverse material and manner for the contemplation of his Beloved. And, therefore, because he followed an art in his contemplation, did Blanquerna so abound in the contemplation of his Beloved that his eyes were ever in tears and his soul was filled with devotion, contrition and love.

CHAPTER III

OF ESSENCE

BLANQUERNA began to contemplate the Divine Essence together with the Divine virtues; and, remembering, comprehending and loving the virtues, he said these words:

2. "Divine Essence! So great art Thou in goodness and eternity, that between Thyself and Thy goodness, greatness and eternity is no difference soever. Thou art Essence, and Thou art God, for between Deity and God there is no difference. I adore Thee as One and the Same, as Deity and God, as Essence and Being. For if as Deity and God, as Essence and Being, Thou wert not One, without difference soever, Thy greatness would be finite and determined, inferior to Thy goodness and Thy good, Thy eternity and Thy eternal Being. Whence it would follow that Thy Deity was one thing, and God another, and the same of Thy Being and Thy Essence. But since Thy greatness is infinite in goodness and eternity, therefore, O

Sovereign Essence, do I adore Thee and bless Thee in one pure and simple actuality with all Thy virtues."

3. "Of Thy goodness and of Thy good, O glorious Essence, my soul remembers and comprehends that which it can remember and comprehend of no other thing. For goodness and good, greatness and great, abidingness and abiding are not one thing in creatures: were they so, there would be no difference between essence and being in creatures. And, but for this, Thy goodness were not sovereign in greatness as is fitting. Wherefore—to signify the nobility of Thy Being and Essence—Thy Essence and Being are greater as being One, than created essence, and created being, wherein greatness is lacking; by which lack we have knowledge of Thy infinite greatness, and this I praise, holding suspended all the greatness of my will in adoring, contemplating, praising and serving Thy glorious Essence."

4. "In the creature is essence distinct from power, knowledge and will created. For one thing is power, another is knowledge and yet another is will. Wherefore essence cannot be one self-same thing with power, knowledge and will. But since Thou, O glorious Essence, makest no difference between Thy power, knowledge and will, nor is there in Thy power, knowledge and will any difference soever, therefore art Thou one Essence, and between Thy Being and Thy power, knowledge and will is there in no wise any difference. And since this is so, therefore art Thou Sovereign Good, since all other good lacks power, knowledge and will which is one and the same thing with its essence, and by its nature is inclined to corruption; to the which inclination its nature had been contrary, were there no difference between its Being and its Essence."

5. "O glorious Essence! Thy power can work no defect in Thy Being, but my power can work defect against my being; and this is so because my being is one thing, my essence another, and yet another my power. And, since

my power is far other than my being and my essence, it can work against my being and my essence. But Thy power is Thy Essence and Thy Being without difference soever, and therefore canst Thou do naught against Thy Essence and Thy Being—wherefore, O Essence, hast Thou power eternal, infinite and complete, in truth, virtue, glory and perfection."

6. "After human kind is named humanity, which is of human kind the essence; after the chevalier is named chivalry; after the just man is named justice; and after the wise man, wisdom. In Thy Deity art Thou, O God: he who speaks of Thy Deity, speaks of God, and he who speaks of God speaks of Thy Essence. For Thy Virtue suffices to be Thy Essence and Thy Being in truth, in glory and in perfection. And there is greater truth in that Thy Being and Thy Essence are One and the Same, than in that in the creature essence is one thing and being another, in that the just is one thing and justice another. Wherefore many that are just and chivalrous and human may differ in divers regards under justice, chivalry and humanity. But it is not thus with Thy Being and Essence, for Thy glory and perfection have virtue and truth, wherein is no diversity of Being and Essence."

7. "If there were no justice in the creature it were impossible that the just man should be created, even as it were a thing impossible that human kind should exist if humanity existed not. Wherefore when man and humanity and all things else existed not, there resided already in Thy justice both justice and the 'just,' without there being the 'just' in Thy Essence, nor, in the just that is Thine, justice according to the creature, but rather justice and the just according to Thyself. For even as man cannot be without that which is not man—to wit, elements, matter, form, accidents, nature and cause—even so in Thy Essence there could be neither justice nor the just, if therein there could be accident or quality or difference of Being and Essence

nor, if Thy justice had need of aught but God and Divine Essence, could it be infinite, eternal, full of virtue, perfect and complete."

8. "Divine Essence! Ere ever he was made on whom Thou dost bestow Thy gifts, there was in Thee liberality; for if Thou art liberality and liberality is Thyself, Thy liberality is in no wise behind Thy Essence in Thy eternity and infinity. And the same is true of Thy mercy and of the remaining virtues. Neither now, when there are creatures on whom Thou dost bestow gifts and forgiveness, are Thy mercy and liberality any greater. And were there difference between Thy mercy and liberality in Thy Essence, then hadst Thou not been liberal nor merciful till Thou hadst made the creature. And it were impossible that Thou shouldst have created any thing, hadst Thou not had mercy and liberality before creation was."

9. Blanquerna considered that humility, dominion and patience are in the creature qualities, but in God are Essence; and since these qualities are distant far from Essence, in comparison with the humility, dominion and patience which are Essence, therefore Blanquerna adored humility, dominion and patience, as Divine Essence and Being, and said these words: "Humility that humbles not, and dominion that has no domain, and patience that is not patient cannot of their nature be Sovereign Essence in goodness and greatness that are eternal and to all creatures. Neither does it beseem the Essence of God that there should be humility as between greater and less, nor that there should be lord or vassal, doer or sufferer according to the rule of less and greater." Now, while Blanquerna contemplated in this wise, he became troubled, and feared lest he should utter a contradiction; but, by reason of the height to which his understanding had risen in his contemplation, he knew that his imagination sinned in making a comparison falsely, and his memory recalled that to God must be attributed all good things that are in the creatures,

inasmuch as they must of need be every one in the Divine Essence, lest it should follow that there were any imperfection in God. And since humility, dominion and patience are good things in the creature, they must likewise be in the Divine Essence; but since in creatures they are not in so great perfection as in God, we must needs understand that in another and a nobler way humility, dominion and patience are in the Divine Essence—a way unlike that in which they exist in the creature, wherein they are qualities of accident, having beginning and end.

10. As he contemplated, Blanquerna said that the Essence of his Beloved is immovable, in that He comprehends and is comprehended not; and unchangeable, in that He is eternal; and incorruptible, in that eternal are His power, His will, His knowledge, His virtue, His perfection, His justice. And therefore ought that so glorious Essence to be more often and more firmly in his remembrance, understanding and will, than any other essence or essences whatsoever.

11. "The king, with his dominion, and with his strength, beauty, wisdom, power and justice, and with his other attributes likewise, has no more of human essence than the man that is of an ill-favoured countenance, and a vassal, and a poor man and of small power and knowledge; and this is so because the king may lose all these things aforesaid. But of the Essence of God and of His virtues is it not so; for, since this Essence and these virtues are one and the same thing in goodness, greatness, eternity and the rest, no other thing may have the virtues of God, nor be His Essence. And therefore the Divine Essence is in virtue, in presence, in wisdom, in power, and in all that pertains to His Essence, in every place and through every place, in every time and through every time; and this thing may not be save in the will of God alone."

12. In this and in many another wise did Blanquerna contemplate the Essence of God, uniting virtues in turn

with others, that he might make new argument and lengthier matter for the contemplation of His Essence. And, when he had ended his prayer, he wrote down the substance of his contemplation, and afterwards read that which he had written; but in his reading he had less of devotion than in his contemplation. Wherefore less devout contemplation is to be had in reading this book than in contemplating the arguments set forth therein; for in contemplation the soul soars higher in remembrance, understanding and love of the Divine Essence, than in reading the matter of its contemplation. And devotion accords better with contemplation than with writing.

CHAPTER IV

OF UNITY

BLANQUERNA turned his thoughts and considerations with his love to the contemplation of the Unity of God, and he said these words: "Sovereign Good! Alone is Thy Goodness in infinite greatness and in eternity and in power, for there is none other goodness such as can be infinite, eternal and of infinite power; wherefore, O Sovereign Good, I adore Thee alone in one God Who is Sovereign in all perfections. Thou art one only Good whence all other good descends and springs. Thy Good of Itself alone sustains all good beside. Thy Good alone is the source of my good, wherefore all my good gives and subjects itself to the honour, praise and service of Thy Good alone."

2. "O loving Lord! Greatness that art without beginning and end in Thy Essence full of virtue and complete in all perfection, Thou dost accord with one God alone and not with many, because eternity that is without beginning or end in its abidingness, accords well with greatness which in essence and virtue has neither beginning nor end, but is itself both beginning and end in all its fulness. And

were it not so, O Lord, it would follow that justice and perfection were contrary things in eternity, if eternity, which has neither beginning nor end in duration, accorded also with greatness in essence, which has finite and determined quantity. And since Thou, my God, art One with Thy justice and perfection, thereby is it signified to my understanding that Thou art One God eternal and alone."

3. The memory of Blanquerna remembered the goodness, greatness, eternity, wisdom, will and power of God. By His goodness he understood a power with more of goodness than any other; by His greatness, a power that was greater; by eternity, a power more abiding; by wisdom, a power more wise; by will, a power more gracious than any other power soever. Wherefore, when the understanding had comprehended Divine power, the memory thought upon one power alone, above all others Sovereign, and therefore the understanding comprehended that God was One and One only, for, were there many gods, it were a thing impossible that the understanding could comprehend a greater and nobler power than all beside.

4. Blanquerna considered the virtue that is in the plants and in things which Nature orders to one end, and his understanding comprehended that every thing that is in nature has one virtue which is lord over all other virtues that are in that body; and therefore Nature in each elemental body has natural appetite rather to one end than to another, since one end—that is, one perfection—has below it all perfections beside. While Blanquerna considered this, his memory bore his understanding to the comprehension of the end for which all men are made and created, and of how beasts, birds, plants, metals, elements, heavens, stars have one end only, namely, to serve man; and thereby is signified, according to the perfection of power, justice, wisdom and will, that all men are to honour and serve one God alone; for were there many gods, each god, according to his perfection and justice and power,

knowledge and will, would have made and created men and creatures for many ends. As Blanquerna contemplated the Unity of God according to the manner aforesaid, he felt himself to be uplifted exceedingly in his memory and understanding and will.

5. To man is given will, whereby he wills to possess for himself alone his castle or his city or his kingdom, or his possessions or his wife or his son, or his memory or his understanding or his will, and so of other things. And when to his hurt he finds his peer in these things, he is moved to passion thereby, which is contrary to glory and dominion. When Blanquerna had remembered all this, he remembered the glory and the dominion of God, and comprehended that if there were many gods and lords of the world, their glory and dominion could not be so great as is that of one God alone. And since there must needs be postulated of God the highest glory and dominion, there was demonstrated therefore to the understanding of Blanquerna that God is One and One only. And, that his understanding might rise to greater heights of comprehension, his will was greatly exalted in fervour to the contemplation of his Beloved, the Spouse of his Will. And he said these words:

6. "True is it, O Lord God, that there is no other God save Thyself alone. To Thee alone I offer and present myself, that I may serve Thee. From Thee alone I hope for pardon, for there is none other liberality to give nor mercy to forgive, save Thine only. Humble am I indeed if I humble myself to Thee. Lord am I, if I am Thine alone. Victory have I above mine enemies if I can only suffer for Thee. Wheresoever I may be, with all that I am, I give myself to Thee alone, and Thine alone I am, a guilty sinner. Of Thee alone I beg forgiveness, in Thee I trust, and for Thee I incur perils. Whatsoever may become of me, let it be all to one end, to wit, Thy praise, honour and glory. Thee alone do I fear, from Thee alone is my

strength, for Thee I weep, for Thee I burn with love, and none other Lord will I have, save Thee only."

CHAPTER V

OF TRINITY

BLANQUERNA was fain to contemplate the holy Trinity of our Lord God, wherefore, at the beginning of his prayer, he begged of God that He would exalt the powers of his soul that they might rise to the contemplation of His virtues, whereby he might contemplate His glorious Trinity. And therefore he said these words: "Divine Essence, glorious and holy, in Whom is the Trinity of Divine Persons! I ask of Thee this boon, that it may please Thee to humble Thyself that my soul may rise to contemplate Thy Trinity with Thy virtues proper, essential and common to the three Persons, and Thy three properties personal and essential. I am not worthy to ask of Thee this boon, nor to receive it; but since Thou canst give it, and I therewith can the better love, know and praise Thee, for this cause I ask it of Thee, for my soul desires to know and love all these things, that it may the better love and know, praise and serve Thee, and make Thy glories and honours loved and known."

2. Blanquerna trusted in the help of God, and said these words: "Never was it in creatures, nor is nor shall be, that infinite and eternal Good should proceed or be engendered, seeing that all created good is finite and determined in greatness and eternity. If in the creature there were a Good which was infinitely great in eternity, knowledge, power and will, it would indeed be possible that one infinite Good should engender another; for were it not so, it were impossible that in the creature there should be such an infinite Good as we have postulated above." When Blanquerna had committed this to his memory, understanding

and love, he remembered and understood that if the Sovereign Good exceeds created good in greatness, eternity, power, knowledge and love, It must needs have also a higher and nobler work and actuality; for, had It not this, it were impossible that It should exceed created good in infinity of goodness, greatness, eternity, power and wisdom.

3. When Blanquerna, by the help of God, had lifted up the powers of his soul, even to the highest degree to which he had been able to raise them, he strove after another manner to raise them yet higher. And he fell to considering how great a good it is that God should be engendered, Who is Good, infinite and eternal, powerful, wise, loving, virtuous, true, glorious, perfect, just, liberal, merciful, humble, patient, and over all things Lord. When Blanquerna had considered this for a great space of time, he thought again how great a good it is that to God should be attributed a procession of all these virtues aforesaid which are common to the Persons. And yet again he considered how great is that Good whereby God is engendered, and whence proceeds God, the eternal and infinite. When Blanquerna had considered all these things, he considered after the manner of negation how the good of which he had thought might not be in the Sovereign Good. And immediately he felt his soul to be void of devotion and understanding, and returned to the consideration of that upon which he had thought by affirmation, and then he felt his soul to be full of remembrance, understanding and love of the Sovereign Good, and he fell to weeping and praising God Who granted him so high a degree of contemplation.

4. Blanquerna had remembrance in his soul of created virtue and was fain to lift it higher through the potency of virtue uncreate. And his memory recalled these words: "Philosophers have said that the world is eternal, and this they have said with intent to honour virtue uncreate which must needs work in a manner both infinite and eternal.

Wherefore, as they knew not in God His Trinity and His eternal work, they attributed to God an infinite and eternal work in the world, and in those things whereof the world is made. But it better beseems the virtue of God to perform in Himself an eternal and infinite work in power, wisdom, love, perfection and glory, than in any other thing that is not God Himself." And therefore the perfect justice, wisdom, glory and truth of God signified to Blanquerna that the world had had a beginning, and that the work of the Divine Essence in Itself, whereby the Father begat the Son, and the Holy Spirit proceeded from the Father and the Son, is a work infinite, eternal and wholly perfect. And were it not so, it would follow that the world, in receiving eternity, would have just so much infinite virtue as has the Divine power in giving out virtue unto eternity; and this is a thing impossible. When this impossibility was shown to Blanquerna, his understanding was so greatly exalted that his will soared high in love to the Trinity; so that love gave afflictions to his body, to his eyes tears, to his heart sighing and devotion, to his mouth prayers and praises of his glorious God.

5. Fearfully did Blanquerna pronounce these words to the Holy Trinity with lips and mind: "Sovereign Trinity All-Excelling, through Thy common virtues my understanding soars that it may contemplate and love Thee, and in Thy virtues personal and proper my understanding fails me when it has knowledge of Thee. But my will, illumined by the light of faith through Thy blessing, soars to love Thee, wherefore am I contemplating Thee by intellect and by faith without there following any contradiction."

6. While Blanquerna contemplated thus the Sovereign Trinity, Error and Ignorance were fain to incline him to believe no longer in the Trinity of God, and he considered how in all trinity there was composition. Then Blanquerna thought once more upon the infinite greatness in power, perfection and eternity, and comprehended thus how it be-

seemed not that, if plurality and eternity created could not be without such composition, it should follow that the Sovereign Trinity must needs be compounded. For as the Sovereign Trinity and Plurality is superior to plurality and trinity created, in goodness, greatness, eternity, power and the rest, It must needs be above it also in simplicity; for, if the Unity of God is in simplicity Sovereign over all unity created, the Sovereign Good must needs have plurality that It may be in simplicity above plurality created.

7. "O Holy Trinity! In that I comprehend Thee not Thy greatness is the greater and my understanding the less, and in that I believe without comprehending Thee is my faith greater than my understanding, and Thy greatness than my faith. And this is so because Thy greatness is infinite in all perfection, and my faith and understanding are limited and bounded by Thy greatness. Wherefore, since through believing in Thee I am greater by faith than by understanding, if I understood Thee I should be greater in loving than in believing. And, were this not so, it would follow that love agreed rather with ignorance than with understanding, in the which case love would of necessity be less in the heights of understanding, and greater in its deeps. And this is impossible, unless there should follow contradiction of merit or of understanding through faith, which remains that which it was, according to the diversity of objects between faith and understanding. This diversity we have signified above in the Divine virtues common to all three Divine Persons and according to the properties both personal and Divine."

8. To the end that he might use the art of contemplation, Blanquerna considered within himself generation in infinity and eternity, that he might not think Divine generation to be like to that which is in creatures, which he could not conceive in his mind to be a thing of infinity and eternity. And hence he comprehended in Sovereign generation simplicity without composition or corruption,

and in the lower generation he could not believe there was neither corruption nor composition, because his understanding had knowledge that the generation of the creature cannot increase perfection in eternity and infinity, in his understanding and memory.

9. "O Holy Trinity! If Thou wert not, wherein would God be like unto man? Or how would that word be true which says: Let us make man in our image and likeness? And if Thou, O Trinity, art unlike any trinity of ours, it is that Thou art a Being infinite and eternal in Wisdom, Power and Perfection." Thus did Blanquerna contemplate the Holy Trinity, and thereto did he lift up the powers of his soul, even to such heights as he could, that he might be obedient to the commandment of God which commands man to love God with all his strength, and with all his mind and with all his soul,—that is to say, with memory, intellect and will.

CHAPTER VI

OF INCARNATION

Blanquerna remembered the holy Trinity of our Lord and God, that his understanding might comprehend how through the influence of the great goodness of eternity, power, wisdom and will of the glorious Trinity, God should perform a work in the creature which should be of great benignity, abidingness, power, wisdom and charity; and for this cause his understanding comprehended that according to the operation which is in the Divine Persons, it was fitting that God should take our human nature, in which and through which might be shown forth His Divine virtues and His works which He has in His Divine Persons; and that thus the wills of Blanquerna and all men beside might love God and His works. Wherefore Blanquerna spake these words;

2. "Divine Virtue," said Blanquerna, "Thou art infinite in goodness, greatness, eternity, power, wisdom, love and all perfection; wherefore if there were aught else infinite in greatness, eternity and patience, Thou couldst infinitely work therein through greatness, eternity, action and the like, since Thou hast the power to work, as that thing would have power to receive. But inasmuch as all virtue is finite, save Thine, therefore neither in eternity nor in infinite greatness is any thing sufficient to receive the impress of Thy work, without beginning of time or quantity. Now to show forth all these things Thy wisdom willed to create a creature greater in goodness and virtue than all other creatures and virtues created, and the Son of God willed to be one Person with that creature, to show that Thy goodness had been able to give Him greater virtue than all creatures else, even as He could make Him greater than the creature and than all other creatures."

3. "Thy human nature, O Lord, has a glory greater than all other glories created, and this because its perfection surpasses all other perfection; and since Thy justice, O Lord, has greater goodness, power, wisdom and love than any other, therefore it was fain to give greater glory and perfection to Thy humanity than to any other nature created. Whence, since this is so, it is most meet that all the angels, and all the souls of the saints, yea, and all the bodies of the just when the resurrection is past, should have glory in Thy human nature, and thereby rise to have greater glory in Thy Divine Nature."

4. When Blanquerna had considered for a great space of time the things set down above, he felt his memory, understanding and will to be greatly uplifted in contemplation. Yet even so his heart gave no tears to his eyes that they might be bathed in weeping, and therefore did Blanquerna prepare to uplift the powers of his soul still higher that they might multiply devotion the more in his heart, and fill his eyes with weeping and with tears; for

high contemplation goes ill save with weeping. Wherefore Blanquerna caused his memory to descend, and to think upon the vileness and the misery of this world, and the sins that are therein, and the great wickedness committed by our father Adam against his Creator, in disobeying Him, and the great mercy, liberality, humility and patience of God, when it pleased Him to take human flesh and when He willed to give His Body to poverty, scorn, torments, trials, and to vile and grievous death; although He had no guilt nor sin such as are ours. While the remembrance of Blanquerna called these things to mind, his understanding was lifted up to comprehend and follow his remembrance, and together they contemplated the lofty and Divine virtues, to wit, goodness, infinity, eternity, and the rest. And therefore the will had so much devotion from the nobility of the virtues and the Passion and Death of the Nature of Jesus Christ, that it gave to the heart sighs and griefs, and the heart gave to the eyes weeping and tears, and to the mouth confession and praise of God.

5. For a great space of time did Blanquerna weep as he contemplated the Incarnation of the Son of God after the manner aforesaid; but, as he wept, the imagination strove to represent the fashion wherein the Son of God conformed Himself to human nature; and since he might not imagine it, the understanding had no longer knowledge and Blanquerna fell to doubting, and his tears and sighs ceased by reason of his doubt, which destroyed his devotion and made it to vanish. When Blanquerna felt to what state his thoughts had descended, he lifted up once more his memory and understanding to the greatness of the goodness, power, wisdom and perfection of God, and in the greatness of these virtues his understanding comprehended that God may conform to Himself human nature, though the imagination know it not neither may imagine it. For greater is God in goodness, power, wisdom and will than is the imagination in its imagining; and in remembering and understanding

thus Blanquerna destroyed the doubt which he had had concerning the Incarnation; and devotion and contrition returned to his heart, and weeping and tears to his eyes, and his contemplation was loftier and more fervent than at the beginning.

6. Long did Blanquerna contemplate the Incarnation of the Son of God after the manner aforesaid. And when he felt that his mind was wearied by one matter he took another, that through the renewing of the matter his mind might regain strength and virtue for contemplation. So Blanquerna remembered how the holy Incarnation and Passion of the Son of God are honoured in the goodness, greatness, eternity, power, etc., of God, and how in this world He has honoured with His grace many men who render Him not the honour which they might. After this he remembered how many men there are in this world who are unbelievers and honour not the human nature of Jesus Christ which God in Himself has so greatly honoured, but believe not, and blaspheme that same nature, and hold that sacred land wherein He took that nature, and wherein, to honour us and restore us to the Sovereign dominion which we had lost, He suffered Passion and Death. Then, after Blanquerna had fixed the powers of his mind upon that matter, his devotions, sighs, tears and griefs were renewed within him, and his mind soared higher and yet higher in contemplating the sacred Incarnation of the Son of God. And therefore he said these words: "Oh Lord God, Who hast so highly honoured and exalted our nature in Thy Divine virtues! When comes that time wherein Thou wilt greatly honour our remembrance, understanding and will, in Thy holy Incarnation and Passion?"

7. So lofty was the contemplation of Blanquerna that the powers of his soul discoursed with one another within his mind. Memory said that great goodness performed a great work, and great power worked great might. Understanding answered that great mercy, humility, liberality and love

conformed lesser virtues to greater. And Will said that above all creatures he must needs love his Lord Jesus Christ. But at one thing he marvelled,—to wit, how that Jesus Christ so greatly loved His people, and willed to suffer for them so great Passion, and how God willed so greatly to humble Himself, and how in the world there are so many men, unbelievers, idolaters and ignorant of His honour. Understanding answered and said that that thing was matter for the will, how that it should have such devotion as to make a man desire martyrdom that the Incarnation should be honoured; and that it was matter for the memory, how that it should have remembrance so lofty of the virtues of God that He might be exalted in such necessary demonstrations as should show forth to unbelievers the sacred Incarnation and Passion of the Lord Jesus Christ.

8. By the Divine Light the spirit of Blanquerna was illumined and inflamed, and he spake these words: "O Incarnation, O greatest truth of all truths, uncreated and created! Wherefore are greater in number the men that scorn thee, and know thee not, neither believe thee, than they who honour and believe thee? What wilt thou do? Wilt thou punish so great and mortal failings? O mercy wherein is so great benignity, love, patience and humility! Wilt thou pardon them?" So Blanquerna wept, and between fear and hope he sorrowed and joyed, as he contemplated the sacred Incarnation of the Son of God.

CHAPTER VII

OF THE *PATER NOSTER*

BLANQUERNA called to mind the Divine virtues, and through them was fain to contemplate God in the *Pater Noster*, and to set the virtues and the *Pater Noster* in his memory, understanding and will. Wherefore he spake to God these words: "O Father, Thou art Lord over us—that is, God the Father is Father of God the Son, Who is infinite and eternal in goodness, power, wisdom, love, perfection and all His other attributes, and Thy Divine Essence is Father of the human nature of Jesus Christ by creation and by benignity, mercy, liberality, humility and charity. And therefore said Jesus Christ, when He made the prayer of *Pater Noster*, that in Thee is the personal Father, Father, rightly so called, of God the Son, and that Thou art that Essence, which is Father of His humanity, and likewise of all other creatures. Because, then, the Apostles were creatures, and because they believed in His Trinity and Incarnation, therefore our Lord Jesus Christ commanded them that they should say the *Pater Noster*."

2. "Thou, O Lord, art in the heavens God the Father of God the Son, which heavens are Thy infinite greatness, goodness, eternity, power, wisdom, love, etc., and these are Essence wherein is God the Father Who begat God the Son; and, since infinite perfection is in Thy Essence in goodness, greatness, eternity, etc., therefore with the heavens, which are high, may be compared Thy virtues, which are so high that none others save Thine alone suffice to reach heights so exceeding great. By which heights and excellences Thou dost make known in the *Pater Noster* that Thou art Father, because Thou art higher than all creatures, and because in Thy heavens are Thy works, whereby Jesus Christ called Thee Father, of Himself and of us. Wherefore, if Jesus Christ, Who is God and Man, in the heavens and equal with Thee as touching His Godhead, and upon the earth as touching His Manhood, bears Thee witness that Thou art His Father and ours and art in the heavens, it is meet and right that we, who are here below on earth, should believe His witness and say this prayer of *Pater Noster*."

3. "Hallowed be, Lord God, Thy holy and glorious Name, in Thy goodness, greatness, eternity, power, etc., which is the Name of the Father, Son and Holy Ghost,

through generation and procession, without which generation and procession there could not be in Thy Essence these proper and diverse Names eternally and infinitely in goodness, virtue, truth and perfection. But since the Father is eternal, the Son eternal and the Holy Ghost eternal, and each one of these Persons is infinite in perfection, therefore are there in Thy Essence Names eternal and infinite in perfection, and therefore is it worthy and meet that Thy personal Names should be hallowed in Thy Divine Essence, eternal, infinite and complete."

4. "Not alone, O Lord, does justice require that Thy Name be hallowed in Thy virtues, but of reason also it is worthy and meet that It be hallowed among us here below throughout all the world; and therefore hast Thou, O Lord, established upon earth the Holy Roman Church, that Thy Name may be named and known throughout all the world, and hallowed in the souls of men and in the holy Sacrament of the Altar. And that the Pope and his colleagues the Cardinals and the other prelates may not be neglectful, nor for other business cease to strive for the hallowing of Thy Name, therefore hast Thou given us commandments with Thine own mouth in the *Pater Noster* and at the hour of Thy passing from this world, which commandments Thou didst make to Thy ministers the Apostles after Thy passing."

5. "Thy kingdom, O Lord, is Thy very Essence and Thy personal properties, wherein are goodness, greatness, eternity, etc. May that Kingdom come, O Lord, to our souls, through remembrance, understanding and love of Thy universal properties and Thine own personal properties, to the end that Thy Kingdom may be honoured among us here below and we ourselves may rise to dwell in Thy glorious Kingdom perpetually."

6. "Thy will is done, O Lord, in the heavens and on earth. In the heavens it is done, because Thy Essence is goodness wherein are goodness and will which issues from the infinite Father and Son in goodness, greatness, eternity,

etc. Perfected is Thy will, O Lord, in the Son that is begotten eternally and infinitely in all perfection; and therefore is it the will, O Lord, of justice, perfection, virtue and truth that Thy will be done on earth, that is, in the human nature which Thou didst take, wherein is earth corporal and elemental. And this Will was done by the work of the Holy Ghost when He gave Thee flesh in the womb of the glorious Virgin."

7. "O Lord, so lofty and so marvellous is Thy Will that throughout this whole world Thou art to be obeyed through Thy goodness and Thy power, Thy justice and Thy perfection. Thou art obeyed, O Lord, through Thy goodness, humility, patience and mercy, in those who desire to serve Thee, and who upon earth withdraw apart their memory, understanding and love, that they may contemplate and serve Thee. And Thy will is obeyed, O Lord, through Thy justice, dominion, power and truth, in the punishment with pains of hell of those who may not flee from Thy sentence and domination, and who fix their remembrance, understanding and will upon earthly vanities, despising the blessings of Heaven."

8. "Our daily bread, O Lord, is Thy sacred and glorious Body sacrificed upon the Altar. Thy Body is in the heavens, yet daily It is among us here below in this Sacrifice, which in our minds we see through the working of Thy great benignity, wisdom, power, humility, mercy and will. For as the eyes of our body and our other senses fail us when we see this Bread—that is, Thy Body and Blood—even so, O Lord, may the powers of the soul suffice, Thou Thyself helping us, that we may see this our Bread through the working of the virtues of Thine Essence. For if Thy power is great in infinity, it follows that under the form of bread may be sacrificed one Body of Flesh and Blood in divers places, signifying Thy power to be infinite. And if Thy benignity, humility, will and liberality are infinitely great according to the infinity of Thy perfect justice,

it is signified thereby that Thou wilt give us our daily bread in this world which is to-day, for this is the day of choice between damnation and salvation, which day for every one of us will pass away."

9. "Forgive us, O Lord, the debt that we owe Thee, for we can never pay Thee, being sinners every one in our father Adam. So great are our debts to Thee that we can never pay Thee, for Thou didst create us, and didst will, through love of us, to become Man, to be tortured and crucified for us, and to die. And since Thy perfection is infinite in Thy goodness, greatness, eternity, etc., Thou needest not, O Lord, that we should pay Thee; for didst Thou so need, there would be in Thee want of perfection. And since we resolve[1] the debts which we owe to our sensual natures, in mortifying them with fastings, afflictions and prayers, even as we mortify our understanding by believing the marvels which Thy virtues work, then if Thou, O Lord, forgavest and pardonedst us not our debts, as we for love of Thee forgive our debtors, there would be in us greater justice and perfection than in Thyself. And this may not be; whence, O Lord, it is fitting that Thou shouldst not require of us our debts, which we could in no wise pay Thee."

10. "Well do we know, O Lord, that Thy great goodness, love, liberality and mercy make Thee to desire us to have great merit, that Thy justice may with reason give us great glory and perfection, and therefore dost Thou allow us to be tempted by the world, the flesh and the devil. And since we are poor in memory, understanding and love, it befalls us many a time to be conquered and overcome by our temptations. Wherefore since Thou, O Lord, art so great in benignity, mercy, liberality and humility, give Thou to us that which we merit not, if we endure, but

[1] The original has *lexam*, from a verb which occurs throughout the paragraph in the double sense of "loose" and "forgive." It is difficult to bring this out in the English.

conquer not, our temptations, for it suffices us that we are in Thy kingdom and have Thy glory without merits of our own."

11. "Deliver us, O Lord, from the evil that we have when we know Thee not and love Thee not and forget Thee; for in this evil all others have their beginning. And since that deliverance is to be effected, O Lord, by the remembrance, understanding and love of Thy goodness, greatness, eternity, power, etc., if Thou Who hast created us and canst aid us defendest us not neither deliverest us from evil, Thy mercy and humility will be without love, and we shall be creatures without a Lord Who loves His subjects, and this is ill-beseeming. Wherefore my memory hopes, O Lord, in Thy succour." Thus and in many other ways that can neither be told nor written did Blanquerna contemplate in his soul the virtues of God together with the *Pater Noster*.

CHAPTER VIII

OF *AVE MARIA*

BLANQUERNA was fain to contemplate the Queen of Heaven, and of the earth and sea and all that is, with the virtues of her glorious Son, our Lord God. Wherefore he spake these words: "Hail, Mary! The goodness of thy Son, Who is infinitely great in eternity, power, wisdom and love, gives thee salutation, because the Son of God took thy nature, wherewith He is yet one Person only, equal in goodness, greatness, eternity, and the like, to the Father and the Holy Ghost and to all essence in goodness and virtue."

2. "Full of grace! Power, Knowledge and Will, which are one power, knowledge and will in essence, and one power, knowledge and will in filiation, have been incarnated in Flesh of thy flesh and Blood of thy blood. This Power, Knowledge and Will is one Son and one only of the Sovereign Father. And through this Son there is

created, within thee, a Son Who is Man, one Person in unity with a Son Who is God. And therefore, O Queen, art thou filled with grace through the Son of God and thy Son that is Man. And the Son that is God is thy Son, Who is one Person with the Son of God. Wherefore, since this is so, from the inflowing of the fulness of grace whereof thy Son is full, art thou, O Queen, full of grace which is greater than we can remember or comprehend or love. And from thy fulness of grace comes an inflowing to the memory, understanding and will which contemplate the fulness of thy grace. Blessed then, O Queen, be thy grace, which is so full that it fills all those who through the same shall attain perpetual fulfilment."

3. "The Lord is with thee, O Queen, namely Virtue, Truth and Glory—that is, the Son of God. This Virtue, Truth and Glory have infinity in power, knowledge and will. This infinity is Sovereign Good in eternity. The Lord within thee, O Queen, is God and Man: God, through His Divine Father, and Man, in that He took of thee flesh and blood. And that this Lord is within thee, O Queen, makes thee to be in great virtue and truth, who after thy Son art pre-eminent in virtue, truth and glory over all other creatures. And this is the reason thereof, that, excepting thy Son, the Lord is in no creature so virtuously, truly and gloriously as in thee, for to no other creature has He given such power to receive His virtue as to thee. Therefore, since by His virtue thou canst receive greater virtue than any other creature, His glory is more truly in thee than in any other."

4. "Blessed art thou, O Queen, among women; for greater perfection, greater justice, greater liberality is given to thee than to any other woman soever—yea, than to all men and to all angels and to all other creatures. For the perfection, justice and liberality which are given to thee, are Christ thy Son, Who is perfection of all other perfection, and justice of all other justice, and liberality of all other

liberality; and beside thy Son there were none who should have such Being or perfection. From this perfection, O Queen—to wit, thy Son—comes it by justice that thou art blessed above all women, because thou hast more of perfection than they all. Then since in thee is such perfection, that perfection which is of justice and liberality wills that thou shouldst give perfection to every soul—in its remembrance if it remember thee, in its understanding if it understand thee, and in its will if it love thee. And were this not so, there would be a lack of justice and liberality in thy Son, as also in thee, which is a thing unbeseeming and impossible."

5. "Blessed is the fruit of thy womb, O Queen, with mercy and humility, which have united that fruit with the Divine Nature, a union greater than any other that may be between God and the creature. And therefore, O Queen, to no other creature, nor to all other creatures, has the Divine Nature given so much of mercy and humility, as to the Fruit of thy womb. For this thy Son, glorious Man, is Man in the Son of the glorious God, Who makes Him to be Man, while He is yet with Himself one Person, namely God and Man. And that Person, Who is God, and is infinite mercy and humility in goodness, eternity, power, wisdom, love and the like, has blessed thy Son in His being one with infinity of mercy, humility, goodness, eternity, power, etc. Wherefore, as this is so, O Queen, what fruit may be so blessed or more blessed than the fruit of thy womb?"

6. "O Queen! So great is the brightness of the sun, that it gives radiance to the moon, the stars and the air; and since mercy and humility are greater in thy Son than is the sun's brightness, therefore, O Queen, there comes to ourselves and to the angels an influence from the blessing of the fruit of thy womb, greater than is the brightness of the sun and of all other lights created. And since in thee, O Queen, mercy and humility have so greatly exalted thy

Fruit, and have set thee in such excellent places, it is right that thou shouldst remember us according to thy greatness in mercy and humility. If mercy has been pleased to honour thee, do thou by thy mercy be pleased to remember us. And if humility willed to incline itself to thee that thou mightest be exalted, do thou incline thy thoughts to us that to them we may rise and receive the blessing of thy womb."

7. "The Holy Ghost has come upon thee, O Queen, and has overshadowed thee with the power of the Most High. That Holy Spirit, O Queen, has come upon thee with the Lord of all the world—yea, and of the world to come. He has overshadowed thee with a virtue which comprehends all virtues, and with virtues which are one virtue. The nature which He has taken in thee He has overshadowed with infinite goodness, greatness, eternity, power and the like, and thee has He overshadowed with that nature which He has taken in thee, through the which thou art mother of every virtue and of all virtues created. All of these derive brightness from thy shadow, and through thy shadow they are guided to the brightness of thy Son. By thy shadow, o'ershaded by shadow human and divine, the Saints in glory are in eternal shade, being shielded from the perpetual fire, in which is no shadow of respite from the heat neither of forgiveness."

8. "O Queen of Heaven! Thy Son for reasons twain is Lord over every creature: the first, in that He is God; the second, in that He is Man conformed to God and made one with Him. Then as thy Son is doubly Lord of all the world, thou thyself for reasons twain must over all the world be lady pre-eminent: the first, in that thou art Mother of God; the second, in that thou art Mother of that Man Who is made one Person with God. And as this is so, do thou, O Lady, have remembrance of that whereover thou art placed, that He Who hath placed thee there may have pleasure therein, and that we ourselves may be exalted in the nobility of His dominion."

9. Thus in the *Ave Maria* did Blanquerna contemplate Our Lady with the virtues of her Son; and, while he contemplated, his remembrance and understanding and will were so highly exalted that he took no knowledge if he were weeping or no. And when he had ended his contemplation, he knew and remembered that his heart had given no tears to his eyes, that they should be in weeping and tears as he contemplated. And since it was ill-beseeming that he should contemplate Our Lady without weeping, therefore Blanquerna fell to contemplating her anew and to remembering the patience of her glorious Son on the day when He was stripped of His garments, spat upon, beaten, crowned with thorns, nailed to the Cross, wounded and killed. He remembered how that Our Lady loved Him with wondrous love, and that, while men tormented Him, He looked upon her, and she upon Him, with looks devout and sweet. How that Our Lady lamented over her Son when she saw Him die; how that she was sore afflicted, as she saw herself divided from Him by death; how that she knew Him to have done no wrong, but to be Lord and God. And while Blanquerna thus contemplated, and led the powers of his soul to consider the virtues of God and of Our Lady, his heart was so moved with devotion that his eyes thereby had abundance of weeping and of tears.

CHAPTER IX

OF THE COMMANDMENTS

BLANQUERNA remembered in the Gospels the answer that Jesus Christ had given concerning the Commandments, and he was fain to contemplate these with the Divine virtues of God. And he said these words to his will: "Thou shalt love thy Lord God, for thou art commanded thereto by the goodness, greatness and eternity of God. Whence if thou, O Will, wert so great that eternally, without beginning or end, thou couldst love God, thou wouldst be constrained thus to obey His Commandment, for the Lord Who commands thee thus is infinitely good and eternal. But since thou hast a beginning, thou couldst not love before thou wert in being; yet now that thou art, thou art constrained to love, and, if thou lovest not, thou art disobedient to infinite and eternal goodness; for the which disobedience He will doom thee to infinite and eternal affliction and torment."

2. The Understanding said to Blanquerna that the power, wisdom and love of God commanded the will to love God with the whole heart. And as he understood that the will could love God wholly through His power, knowledge and will, he said that the power which it had of not loving God in its totality was not of the power, knowledge and will of God, but was of guilt, fault and sin, inclining to powerlessness whatsoever wills not to be power in the power, knowledge and will of God, by Whom is sustained, kept and defended power created against power of guilt, if all created will gives itself to love and obey the commandment of God.

3. While the Understanding of Blanquerna reflected, and mentally spake to his Will the aforementioned words, the Will replied by asking if it were a licit thing to love naught else save only God. The Understanding answered and said that it might love all things created so that it loved them with respect to God—that is to say, if it loved them that it might the better love God.

4. As the Understanding and the Will of Blanquerna thus discoursed, the Memory recalled how in the Commandment it is said that man is to love God with all his soul; and being itself one of the three powers of the soul it held itself obliged with all its might to remember virtue, truth and glory. And Memory said to Understanding that she recalled how that he, being one of the three powers of the soul, was wholly constrained to comprehend the virtue,

truth and glory of God. When Understanding had comprehended the argument which Memory recalled and related to him, he was conscious of the many times that he had failed to comprehend the virtue, truth and glory of God, that Will through faith should have the greater merit. And since to Understanding in his totality has been given as great a commandment as to Will, therefore the Understanding exalted himself in all his power to comprehend the virtue, truth and glory of God, and besought forgiveness because through ignorance he had gone astray, that faith might be greater in Will.

5. Blanquerna said to God that His Justice was perfect, and that therefore the commandment which He gave must be just and perfect to all thought; which commandment would have no perfection if it commanded human thought otherwise than to love wholly the justice and perfection of God, since thought is wholly created and dowered by the justice and perfection of God. While Blanquerna thus spake concerning thought, and concerning the justice and perfection of God, Will said to Understanding that she set her love more firmly upon the greater part of that which he comprehended when he comprehended with all his power. Thus was Understanding reproved as to that in which for long he had erred—to wit, that he had not risen to comprehend all that he might, that he might have the greater glory. For the commandment is given to the whole of thought, which signifies all the power of the understanding. As Will said these words to Understanding, came contrition to her, with consciousness that she had not commanded Understanding to love God with all his power, as commandment was given to her. Then, since Will had contrition, Memory recalled that many a man disobeys the commandment of God, yet thinks that he obeys it, by exalting faith and mortifying the understanding, through which mortification comes error, sin and ignorance.

6. Again Blanquerna considered the commandment of God to the Will, to wit, that man shall love God with all his heart; and then, that he shall love Him with all his soul; and again, that he shall love Him with all his thought. Wherefore in these three times in which the commandment is made, has man knowledge of the liberality of God which brings mercy to his understanding, that it may comprehend divers works in the three powers of the soul, according to the diversity of the three commandments aforesaid. For in that God commands man to love with all his heart is signified faith, whereby the will may love above that which the understanding can comprehend. In that He commands man to love Him with all his soul is signified that all three powers of the soul should be fixed equally on some end equally remembered, comprehended and loved. And in that He commands man to love Him with all his thought is signified that God commands man wholly to exalt his understanding, that in remembering God he may have greater remembrance, and in loving Him greater will. And the greatness of these lies in the exaltation of the understanding, whereby God loves to be widely known.

7. Blanquerna said to his soul that to love God with all his heart and soul and thought is the first commandment; wherefore the understanding comprehended the second commandment in its relation to the first, in the which second commandment was signified equality of love between Blanquerna and his neighbour, in that God commands the will that man shall love his neighbour even as himself. And since He says not " with all his soul and all his thought " nor even " with all his heart," there is made a difference between the first commandment and the second, by the which difference is signified that the first has precedence over the second, and that the second is subjected and must be ruled by the first; so that man, in loving, comprehending and remembering God above himself and his neighbour, may do obedience

and reverence in honouring the humility and dominion of God.

8. To love, remember and comprehend God above all beside, and one's neighbour as oneself, are two commandments which are the beginnings of the others. He that in these two commandments is obedient, obeys God in all the rest; and he that in any of the others is disobedient to God disobeys Him in the first two commandments; and he that loves himself and his neighbour equally with God is disobedient to the first commandment and to all the rest.

CHAPTER X

OF THE *MISERERE MEI DEUS*

WITH the virtues of our Lord God Blanquerna contemplated God in His Essence and Trinity and Incarnation in the sayings of the holy Prophets, as exemplified in these words: " David begged forgiveness of God according to His mercy, and therefore at the beginning his soul considered together grace and mercy, with goodness and eternity; for the goodness of God is greater than any other goodness, and His eternity than any abidingness soever. And since goodness and eternity accord with greatness, and the mercy of God is great over all other mercy, therefore David besought goodness for the great good of piety, of gifts and forgiveness; and he besought eternity that such gifts and forgiveness might be eternal and without end. And this petition he made because in the Divine Persons there is conformity in personal properties, which are in Essence goodness, greatness, eternity and mercy."

2. " It beseemed not David to make distinction in the Essence of God between greatness, mercy and justice; for these are one thing only. In praying that God would pardon him according to His great mercy, he signified His great justice; for it beseems great mercy according to

great justice to give and to pardon, and this signifies that it is greater justice that great mercy should forgive great faults and bestow great gifts than that lesser mercy should grant gifts and forgiveness. And, were this not so, it would follow that great mercy and great justice would have between each other no concord or agreement."

3. When Blanquerna considered the words aforesaid, his soul rejoiced greatly in his hope of the mercy and justice of God and of their greatness; and therefore he understood how great good, both endless and eternal, was prepared for the man that begs for mercy from the greatness and justice of God. When Blanquerna in the Essence of God had contemplated goodness, greatness, eternity, mercy and justice, he entered into another consideration, and contemplated the virtues aforesaid in the three Divine Persons, saying these words:

4. "O Lord God Who art Father, great in Thy power, knowledge and will, by virtue of Thy goodness, eternity, mercy and justice! Behold David, in the person of the Roman Church, beseeches Thy Son, Who is great in power, knowledge and will by virtue of goodness, eternity, justice and mercy; for in that he besought Thee to have mercy according to Thy greatness, Thou must needs have mercy with greatness as mighty as is Thine Own, which we ourselves could not receive but with that which is equal to Thy greatness, namely, Thy glorious Son, Whom Thou didst give us in the Incarnation and Redemption. Through this Thy Son is signified to us Thy glorious Trinity and Incarnation; for if in Thy Divine Nature there were no distinction of Persons, Thou couldst neither give nor pardon according to Thy great mercy, for we should have no strength to receive it. But since Thy Son was pleased to take our flesh, therein could our poor nature receive it, since in that Thy Son is God, He is equal in virtue with Thy greatness, and in Him and through Him Thou, even as Thou art, canst give and pardon and judge."

5. Blanquerna remembered truth, glory and perfection in God, and through the words of David he comprehended that greatness accords with truth, glory and perfection, which greatness must needs be infinite, for were it finite it would not accord with truth, glory and perfection, which are virtues infinite in God. Whence, as greatness and mercy are infinite virtues, and as David besought mercy according to the greatness of God, it is signified thereby that the Son, in Whom is truth, glory and perfection, besought the Father that His gifts and forgiveness might be equal to the infinite grace which the Father has in truth, glory and perfection. Whence, as this is so, it is signified thereby that David besought God for His gifts and forgiveness in the person of the humanity of Jesus Christ, to the which humanity they could not have been given had union not been made between it and some Person of equal truth, glory and perfection, and further, with some Person residing in the Divine Essence.

6. "Liberality, humility, dominion and patience, O Lord God," said Blanquerna, "are in Thee virtues infinitely great; for, were they not so, they would be contrary to Thy mercy, which is infinite, and it would follow that David would have begged of Thee gifts and forgiveness which Thou couldst not have given him through defect of Thy virtues. And since it is impossible that in Thee there should be any defect at all, Thy liberality must needs have within it a gift proportionate to itself; in Thy humility there must be that which is humble wherein all may humble themselves; and Thy dominion must have that which is proportionate to itself, that Thy mercy, likewise so proportioned, may have a Lord Who can give. And it is beseeming that Thy mercy have patience in giving the same patience that is in itself. And were this not so, David might have asked for greater Mercy than Thou couldst have or give him, which is a thing wholly unbeseeming."

7. According to the manner aforesaid, Blanquerna contemplated God in His Essence, Trinity and Incarnation, with his art, expounding the words of David together with the Divine virtues. By this art man may reveal the secrets and the dark sayings which were written by the Prophets to the end that the understanding might exalt itself to search the deep things of God, that its comprehension might be higher, and in the heights of the understanding the will might be lifted up to love God greatly in His Essence, in His Trinity, in His Incarnation and in all His works.

CHAPTER XI

OF THE SEVEN SACRAMENTS OF HOLY CHURCH

In the Sacraments of Holy Church Blanquerna was fain to contemplate the virtues of God, and he spake to God in these words: "O Lord God! In the Holy Sacrament of Baptism willest Thou to show forth the greatness of Thy power, knowledge, will and virtue; for by great virtue of power, knowledge and will dost Thou reveal to our human understanding a most strange and marvellous work in Baptism, when, by water and by the words of the priest and by the faith of the sponsors, the infant, who may not use understanding or will, is in the Sacrament cleansed and purified from original sin. This work, O Lord, is great and marvellous above all works of nature, signifying that Thy virtue is so great in power, knowledge and will that Thou hast power, knowledge and will to work in supernatural wise all that which is of Thy good will and pleasure."

2. "As in a city, Lord, there are many and various offices, even so in the city of Holy Mother Church are the offices of the seven Sacraments. As all these offices serve to ennoble the city, so the seven Sacraments serve to demonstrate the noble use which Thy glorious virtues have in the creatures, as is therein shown forth and revealed.

And therefore, Lord, the goodness and greatness of Thy dominion prove how all creatures are obedient in the seven Sacraments to Thy power, knowledge and will."

3. "Glorious God! As the infant has no eyes of reason till he is grown, the sponsors must needs have the virtue which Thy virtue gives and renders to the infant when he is of the age to be confirmed and to perform that which his sponsors have promised for him. That the sponsors should have such virtue, that at the confirmation of the child their obligation should be fulfilled, and that the child should receive virtue through his confirming by the Bishop—all this is significant of great virtue, truth, perfection and dominion, which in the Sacrament of Confirmation perform all that Thy will demands, without opposition of any other power, which is powerless against Thine."

4. Blanquerna was fain to enter into contemplation of the Holy Sacrifice of the Altar with the Divine virtues; and therefore at the beginning he directed the powers of his soul towards that contemplation, to the end that, when he should be engaged therein, he might not be impeded by insubordinate remembrance or will, nor yet, through his bodily senses, be disobedient to the Divine virtues. And therefore he said to his soul these words:

5. "O soul, my friend! Thou knowest that the humility of God is great, and great equally therewith is His Power; and since humility and power are one thing in virtue with wisdom, will, truth and perfection, the bodily eyes which see bread made Flesh in the Sacrifice of the Altar are little prone to be disobedient to the Divine virtues aforesaid, which are so great that they have power and will and knowledge, that beneath the form of bread there may be Very Flesh and Very Blood of the Body of Jesus Christ. And if this could not be so, it would follow that the eyes had truer power to take for objects corporal things than hast thou, my soul, to take Divine virtues and their works. Furthermore it would follow that there would be lack of

greatness in the virtues of God, and that truth would accord better with bodily things than with spiritual. And this is a thing ill-beseeming, since God is spiritual Essence and His virtues are spiritual, and the body and the bodily senses are things corporal and corruptible."

6. For a great space Blanquerna conversed in his mind with the three powers of his soul. Understanding answered him, saying that he comprehended such greatness in the virtue and the power of God that He could cause Very Flesh and Very Blood to be, under the form of bread; but he comprehended not the reason why God should will to make that Sacrament nor why He had need to make it. Blanquerna answered Understanding, saying that he should unite in his comprehension the great goodness, wisdom, love, perfection, humility, liberality, mercy and patience of God, and comprehend how great is the power shown by God in that there may be accidents without substance, and substance without accidents. So great a work cannot be performed in the course of nature; therefore, if it be performed by the power of God, that power is seen the more clearly to be above nature. And since the will desires this in order that the power may be seen to be the greater and nobler, it is shown to have more of love than has power; and if neither the power could work it nor the will desire it, so great a good would not accord with knowledge, nor would humility be so great towards us, nor would mercy, liberality or patience accord so well with goodness and greatness; and because in this work we may know that the nobility of the Divine virtues accords best with greatness, virtue and truth, hereby is signified the reason why God has willed to create and order the Holy Sacrament of the Altar.

7. "Understanding, my friend!" said Blanquerna, "Strive thou in virtue, for thou hast more virtue in understanding, than have the eyes of the body in seeing, or the senses of taste and touch in tasting and touching, for in

many a thing dost thou see these err and fail daily. Let not thyself be vanquished by the bodily senses, but defend thyself from them by the Divine virtues. Comprehendest thou how wondrous a work is the Trinity in God, and how far above nature is the Incarnation of the Son of God? To show forth the wonder of this work, God was pleased to institute the Holy Sacrifice, that thereby we might have daily remembrance of the wondrous and supernatural work of the Divine virtues. For as we ourselves, corporally and physically, make the sign of the figure of our Lord God Jesus Christ on the Cross, even so in the Sacrifice of the Altar is made the sign of the miraculous and spiritual work which is performed by the Divine virtues."

8. Understanding considered deeply the words which Blanquerna spake to him, and comprehended by these words that the imagination had for long impeded him from comprehending the Sacrament of the Altar, because it caused him to represent it to himself more powerfully in its physical and natural aspect than as in the virtues and the works of his glorious God, to which virtues and works imagination could not soar. And therefore Understanding performed the words of Blanquerna, and he soared aloft in adoration and contemplation of the Holy Sacrament of the Altar.

9. There was debate between the Memory of Blanquerna and his Understanding, which Sacrament was more opposed to the bodily senses,—the Sacrament of the Altar or the Sacrament of Penance. For the Memory recalled that man has sinned against God, and that the Holy Apostolic Father is a man, and that men are his ministers who absolve and pardon and give penance to their fellowmen. And Understanding said that the Sacrament of the Altar manifests itself in bodily and sensible form, having indeed bodily form, but a form invisible to the bodily senses. For a great space Understanding and Memory held debate upon this matter, and they came to Blanquerna for judg-

ment. And Blanquerna said that the Sacraments were equally opposed to the senses, for by the Divine virtues, which are incorporeal, were created and instituted the two Sacraments aforesaid and likewise the rest, all of them supernatural, that their sovereignty over virtue natural and created might be shown. And when Blanquerna gave this sentence, he spake these words:

10. "As the Divine virtue causes the virtue of Flesh and Blood to exist under the form of bread, so also It causes the virtue of pardon to exist under the form of a man,—to wit, the priest. And as the virtue which is of Flesh and Blood, under the form of the Host, is not of the Host, but of God, so the virtue of the priest in pardoning is not of the priest, but under the form of the priest is the Virtue of God."

11. "Blanquerna!" said Remembrance, "As thou dost speak thus subtly, couldst thou prove to me that since God has power to make the Sacrament of Penance He must needs will that this Sacrament should be, for God can do many things which His Will desires not to perform?" Blanquerna answered, and said that as in the great goodness, mercy, humility and virtue of God and in His other attributes it is signified that God wills and needs must will according to the greatness of His justice, which wills that the virtues be shown forth in exceeding greatness through the Sacrament of the Altar, so by that same ordinance, great justice wills, and must needs will, that the Sacrament of Penance exist, that the Divine virtues may be shown forth, and men may be directed in contrition, penance, restitution, counsel, affliction, repentance, hope and other things like to these, which could not be without the Sacrament of Penance.

12. To signify the order which is in the three Divine Persons, and how by means of this order the Person of the Son came to take our human nature, and how lack of order beseems not Baptism and Confirmation, the Holy Sacrifice,

Penance, Matrimony and Unction, therefore is it fitting that there be an Order of Priesthood whereby may be ordered each one of the Sacraments aforesaid. And this is signified in the Divine virtues and in the greatness according to the which they are signified and demonstrated to us.

13. In the virtues aforesaid Blanquerna perceived the Order of Matrimony, even as he had seen in them the other sacraments. And he saw that as justice signified that in temporal things a difference is made to divers men, so also it made it meet that a difference should be made between man and woman, that chastity and virginity should be contrary to lasciviousness, and that from sensual things the powers of the soul may take order and arrangement, and the commandments of the Divine Sovereignty may be obeyed.

14. "In the Earthly Paradise," said Memory to Will, "God created matrimony, and in significance of that matrimony He wills that in this world the Sacrament of Matrimony shall exist; for, if it were not, the wisdom and will of God would not unite with perfection in showing forth the great glory of God which accords with justice, to the which is opposed irregular union between man and woman. Through such irregularity man is unworthy of coming to the glory of God, for it would be against both greatness and perfection if man, after irregular union between man and woman, came to the truth and glory of God. And Divine Wisdom and Virtue would have placed greater virtue in the bodily elements which duly join and unite, that a body may be duly begotten, than in the wills of man and woman, to the end that children may be begotten and the human race preserved in the world."

15. Blanquerna remembered that in this world man has a beginning, a mean and an end, and that for this cause, to signify the eternal dominion of God, Divine Wisdom has ordained that at the entrance of man into the world the first sacrament should be Baptism, and that Extreme

Unction should be the last; and thus is signified the submission wherein man has lived in the world, in his obedience to the first sacrament and to the others which are between the first and the last. And since justice has greater reason to judge one that is obedient unto law, and mercy to pardon him by Confession, Contrition, Confirmation and the other sacraments from first to last, therefore the great Justice and Sovereignty of God wills that Extreme Unction may be a sacrament, that thereby a seal, as it were, may be set upon all the other sacraments, and the sacrifice shown forth of the Body of Our Lord God upon the Cross, which Body was anointed with His sacred Blood, with the tears which flowed from His eyes, and the sweat which came to Him in the agony of His death.

CHAPTER XII

OF VIRTUES

Blanquerna remembered the seven virtues which many a time had aided him against the Spirit of Evil, and in them he was fain to contemplate the Divine virtues which the seven virtues had revealed to him. Wherefore he said these words: " O Faith, that art worthy of all love, great art thou in believing great things of God, and good art thou, since by thee man comes to eternal happiness; illumined with Divine wisdom art thou through the light of grace; that which is true dost thou love, for the love of the King of Heaven makes thee to love His virtue and truth, His glory and perfection."

2. " O Faith, my friend! Thou dost believe in God, in Unity of Essence and Trinity of Persons. A great thing is it to believe in things invisible, to believe that infinite Good is that which is infinitely and eternally engendered from infinite and eternal Good. And to believe that from both issues infinite and eternal Good is a belief truly great

and marvellous, and illumined with the wondrous brightness of the light of grace. And therefore, O Faith so lovely, since thou art great, my soul must needs give great thanks and render a tribute of great love to the Eternal Greatness and Goodness which has made thee to be so great, and in thy greatness has made me great likewise."

3. "Through thee, O Faith, I do believe that by great charity, power, knowledge, humility and mercy, the Son of God took flesh of our Lady Saint Mary, which flesh He united with Himself, becoming therewith one Person having Natures human and Divine without corruption, alteration, composition and accident of Divine Nature, and without change of the human nature which He assumed. Wherefore I believe these things so great and marvellous by the exceeding greatness and virtue, doctrine, mercy and benignity of the Sovereign Good; and therefore my soul is greatly constrained to remember, comprehend, love, honour and serve the Divine virtues which thou, O Faith, dost make to shine in me so numerously and with so great grace and such brightness."

4. Blanquerna discoursed in his soul with Hope, and said that of great things man should have great hope; for from such great goodness, greatness, eternity, power, wisdom, love, virtue, truth, glory, perfection, justice, liberality, whence is engendered and whence issues such great good as the virtues aforesaid, should be hoped and desired great happiness. For it is impossible that from such great and noble things as those aforesaid there should not flow an influence exceeding great of so great happiness to lovers of the Divine virtues.

5. "Consider, O Hope, how great a thing it is that the Son of God, Who is so great in virtues, should unite Himself with man's own human nature, which is a thing created, and to give that creature to death and torment for us sinners and that thou mayest be greater in trusting in the virtues of the Sovereign Good. See, O Hope, how that God has

created things great and many and various and beautiful and virtuous and good: angels, heavens, sun, moon, stars, earth, sea, men, beasts, birds, fishes, plants, metals and other things created. Wherefore, as these things aforesaid are so many, so noble and so great, therefore, O Hope, it behoves thee to trust and hope in goodness, greatness, eternity, power, etc., for great blessings and graces."

6. "O Hope, were there no Trinity or Incarnation, thou couldst not hope for such great gifts and blessings from God as now thou canst. For the virtues of God would not show themselves to be so great in our sight as in fact they show themselves, seeing that Trinity and Incarnation exist. And if Resurrection were not, thou wouldst be less than thou art, for we should not see the charity nor the power, nor the mercy, humility, dominion and patience which in God are so great, as we see them in believing the Resurrection to be true. And therefore, O Hope, we see, thou and I, together with the Divine virtues, Resurrection, and the greatness of the Divine virtues together with the Resurrection. And therefore, O Faith and Hope, do ye agree in being the greater in yourselves, and we are the greater in you, and we have greater agreement thereby with belief."

7. "O Divine Love, that hast within thyself a Lover infinite and eternal in loving! From Thee, that art so great in Thy heights in all perfection, shall come all graces; for if in Thine Essence there are Persons three, Beloved and Loving, Eternal and Infinite in power, knowledge, will, virtue, perfection and glory, from that great inflowing of love which is in Thee will so much come to us here below that we shall love to honour and serve no other, save Thyself alone."

8. "It is the nature of good that it shall engender other good, and it is the nature of power that it shall engender other power; and the same is true of virtue, glory and perfection. Wherefore, since thou art so great and so noble,

O Love, for thou art infinite in goodness, eternity, wisdom, power and the like, how may it be that we, who are thy creatures, created by thee anew, thy slaves whom thou hast bought, are not enamoured of thee more strongly? Wherein, O Love, is the accord which thou hast with liberality, mercy, humility and patience? For with such accord must there needs be pity in thee, and in ourselves must there be happiness, hope and love."

9. " O Divine Justice! Among ourselves justice is predicated of the just; and in Thee just and justice are one and the same thing. Then, since Thou art just and justice infinite in Being and Essence without difference, and since that which is in Thee just and justice, Being and Essence, is goodness, eternity, power, wisdom, love, virtue, truth, glory, perfection, mercy, liberality, humility, dominion and patience, it must needs be, according to such universal virtues and properties, that Thou art to ourselves just and justice, with mercy, humility, charity and patience, and that of Thee we have justice, whereby we may live justly, praising, honouring and serving Thee. And if in ourselves there is no justice of that justice which is in Thee, where then is the influence which from Thy justice comes to us? And where is the accord that is between Thy justice and Thy goodness, charity, mercy, humility, liberality and patience?"

10. " O Divine Essence! The great justice which is in Thee causes the Just, Infinite, Eternal in goodness, power, wisdom and charity to engender Another Just, Infinite, Eternal in goodness, power, wisdom and charity, and from both of these Just aforesaid proceeds Another, Eternal and Infinite in goodness, power, wisdom and charity. Wherefore, as this is so, there proceeded from this Thy justice so great an influence that it made One of ourselves to be one Person with One of the Three that are in Thyself. Whence, from the great inflowing of justice which came to One of us with charity, mercy and humility, there will come to us

all that whereby we may become just in loving, knowing, honouring and serving Thee. And if this Thou dost not, where is the influence of humility, patience, charity and liberality that is in Thee? Or Who is that Lord that is ours, since it is a reasonable thing that a lord should love, help and bestow gifts upon his subjects?"

11. "I pray Thy power, knowledge and will, O Lord God, for prudence, which Thou wilt give me through the benignity which is in Thee, according to justice and mercy. Through Thy power and knowledge canst Thou give it me, and since I ask it therewith to love Thee, therefore truth and justice should make Thee to love prudence in me, that thereby I may know Thee, and knowing, love Thee, and through this knowledge and love may know and will to praise, honour, obey and serve Thee."

12. "O Greatness of justice! If Thou wilt have this justice, O Lord God, upon us sinners to punish us, then mayest Thou exercise it the better if Thou dost punish us who know Thy Trinity and Incarnation and yet honour, love and serve Thee not, rather than those who know not Trinity in Thee, and who knowing not the Incarnation, believe it not. And if Thou wilt have mercy, humility and pity on us, Thou mayest the better have it if we know Thee and love Thee, than if we are disobedient to Thee through ignorance. Wherefore, as this is so, then, according to all these reasons and many besides, Thou wilt give prudence to ourselves, faithful Christians, and to unbelievers alike, that we may know and love Thee, since Thy liberality accords with Thy will, which has created us principally that we may know and love Thee before all things else."

13. "Ah Temperance, my friend! Daily do I need thee against my enemies, who hinder me from contemplating the virtues of my Lord, for Whose sake I have come to this hermitage. I beg for thee of the virtues of the Lord Who has created thee, for I need thee in order

to serve them. Father and mother, kindred and wealth have I left, that in this hermitage I may company with thee. Without thee can man do naught against gluttony or drunkenness, though he wear honest raiment or embrace the estate of the hermit or the religious life. And I may not have thee without the goodness, greatness, wisdom, power, love, virtue, humility, mercy, and liberality of the Lord, in Whom are all these virtues."

14. "O Temperance, man cannot overmuch remember God, nor understand nor love Him; but by surfeit of remembrance, understanding and love with weeping and fasting, afflictions and vigils, the body weakens and languishes and dies, and the soul may not as fervently or continuously contemplate the virtues of God. Therefore, O Temperance, do I need thee both in body and spirit: give thyself to me that thou mayest possess me and be my ruler, and no longer be in the servitude of my gluttony and my belly." In this manner and in many another did Blanquerna pray for virtues created to virtues uncreate that he might therewith serve God.

CHAPTER XIII

OF VICES

BLANQUERNA remembered the seven deadly sins whereby the world is in disorder, namely the world created by the virtues of God. And therefore Blanquerna enquired of Divine Goodness: "Whence come these demons aforesaid, to wit, the seven deadly sins, which destroy the world?" Wherefore Blanquerna said these words: "Sovereign Goodness, that art so great in virtue and perfection, and that in eternity and nobility art above all creatures! Whence have come gluttony, lust, covetousness, sloth, pride, envy and anger? For these seven beasts destroy, corrupt and ruin the good things which are Thine by creation and sovereignty. And since Thou art so powerful, wise, loving and virtuous, wherefore dost Thou suffer that so much evil, deception, error, affliction and ignorance should be in the world through the seven demons aforesaid?"

2. "If Thou, O Goodness, wert evil or defect of good, these seven deadly sins might have come from Thee. Wherefore, since Thou art fulness of all fulness, and since perfection is contrary to defect, and since all sin and evil must needs have a beginning, let Thy Eternity, then, which existed before such beginning was, tell me whence have come sin and defect."

3. Blanquerna contemplated Sovereign Goodness in greatness, eternity, power, wisdom, love, etc., according to the manner aforesaid, and he felt in his soul that Memory and Understanding were holding converse. Memory said to Understanding that she recalled how that Will desired gluttony, lust and their companions. And Understanding answered that the desire that desired gluttony or lust or other vice is born of the will, and therefore the will is to blame because from it proceeds the desire which desires sin, and through that desire the understanding which comprehends sin is to blame, and the desire and the free will with that will inclines to desire sin. And therefore the memory which recalls all these things is to blame. And since Memory, Understanding and Will are creatures of Sovereign Goodness, and give occasion to remember, understand and love sin, therefore said the Understanding of Blanquerna to his Memory, justifying the goodness of God, that the seven demons have their beginnings in the works of remembrance, understanding and will, which treat of things displeasing to the goodness of God.

4. "O Divine Wisdom! Thou that art Light of all lights, show me the manner and the art whereby I may mortify the seven vices in my memory, understanding and will." Then Memory recalled the Divine virtues; Under-

standing comprehended the shortness of life in this world and the pains of hell; Will loved God and all His virtues, ceased to love sin and prayed for pardon, and despised the vanity of this world. And Blanquerna felt in his soul that his vices and sins were mortified through the working of his remembrance, understanding and will. And therefore he spake to Divine Wisdom these words:

5. "O Sovereign Doctrine! From Thee comes virtue, from Thy power comes power, and from Thy love comes desire to the soul which desires to remember, comprehend and love Thee. When memory desires not to remember Thee, nor understanding to comprehend Thee, nor will to love Thee, come wrongs and faults from that which the will has no will to desire, and from that which it wills to desire in remembering, comprehending and loving or loving not. And therefore, O Sovereign Doctrine, be Thine all my remembering, understanding and desiring, together with my memory, understanding and will, that I may contemplate, remember, comprehend and love Thy virtues, and cease to love vices, wrongs and sins, to the end that Thy praise, Thy honour and Thy dominion may daily be in my memory, understanding and will."

6. "O Sovereign Liberality and Mercy! Thou hast given me memory to remember, understanding to comprehend, and will to love Thy virtues. But these suffice me not if Thou give me not remembrance in remembering Thy virtues, understanding in comprehending them, and will in desiring them, and if Thou give me not the seven virtues which are opposed to the seven deadly sins. I pray Thee, too, to give me remembrance, understanding and will to remember, understand and cease from loving gluttony, lust and the other vices. Wherefore, since Thy power can give me all these things which are so needful to me, and since for all these things Thou hast created me, I pray Thee to grant me gifts whereby all my powers may honour Thy graces."

7. " O Glory and Perfection! To give the power to sin is to give occasion for having faith, hope, charity and the other virtues. The gift of the power to have faith, hope, charity and the like, is a gift against gluttony, lust and the other vices. Wherefore I pray Thee to give me these virtues, and therewith freedom as to sin, that Thou mayest grant me to remember, comprehend and love Thy graces, and to remember, comprehend and cease to love my sins and the vain delights of this world." Blanquerna wept and sighed as he prayed for these gifts, and God granted him that which he desired, and Blanquerna rendered Him thanks with tears. The contemplation and devotion which Blanquerna had, and the art and manner thereof, none can tell it neither explain it, save only God.

ENDED IS THE BOOK OF "THE ART OF CONTEMPLATION"

CHAPTER C

OF THE END OF THE BOOK

One day Blanquerna was contemplating God, and he had with him the *Book of Contemplation*[1]; and there came to Blanquerna a jester,[2] full of tears, and giving signs in his features that the sorrow of his soul was very great; and he spake to Blanquerna these words: "Blanquerna, my lord! The fame of thy holy life has gone out through all the world, whereat my conscience torments me with contrition of soul, for the faults which I have committed in my office; wherefore have I come to thee that thou mayest give me penance." Blanquerna enquired of him what was his office, and he answered that he was a jester. "Fair friend!" said Blanquerna: "The office of jester was made with good intent, namely, to praise God and to give solace and comfort to them that are tried and tormented in the service of God. But we have come to a time wherein scarce any man fulfils the final intent for the which all offices were in the first place ordained; for the office of clerk was founded first of all upon a good intent, and the same is true of the office of knight, jurist, artist, physician, merchant, religious, hermit and every other office; but now have we come to a time wherein a man fulfils not as much as he might the intention for the which the offices and sciences were made. And for this cause the world is in error and strife, and God is neither known nor loved nor obeyed by those that are bound to love and know and obey and serve Him. Wherefore, fair friend, I give thee this penance, that thou go throughout the world, crying out and singing first of one office and then of another, and making known the intent for the which were made in the beginning the office of jester and all other offices. Thou shalt bear with thee likewise this romance of Evast and Blanquerna, wherein are signified the reasons for the which in the beginning the offices aforementioned were established; thou shalt reprove

[1] See note, p. 407. [2] *juglar*. See note, p. 175.

and correct all such as use not their offices well, according to thy power, and according to time and place and opportunity; and fear thou not reproofs, neither trials nor death, in being pleasing to God." The jester took this penance of Blanquerna, and received the office which he had given him, and went through all the world relating the intent wherein were made the offices of theology, clerkship, religion, chivalry, prelacy, lordship, merchandise, medicine, law, philosophy and other things like to these; and he reproved those that kept not the final intent for the which these things aforementioned were established, and in public places and in courts and in monasteries he read the romance of Evast and Blanquerna to the end that devotion should be increased, and that he might have the greater strength and courage of mind to perform the penance which Blanquerna had given to him.

2. We have related the romance of Evast and Blanquerna, and the tale now returns to the Emperor whom Blanquerna found in the forest; the which Emperor had made ordinance concerning his empire to his son, for whom he made the *Book of the Doctrine of Princes*, according to the which he should rule his house and his person and his land; and after all these things he forsook the world, and went to seek Blanquerna, to the end that they might together live the lives of hermits and contemplate our Lord God.

3. While the Emperor went in search of Blanquerna he met a Bishop who was going to the Court to expound the *Brief Art of Finding Truth*, the which Bishop purposed to plead with the Lord Pope that this art might be read and expounded in all seminaries of common studies, to the end that through exaltation of the understanding there might be greater devotion in the world to the love and honour and service of God, and that greater knowledge of Him might be given to the unbelievers who journey in ignorance to eternal torment; and to the end that this task might be accomplished, the Bishop purposed to give up all the days

of his life and all the income of his diocese. When the Emperor and the Bishop had met, they made the acquaintance the one of the other, and greeted and welcomed each other very courteously. Each enquired of the other concerning his estate and his purpose, and each gave the other fitting answer. Great pleasure had the Emperor at the devotion of the Bishop and the Bishop at the devotion of the Emperor, the which Emperor prayed the Bishop to be an advocate, in the Court of Rome, of Valour, who by so many persons has been wronged and prevented from giving due praise and honour to God; and he begged him to command the Jester of Valour to sing these stanzas in the Court, to the end that the Pope and the Cardinals might have the better remembrance of the lives of the Apostles, in whose time there yet lived holiness of life and devotion and valour:

¶ O God, true Lord, our glorious King,[1]
Who with us men dost deign to be,
Remember those that to Thee sing,
Who fain would suffer death for Thee.
O, make them worthy praise to bring,
And service to Thy Majesty
With all their might,
For all they wish and hope must be
Good in Thy sight.

¶ Once more is born a fervent zeal,
Once more an apostolic love,
In those who as they praise Thee kneel
The sweet assault of death to prove.
Let him go forth whose faith is real
The wondrous power of God above
O'er earth to cry—
For God all-wise, our hearts to move,
Came from on high.

[1] The metre and rime-scheme of these verses correspond exactly to that of their original,—as also do those of the verses on p. 300,—except that in the Catalan the two final quatrains have the same rimes as the latter half of he stanza preceding them.

¶ The Minorites from near and far,
Remembering God's blessed Son,
Who calls us to a holy war,
And bids us work with Him as one,
Have made the house of Miramar,
By fair Majorca's king begun
The Moors to save,
For whom our God great things has done
Their souls to have.

¶ But what see we the Preachers do
That love so much to serve[1] our Lord?
Where do the priors and abbots go,
Bishops, that great possessions hoard,
Prelates, that prize this world below,
Kings sleeping with unbuckled sword
In sloth so base,
Yet thinking to have Heaven's reward
And see God's Face.

¶ Both great and small, both young and old,
Delight to scoff and do me wrong,
While sighs and tears of love untold
My body make to suffer long.
But memory, will and mind are bold,
And joyfully I'll sing this song
Throughout my days;
To Him alone will I belong
And tell His praise.

¶ Sweet Mary would I serve right well,
As I have done.
Through her I lost all fear of hell
And new love won.

¶ Blanquerna! Who can show thy cell?
Where art thou gone?
Fain would I be where thou dost dwell
With God alone!

4. "How, lord!" said the Bishop to the Emperor: "Hast thou likewise knowledge of Blanquerna?" The Emperor answered him and related how that he had met

[1] *servir* (P, D). The other versions have *fruir*, "have fruition of."

Blanquerna one day when he was going alone through that forest wherein Blanquerna sought his hermitage, and how he had promised him that he would make satisfaction to Valour for the wrong which he had done her. The Bishop recounted to the Emperor the holy life of Blanquerna, and showed him the parts wherein he could find the place where Blanquerna lived the life of a hermit. Right pleased was the Emperor at that which the Bishop had related to him concerning Blanquerna, and that he had shown him the ways whereby he might find him. The Bishop took the stanzas, and bade the Emperor very courteously adieu, and commended him to the benediction of God.

¶ ENDED IS THE ROMANCE OF EVAST AND BLANQUERNA WHICH IS OF THE LIFE OF MATRIMONY AND OF THE ORDER OF CLERGY, TO GIVE DOCTRINE WHEREBY MAN MAY SO LIVE IN THIS WORLD THAT IN THE NEXT HE MAY DWELL ETERNALLY IN THE GLORY OF GOD.

APPENDIX I

ADDITIONAL PARAGRAPHS OF THE "BOOK OF THE LOVER AND THE BELOVED," FOUND IN CERTAIN VERSIONS ONLY

THE Lover entered a delightful meadow, and saw in the meadow many children who were pursuing butterflies, and trampling down the flowers; and the more the children laboured to catch the butterflies, the higher did these fly. And the Lover, as he watched them, said: "Such are they who with subtle reasoning attempt to comprehend the Beloved, Who opens the doors to the simple and closes them to the subtle. And Faith reveals the secrets of the Beloved through the casement of love."

The Lover went one day into a cloister, and the monks enquired of him if he, too, were a religious. "Yea," he answered, "of the order of my Beloved." "What rule dost thou follow?" He answered: "The rule of my Beloved." "To whom art thou vowed?" He said: "To my Beloved." "Hast thou thy will?" He answered: "Nay, it is given to my Beloved." "Hast thou added aught to the rule of thy Beloved?" He answered: "Naught can be added to that which is already perfect." "And wherefore," continued the Lover, "do not ye that are religious take the Name of my Beloved? May it not be that, as ye bear the name of another, your love may grow less, and, hearing the voice of another, ye may not catch the voice of the Beloved?"

They asked the Lover: "What is the world?" He answered: "It is a book for such as can read, in the which is revealed my Beloved." They asked him: "Is thy Beloved, then, in the world?" He answered: "Yea, even as the writer is in his book." "And wherein consists this book?" He answered: "In my Beloved, since my Beloved contains it all, and therefore is the world in my Beloved rather than my Beloved in the world."

"Say, O Lover, who is he that loves and seems to thee as a fool?" The Lover answered: "He that loves the shadow and makes no account of the truth." "And whom dost thou call rich?" "He that loves truth." "And who is poor?" "He that loves falsehood."

They asked the Lover: "Is the world to be loved?" He answered: "Truly it is, but as a piece of work, for its artificer's sake, or as the night by reason of the day which follows it."

The Lover gazed at the rainbow, and it seemed to him as though it were of three colours. And he cried: "O marvellous distinction of three, for the three together are one! And how can this be in the image, unless it be so of itself, in truth?"

Two men were disputing concerning simplicity, the one against the other. And the one said: "The simple man is he that knows naught." The other said: "The simple man is he that lives without sin." And the Lover came and said: "True simplicity has he that commits all his ways to my Beloved. For simplicity is to exalt faith above understanding, which it so far exceeds, and in all that pertains to my Beloved it is to avoid completely all things vain, superfluous, curious, over-subtle and presumptuous. For all these are contrary to simplicity."

Another time they both enquired of him, asking that he would tell them if the science of the simple is a great one. He answered: "The science of great sages is as a great heap of a few grains, but the science of the simple is a small heap of numberless grains, because neither presumption nor curiosity nor over-subtlety is added to the heap of simple men." "And what is the work of presumption and curiosity?" The Lover answered: "Vanity is the mother of curiosity, and pride is the mother of presumption, and therefore is their work the work of vanity and pride. And the enemies of my Beloved are known by presumption and curiosity, even as love for Him is acquired by simplicity."

Many lovers came together, and they enquired of the Messenger of Love where and in what thing the heart was most ardently inflamed with devotion and love. The Messenger of Love answered: "In the House of God, when we humble ourselves and adore Him with all our powers; for He alone is Holiest of the holy. And they that know not how to do this, know not what it is truly to love Him."

The Lover thought upon his sins, and for fear of hell he would fain have wept, but he could not. So he begged Love to give him tears, and Wisdom answered that he must weep earnestly and often, but for the love of his Beloved rather than for the pains of hell; for tears of love are more pleasing to Him than tears shed through fear.

The Lover obeyed Wisdom; and, on the one hand, he shed many and great tears for the sake of Love, and, on the other, few and small tears for fear, that by love and not by fear he might honour his Beloved. And the tears which he shed for love brought him solace and repose, while the tears of fear gave him sorrow and tribulation.

They asked the Lover in what manner the heart of man was turned towards the love of his Beloved. He answered them and said: " Even as the sunflower turns to the sun." " How is it, then, that all men love not thy Beloved ? " He answered: " They that love Him not have night in their hearts, because of their sin."

The Lover met an astrologer, and enquired of him: " What means thy astrology ? " He answered: " It is a science that foretells things to come." " Thou art deceived," said the Lover; " it is no science, but one falsely so called. It is necromancy, or the black art, in disguise, and the science of deceiving and lying prophets which dishonour the work of the sovereign Master. At all times it has been the messenger of evil tidings; and it runs clean contrary to the providence of my Beloved, for in place of the evils which it threatens He promises good things."

The Lover went forth, crying: " Oh, how vain are all they that follow after lust of knowledge and presumption! For through lust of knowledge do they fall into the greatest depths of impiety, insulting the Name of God and with curses and incantations invoking evil spirits as good angels, investing them with the names of God and of good angels, and profaning holy things with figures and images and by writings. And through presumption all errors are implanted in the world." And the Lover wept bitterly for all the insults which are offered to his Beloved by ignorant men.

One day the Lover was looking towards the east, and

towards the weſt, towards the south and towards the north, and he espied the Sign of his Beloved. And therefore he caused that Sign to be engraven, and at each of its four extremities he had a precious jewel set, as bright as the sun. That Sign he wore ever upon him, and it brought the Truth to his remembrance.

The Lover passed through divers places, and found many men who were rejoicing, laughing and singing, and living in great joy and comfort. And he wondered if this world were meant for laughing or for weeping.

So the Virtues came, to pronounce upon that queſtion. And Faith said: "It is for weeping, because the faithless are more in number than the believers." Hope said: "It is for weeping, because few are they that hope in God, whereas many put their truſt in the riches of earth." Charity said: "It is for weeping, because they that love God and their neighbour are so few." And there followed the other Virtues, and so declared they all.

The lovers sought to prove the messenger of Love, and they said that they should go through the world, crying that worshippers muſt honour servants as servants and the Lord as a lord, that their requeſts might better be heard, and because there needs not to love, save the Beloved, nor to truſt, save in Him alone.

They asked the messenger of Love whence came to the Beloved so many useless servants, viler, more abjeƈt and more contemptible than secular men. The messenger of Love answered and said: "They come through the fault of those whose task it is to furnish their Sovereign,—the King of Kings,—the Beloved,—with servants. They make no queſtion, as they ought, concerning the wisdom or the lives or the habits of those whom they choose. And those whom they will not take for His train they allow to serve the Eternal King in His palace, and in the moſt holy miniſtry of His Table. Wherefore ougth they to fear the severeſt retributions when they are called by the Beloved to their account."

They asked the Lover this queſtion: "Wherein dies

love?" The Lover answered: "In the delights of this world." "And whence has it life and sustenance?" "In thoughts of the world to come." Wherefore they that had inquired of him prepared to renounce this world, that they might think the more deeply upon the next, and that their love might live and find nourishment.

APPENDIX II

INDEX TO PRINCIPAL WORDS UPON WHICH NOTES ARE TO BE FOUND IN THE TEXT

But Gesualdo falls foul of the rigid class structure in mid-19th century Sicily. His title 'Mastro-Don', 'Worker-Gentleman', is ironic in itself. Peasants and gentry alike resent his extra-ordinary success. And when the pattern of society is threatened by revolt, Gesualdo is the rebels' first target . . .

Published in 1888, Verga's classic was first introduced to this country in 1925 by D.H. Lawrence in his own superb translation. Although brough in scope, with a large cast and covering over twenty years, *Mastro-Don Gesualdo* is exact and concentrated; it cuts from set-piece to set-piece — from feast-day to funeral to sun white stubble fields — anticipating the narrative techniques of the cinema.

SHORT SICILIAN NOVELS — Giovanni Verga (translated by D.H. Lawrence)

Short Sicilian Novels have that sense of the wholeness of life, the spare exuberance, the endless inflections and overtones, and the magnificent and thrilling vitality of major literature.

-New York Times

"In these stories the whole of Sicily of the eighteen-sixties lives before us — poor gentry, priests, rich landowners, farmers, peasants, animals, seasons, and scenery; and whether his subjects be the brutal bloodshed of an abortive revolution or the simple human comedy that can even attend deep mourning, Verga never loses his complete artistic mastery of his material. He throws the whole of his pity into the intensity of his art, and with the simplicity only attainable by genius lays bare beneath all the sweat and tears and clamour of day-to-day humanity those mysterious 'mortal things which touch the minds'."

-Times Literary Supplement.

THE GOLEM — Gustav Meyrink

'The Cabala . . . found in the ghettos a suitable home for its strange speculations on the nature of God, the majestic power of letters and the possibility for initiates of creating a man in the same way God created Adam. This homunculus was called The Golem . . . Gustav Meyrink uses this legend . . . in a dream like setting on the Other Side of the Mirror and he has invested it with a horror so palpable that is has remained in my memory all these years.'

-Jorge Luis Borges

"What holds us today is Meyrink's vision of Prague, as precise and fantastic at once as Dickens's London or Dostoevsky's St. Petersburg.'

- Times Literary Supplement (1970)

When **The Golem** first appeared in book form in 1915, it was an immediate popular and critical success, selling hundreds of thousands of copies. It has inspired three film versions. Admirers of the book have included Carl Jung, Hermann Hesse, Alfred Kubin and Julio Cortazar.

LES DIABOLIQUES (The She Devils) — Barbey D'Aurevilly

The publication of LES DIABOLIQUES in 1874 caused an uproar, with copies of the book being seized by order of the Minister of Justice as it was a danger to public morality. Scandal made the book an immediate success, a century later it is now firmly established as a classic and studied in French Schools.

"The book is a celebration of the seven deadly vices and shows no counter-balancing interest in the seven cardinal virtues. Even more, it is a celebration of pride, the pride of the ancient aristocracy of evil. Those who have the style to carry off their vices have also the right to do so."

Robert Irwin

"Les Diaboliques is intended to be a collection of tales of horror and this horror is, in each case, well built up and sustained."

Enid Starkie

LÀ-BAS (Lower Depths) — J.K. Huysmans

Là-Bas follows immediately on from "A Rebours" (Against Nature), and takes Huysmans' quest for the exotic and extreme situations a stage further. The novel's hero Durtal, investigates the life and times of the fifteenth century sadist, necromancer and child-murderer Gilles de Rais. But these dabblings, and table talk of alchemy, astrology and spiritualism lead him on to direct experience of contemporary devil worship and sexual magic.

Bizarre and blasphemous, Là-Bas is even so a lightly fictionalised account of Huysmans' own experience in fin de siècle France. It is the classic work of fiction on nineteenth century Satanism and establishes Huysmans' reputation as one of the major novelists of his century.

THE ARABIAN NIGHTMARE — Robert Irwin

"The Arabian Nightmare is an engaging and distinctive blend of the seductive and the disturbing, its atmosphere constantly shifting from sumptuously learned orientalising to grotesque erotic adventure and dry anarchic humour. As a feat of erudite philosophic fantasy it bears comparison with Eco's The Name of the Rose. — CITY LIMITS.

"Robert Irwin is, indeed, particularly brilliant and beauty of beauties, the book is constantly entertaining." — THE GUARDIAN.

"somewhere between a Borges "Labyrinth" and a Bunuel movie." TIME OUT

"Robert Irwin wittily juggles oriental thought with western theology and sexual fantasy and comes out laughing. — THE TIMES

"It is certainly one of the best fantasy novels of the last twenty years and in time to come will surely be rediscovered and elevated to classic status." — FANTASY

Also by Robert Irwin, Limits of Vision, which was published by Dedalus in conjunction with Penguin Books in the Spring of 1986.